TWO SOULS

Visit us at www.boldstrokesbooks.com

By the Author

Awake Unto Me

Forsaking All Others

A Spark of Heavenly Fire

Warm November

Two Souls

TWO SOULS

by
Kathleen Knowles

2016

This Trade Paperback Original Is Published By
Bold Strokes Books, Inc.
P.O. Box 249
Valley Falls, NY 12185

First Edition: November 2016

Credits
Editor: Shelley Thrasher
Production Design: Susan Ramundo
Cover Design By Sheri (graphicartist2020@hotmail.com)

Acknowledgments

I received help from Yolanda Bustos, archivist of the California Academy of Science, and from the librarians in the History Room at the San Francisco Public Library. Historical novelists need librarians and archivists and we owe them gratitude.

Alice Eastwood, a towering figure in the history of the Cal Academy and the history of the 1906 San Francisco earthquake, is the basis for Abby Eliot. I don't know if Alice was a lesbian or not, but she certainly makes a fascinating character in her own right. I got the idea for this book when I heard about Alice during a "backstage" tour of the Academy botany collections.

So I want to recognize my debt to Alice Eastwood.

As always, I got great support from my family; my spouse, Jeanette; and my sister, Karin. My friend and fellow writer, Katia Noyes, was an important sounding board. My friends Marcus and Kent don't mind me babbling about my latest book.

Thanks as always to the BSB team: Shelley—my esteemed editor, Radclyffe, Sandy, Cindy, and the rest of you. You make the making of books lots of fun.

Dedication

To Jeanette, who keeps me grounded and steady,
earthquakes or not.

Chapter One

January 15, 1906
Somewhere in Nebraska

Norah sprang awake when the train took a curve a little too fast. She had been sleeping soundly in the upper berth of a sleeper cabin on the Central Pacific Railroad Special to San Francisco when the motion almost threw her out of her berth, but she'd become tangled in the privacy curtain. She caught her breath, happy she'd not been thrown on the floor, but she couldn't fall back asleep right away. From the sound of light snoring, she deduced the train's sudden swerve had presented no problem to the lady in the bunk below her.

Norah adjusted the thick damask curtain and groped around in the dark for her small lantern. It was in her travel bag, right next to the two letters she'd carried with her ever since receiving them within a few days of one another some six weeks previous. The letters were the reason she was on a train traveling from New York City to San Francisco. She lit the lantern and, by habit, read the more official letter first.

Dear Dr. Stratton,
It is with great pleasure that we offer you the position of second attending physician in the Infectious Disease Department of the City and County Hospital, Department of Public Health, San Francisco, California.

It was signed by the hospital director and contained a few other sentences of necessary bureaucratic trivia.

She folded it neatly, returned it to its envelope, and drew the second letter out. This one was handwritten, rather than typewritten, because it was a letter from a friend. Norah smiled at the headlong, impatient, but firm hand of her friend Esther Strauss. So like Esther's personality, she reckoned. There was perhaps something to handwriting analysis, a skill whose efficacy May had tried mightily to make Norah subscribe to. Norah tightened her grip on the two linen-paper pages in her hand. She didn't want to think of May, but it seemed as though the slightest thing would send her thoughts veering in that direction, and once sent on their way, they would travel that weary and painfully dispiriting journey until their inevitable and bitter end.

Norah shook her head and put the lantern near to the pages she held.

My dearest Norah,

We'll be seeing each other soon, but I cannot wait until that day and must send you my warmest congratulations on attaining your new position. It will be wonderful to see you again and, most of all, to resume our working relationship. My move to the West several years ago caused me to lose touch with all sorts of people, but thankfully you weren't one of them. It seems fated that you should accept this position. I can't take too much credit since you are eminently qualified, but I can say with some truth that I put your name forward after you'd written me that you wouldn't mind of a change of scene. Addison was favorably impressed by my opinion, but that wouldn't have been enough. The letters from your superiors at Bellevue cemented his decision.

Our department is growing, one of the few in the City hospital to expand. We find ourselves busier than ever and...

Esther's letter went on to offer her home as a temporary refuge until the time that Norah could seek lodging elsewhere. Norah re-folded it and returned it to its place. She extinguished the lantern and settled herself back on her pillow, willing sleep to come, and it did, but not for a very long time. Yes, she'd been offered a new post, but the real reason she'd sought to leave New York City was to try to escape her memories of the failed love affair with May Tillinghurst, her first and only love affair, so far. She tossed impatiently, trying to quiet her mind, but it was a long time before she could sleep.

❖

Three days later, Norah alit from the train and searched the crowd on the platform at the San Francisco train station until she spotted Esther waving at her vigorously from several feet away. In spite of the intervening years since their last meeting, Esther was unchanged. She still radiated confidence and energy, though perhaps she seemed a little more settled. Standing next to her was a dark-haired, bearded man looking slightly confused. This must be the famous Addison Grant, Norah thought, smiling: the one man who seemed to have captured Esther's heart, though not her hand in marriage. That, Norah reflected, was unlikely to ever happen. Once she decided something, Esther wasn't one to change her mind. About anything.

She made her way toward the couple and within a moment was wrapped in Esther's arms and soundly kissed on both cheeks. Esther's black eyes shone, and Addison looked on with a kind, indulgent expression. When Esther leaned back with both of Norah's hands in hers, he said, "My dear, you might introduce us."

"I was about to do that, Addison. Goodness, give Norah a chance to catch her breath."

To forestall further argument, Norah extended her hand to Addison. "I'm pleased to make your acquaintance, Doctor Grant. I've heard so—"

"Ha. Please call me Addison. We're not formal out West. And as a dear friend of Esther, you'll always be Norah." He grinned and pumped her hand.

They stood looking at one another, with Esther beaming at them for several seconds.

"My word. Let's not stand here a moment longer." Addison dropped her hand. "I'll go fetch the motor."

Norah raised her eyebrows as she caught Esther's eye. Esther rolled her eyes just a bit but smiled.

"Addison bought this auto from Whit last year and never goes anywhere without it. We're sorry to not have Clover and Princess to take us around in the carriage any more, but the automobile is a godsend."

Addison said, "Esther, can you help Norah retrieve her luggage?"

"Of course, my dear. Shall we meet you at the corner of Townsend and Fourth Street?"

Addison was already walking away swiftly and turned to call out, "In about ten minutes, love!" Then he disappeared into the crowd.

With the help of a porter, Norah and Esther located Norah's two suitcases. They were so heavy, the two of them were obliged to drag them along the platform, out through the lobby, and onto the street, pushing and pulling the unwieldy objects until they finally made it to the appointed spot, and while they waited, Norah took in the scene as she and Esther talked. The streets were jammed with people of all descriptions and all nationalities. Within the space of a moment, Norah spotted Negroes, Chinese, Italians, some dark-skinned folk she deduced must be Mexicans, and Europeans of every type. There were some obviously wealthy couples, but a large portion of San Francisco's citizens appeared to be the working poor. She was unruffled by the scene, since her last place of employment was Bellevue Hospital in Manhattan, whose patients crossed every conceivable strata of New York's citizens. There, she'd lived in an apartment building where the tenants were mostly Jewish.

The buildings surrounding the train station were ramshackle and poorly constructed, as though all had been thrown up in haste with no thought and no care. She noticed shoddy hotels, warehouses, and saloons. The sidewalks and streets were paved, but otherwise, the neighborhood looked every inch the Wild West of popular imagination.

"—in City, we have too many patients and not enough room and—" Norah caught the tail end of Esther's sentence.

"I'm sorry, Esther. I lost track of what you were saying."

Esther regarded her seriously, her gaze sharp and probing. That hadn't changed either.

"Oh, I'm merely complaining, as Addison says I do far too often, about the City and County Hospital. He's not one to dwell on its shortcomings. But I don't wish you to harbor any illusions. It's worse than Bellevue, if you can imagine, with even less money to support it. San Francisco has no shortage of wealth, believe me, but the politicians are more corrupt than those in New York."

"That doesn't concern me, Esther. You remember we always told one another it was necessary to shut out the 'noise,' as you called it, and focus on the patients."

"I did say that, didn't I? I still believe it, but the older I get, the harder it is to achieve. I wouldn't have encouraged you to accept the position if I didn't think it would ultimately be suitable for you. Even my selfish longing to see you wouldn't be enough reason to uproot you from your life and drag you all the way across the country. But you assured me you were ready for a change." Esther fell silent and looked closely again at Norah. Norah would tell her the whole story in due time. She couldn't let her grief and shame prevent her from telling Esther the truth, though she would have been happy to sweep it under the proverbial rug.

"No. I wanted to see you and I wanted to leave New York, and that's that. It couldn't have been a more welcome opportunity."

"Here's Addison." Esther gestured as a sturdy black sedan pulled up beside them. Clearly very proud of his auto, Addison jumped out without turning the motor off and loaded them and Norah's suitcases into the vehicle.

Addison drove north on Fourth Street until they reached a large, wide boulevard. MARKET STREET read the street sign, and it was jammed with vehicles of all descriptions: carriages, wagons, autos, and streetcars. Pedestrians thronged the sidewalks and milled, seemingly at random, across the streets as horns blew. It was as chaotic as downtown Manhattan, with several tall buildings but not quite as many as in New York. They'd turned left and, unlike in Manhattan, where buildings stretched as far as the eye could see, at the end of Market Street, surprisingly, stood two mountains. That was certainly a welcome change in scenery.

As they made their way up the street, Addison had to shout to be heard over the traffic noise. "We've left the Financial District and are moving into mostly residential areas." He waved at a hill to their right. "There's Nob Hill."

"I've heard of that," Norah said.

"Indeed. Most have. The richest of the rich live up there, but plenty more well-to-do people live in other parts of the City."

"Not so many down by the train station," Norah said.

"No, not at all. South of the Slot is the opposite. It's an eyesore, to say the least."

"South of the Slot?" Norah was mystified.

"He means the cable-car tracks on Market Street," Esther said. "That's what the people of San Francisco call it. South of the Slot is the poor neighborhood."

Addison swerved to avoid a bicyclist but, unperturbed, continued speaking. "My dear, we should be grateful that so many poor people live in San Francisco. They provide a never-ending supply of people whose ailments we can study."

"You're right, my love. And now we have another pair of hands to assist us." Esther beamed at Norah.

❖

Esther poked her head through the doorway of Norah's bedroom. "May I come in?"

Norah looked up from her open suitcase. She'd been debating how much to unpack. She wanted to find lodging sooner rather than later so that she wouldn't be a burden on her hosts. At supper, she'd met another member of their household, Beth Hammond, and heard about the fourth member, Beth's companion Kerry, who was at work. She made five in the house, and in her mind, that was too many people for one household.

"Certainly."

Esther sat down on the bed and clasped her hands around her knee, which she crossed over her opposite leg. Norah marveled at how ladylike Esther seemed even when she took such positions.

"Are you comfortable? Do you need anything?" Esther asked, again looking closely at her as though she had a question other than those she'd just voiced.

"Oh, yes. I'm very grateful to you for taking me in. I plan to find my own rooms as soon as possible."

"Please don't worry yourself. We're glad to have you."

"I appreciate that, but I should be on my own." Norah folded several articles of clothing and stowed them back in the suitcase. Esther wanted her to talk, and she found herself reluctant to do so. She didn't want Esther to think her foolish, though that was how she felt. But she wanted to talk about May to someone who'd understand.

To stall for time, she said, "Addison is exactly how I pictured. He's a dear."

"That he is. For the most part."

"What could possibly be wrong?"

"He still wants us to marry."

"Oh, Esther dear, why ever not? It's not as though you'd suddenly have to turn into a dutiful, housebound wife."

"I don't think so but one never knows. Something happens to men when they finally succeed in having that gold ring about their beloved's finger. They are no longer tender and gallant and accommodating but instead turn into horrid tyrants. Legally, that is their right. I've told him that marriage is not only not necessary for me, but it's most unwelcome."

"Surely that wouldn't happen to you and Addison."

"I've no such assurances. I'm quite content with my lot. But enough of me. How have you been since the break with May?"

"I've prevailed. It's not something I think about." Norah tried to make her tone light, but her friend would have none of it. Besides, it was a lie.

"Please, dear Norah. Don't try to deceive me. It was a blow to you, I know. You're not a woman who can take betrayal in stride. None of us can. Not even me. Don't forget that I'm well acquainted with Miss May, and I'm sure she tried to soothe you with honeyed words and ardent kisses."

Norah blushed because that was exactly what had happened. When she had confronted May with the evidence of her mischief, she was furious, but somehow nothing was solved, nothing was apologized for. Instead, she was drawn into bed and forgot all about it until she woke up the next morning, ashamed and depressed. She was in love with someone who was, while beautiful and seductive, entirely unworthy and unreliable. Norah was appalled at her own weakness. She'd had to make a break, and leaving New York was the only way she could keep herself from May.

"Yes, but I finally could endure no more. Your offer couldn't have come at a better time."

"That was my hope, though you aren't someone to dwell in misery for long. We've work to do at the City hospital, but more than that, I believe you can find happiness here in San Francisco."

"I wish I could share your optimism, but I'm not certain that my heart is even open to another."

Esther stood up and brushed her skirt neatly. "Well. We cannot say for sure, but perhaps you needn't look so much as to just wait and see what and who comes your way. Now, I'll leave you, since you must be tired."

"I am a little, thanks."

Esther embraced her and patted her back tenderly.

Norah fell asleep, for once not thinking of May but of a new beginning.

❖

Kerry O'Shea straightened her chef's toque and made sure the sleeves of her pristine white jacket were rolled to precisely the same length on each arm. She entered the huge kitchen of the Palace Hotel, where ten cooks labored at top speed to finish the dishes for the luncheon banquet they would present in less than hour. Kerry was still, technically, a line cook, but her boss, Chef Fermel, had finally, albeit begrudgingly, given her more responsibility. She'd demanded a higher wage and had gotten that too. Fermel didn't want to be in charge of lunch banquets the Palace had instituted to make more money for the restaurant. Kerry had volunteered, and the stubborn French chef had finally agreed, but only because he saw prestige to be gained with no effort on his part.

She walked the line, tasting everything. She said, as she walked, "More salt but not too much" and "Glaze that immediately—are you asleep?" and gave other pointed directions. The cooks might grumble but they obeyed. Fermel had threatened them with the boot if they didn't listen to her.

She went to the middle dining room, where the placard outside the door read SAN FRANCISCO NATURAL HISTORY SOCIETY ANNUAL LUNCHEON THE TWENTIETH OF JANUARY, 1906 and listed the dishes to be served. The pièce de résistance was an enormous baron of roast beef au jus, cooked so that all preferences for doneness could be catered to. She had directed the roasting personally and, after checking the banquet room itself to ensure its readiness, returned to the kitchen and issued her final directions.

At precisely one p.m., Kerry stood at the end of the buffet tables next to the roast beef and smiled as she greeted the attendees of the luncheon party. A staid lot, they all seemed to be grizzled men, mostly wearing spectacles, whether they were young or old. Kerry didn't know what the San Francisco Natural History Society was and didn't much care, as long as they enjoyed their luncheon. Near the end of the shuffling line, one Society member who didn't resemble the rest of them caught her eye.

She was well above medium height for a woman. She was, in fact, the only woman save one present. She neither resembled the male Society members nor the other female present in the least. She moved swiftly and surely, with enviable vigor, choosing this or that morsel and filling her plate. She arrived at the roast-beef station and paused.

Kerry caught her eye and smiled. She was, on closer look, middle aged, and her face was tanned as though she spent much time out of doors. Her tawny hair was done up in a bun from which several hairs fell haphazardly. Her clothes were not fashionable but appeared to be sturdy and utilitarian, with the skirt short enough to show her ankles, though they were encased in lace-up shoes also clearly worn for comfort. She scrutinized the baron of beef with some interest.

"Where was this meat obtained?" she asked. Her tone was brisk, not impolite, but she spoke in the manner of someone who got to the point and expected everyone to whom she spoke to do the same.

"The Palace Hotel buys its meats from the Macmillan Wholesale slaughterhouse on Folsom Street, where we—"

"Not where it was slaughtered, Chef. What ranch raised the cow from which it came?"

"Ah, I don't know that, but I believe MacMillan buys its beef cows from various ranches in northern California." Kerry was a bit put off but also intrigued. She also liked being called Chef. Though she didn't have that special title, she saw no reason to correct the lady.

"Which ranch makes a difference, you know," the lady said. Though "lady" wasn't exactly the word Kerry would apply to her. She wore her skirt with the air of someone who would be more comfortable wearing trousers.

"Well, I'm sure that's true, but I believe MacMillan would not accept animals of inferior quality. Which cut of the roast would you prefer?" Kerry tried out a smile, which she was pleased to see elicited one back from the lady.

"Rare. If it's going to be tough, I'd rather have a piece which is not overcooked to the texture of saddle leather.

Kerry decided it wouldn't do any good to be offended. She motioned to the cook to serve the strange woman.

"You have experience with beef cattle? Are you a rancher?" Kerry was hoping to engage the woman in conversation.

The woman laughed with such an unforced and open expression of cheer, Kerry was charmed.

"Good heavens, no. I'm a botanist. But I've spent a good deal of time at various farms and ranches all over the West, and my hosts have kindly educated me on the variations in taste and texture of meat depending upon where the cattle graze."

Kerry wondered what in the world a 'botanist' was, but she needed to keep the line of guests moving.

"Well, please enjoy this roast beef, wherever it may have come from." She beamed with what she hoped was hospitality.

"I certainly hope I shall." With that, the woman walked off in conversation with a tall gentleman and found a seat.

❖

Abigail Eliot hadn't especially wanted to attend the annual luncheon. She'd been absorbed in cataloguing and preserving more than three-dozen plants she'd returned home with from a trip to Washington State the previous week. But it would be impolitic not to do so. She reluctantly had left her workroom on the sixth floor of the San Francisco Natural History Society's headquarters at Market and

Fifth Street in downtown San Francisco to walk the six blocks east to the Palace Hotel.

This was the first occasion that the Society had chosen the Palace for its annual party. They'd previously patronized a restaurant farther into the Financial District north of Market Street.

She ate lunch and chatted amiably with the other guests, most of whom she'd known and liked for years. The exception was Howard Sellars, the deputy director. He was not as companionable as Society members usually were. In fact, in her view, he was wholly unsuited for his position, as he possessed not an ounce of charm and very little appreciation for science. He was old-fashioned and disdainful of women, which increased her dislike. The Natural History Society had a tradition of accepting members of both genders. Though he never said anything, Abby was aware of his disdainful attitude toward her.

Abby was, however, intrigued by the chef she'd conversed with. On first look, she appeared to be male, but when speaking with her Abby had realized she was not. She was merely a masculine woman of a type that Abby was not unfamiliar with. The ranchers and farmers who were so kind to give her lodging when she was on a collecting trip were not society dames. They were tough, no-nonsense women who worked hard, didn't take on airs, and didn't expect deference. This chef was of that ilk. Abby had caught her frankly appraising look, but it hadn't bothered her. What others thought of her was of no consequence to her other than the professional esteem she garnered in recognition of her work.

The luncheon dragged on through dessert, coffee, and a few speeches by officials who should have known better than to keep the scientists away from their work too long. The guests were happy to eat the very delicious food, but then they wished to return to their workrooms and their researches. Abby certainly did, and she especially didn't care to listen to unctuous, insincere, and boring words from Howard Sellars.

Before she left, Abby stopped to thank the chef. She had enjoyed the food and wanted to say so, but she also wanted another chance to speak with this interesting woman. She surmised that a big restaurant kitchen wouldn't be especially hospitable to a woman, but perhaps as in science, competence could overcome men's prejudices.

"Thank you so much. I quite enjoyed the roast of beef and the stewed tomatoes and the new potatoes. Well, everything. I commend your abilities."

"You're quite welcome. I certainly hope you feel moved to patronize our restaurant. We've a lovely Ladies' Grill. It would be my pleasure to cook for you."

Abby was taken aback but, again, charmed. She generally ate a hasty home-assembled luncheon at her desk. She was mostly indifferent to food as long as it had some taste and was filling. She needed fuel when she was out in the wilderness pursuing plants.

To her surprise, she found herself saying, "I would be honored. Shall I call ahead?"

"Please do, and ask the manager to inform Kerry O'Shea. I'll prepare something especially for you." Kerry bowed slightly from the waist, and her grin was rakish. Abby couldn't help but grin back.

Beth Hammond settled her stethoscope in her ears and listened to the heartbeat of the woman in the bed before her. She was weak and pale, and her swollen belly looked out of place on her thin frame. She'd come to the hospital complaining of a headache and fever, and she was likely ill with typhoid. This would not be good for her unborn child, but Beth could do nothing more than treat her fever and hope for the best.

In the year since she'd finished medical school, Beth had been educated in the vast difference between the theory of the classroom and the reality of sick people. She loved to comfort people, to heal them, make them feel better. She'd instinctively done that as a nurse. Now, she had to do much more and had much less time for the emotional needs of her patients. She had to determine what was wrong, and then she had to take steps to remedy it. She had to be smart and decisive, and she had to be correct. One mistake could mean that someone died or was severely impaired.

She'd thought many times about returning to nursing, where that responsibility was more the doctor's and she had only to follow doctor's orders, comfort, and clean. But in the end, she'd decided to stick it out. She had Addison and Esther as her mentors and didn't want to disappoint them. When she made the right diagnosis, the feeling was transcendent. She'd never had that much gratification when she was a nurse. Each new patient presented a new mystery or more than one mystery to solve.

And as she well knew, the patient might or might not know how to behave in her best interest or even tell her doctor the truth.

She kept her stethoscope in place and studied her patient's face. The woman's eyes were bright and feverish. She sat up suddenly and coughed, her face bright red. Beth discreetly turned aside to avoid contagion.

"I think we can say definitively you've contracted typhoid fever. Tell me about the sanitary arrangements at your home. Where do you live?"

"Doctor, I got to get home and take care of my husband and our little Joey. He's not but six year. My husband, he works all night at the dock and he has to sleep during the day. He ain't going to be able to do that with Joey pesterin' him. What can you give me to get me better?"

"Mrs.—" Beth looked at her chart. She could barely keep the names straight of her patients. "Williams, you must stay here for a couple weeks until we can get you well. Typhoid is a very dangerous disease. Do you have a neighbor who can help out with your boy?" Beth knew that the poor working people of San Francisco had little in the way of resources except one another.

"I dunno, Doc. Maggie across the hall could maybe take him. My man is not partial to Maggie, but I got to figure something." She kept talking, and as usual, Beth let herself get sidetracked by the patient's litany of woe and didn't receive an answer to her question. If their water source was contaminated, other people in the area would sicken.

Beth took Mrs. Williams's wrist to check her pulse. A simple action like that could serve to distract the patient from her fretful fixations, and Beth could artfully uncover the information she needed,

"You've got a privy in the backyard?"

"Uh-huh. But there's too many people sharing it."

"Where does your water come from?"

"It comes from a well a little ways away."

If Beth was right, it was likely the privy wasn't far enough away from the well and could contaminate the neighborhood water source. Addison had taught her to look at the patients' environment as well as their symptoms.

Beth lowered Mrs. Williams's wrist. "We must keep you here for a few days."

"Oh, Doctor, what'll I do with my husband and my son and—"

"Is Mr. Williams coming to see you today?"

"He'll come later before his shift. He'll wanna take me home."

"We'll speak with him as soon as he arrives. Please tell Nurse Davis, and she'll find me. And, Mrs. Williams, try not to worry. You must rest so that you can get well." Beth patted her hand and looked at her earnestly. She could sometimes use both her authority as a doctor and her empathy as a woman to induce the correct response from recalcitrant patients.

She was pleased that Mrs. Williams nodded, lay back on her pillow, and closed her eyes. Beth went to wash her hands and reflected that was but the first step. Next would come convincing Mrs. Williams's husband that he had to accommodate his wife's illness and not insist she come home to resume her normal duties. When the time came, she'd see if the man was of a loving and sympathetic bent or self-centered, lazy, and argumentative. She went on to the next bed, the next complaint, the next set of personal problems.

CHAPTER TWO

Norah leaned back on the sofa and accepted a cup of tea from Esther. They were at home in the big house on Fillmore Street while the rest of the household was still out at their various occupations. Addison remained at the hospital with a patient in crisis. Beth was busy as well. She'd recently started to consult in the children's ward as well as the women's. She was attempting a study of some of the common diseases of the South of the Slot neighborhood and had interviews to conduct. Esther and Addison were very proud of their protégé. Kerry was downtown cooking at the Palace, as usual. Norah reflected that for such a house full of folks, they were rarely all at home at the same time.

She had been there only a few weeks, but she felt at home and integrated into the commune, as they called it. She had Esther's full disclosure of the nature of the residents in one of her letters. She was very taken with Kerry and Beth, who couldn't have been more different from one another but seemed a quite harmonious duo. She wanted to hear more about them at some time but didn't want to pry.

Esther grinned at her over the rim of her teacup.

"Well, I believe you've received a fair picture of what we must contend with."

They'd spent part of their day in a long, drawn-out meeting with the director of the hospital, the chief of the hospital's infectious-diseases department, Addison, the chief nurse, and the hospital accountant, arguing about the costs of implementing the vaccination program. Esther and Norah were in favor of taking a visiting-nurse approach and sending them out to the neighborhoods of San Francisco to meet people on their home fields instead of making them come to the hospital. As usual, the argument centered on the cost of prevention versus that cost of treating sick people. Norah was sure they'd not receive what they requested in resources but would get something. She was grateful for Esther's advocacy. A forceful speaker, she knew the various interested parties and could frame her appeals to suit her audience. Norah sat listening and marveling at Esther's speaking ability. In the end, they reached an agreement. Norah would have another physician and two nurses who would help with the outpatient vaccination program. They would preserve the weekend clinic as well.

"I'm doubly in your debt, Esther. Maybe triply, if I count your obtaining the job for me, giving me a place to live, and then arguing on my behalf with the City people."

"You must think of it as you helping me, my dear Norah, and not the other way around. I'm determined to press ahead with our public-health work. Addison and Beth are keen to help out, and with you and Doctor Denny, that makes five." The telephone in the kitchen rang.

Esther hurried to answer it. She'd told Norah they'd had it installed the previous year, thinking it would be helpful for City and County to be able to summon them at once for any problem. It was a mixed blessing, Esther said, for though it could ease communication, it tended to ring far too much. The Palace would call for Kerry. Many of their friends and acquaintances called as well instead of simply coming over.

Esther returned in a few moments. "Beth's friend Scott. He wishes to leave a message for her."

"What sort of friend?" Norah assumed that Beth, like herself, had to contend with the attentions of young men who saw her as marriage material in spite of her profession.

Esther raised her eyebrows. "Oh, nothing like you think. They attended the University of California Medical Department together. He's not a suitor. Quite the opposite. Let's just say he's much like Arthur from the Bellevue fund-raising office." She referred to their former colleague, whose expertise in making well-to-do, would-be hospital patrons part with their money was legendary.

"Oh. I understand." Norah grinned.

"And he is charming, of course, though Beth is disappointed that he not only went into private practice but joined the practice of a Nob Hill physician who took quite a fancy to him." Esther rolled her eyes. "Beth and he were inseparable in medical school, and I'm sure she assumed he would follow her into public service, or at least take up a practice that included some charity patients. But it wasn't to be."

"You and Addison mentioned Nob Hill on our trip home from the train station."

"Yes. Just substitute 'Park Avenue' and you'll grasp what I'm saying."

"I see. He's going to become almost as wealthy as his patients," Norah said.

"So he hopes, I imagine. Beth doesn't think it's right for him, but she loves him too much to break their friendship over it. Doctor Scott Wilton is quite the society doctor, but he's still welcome here."

"Beth isn't the type of woman to throw over a friend for a disagreement. I can see that."

"Not at all. She's loyal to a fault. Unlike some we know." Esther grimaced, and Norah knew she was referring to May.

Norah was silent and Esther looked at her sharply.

"I've not troubled you, have I? That wasn't my intention. I was trying to induce you to laugh a little, or at least see that May was unworthy of you and it's best that your connection is severed and that you're well away from her and have begun a new life."

"I know all of that is true, Esther but I'm still lonely and regretful. It's not as simple for us as it is for you. Finding and keeping love is more an exception than a rule."

"I would submit that is true for everyone. Loveless marriages are quite common."

"So I see. I assume that's one reason you and Addison haven't married."

"Not precisely. I don't believe marriage in itself destroys love. I just believe that its legal framework that gives men power over women is abominable, and I'm afraid that, even as compatible as we are, if we were to marry, Addison would wish to take up his prerogatives, which would not do for me. That would surely destroy our happiness or, at least, *my* happiness." She chuckled.

"Oh, surely not. He behaves with you as though you're his equal in all ways."

"He does, but that's because we're not married." Esther laughed, a little grimly, Norah thought. "But back to you, my dear friend. What can we do to increase your social prospects? I'll have to think on it. We have some staff members at City that I suspect may be of your bent, but I can't say for sure."

"I may know to whom you refer, but how would I find out?"

"That I don't know, but at least perhaps we could make a party where we pull folk out of the hospital milieu and into a more social atmosphere and see what transpires. What do you think?"

"I don't know, really. I'd rather wait a little while, if you don't mind." The prospect terrified Norah. She was still smarting from May's betrayal and couldn't imagine taking up with someone new, never mind the difficulty of even finding a suitable woman.

"Oh course, dear. I'll not nag you about it. The time will come when you'll feel like meeting new people. Oh, goodness. I think that's Addison now." The front door opened, and Norah could hear Addison calling, "Anyone home?" Esther gave her a smile over her shoulder as she hurried to greet her paramour and welcome him home. Norah was happy that Esther was happy but also envious. She feared she would never have the brand of happiness that sprang from deep love shared with a compatible partner.

For a while, it seemed that she and May would enjoy it. For a very short while. It was quite possibly her inexperience that had led Norah to become emotionally entrapped by a person like May. Perhaps she assumed that because her suitor was female, matters would be different, but it wasn't so. Norah felt like an enormous fool and wondered when that feeling would go away, if ever.

❖

"You'll never guess who I saw today," Kerry said to Beth.

Beth was sitting at the dining-room table with stacks of forms surrounding her, tabulating the answers to questions she'd devised for the City patients from the South of Market area. She was hoping to give a paper on it at a doctors' convention that would occur in a few months. She had to drag her attention from her work to Kerry.

"Who was that, dearest?"

"Abigail Eliot, the botanist," Kerry said, with considerable self-satisfaction. "She came to the Palace to have lunch, just as I asked her to. I made sure to speak with her, and she told me all about her work at the San Francisco Natural History Society. I don't know as I can see why someone would care so much about dead plants, but I'm positive she's not married. She never once mentioned a husband. She has that air—you know what I mean, love."

"I suppose. Kerry dearest, I must finish this before I go to bed."

"Oh, all right, Bethy. I'll leave you be. But I was excited and wanted to share with you."

"I know, love. We'll have to talk later."

Kerry nodded, looking bereft. She'd become eager to find those she considered like herself and Beth: women who preferred women. They saw Marjorie and Florence on occasion, but Kerry still had reservations about the way Marjorie treated Florence and only agreed to socialize with them for Beth's sake.

Beth counted the forms she still had to review and went to get another coffee from their kitchen. Their cook had made a huge urn of it as soon as she arrived for the afternoon. They'd finally had to hire someone because, though Kerry tried to keep up with their meals, she was often far too busy at the Palace. They'd have starved if they hadn't had someone in to cook.

Beth hoped that she'd get more recognition if she could publish some scholarly articles. She'd get speaking honorariums, and perhaps the City and County Hospital would increase her salary. She and Kerry were still struggling to save money for their house and to repay Beth's loans for medical school.

❖

Kerry had cooked a tasty lunch for Abigail on the day she came to lunch. As she sat and talked with her for a short while, she watched Abby closely and listened for clues as to her marital status. The absence of mention of husband, plus Abby's cheerful obsession with finding, preserving, and cataloguing plants, convinced Kerry she was potentially a lesbian. Esther had taught her that word, along with much more information. It was quite momentous news to Kerry that New York seemed to harbor large numbers of such women. She'd been slightly suspicious of Esther at first but had quickly warmed up to her as she found that she was the exact opposite of Laura, Addison's former and unmissed wife.

She was eager to tell Beth all about Abby, but Beth wasn't in the mood to chat, so she went off to find Esther. Esther had proved to be one of the most convivial people Kerry had ever met.

She was also working, as did Addison and Beth at home after their hours at the hospital. But she was reading something in the parlor and looked up, smiling, when Kerry entered. Kerry had brought her a piece of pie as an extra bribe. Beth was often, to Kerry's dismay, entirely indifferent to food.

"Oh, my," Esther said, "Did you make the pie or did Mrs. Hughes?"

"I did, and I assure you it's far superior to anything Mrs. Hughes could manage." Kerry grinned and presented it to Esther with a flourish. "Where's Addison?"

"Oh, still at City. He said he'd rather work in his office than try to concentrate with a houseful of women." She laughed and Kerry echoed her. Addison often complained in a teasing way of his status as the sole male. They both knew he truly enjoyed it rather than the opposite.

"How's Beth?" Esther asked, her black eyes dancing.

"How else? Working." Kerry sighed.

"You must be patient, Kerry. Beth wants to advance professionally. It's good for her, and in time it will be good for you both." Esther had helped them understand one another better and become more compatible and more patient with each other, and she knew all about their future plans.

"I know. I just miss her."

"She misses you as well, but matters will improve."

"I want to tell you about someone I met." Kerry sketched a picture of her new acquaintance.

"How very interesting. If I can convince Norah, I want to make a party very soon to welcome her, and we shall have to invite this Abigail."

"Oh, yes. We ought to. I wonder about her true story, but in any case, she's friendly. She loves my cooking anyhow." Kerry laughed, recalling how much Abby had praised the food she'd served her and compared it to her usual fare.

"She's odd. She works up the street at the natural-history place where they're all scientific types. Everyone studies some little part of nature. She's the curator of botany." Kerry enunciated this title carefully.

"Well, that's quite a grand title."

"But she acts like a regular person, even though she goes all over the western states on trips and looks for her plants. She must be really smart. She started spitting out Latin names of plants like it was nothing."

"She sounds like a gem. Yes, we can certainly invite her. We'll need to ask some of the folks from the hospital. And Scott, of course, and Whit too, I suppose. Not a large party. We don't want to overwhelm Norah."

"No, not at all. I like her very much." It was true. The melancholy but lovely dark-haired doctor was a pleasant houseguest, modest and undemanding. Kerry wondered about her air of sadness and decided to ask Esther, who undoubtedly knew, as she seemed to know everything about everybody, including her.

"Norah seems very unhappy, even though she's always pleasant to all of us and especially loves to talk to Beth."

"She had an unfortunate love affair in New York. With May, whom you remember me telling you about? May's quite vivacious and pretty but, like many of that ilk, a butterfly, flighty and inconstant. She loves the chase, but once you've caught her, she wishes immediately to get away. Norah was quite enamored of her, I understand, and took their break very hard."

"That's unfortunate, but she's here, and we must try to cheer her up and show her San Francisco is a much superior city to New York."

"That we must. Off with you and leave me to my journal-reading. We'll plan the party soon."

❖

Abby had a practice she loved to engage in when she went to work in the morning. She traveled the fourteen blocks from her home in Russian Hill down to Market Street, and as she walked she counted the little plants that sprang up between the cobblestones. She planned on a more rigorous cataloguing of them when she was able, but in the meantime, she counted them and admired their adaptive abilities among the stones. Fortunately, Russian Hill was too steep for horses to ascend safely unless they were beaten and forced to climb.

She loved the fact that plants could and frequently were able to live just about anywhere. From the cultured environs of Golden Gate Park to the rocky vastness of the Sierra, living things gained a foothold and thrived. They were admirable and they were lovely, all in their own ways. She appreciated the animals and birds as part of God's great creation, but the flowers and the trees in their humble but infinitely varied lives moved her the most. She was grateful every single day of her life that she could devote herself to them. Few people indeed were as blessed as she was to be able make her life's work of what she loved best. It was a singular gift, and she was deeply aware of how unusual it was. Her colleagues at the Society aside, most people to her mind were forced to make their living either in hard labor or engaged in trade, politics, or financial pursuits, none of which held the least interest to her.

She tramped downhill, keeping a good pace. As a dedicated walker, she could not only keep up with most men out on the trail but surpass a good many of them. Her walk back and forth to work every day was but a mild stroll compared to what she was used to on mountain trails. It would be time to plan a trip soon, as it was early spring and time for the wildflowers to bloom in the Sierra Madre.

Some might say her life was incomplete because she had no home, no husband, no children, but she disagreed. Her life was as rich and as full as that of any married woman and a good deal happier, as far she could tell. She was self-sufficient but friendly. She had hosts of friends up and down California and within the ranks of botany enthusiasts from all over the world. She associated love with friendship, had never had a special person, and had no feeling of lack on her part.

She didn't mind the bustle of the City, where the Society kept its headquarters, as it was necessary for them to maintain a central facility with easy access to San Francisco's many attractions as well as the wealthy donors who supported their work. Her true home was in nature: in the mountains or the forest, and even in the desert. She had read John Muir's writings and agreed with him wholeheartedly.

Abby entered the front door of the Society, walked past the stuffed mastodon in the foyer, and climbed its grand marble staircase to her workrooms on the sixth floor. There, she put her jacket and bag in the small office adjoining the workroom and then went to the lavatory to wash her hands before handling her plant specimens.

She was still describing, preserving, and cataloguing the material she'd brought back from Monterey three weeks before. She took one plant from the heavy papers it was pressed between, and with her magnifier and her identifying key, she carefully and minutely examined its features. In her notebook she had recorded the exact location, date, and time of day that she'd collected it. It could turn out it to be a completely different species than the ones already described in the literature. If that was true, she could be the one to describe it, name it, and get credit for it in the botanical world. She'd had three such successes in her life.

It was immensely gratifying to discover something new, some flower no one had seen or some shrub that was found in a completely new environment. She bent to her work, her mind alive and alert as she recorded notes in her clear handwriting. She sat surrounded by the Natural History Society's enormous collection of plants. They lay silent, treasured and preserved in the vast wooden cases, drawer upon drawer. If Abby couldn't be in the wilderness looking for new specimens, she was nearly as happy in this room surrounded by her favorite companions.

❖

It was time for Norah to think of finding her own place to live. She enjoyed the hospitality of the commune but needed some independence. Part of her wished to remain with Esther, Beth, Addison, and Kerry indefinitely. She was much less lonely and bereft than she'd been in the weeks after May left. They were all in and out of the house and full of their plans and their work, but at least once a week, the whole household had a dinner together, and in their company, Norah would experience something close to happiness, though seeing the interaction of two devoted couples made her wistful and sorry for herself sometimes.

If only things had turned out differently with May. She'd still be in New York, and they would be happily domiciled together, sleeping together every night and loving every day. Now she was in her bedroom sitting near the window to read a book by the afternoon light. At such times her memories would intrude on the present and send her into a funk.

They'd met at a party, of course. Esther had brought her around to meet her anarchist friends, Miss Goldman's followers. The great lady herself would be in attendance, and many guests were expected. Norah was shy and had a difficult time talking unless spoken to first. May sat down next to her on a settee with a glass of sherry in her hand and started conversing with Norah as though they were already acquainted.

"Oh, forgive me," she had said merrily. "I've a bad habit of prattling away before properly introducing myself." To Norah, it sounded as though she was not at all sorry that she behaved this way, and Norah was disposed to forgive her. It was much later when Norah discovered that May had a great many characteristics for which she needed to apologize but never did.

She was curly haired, blond, and had the rounded hourglass figure so beloved of fashionable magazines. Norah was consumed by her beauty before the evening had ended. May would leave her to fly across the room to greet someone else effusively, but she always returned to Norah's side. Her gaze, direct and unwavering, caught Norah and held her, mesmerized and immobilized. She'd never met such a creature, whose effortless attractiveness engaged both sexes and all ages and manner of people.

At the end of that evening, May presented her with a card and asked with the air of someone who knew the answer to her question, "Would it be possible we may meet again sometime? For tea or for meal or a concert? I do so much wish to know you better."

And for Norah, the answer had been a foregone conclusion. And so it began.

Norah closed her book, sighed, and looked out the window down at the street. Fillmore Street was well out of downtown San Francisco and quiet in the late afternoon. Would she ever truly begin to feel at ease again, to experience happiness and contentment? She put her book aside and went to straighten her hair in the looking glass. Her dark-brown hair was thick and heavy and tended to become unmoored from the pins that she used to tame it. As she neatened her hair and repinned it, she suddenly recalled the first time May had touched her hair, murmuring about its beauty and its texture so that Norah became nervous and warm at the same time.

She gave a grunt of frustration, patted her hair one final time, and went downstairs to see if the evening paper had been delivered so that she could scan the ads for rooms to let.

Beth had seen Scott perform the same ritual countless times. He removed his overcoat and handed it to the coat-check man, at whom he grinned with far too much familiarity until the man responded with his own grin. He placed a hand on Beth's back and guided her as they followed the headwaiter to the table, pulled out her chair, and pushed it in as she seated herself, then sat down across from her, straightened his silverware, and shook out his napkin before turning his sparkling green eyes to her face with a jovial smirk.

They were at Delmonico's, an extremely expensive restaurant that was one of the chief rivals of the Palace Hotel. The establishment made Beth uncomfortable, but Scott had chosen it and he was paying, so she kept silent. She fought to keep her disquiet at bay because she had no wish to pick a fight with him, no matter how much he irritated her. He was her closest friend and she felt she must overlook his idiosyncrasies, but it was becoming harder all the time.

He snapped his fingers at the nearest waiter in an imperious fashion. The man came over to their table and Scott ordered a bottle of wine, an expensive one.

When Beth held up hand to stop him from pouring her a full glass of wine, he said, "Don't be concerned, Miss Beth. I'll see you safely home as I always do. Please don't worry if you drink too much. Enjoy yourself for once."

"I enjoy your company, Scott, and I don't need large amounts of wine to make me merrier."

He shook his head and sipped his glass of wine as they looked over their menus.

"I hear the roast duck is superior here," Scott said.

"I'm not very hungry and duck is a bit rich for me." Beth anticipated indigestion. "I think perhaps a veal cutlet without any sauce."

"I swear, Miss Beth, you're becoming more like your patients every day."

"Whatever do you mean by that?"

He leaned back and crossed his legs, drumming his fingers on the table. She knew that tic from their student days when he was impatient with something he heard that he considered silly.

"You know. You're behaving as though, like them, you have to live in a scratched manner, that fine food and drink are beyond your means."

"It's not that. I just don't like to overeat or drink too much. Either makes me feel unwell."

"Indeed. Well, I'll have to make up for your lack."

"How's the practice?" she asked to change the subject. He enjoyed nothing more than boasting about his wealthy patients.

"Couldn't be better. You wouldn't believe the referrals we receive. I think Mrs. A.N. Townsend is going to ring us up very soon. Mrs. Collis P. Huntington promised she'd recommend us to her."

"Who's that?" Beth knew Mrs. Collis P. Huntington was the wife of a big railroad tycoon, but the other name was unfamiliar to her.

"Who's that, you ask. Mrs. Townsend is the widow of the vice president and general manager of the Central Pacific Railroad." He seemed irritated that she didn't recognize the name.

"Congratulations, Scott. I'm glad to know you and Whit are acquiring so many patients." The older doctor Scott had been taken into practice with had a name almost as imposing as those of his illustrious patients: Anderson Whitmore Ellsworth, III. Scott had also fallen in love with him. Their medical partnership provided a perfect cover for them to be together. They maintained separate houses, but it was all for show. Beth liked Whit but thought him shallow and greedy, and Scott, between love and ambition, had taken on many of Whit's characteristics, much to Beth's dismay.

"We may have to hire another associate soon, but I hope not. We need to find ways to efficiently care for everyone without taking too much time. Whit's certain that we could make more money if we advertised to cure hysteria."

"What does that mean?"

"Whit talked to a doctor from Chicago, who told him that his female patients who complained of nerves and depression were suffering from the peculiar female ailment of hysteria. It's necessary to massage their female parts to ensure their wombs are in place. Enough of that and they experience a paroxysm and go away calm and happy." He leaned back, looking smug. "Whit thinks we ought to start offering that service."

Beth was aghast because it dawned on her what he was talking about. "Perhaps if their husbands were more attentive and competent lovers, they'd have no need of your hysteria 'treatment,'" she said tartly.

Scott guffawed. "Ah, to be sure, but that isn't likely to occur, so in the meantime, we doctors must do our best." He grinned at her, and Beth was certain he was thinking *she* would be very good at this treatment but was not indiscreet enough to say so, for which she was grateful.

"Prescriptions are also an excellent way to go. Many of the ladies are happiest when they leave my office and return home with a new medicine."

Beth found all of this news horrifying, and it must have shown on her face, because Scott, always so vigilant about her moods, noticed and fixed her with a searching look.

"Tell me, Miss Beth. Does something concern you?"

"Scott! That's no way to practice medicine. You're doing your patients a disservice by not being honest with them and taking their money for nothing! I can scarcely believe I'm hearing you talk this way."

"Oh? Is that how you see it? Well, I don't. I'm not slaving away in a charity hospital, underpaid and underappreciated. My patients go away happy after they see me, and no one is hurt."

His reference to her employment offended her, but she decided to let it pass. Though he'd changed so much from their medical-school days, he was still her beloved Scott, who could be gentle, charming, and funny. She wished those sides of him were more in evidence more often.

She changed the subject again. "I understand your position. How is Whit getting along these days?"

"Whit is absolutely magnificent in every way." Scott sighed theatrically.

Beth had to laugh. It made a real difference that Scott had found love. He'd gone through medical school without it, and she'd felt sorry for him. She just wished he'd not fallen in love with someone like Whit, but she never said so.

"I'm happy to hear that, and when is your next visit back to Charleston?" That question sent Scott off on one of his hilarious recountings of his large family's crazy personalities and mishaps. She could listen and be entertained and not have to worry about starting an argument.

When dinner was over and they were on their way back to the commune, Scott seemed subdued. He stopped the car in front of the house and hugged Beth.

"Thanks for being my friend. I don't know what I'd do without you. You're the only friend Whit isn't jealous of because he knows you won't take me away from him."

"But doesn't he trust you?" This information appalled Beth.

"No, but I may have given him reason." Scott sat with his chin on his chest. "I was a little too charming to the son of one his wealthiest patients."

"Oh, Scott."

"So he's quite suspicious of my friends. Even old Tom Trenton. You remember him." Scott referred to one of their classmates, a homely but intelligent and companionable man. Beth could only shake her head.

Whit and Scott, of course, had an auto, much more luxurious than Addison's second-hand vehicle, which he had bought from Whit, who had had their fancy car shipped over from Great Britain for an enormous sum.

"Good night, Scott. Thank you for dinner and be well. I hope to see you soon."

"My pleasure, Miss Beth, and please tell Kerry I want to partake of her cooking sometime soon."

She gave his arm a squeeze and left him.

Norah walked into the foyer of the commune, removed her coat and hat, and hung them up on one of the many hooks near the door. She was tired after her day at the hospital. She'd been preparing all week for the Saturday clinic and keeping an eye on several patients at the same time. Esther was at home, she noticed. Her coat was there on a peg. She had seen her early in the morning just in passing. The house staff was always busy, as was customary in a big public hospital. But their paths hadn't crossed for the rest of the day, which was unusual.

She went to the foot of the staircase and called out, "Esther, dear? I'm home." She heard a faint murmur and was surprised. The Esther she knew would have arrived at the top of the staircase to answer her cheerfully. She mounted the stairs to the third floor, where Esther and Addison's bedroom was situated.

The door was open, and there lay Esther on the quilt on the big four-poster bed with a cloth on her forehead.

"Esther! Whatever is the matter? Are you unwell?" She crossed the room to stand next to the bed.

"Ah, Norah, I'm not feeling too well today. I vomited earlier and I'm so nauseated, I was afraid to try to eat again. That made me feel light-headed, but now I'm hungry. Very hungry."

"Let me fix you some tea and toast. Goodness, you must eat something. Have you acquired some bug from one of your patients?" Norah thought this unlikely, since Esther was one of the strictest followers of cleanliness she knew.

"I doubt that. Yes, if you wouldn't mind, I'd love some tea and toast." She put the cloth aside and struggled to a sitting position.

"I'll go prepare something and I'll be right back."

When she came back to the room bearing a tray with the light meal, she pulled a chair over to sit with Esther as she consumed it.

"Ah, this is much better. I'm afraid that I'm unused to being a patient. After I had that bout of bubonic plague some years back, I thought I'd never get sick again. Yet, that's absurd." She took a gulp of the tea and frowned.

"Well, I hope it's nothing serious. You're not feverish, thank God." Norah felt her forehead, then automatically checked her pulse, which beat strong and steady.

Esther sighed, looked at the ceiling and then back at Norah, her mouth closed in a straight line.

"My monthly is late," she said. This apparent non sequitur confused Norah.

"Your—"

"That, and my mornings are plagued with nausea that often erupts in vomiting. I don't think I need to be a doctor to diagnose my problem." She snorted and looked away, and it dawned on Norah what she was talking about.

"You're pregnant? But, I thought—"

"Last month, Addison and I attended a birthday party, and well, we both drank a bit more than usual, and when we returned home, you can imagine. We were so tipsy, Addison forgot all about putting on a safe, and I forgot to remind him. I thought it wouldn't matter because I assumed I was barren. But now I perceive that I'm not." She laughed without mirth.

"Have you told Addison?" Norah watched her face and couldn't divine if Esther was happy at the prospect of being a mother. Though she was a loving, compassionate doctor and devoted friend, Norah didn't see her as a mother of children. This couldn't be welcome news.

"No, not yet. I dread telling him, for it will renew his pleas for us to be married."

"You will bear the child?"

"Of course. He would want the baby, and I cannot break his heart. I couldn't bear that. But I may have to disappoint him anyway."

"But surely, now, after so many years, you could see your way clear to be married."

"I'm afraid, Norah. I'm afraid to be a mother and a wife. I never wanted to be either of those things."

Esther, afraid? That was a truly surprising admission. "But you will excel at those roles as well as you excel at being a doctor. You could do no less." Norah spoke as forcefully as she could.

"I doubt that. My personality is ill-suited for either. But let's not dwell on this. My pregnancy will not be evident for several more weeks. I'm feeling much better. You'll be leaving us soon for your new lodging. We must make a party for you. Please go fetch my notepad and pencil. Let's make a plan."

Norah shook her head. She didn't want a party, but it seemed churlish and ungrateful to refuse. She could tell Esther had no wish to discuss her new circumstances any further at that moment. She had to indulge her so she did as she was asked, and they spent the next half hour planning when and whom to invite and what food to prepare.

Chapter Three

In her bedroom, Norah dressed for the party and attempted to generate some enthusiasm for the event. She was grateful to Esther for coming up with a plan to improve her social life and touched by the rest of the commune's efforts to make it a success, but she just didn't feel very social. She had been plagued by shyness as a child, and only through determination had she overcome it enough to function as a professional. Social situations still frightened and enervated her. The memory of the occasion that had led to her affair with May was also fresh in her mind and contributed to her unease.

In any case, she had to put on her social persona and make the best of it. The opportunity to socialize with other members of the City hospital staff would be beneficial, she supposed, as she had to work with them. She also was newly arrived in San Francisco, and if she expected to make it her home, she ought to get on with the business of integrating herself into its social life. So far, she noticed that its citizens were seemingly easygoing and not suspicious of strangers, entirely unlike New Yorkers.

She gave her hair one last pat and smoothed her dress. For the occasion, she had chosen a simple dark-blue linen, which she'd been told made her eyes bluer. She wished her hair would be more cooperative, but it wasn't to be.

Downstairs, Beth, Kerry, and their cook labored in the kitchen preparing the party food, all chosen by and prepared under Kerry's direction.

"May I help?" Norah asked.

Beth grinned and made a shooing motion at her. "Not at all. Go out to the hall and help Esther greet the guests and get introduced to everyone. You're the guest of honor."

"Very well." Norah wished she could stay in the kitchen and cook, not that she was very good at it.

She joined Esther in the foyer just as a new arrival was removing her coat and hat.

"Norah, this is Kerry's friend from the Natural History Society, Abigail Eliot."

The woman nodded with a brief smile as she handed the items over to Esther.

"Abigail, this is our friend and colleague, Doctor Norah Stratton, newly come to work at the City and County Hospital. She, like me, hails from New York City."

"How do you do?" Abigail said, offering a hand to shake.

Norah met the woman's direct but friendly gaze, briefly noting that her hand and wrist were brown and her grip quite strong.

"Very well, and I'm pleased you could come." She tried a smile and was rewarded with a brilliant grin from her new acquaintance.

"You can thank Kerry for persuading me. Is she in the kitchen?"

"Why, yes, she is." Norah enjoyed the woman's brisk but good-humored tone. She appeared to be completely without pretense, her gaze frank and direct.

"Would you like to say hello to her?" Norah asked to be polite.

"Perhaps in a moment. I could use something to drink."

"Norah, I'll take care of the greeting," Esther said. "Please show Miss Eliot where she may obtain liquid refreshment." She looked squarely at Norah, and Norah took her meaning.

Abigail Eliot laughed. "Please call me Abby. Being called Miss Eliot reminds me of my students."

"You're a schoolteacher?" Norah asked, confused.

"Oh, no. Though I used to be. Now I'm curator of botany at the San Francisco Natural History Society."

Norah guided Abby down the long hallway to the parlor in the back, where a sideboard held a number of types of drinks, including coffee, lemonade, wine, and a punchbowl.

"That sounds very grand," Norah said in a teasing tone.

"It's not," Abby replied. "Compared to that of a doctor, the life of a scientist is a dull one."

"I don't agree. Taking care of the working poor and their many ailments is time-consuming but hardly exciting."

"What animates you then and serves to keep your attention?" Abby asked.

This was an impressively searching and serious question. Abby waited for her answer as she scanned the offerings on the long sideboard. "I believe it boils down to the fact that I like to help people, to cure them of disease, ease suffering, and make them feel better." Norah watched Abby's face as she took this comment in.

"Medicine is a noble profession. But not an easy one for a woman, I imagine."

"It can be difficult, especially when I first graduated from medical school. I went to the Women's Medical College of Pennsylvania, which was devoted to educating women to be doctors so, as you can imagine, the atmosphere was affirming. Then I went to work at a hospital in New York, which was quite different. Esther was the one who really helped me—by her example. She'd graduated the year before me. But what about you? What is it that you do, exactly?"

"Ha. Good question. I'm in charge of the Natural History Society's plant collections, so that requires me to both preserve and to add to them as much as I can. The collecting aspect, which we call botanizing, is what I enjoy the most."

"What does that mean?"

"It means making trips all over California in search of new material." She took a sip of punch and made eye contact with Norah so directly, it made her uncomfortable, yet this just seemed to be her way and didn't mean anything special.

"And when you find your material, what do you do?" Norah was slightly surprised that she'd adopted a cheerful, nearly flirtatious tone.

"I carry it back to the Society on Market Street."

"And then?"

"Identify and preserve it carefully. Also, if I suspect that I have a new species, I have other experts review it. I lecture and write articles for many different journals and also for popular periodicals. It all keeps me gainfully occupied."

"I see. But what is the goal of all this?" Norah posed this question quite seriously, but she was barely aware that underneath lay a hint of teasing skepticism.

"I'm not sure what you mean," Abby said, knitting her brows, but her voice also carried an undercurrent of teasing.

"You have told me all about what you do and how it's done, but not why. I too have a myriad of tasks to perform and other doctors with whom to consult and treatment of patients to direct and manage, but the reasons are very clear. My *aim* is to heal and relieve suffering."

"Ah. I see. You're wondering what's the good of all this knowledge. I understand some folks have no use for anything they don't consider practical."

Norah was taken aback because that's exactly what she thought.

"Some may think the attention I devote to dried-out plants the epitome of wasted effort, but that's hardly the case."

Norah considered that statement. "I assume you're putting *me* in that category of person. But I'll wait until I hear more before I form my opinion as to the usefulness of what you do." Norah was unhappy that a tart note had crept into her voice and didn't like it, but she was seemingly unable to moderate it.

Abby, however, was apparently unconcerned about what Norah thought.

"Very well. As to your question: the natural world is replete with things we don't understand. I believe man's soul, his very existence is enriched by both exposure to and by striving to understand the mysteries of God's creation. That, I think you may agree, is a worthy endeavor."

Before Norah could answer, she heard raised voices from the drawing room at the front of the house. Abby heard them as well. They caught each other's eye and, without another word, walked down the hall together, following the sound.

It was the most crowded room since it held the buffet table. There, two men, one of them Addison, the other unknown, stood in the center of the room arguing. The rest of the guests stood around awkwardly, pretending not to listen, but the disturbance was impossible to miss. Norah spotted Beth standing behind a slender and strikingly handsome fellow, who was watching the two men intently.

The man arguing with Addison was not good looking, but he was tall, well-dressed, and self-assured. Addison seemed to be directing most of his ire at the taller man.

Waving his hand for emphasis, he said, "All I'm asking is that you use your influence as a doctor for the public good. You have well-to-do patients who could command the ear of the mayor and the City supervisors and at least add their voices. Some of the matrons are surely involved in charitable works, are they not?"

"Addison, you entirely mistake my relationship with my patients. I'm not their social equal, no matter how pleasantly they treat me and how much they depend on me," the tall, elegant man said.

The handsome onlooker addressed him. "But Whit, Mrs. Huntingdon is always talking about orphans and fallen women and the like. Maybe Addison's right and—"

"Scott, my dear fellow, please don't speak of things you don't understand." Whit sounded exasperated and bit condescending.

Scott shut his mouth but looked troubled. Beth touched his arm, and he turned to her and patted her hand. Norah thought of Esther's words about Beth and her friendship with Scott.

"I'm very sorry, Addison, but I'm simply unable to offer you any assistance in your quest." Whit spoke smoothly and entirely without emotion.

Addison stared at him for a moment and then said, "Very well, though I find your attitude craven and unsuitable for a medical man and for someone we consider our friend." He looked at Beth when he said this, then back at Esther, who had come in to stand next to him. She was staring at him, seemingly trying to convey something without saying anything aloud. She surely wanted Addison to not continue to argue.

Scott looked aggrieved. "Addison, I'm shocked you would characterize Whit like that. It's not his fault. He tries."

"Bah. That's not the case and you know it. It's all very well for *you* to defend him."

Esther took Addison's arm and pulled him away, and Beth did the same with Scott, who shook her off and went to a corner with Whit, where they whispered together.

Abby looked at Norah with eyebrows raised in inquiry, and Norah didn't know quite what to say.

Kerry approached the two of them looking distressed. "Are you having a good time? I'm sorry matters got a little heated." She shrugged.

"Please don't worry," Abby said. "A party can be boring without a little conflict."

Kerry shook her head but grinned anyhow. "Guess that's true. Addison's got very strong feelings about some things. Say, what do you think of the food?" she asked eagerly.

Norah knew Kerry was very particular about her cooking and how people liked it.

"Oh goodness, I can't say I've eaten anything as good since, well, since I came to have lunch at your Ladies Grill." Abby laughed heartily.

Norah was quiet, watching their interaction and wondering what Abby made of Kerry's manner and dress. Even in wild and wooly San Francisco, a woman like Kerry would be unusual, but Abby didn't seem to notice.

She heard Esther call out, "Come, everyone. Beth is going to play for us." Esther was so shrewd. She understood people needed a distraction from the unpleasant argument they'd witnessed.

They gathered around the piano as Beth settled herself on the bench and looked through the sheet music on top. She often played after dinner in the evening. After a long day's work, the commune members were soothed by Bach or Mozart or Chopin pieces. Norah smiled a little to herself, thinking of how Kerry, if she happened to be at home, looked at Beth when she played piano. But this evening seemed to call for a livelier type of music.

"How about something we can all sing?" Beth asked. At the murmurs of assent, she opened a page and launched into "Camptown Races." Everyone joined in, and Norah became aware that Abby was standing close to her and how her voice stood out from the rest. Norah stole a glance from the side and saw that Abby was transformed, her face rapt, her eyes hooded. Beth must also have noticed Abby, for when the raucous song was finished to cheers and handclaps, she pulled another sheet from her pile of music and showed it to Abby.

"This does better, I think, with one voice. Would you mind?"

Abby looked thoughtful for a moment but said, "It would be my pleasure."

Beth played an introduction, then nodded to Abby, who sang,

Alas, my love, you do me wrong to cast me off so discourteously.
For I have loved you so long, delighting in thy company.
Greensleeves was all my joy,
Greensleeves was my delight,
Greensleeves was my heart of gold,
And who but my lady greensleeves.

Norah stared at Abby. Her voice was wonderful, clear and true, not high or low but somewhere between. Norah had no knowledge of music, but it didn't matter. The sound of Abby singing mesmerized her. Norah wondered who she thought of as she sang. The lover's lament made her think of May, and her sad memories threatened to push out the joy she felt while hearing Abby sing.

The song ended and everyone clapped vigorously. Abby nodded, gracious and modest but clearly pleased with her performance. She turned to Norah, her face glowing. In Norah's mind, something whispered. It was something she'd heard before, when May had finally and irrevocably focused on her at that other long-ago party. There were no words but a feeling, a force like gravity that had pulled her toward May, and now she was feeling it again from Abby. Well, not from Abby, but from within herself, and it was impossible to ignore but also impossible to consider responding to.

She inwardly drew back in fear. This couldn't happen for so many reasons. She couldn't allow herself to fall in love again. Abby was not in the least like May, but something about her was so compelling that Norah was unable to resist it. That could explain her earlier prickliness as well. She would need to watch herself. She made herself be pleasant to other guests as she was introduced. Esther steered her toward several women whom Norah found pleasant but unexciting.

A little later, Abby sought her out. "Our conversation was interrupted earlier. Shall we finish it? I'm considering making my good-byes, but I wanted to talk with you before I leave."

Abby seemed mildly embarrassed but sweet. Norah was charmed without really wanting to be, and that unnerved her even more.

"I think I've gotten a fair idea of what it is you do." Her tone was again frostier than she wished, but it was too late to take it back.

Abby's smile faded. "Perhaps I've not really conveyed to you, though, the true worth of my work."

"It seems rather more a hobby than actual work. It's good that you are able to do what you want, what makes you happy." Norah disliked how hateful she sounded, dismissive and superior. It wasn't truly her, but some version of herself that suddenly pushed to the fore of her personality with the express purpose of repelling Abby.

Abby looked more troubled but said only, "I see. Well, perhaps it would be better if I could show you rather than try to describe to you why I do what I do."

Norah was sorry she'd been so discourteous. It was unlike her, but it seemed she was powerless to stop herself. She couldn't think what to say next. Abby, even though she must be hurt, was clearly not discouraged.

"I'm planning a day trip to Mount Tamalpais in March. It's lovely this time of year with the wildflowers blooming."

She looked so hopeful and sincere that Norah relented. "Very well. If you could plan it for a Sunday, then I could accompany you."

"Certainly. It's been a wonderful party. Please thank everyone again for me. I can telephone you a little later this week with the exact date."

They shook hands, and Abby's palm was warm and smooth, her grip strong. Then she was gone, and Norah stared at the front door through which Abby had just exited and tried to make sense of her jumble of emotions. She was sorry she'd been prickly. She was feeling a tug of attraction that she wanted to resist, but she also wanted to see Abby again.

"It's not that I don't like Scott, love. I just don't like the way he lets Whit influence him. He doesn't listen to you anymore. He's absorbed in Whit and their social-climbing."

Beth and Kerry were in bed but still wakeful from the excitement of the party.

Beth sighed, knowing Kerry was right but unwilling to agree. She was being pulled several directions because of her love and loyalty, with no way to reconcile the competing desires and feelings of all her loved ones. She wished all the conflict would go away because she needed to direct all her energy and attention to her work. The meeting at which she wanted to present her research was to be held in April in San Francisco, and since it was late February, she had little time to spare and so much to do.

Kerry was lying on her side with her elbow holding her head up as she simultaneously talked and lightly stroked Beth from her hair to her hip. Beth usually found this type of attention comforting, but not this night. She was too agitated. Scott's rejection of her counsel still rankled her.

She said, finally, "I wish he wouldn't let Whit boss him around so much. When he's not around Whit, he's much nicer."

"But you told me he's not really much of a doctor. You said he cares more about money than about taking care of people."

"I know. He's lost his way but doesn't know it."

"I hate that it hurts you so much. That's what troubles me the most. Perhaps you should break off with him." Beth shuddered inwardly, knowing that might have to come to pass but not wanting to think of it.

"Bethy?" Kerry asked. Beth had been silent for a long time.

"Oh, Kerry, dearest. I don't know what to do. I can't think right now. Let's talk tomorrow. I just want to sleep."

"All right, love. Shall I hold you?" Kerry patted her cheek, and then Beth grabbed her hand. She loved that Kerry always tried to make her feel better and was usually able to comfort her.

"Yes, please." They snuggled together, Beth allowing Kerry's warmth to soothe her. She turned to bury her face in Kerry's neck, and Kerry's arms wrapped her tighter.

❖

Beth offered to accompany Norah downtown to the South of the Slot neighborhood where she conducted her researches so that

Norah could visit some of the places whose addresses she'd culled from her search of the *Call—Bulletin* classified advertisements for rental rooms.

They rode the cable car over Nob Hill to the foot of California Street. It was a marvel to Norah that, in the middle of February, they could make do with light coats and hats. The sun was warm on her face, but the breeze at their backs made Norah pull her coat tighter.

Beth said, "So that we may efficiently make use of our time, show me your list."

Norah handed her a piece of paper, where she'd noted the addresses of boardinghouses with rooms to rent.

Beth scrutinized Norah's list and then consulted her notebook. "Ah, I think I have a rough plan. I hope you don't mind accompanying me to the homes of some of my patients as we go."

"Oh, no. That would certainly interest me."

They set off down Spear Street to Mission Street, Norah noting the remarkable transformation as she and Beth left the prosperous commercial district of Market Street and walked south and then turned on Mission Street. The buildings changed from fine brick edifices to seedy-looking wooden buildings very much like those around the train station farther west. The South of the Slot district was obviously large. The street was paved but indifferently so, with broken sidewalks and missing cobblestones. Norah could smell a myriad of odors: horse manure, cooking, smoke from factories. She had some misgivings but concluded she would be at her lodging only at night. She'd spend most of her time at the hospital and from time to time visit the commune on Fillmore Street.

Beth led her to a three-story apartment building a few blocks from the intersection. There they knocked on the first of many doors, where a careworn mother would answer and they would be ushered into a cramped, seedy flat, generally occupied by several children dressed in ragged clothing with curious expressions on their dirty faces.

Norah had cared for many such patients in Bellevue, but she'd never visited their homes. She thought Beth's project admirable if a little crazy. She sat while Beth conversed with the mothers as to the children's diets, where and how they obtained water, and what the sanitary arrangements were. She would probe the nature of the family breadwinner's work and, subtly, the character of the father. Norah admired Beth's ability to encourage her subjects to disclose information. She wrote everything down in notebooks in meticulous detail.

Their research visits were interspersed with stops at various types of lodging. Some were obviously unsuitable: the premises were filthy or the proprietors exuded the stench of alcohol. But a few seemed clean and respectable, and Norah made her choice and paid a deposit, agreeing to move in three weeks at the beginning of March.

Back on the street after an interview, Beth said, "I'd be quite concerned that you may be assaulted in the middle of the night."

"I've thought of that and have determined to purchase and install my own lock on the door of the place I've chosen."

"You will need to be careful on the street as well."

"And so I shall be. Remember, I've lived in New York City, where all types of people may be encountered. I'm not an innocent."

Beth grinned and nodded as they walked in silence for a few minutes. "Kerry is very eager for you to take your outing with Abby Eliot."

Norah looked at her briefly before responding. "And why is that?"

Beth cleared her throat. "Kerry believes that Abby is of our ilk, but she's not sure."

Norah turned this news over in her mind and said, with finality, "I very much doubt it."

"You're certain? Yet you've met her only once."

"I'm positive."

Beth shrugged. "Well. It's sort of Kerry's hobby to try to puzzle these things out, but she's not necessarily right."

"I don't believe Abby Eliot cares for anything or anyone but botany."

Beth laughed, but then she turned serious. "We all may have our enthusiasm for our work, but it's not the total object of life, after all."

"For you, that's clear, but you're lucky you have Kerry."

"I am lucky. I agree." Beth's expression showed that she'd been visited by some pleasant thought of her beloved.

Norah envied her, but she pushed her own feeling of longing away. "I intend to throw myself into work. I have no need for distraction except the friendship offered by you and Kerry and Addison and Esther. That will suffice for me."

Beth looked skeptical, but she nodded pleasantly and directed them toward yet another rickety wooden building that was in need of paint and lacked a door knocker. Beth pounded smartly on the door.

As they waited, Norah thought briefly of May again. Yes, that experience had been enough to teach her the value of protecting her heart. Not that her heart would need protection from the likes of Abby Eliot. Yet another harried mother opened the door and invited them in to enjoy a cup of weak tea as Beth questioned the tenants.

❖

On the Friday before Norah's outing to Marin County with Abby, the household, minus Kerry, convened for supper in the evening. Norah hadn't seen much of either Addison or Esther during the workday, as she'd been very busy making the final arrangements for the Saturday vaccination clinic.

At the table, Esther took up conversation with Norah, questioning her on her expectations for the next day. It was absorbing, and dinner was nearly over before Norah noticed that Addison had said nothing during the meal, which was quite unusual. He sat in his place at the head of the table and stolidly ate his supper while Esther, Beth, and Norah talked. Then he excused himself before they finished eating, mumbling something about going to his study.

After supper, in the kitchen the three of them cleaned the dishes and put away food.

Beth ventured to ask the question that was on Norah's mind. "Whatever ails Addison? He was so quiet during supper."

Esther emptied a plate of meat scraps into the garbage pail, scraping at it viciously. When she didn't answer for a moment, Beth and Norah glanced at one another.

"He's unhappy with me. I can't say as I blame him, but I can't provide any relief."

"Did you—" Beth asked.

"Yes, I had to, finally. He grabbed my arm before luncheon break and sat me down and asked me what was wrong. I think he knew the answer and was already unhappy that I'd not said anything." She took a breath and set her mouth.

"I said, yes, I'm with child, but no, we are not to be married. He pleaded with me for a few minutes. Then, in the face of my answers, he became angry."

"But what will become of you?" Norah asked. "You can't have an illegitimate child!"

"I can and I will. I'm not worried that he'll not care for the baby. He was happy at first and said his wish had come true."

"You'll have to cease working at the hospital," Beth said.

"Not for a long while yet. I'll stay home for a bit after the child's born to see it properly on its way, but then I'll return. We'll have to find a nurse, but it shouldn't be difficult."

Norah was aghast at Esther's dispassionate response to her predicament and couldn't imagine how Addison felt. Esther seemed to not care overmuch about him. Nor did she appear to be particularly happy at the prospect of being a mother. Norah had long known Esther was a self-contained woman, not one to display her emotions on the surface, but this was extreme. She hoped Esther would change in time.

Chapter Four

A couple weeks later, in her new room at the boardinghouse, Norah prepared for their excursion to Mount Tamalpais according to Abby's specific directions. She chose a heavy but worn skirt and a blouse with a high collar, as well as a wool jacket, and she took gloves.

Abby had said, "We may encounter a little snow at the summit, as it is a higher elevation, but it won't be too troublesome. Dress warmly, as we'll spend most of time out of doors."

That was certainly what Norah looked forward to the least. She'd never been anywhere wilder than Central Park. She had never found a good reason to visit the country outside of New York, and in any case, until she'd met Abby Eliot, she knew no one who would invite her. It would have not occurred to May to leave the island of Manhattan. Norah was not quite sure if May even conceived of life elsewhere.

She wasn't sure *why* she'd agreed to this excursion, but Abby's offer to show her why she pursued plants the way some people pursued love piqued her interest.

She was adjusting her hat and attempting without success to get her hair firmly tucked in when she heard a knock on the door. She flung it open and there stood Abby Eliot, attired in a most peculiar fashion.

She wore a flat-top bonnet anchored under her chin, carried a sturdy wool coat, and had on a white blouse under a bolero vest oddly turned inside out. Those articles of clothing were not remarkable, but it was her skirt that drew Norah's attention. For one thing, it was short, barely reaching past her ankles, brushing the tops of her stout lace-up shoes. Finally, looped over her back, was a packet of boards with papers between them, tied together with twine, and crossed over her other shoulder was a large sack.

Abby stood unperturbed until Norah concluded her examination. "Greetings. I hope this morning finds you well and ready for some adventure."

"Yes, I believe so. I hope so."

"This lodging house suits you?" Abby looked about with interest.

"I think so. I wanted some place cheap but clean, and this one meets my specifications. It's also not too far from the City and County Hospital, perhaps a mile and a half. Tell me, what is that on your back?"

"That is how I can preserve and transport my specimens back to the Natural History Society. I'll show you when we're on the trail."

"Trail?" Norah didn't care for the sound of that. It smacked of snakes, holes, and climbing, none of which was remotely appealing. She wondered again why she'd agreed to this outing.

Abby laughed at her discomfited tone. "Please don't be concerned. I promise I'll not torture you and that we'll enjoy ourselves. Come along, though. We have to make the next Sausalito ferry in a half hour. We've just enough time."

Off they went from Mission Street north to Fourth Street and then to Market. The hubbub was less, for it was a Sunday, and even in so-called wicked San Francisco, people still went to church. As they hurried along, Norah wondered if Abby was a churchgoer.

It took all her energy to keep up with Abby's stride. It was clear she was a veteran walker. She marched steadily down the sidewalk, and they didn't talk much until they boarded the ferryboat on the pier just behind the ferry building. As they strode down Market Street, Norah admired the tower with its ornate clock that loomed ever closer.

Norah hadn't had any occasion to leave the City since she'd arrived six weeks previously. In spite of the brisk wind that blew in their faces, she liked the view. New York's harbor was not lovely, though the view was dramatic because of Staten Island and the Statue of Liberty. As they sailed farther away, San Francisco became fairy-tale like. The two hills west of downtown towered over the buildings, and the houses clinging to the sides of the hills looked like toys with spots of green grass and reddish-brown rocks poked up amongst them. As Norah recovered her breath from their brisk stroll, she began to feel an unfamiliar happiness, the joy of a moment in time where she was unconcerned about the past or the future. She was content to exist where she was, gazing at the jewel-like city as their ferry steamed toward the northern shore of the San Francisco Bay.

Abby came to stand next to her at the railing, and her reverie broken, she turned toward her. Abby seemed to be watching her reaction to the scene before them.

"Come to the other side and I will show you our destination."

Norah obeyed.

At the bow of the ferry, they stood side by side. "There is where we will dock, the village of Sausalito."

Norah had the vague impression of a collection of boats anchored at docks, a small number of houses clustered behind them.

Abby raised her arm and pointed, and Norah naturally followed her hand.

"Out there is the mountain—the Sleeping Maiden. That's where we're headed."

Norah stared. It was tallest point of land she'd seen so far, oddly shaped and bright green.

"The Indians who lived around here, the Miwok, named it, because if you look closely, you can see the outline of a woman. Look. There is her head and then her breasts."

Norah glanced back at Abby, who was also looking at the mountain as she talked. She must have noticed Norah staring at her because she turned to meet her eyes. Norah, to her dismay, blushed. It wasn't as though she'd never heard the word "breast" before, but for some reason, hearing Abby say it had an untoward effect on her. Abby looked back at her seeming unconcerned.

"Ye-ss. I believe I see what you mean." She was chagrined that she'd lost her composure.

"Well, it's just a description. So we're going to the very top."

"We are?" Like the word "trail," the word "top" applied to what looked to be a very big mountain alarmed her all over again. Her reaction must have showed because Abby laughed the same way she had before. Norah was seriously put upon because she didn't like the feeling of being made fun of.

"Why are you laughing?" she asked peremptorily.

Abby became serious at once.

"Oh, I beg your pardon. It's just that your expression when I mentioned "trail" and just now when I said we would go to the top of Mount Tamalpais is so, so discomfited. It's rather sweet, but I'm sorry I laughed. Let me reassure you that we'll be riding the Mount Tam railway up the mountain. When we arrive at our destination, we'll visit a tavern where we may obtain refreshment. We'll go out for a short but easy hike. I'm aware that you're not of the Hill Tribe."

Norah was mollified by Abby's sincere apology and relieved at her more detailed description of their trip. She asked, "What do you mean the Hill Tribe? More Indians?"

Abby chuckled and said, "No. It's a hiking club I belong to. I believe I'm the first woman to be admitted. They take their name from the fact that we enjoy hiking up and down Mount Tamalpais."

"I see. So you're the only woman? Isn't that awkward?"

"No. Not in the least. As I said, I go to many places when I'm botanizing. Like-minded travelers are not disposed to worry about the differences between genders."

"Ah. So you are like a man." Norah was instantly sorry she'd spoken as soon as the words came out of her mouth, but again, Abby was unruffled. Nothing, it seemed, disturbed her. That in itself was a bit disturbing but also intriguing.

"Well. Some might say that, but among those who love the out-of-doors and wilderness and the pursuit of knowledge, there's a kind of genderlessness. I don't know how else to put it. We don't notice those common differences between men and women. Around a campfire or climbing a mountain, they're irrelevant. I was chosen as a member of the Hill Tribe because I'm a good walker. I can keep up with the men."

Norah nodded, unsure what to say. Abby was like no one she'd ever met. Even amongst the women doctors, femininity was cherished. They might know as much as men, but God forbid they ever *act* like men. If they did, Norah was sure they'd be ostracized. But Abby wasn't really like a man. She was just a unique kind of woman, one of a kind. She was like Kerry, who, though she dressed like a man, didn't act like one. Norah wondered suddenly if Abby really did like women in the same way she and Kerry and Beth did. She'd detected nothing of that sort of inclination so far. And she'd denied that she noticed anything of that nature to Beth. She forced herself out of her speculations and back to the present.

"You were going to tell me all about these boards you've brought," she said to Abby, who, during the pause after her last statement, had merely waited patiently for Norah to respond.

"Ah. So I was. Well, as I told you, they're for my specimens. They are a way to carry and keep safe delicate plants until I can return to my workroom. I press them between the boards, and this paper keeps them safe from the elements. I'll take back a few today, but not many, as we aren't going on a long trip."

They were headed into the Sausalito harbor so they made sure they had all their belongings and disembarked. Abby led Norah a few blocks away to a train siding, and within another few minutes, they were aboard the local to Mill Valley.

It was a good deal more rural in Marin County than in San Francisco, and also noticeably warmer, Norah was happy to observe. She pointed this out to Abby, who grinned and said, "Certainly. Enjoy this while you're able. We'll be climbing up to 2500 feet, and the temperature will drop. I think the sun will be out, though, so that's helpful."

"I can assure you this is far more pleasant than New York City in early March."

"That I can imagine. I've been up in the Rocky Mountains in early spring, and that's quite as cold as I ever want to be. That reminds me. You've told me next to nothing about yourself and what your early life was like."

"That can wait until we're on our next train. At present, I want to just enjoy where we are." It was true. Once they'd left downtown San Francisco on the Sausalito ferry and Norah was assured that she wouldn't be physically required to climb Mount Tamalpais, she felt much reassured and truly began to enjoy being out-of-doors on an incredibly mild day. The sun and the blue of the San Francisco Bay and the country town of Mill Valley, much to her surprise, delighted her. She noticed the absence of the smells of the City. In contrast, she'd smelt salt water on the ferry, and now, in the little outdoor train station in Mill Valley, she could sense what she assumed was the scent of wood and other vegetation. A number of trees surrounded the train station, some of them very large.

Since she was traveling with a botanist, it seemed appropriate to ask about the trees. And to her surprise, she found she wanted to know about them. She also wanted to hear Abby talk about what she loved.

"What's that tree there?" she asked, pointing at a very tall straight tree with a reddish-brown trunk.

"Ah. Coast redwood. *Sequoia sempervirens,*" Abby said promptly.

"And how about that one there?" She pointed to a much shorter tree with winding gray branches.

"That would be the California black oak, *Quercus kelloggii.*"

"Am I to be blessed with the Latin name of *everything*?" Norah asked and realized that she'd put a teasing note in her voice.

"Occupational hazard for me, I fear. The Latin trips naturally from my tongue. But I could restrain myself and give you only the common name. I wouldn't want to unduly burden you."

Her lips were twitching slightly, as though she was trying hard not to laugh at Norah again. Norah gazed at her, charmed and not minding the teasing.

As the train pulled up and they boarded, Abby said, "I hope heights don't frighten you."

"I should think not." Norah hoped it was true, but she'd never had that particular part of her psyche tested. She didn't want to appear weak in front of Abby, though, and she silently chided herself for worrying about it.

The passenger car was open on all sides with just a canopy on top. For some reason, Norah thought that their journey to the summit would be in a normal passenger train. She tried to quell her sudden anxiety.

As the train chugged out of the station and gained speed, Abby said, "They call this the crookedest railway in the world."

"Why is that?" Norah asked.

"All the switchbacks it makes."

"What are switchbacks?" Norah wasn't sure she wanted to know.

Abby shot her a surprised look. "On a trail up or down a mountain, there are curves that double back on themselves to make the climb easier, more gradual."

"Well. I wouldn't have known that because I've never been on a trail or on a train like this."

"Of course you wouldn't know that. I take it you've lived all your life in a city?"

"Yes. I have. I grew up in Philadelphia."

The train began its climb up Mount Tamalpais, and it quickly became apparent to Norah that she shouldn't look out the downhill side. Every time she glanced to her left, the precipitous drop made her feel dizzy. She didn't, however, want to admit this to Abby. Why she wanted Abby to think well of her, she had no idea. It was likely just her silly ego.

Abby was clearly enjoying herself. She smiled a bit dreamily at the passing scenery. Finally, she focused on Norah again, and her face changed. "Are you all right?" she asked.

"Yes. Why do you ask?" Norah was sounding peevish again and hated it.

"You look a bit pale, that's all. I hope you're not unwell?"

Norah *was* unwell. She felt as though she might fall out of the train car and off the mountain to her death.

"Take deep breaths, and focus upon the horizon." Abby put a reassuring hand on her arm and Norah remonstrated with herself. *Just do as she says. It'll be over presently.*

The ride took a long half hour. At the station at the summit, Abby jumped off nimbly and then turned to give Norah her hand, which she took without hesitation. Back on solid ground, she felt better.

"I was unaware that heights affected me so," she said as they made their way to the tavern.

"I grew up in the mountains in Colorado and Canada, so they've never bothered me. I didn't think to ask you. I hope this hasn't spoiled the trip for you. I'm always with the same companions and never thought this might be difficult for someone who's never experienced it."

Abby's worry about her and how she was doing and how she was feeling touched her, so she resolved to buck up and not focus on her discomfort but to try to enjoy this outing since that was the original idea.

Abby shouldered her pack of boards and motioned her to follow as she set off on a trail behind the tavern.

"We'll walk about for a bit and then come back for a drink. Would that suit you?"

"Yes. That would be fine."

It was, again, difficult for Norah to keep up with Abby's walking pace. She fell behind, and it was a few moments before Abby noticed where she was.

"Oh, dear. I should go more slowly. I confess I don't think of others trying to keep up with me."

They walked on, but when they stopped to look at many of the flowers, Abby would consult the little notebook she carried. From the satchel over her shoulder, various items emerged: a pencil, the notebook, and a sketch pad.

Abby named the flowers as they proceeded, such as "Jewel flower" or "clarkia," which were truly beautiful. Their bright, colorful blossoms stood in contrast to their green stems and the other non-flowering plants that grew around them.

"At this time, in New York, one would never see flowers blooming."

Abby laughed. "No, you wouldn't. But in a few weeks, if you were to venture out in the country, you would see trillium. They sometimes bloom before the first thaw, poking their bright heads above the snow."

"They do? I mean how do you know that?" Norah was charmed by Abby's enthusiasm and her description of the trillium. It was almost as though the flowers were, to her, sentient beings.

"I've made collecting trips in the eastern United States."

"You have?" Abby, it seemed, was more well traveled than she was.

"Yes, and also to many parts of the western states and Mexico."

"All because of flowers?" Norah was dumbfounded, and then she remembered the original purpose of this trip. Supposedly, it was to show Norah the reasons for Abby's pursuit of plants.

"Well, that I suppose is the simplest explanation. Here, let's rest for a moment."

Abby pulled an odd-shaped object from her bottomless satchel. It was circular, a few inches thick, and had a strap. Abby unscrewed the cap and drank from it and handed it to Norah, who took a sip. It was cool water, and Norah hadn't realized how thirsty she was.

"Thanks. I see you come prepared."

Abby stared at her and then raised an eyebrow. "I should think so. Being on a trail without water isn't advisable."

She didn't say this unkindly, but Norah still felt silly and once more was afraid that Abby would think she was silly

"So." She shoved her shoulder against Abby's briefly. "You've brought me all the way out here for a reason?"

"Ah. Yes." Abby screwed the cap back on the water bottle, stowed it back in her satchel, and closed the flap. Norah, though impatient for Abby to answer, was also impressed by her economy of movement. It went with her air of self-assurance and reminded her a bit of Esther, who never seemed at a loss or unsure. Norah had had to cultivate that confident attitude in herself when at work, but it didn't come naturally.

Abby gestured again, inviting Norah to look toward where she pointed. "Look."

Norah obeyed. Abby took Norah's arm and led them to a boulder near the path, where they sat. Before them, the brilliant green hills spread far below them, and to one side was the Pacific Ocean, sunlight glinting on the surface. On the other side, to the east, lay the enormous San Francisco Bay, its striking blue surface dotted with boats, small and large.

Not being in a moving train on a cliff allowed Norah to relax and take in the view. She understood then what the expression "on top of the world" meant.

Abby brought her back to the earth as she pointed to the clump of irises near them. Norah thought the bright bluish-purple flowers quite lovely, but she didn't see what Abby was driving at.

"I'm a botanist, a scientist because of all of this." She spread her arms wide. "Here is God's work. Here is the world. We are but a small part of a vast, interconnected web of life. To see, to know, to comprehend it is my goal." She fell silent but looked intently at Norah.

Norah didn't know what to say. Abby's face was alive with sincerity and ardor. Until this moment, Norah had thought her looks were pleasant but ordinary. But here at the top of a mountain, in her element and describing what moved her, she was beautiful. The wind ruffled her hair, which had come loose from its tie. She'd taken off her bonnet as well. The sun was directly overhead and lit her head and face in a most attractive way. She continued to look at Norah, smiling faintly.

Norah nearly had to shake her head to stop herself from staring. She wanted to respond and was deprived of speech. Another moment passed. She tore her gaze from Abby, once again, embarrassed, and looked out toward the western horizon to cover her unease.

She spoke finally, only to say, softly, "Yes. I believe I understand." What exactly she understood, she couldn't say.

Abby looked behind her, wondering if she was again walking too swiftly for Norah to keep up. Norah was a few steps back, but she smiled to show all was well. They were hurrying back to the tavern and the train station because it had started to rain. In fact, they had literally watched the clouds blow in from across the sea. They'd gone from bright sun to gray in an instant, and rain now spattered on their heads. This was the way of the mountain in winter, changeable and unpredictable. Abby cursed her lack of preparation for rain. She felt responsible for every aspect of this outing, including the weather. Norah's mood could darken at any instant, and Abby wouldn't blame her.

They made it back to the tavern just in time before it truly began to pour and made themselves comfortable at a table and ordered some tea. Abby wondered if she should be bold and suggest an alcoholic drink but couldn't guess what Norah would think of such a thing in midafternoon. When she was out on a trek with the Hill Tribe after a long hike, nothing tasted better than a chilled glass of beer. That was a tradition for the Tribe when they made the climb up Tamalpais. They'd have a few glasses of beer before taking the train back to Mill Valley, tired, slightly tipsy, and very, very happy.

Abby couldn't discern what was going through Norah's mind. She wasn't even sure of her own motives for suggesting this trip. At the commune party, for some reason, she took Norah's skepticism about choosing botany as one's life work as a challenge. She'd never in her life cared about what someone thought of her vocation. True, she spent most of her time around like-minded people so there was nothing to discuss, but she felt she had to win Norah over. She wanted Norah to think well of her, to understand her in some profound way. She couldn't tell, though, if she was accomplishing her mission. Norah's moods veered from frightened to amused to thoughtful to silly and then back again. She couldn't even tell whether Norah was enjoying herself.

"Tell me more about yourself and how you ended up as a botanist," Norah said.

Well, it was a relief to see that all was apparently well with Norah for the moment, though she looked tired. She wasn't a lover of the out-of-doors. Abby hoped the rain would stop before it was time to board the train back to Mill Valley and then the ferry back to the City.

Abby said, "An uncle of mine gave me a book on flowers when I was around ten. I devoured it and learned all the names of the local Denver plants. When my mother died, my father put my sister and me into a Catholic orphanage for several years so he could concentrate on earning money."

"Oh, goodness. How awful."

Abby chuckled. "Well, it wasn't horrible. We were well cared for. I suppose it may explain my lack of religious feeling."

"But you talk of God's creation," Norah said.

"Yes. But there's a difference between believing in God, appreciating His works, and going to church. I noticed that you don't attend church—at least not today."

"True. My parents were indifferent to religion. You aren't Catholic even though you were raised by nuns?"

"No. The sisters weren't unkind, but they weren't especially motherly. They were mainly concerned with instilling Catholic teaching into us. They succeeded with my sister but not with me."

"I see. Tell me what happened when you grew up." Norah fixed her blue-gray eyes on Abby's face.

The sensation of being listened to closely was new to her. She sensed Norah wanted to know more of how she viewed her life than hear her merely recite the events. It was unnerving, actually. Abby was used to exchanging factual information and reaching agreement on plans for an outing or debating a point of science. She wasn't often required to talk about her feelings except in the most superficial manner. Norah clearly expected more.

Abby recited the facts of her life more or less and then struggled to verbalize how all of it had led up to the present moment. Norah didn't say much until she'd reached the end of her story.

"So you never wanted to marry and have a family?" Norah asked.

Abby had heard that question before and had a stock answer. "I have a very full life. I'm very busy and don't have time for more traditional womanly pursuits. I don't see how marriage would coexist with my travels and studies, let alone child-rearing. Since I served some time as a teacher and as a nanny, I'm well aware of the demands of children, and I wouldn't be a good mother."

"I can see that," Norah said, and Abby realized that Norah understood what she said, which was gratifying.

More conventional women, upon hearing Abby's thoughts, were inclined to draw back from her as though she had a disease that was catching. They seemed horrified, although generally too polite to say so. Norah was clearly not an ordinary woman. She was a doctor, to be sure, but more than that, she seemed different, unusual. That, Abby realized suddenly, was what she was attracted to. Few women crossed her path who weren't the wives of her male colleagues. One exception had been the Branstads, the couple who'd originally brought her out to San Francisco in 1898 to work at the Society. They were an exception, though, devoted to one another and to scientific pursuits. Abby wondered if Norah was in love with someone or had been. There didn't seem to be any evidence of any suitors, but that could be deceptive. But why had she even thought of it? Such things usually didn't concern her.

Though Norah said no more, Abby sensed she had thoughts running through her head. She almost asked Norah some personal questions, but her innate respect for her privacy stopped her. She moved to the window and looked out. "It seems the rain's stopped. Shall we catch the next train down the mountain?"

"I suppose we ought to."

"Do I take it you've enjoyed yourself at least somewhat on this outing?" Abby hoped the answer was yes.

"I did, contrary to my expectations. I am, at least, happy to find out more about you and what animates you."

"I'm glad. I shall take the outermost seat on the train on our journey down and encourage you to watch the passing mountainside instead of looking over the edge. You looked a little green on our ride up."

"Thank you," Norah said, primly. "I assure you, I'll be quite all right."

Abby started to smile again and caught herself. She could understand Norah's wish not to appear weak. It was something she'd confronted early in her career. But it was significant that Norah wanted her to not think ill of her or dismiss her as the city slicker she obviously was. Abby found she was not inclined to do that. In fact, she was amused by Norah's willingness to try something she'd never done before and to be at pains to appear as though things like heights didn't bother her. It wasn't bravado but real courage, and Abby was suitably impressed.

They were quiet as the train made its way down Mount Tamalpais. The rain had passed, and once again the sun shone brilliantly. Abby caught Norah looking out over the horizon a few times, and as she watched her she wondered what she was thinking. This was a new experience for her. She'd never had much curiosity about another's thoughts or feelings. What people said out loud was sufficient. Norah's expression was far away, and near the station in Mill Valley, Norah happened to turn to Abby and their eyes met for a moment. Abby tried a faint smile and received one back from Norah, and that, for some reason, deeply gratified her.

Chapter Five

Abby was quite surprised to look up from the specimen she was identifying as the door opened to reveal Howard Sellars. He approached her with an odd expression, as though he expected to be tossed out. As dearly as she would love to do that, she couldn't. Even if she and he were not the best of friends, he was on the Society's board of governors, actually, the deputy director, and therefore she owed him a bit of respect. Not that he afforded her any more respect than he had to.

"Ah, Miss Eliot. You're here."

Mr. Sellars had a keen grasp of the obvious. If she were not here, then she would be elsewhere, she thought grumpily.

"I trust I'm not disturbing you,"

"Not at all." She hoped he would say what he'd come to say and go away as quickly as possible.

"I would, ahem, like to have you prepare a précis of your, ah, expenses so far this year for review."

A jolt of anxiety shot through her, but she only said, "Yes, of course."

"Please have it prepared for the March meeting. Thank you so much." He bowed and smirked, and then he left.

What was he up to? What an odd request. Everyone in the Society knew she kept meticulous records, not only of her collections but of the money she spent in pursuit of them. She wasn't profligate, and she also didn't draw as much of a salary as the other researchers. She could tolerate that because she had income from her father's properties. She was paid less, she suspected, because for all the Society's vaunted equality of the sexes, they deemed it unnecessary to pay her a full salary because she was a woman and not a man supporting a family.

She slammed her plant-key book shut and arose and went to look out the window.

A few floors down on Market Street, the City went about its complicated business.

Uninvited, a picture of Norah entered her mind. What would Norah have to say about Sellars's request? Did she suffer the same devaluation of her service at the hospital? She could see various emotions play across Norah's features. Shaking her head to dispel the image, she still thought about Norah and wondered if they could meet again. They'd made no plans at the end of the day on Sunday as Abby had walked Norah back to her rooming house. Norah had thanked her, they shook hands, and that was that.

Abby did want to see her again but wasn't sure if she should just write her or call on her at the hospital. As a mutual friend, Kerry could potentially be of assistance.

Beth hadn't seen or heard from Scott since Norah's party and concluded if their friendship was to continue, she would have to take the lead. It wasn't as though *she* had any free time to speak of. She had the hospital every day and was writing the paper to present in April at the medical convention, which was being held in San Francisco. She telephoned Scott at his offices where he and Whit employed a self-important receptionist.

"Whom shall I say is calling?" she asked.

"Just tell him Beth."

"And what is the nature of your call?"

Beth was already irked, and this response wasn't improving her mood. "This is personal. Please, just tell him I called."

"Very well."

Beth could tell this infuriating woman was reluctantly jotting a message. She hoped she had enough sense to pass it on to Scott.

Some hours later, Beth was called to one of the two house phones at City and County Hospital.

"Doctor Hammond," she said, thinking of a dozen different things.

"Doctor Wilton," Scott said. "You telephoned me."

She could tell by his tone that he was irritable, and that annoyed her.

"Scott, dear. We haven't spoken for some time. I was missing you and wondering how you were. Can you come to the house on Saturday for dinner?"

"I cannot fathom why you would think I'd come to a home where Whit wasn't welcomed."

That remark floored Beth. She was disturbed that he would think that.

"That isn't so, you know that. Addison and Whit had a disagreement. That's all. You're still my friend. You both are our friends."

"Whit says he won't come to your house anymore, and he wouldn't want me to see you either."

"Scott! How can that be? You and I have had many years of friendship."

"I'm not at present feeling much evidence of that friendship. I'm sorry, Miss Beth. I don't mean to fret you." He fell back into the speech rhythm of his native South Carolina, which made her feel worse because it reminded her of their medical school days, years before.

"Is it Whit?" Beth asked, knowing the answer.

"Yes. It's Whit. You know I can't go against him. He'd never forgive me." Beth thought that was a weak excuse but didn't say so. What could she say? Scott loved Whit as she loved Kerry. It was a dilemma.

"Well. If that's how things are then, I'll not call you again. If you wish, you may stop by or telephone me when you can."

"I'll be sure to do that. Miss Beth. Please do take care." They rang off.

When she told Kerry about it later, Kerry was angry on her behalf. She liked Scott, but she'd never cared for Whit. She certainly didn't like anyone who troubled Beth.

"He's got no reason to slight you just because you have an opinion about Whit. You ought to wait for him to decide to call you, but what if he doesn't?"

"I don't know." Beth's chin was almost on her chest.

Kerry hugged her. "You'll be fine. You'll miss him, but it's all for the best. He's made his choice."

"He ought not to have to make a choice," Beth said, fuming.

"I know, love. I know." Kerry hugged her and kissed her and patted her, trying to make her feel better. It helped a little bit.

❖

A week after her trip to Mount Tamalpais with Abby, Norah and Esther took their luncheon break together. Since Norah's move to her new home at the boardinghouse downtown, they'd not had much time to talk. Norah was wondering how Esther was faring with her pregnancy and more so about her relationship with Addison.

In the noisy hospital cafeteria, they tried to talk quietly. Esther actually looked quite wonderful. Norah figured her to be in her third month, and she was beginning to show just a bit. Her cheeks and her figure were rounder. She would soon have to buy new dresses or let out the old ones. Norah wondered more how she was feeling.

"We've settled into sort of a truce. We agree to disagree," Esther said, her tone rueful.

"But you will not change your mind?"

"Addison surely hopes I will, but since he's never been able to change it for me, he waits for me with as much patience as he can muster."

"He's a good man. He loves you so."

"That he is and that he does. But I am who I am, and that he also knows. Norah, my dear, let's leave talking about me. I wonder about you." Esther's black eyes glittered and her lips twitched.

"I'm well. I was taken on an adventure not long ago." Norah paused for effect.

"Tell me. What sort of adventure?"

So Norah told her all about Abby and Mount Tamalpais.

"That actually sounds quite lovely. So the botanist is a good guide?"

"She is. I think I understand her much more than I did upon our first acquaintance."

"You have that dreamy look. I recall very well you had it when you first met May."

"I do not!" Norah was appalled. "This isn't the same at all. Abigail is nothing like May. Not in the least!"

"Ah, I would say definitely not." Esther still had that teasing tone, and it irked Norah.

"She's not like May in any fashion," Norah said with deep conviction and knew that Esther would take her meaning.

Esther shrugged. "I suppose you know. She's unmarried, is she not?"

"Yes. She's not married."

Esther had a thoughtful look. She stared at the corner of the table, then back at Norah. "Perhaps Abby doesn't know what or who she truly wants?"

Esther's question struck Norah like a thunderbolt. Was that what Norah wanted to be true of Abby? She didn't know.

She and Esther returned to their work, but later that day when she was back at her doleful boardinghouse on Harrison Street, she ate a bland supper with the rest of the house's inhabitants and retired to her room, where she mulled over what Esther had said.

Norah hadn't understood herself until May had come along. She simply hadn't even the slightest reaction to the tentative romantic approaches of young men, and there had been a couple. She'd never developed any warm or tender feelings toward the brother of one her classmates at the Women's Medical College of Philadelphia who'd sought her company. She'd had the handy excuse of needing to pursue her degree and remembered telling him she didn't see herself as a wife. Much like Abigail considered herself ill-suited for the roles of wife and mother, so did Norah.

She had been too busy to give much thought to the reason until she met May.

May had the gift of making the person on whom she was focused believe every word she said. It wasn't until later that Norah realized she might have just willed herself to believe that they had a profound connection that went far beyond the physical. By the time she'd understood that wasn't the case, it was too late. She'd fallen in love, declared her love, and May had promptly disappeared, leaving Norah to sort out her confusion and belatedly coming to see that her declaration of love and May's disappearance were an example of cause and effect.

But she was left with the stunning perception of her true nature, so in the end she'd tried to see the whole affair in a positive light, but that was difficult. She'd been hopelessly naive, nearly idiotic. Enough people had warned her about May, but she'd failed to listen. She would be the one who was different, and May would be different with her, she told herself.

They had gone to concerts and to dinner, and they'd strolled arm in arm in Central Park in the midst of a riot of autumnal color. When it began to rain, they ran, laughing together into the shelter of the gazebo near the reservoir, and out of breath from the running and the laughter, Norah had turned toward May, who kissed her suddenly, briefly, and tenderly before breaking it off. May had leaned back and cocked her head, apparently waiting to see what effect she'd had.

At the first touch of May's lips, Norah had been surprised, then disbelieving, then finally aroused. In the short space of time of May's kiss, Norah had become aware, excited, and then finally so overcome with lust, when May stopped the kiss, she had experienced it as a deep loss, a deprivation beyond bearing.

May had grinned at her, patted her cheek, and said, "My sweet Norah. My little bashful girl. I want you to keep the memory of my kiss close to your heart." Her eyes narrow and filled with secret knowledge, she stroked Norah's hair and said, "When you fall asleep tonight, think of me. I shall be thinking of you. When we next see each other, which I pray will be soon, you will have many more kisses and much more than simply tender kisses. There is so much you have to learn."

Norah had been speechless and could only nod. And as May predicted, she couldn't sleep for remembering that kiss and for the feverish thoughts of what May might have meant by "more."

In due, time she'd found out.

❖

"It's a tapeworm, I fear," Addison said after he finished examining a man whose belly was swollen and who could never seem to get enough to eat. "You must obtain a fecal sample, and we'll examine it under the microscope with Hemmings." He meant the resident pathologist.

Beth was quite grateful that she could request a nurse to obtain a proper sample and didn't have to perform that task herself. She was relieved to have Addison to turn to in cases where she was unsure. His experience was always useful, and he never regarded her with contempt for merely asking for help, something that other senior doctors sometimes did, though they didn't seem to care if one of the young male doctors asked a question. She was inured to that reaction, but it was still a relief to turn to Addison.

He appeared distracted and unhappy, though, and she felt it wasn't out of the way for her to ask him what ailed him. She suspected it must have something to do with Esther. Nothing else ever seemed to concern him. Prior to Norah's party, Kerry had informed her that Esther was going to have a baby. Beth wondered if that was what was bothering Addison, so she just came right out and asked him when she had the opportunity.

"It's true," he said, but then he said no more.

"But Addison, are you not happy about it? About becoming a father?" She was mystified by his lack of joy. It was so unlike him. For a man who exclaimed with glee when he won a hand at cards to show so little emotion about the impending birth of his child was astonishing.

"It's not that. I'm looking forward to the prospect, I assure you. I dearly hope it's a girl though."

"A girl?" Beth assumed that, like any man, he'd want a son.

"Yes. Then it will not matter that he won't bear my name."

"Your name? Whatever—"

"It's Esther. She refuses to see that we ought to be married, that the child should be legitimate. Good God, she's the most stubborn and self-centered woman in San Francisco."

"Oh." Beth recalled that Kerry had told her something of that nature, but her nose had been buried in her research and she hadn't really been listening.

Addison's dismay was obvious and Beth felt badly for him. She didn't want to take sides though. The four of them struggled to keep their household harmonious and had largely been successful. She didn't wish to upset anyone, though she scarcely could make things any worse if she was correct about the depth of Addison's unhappiness, and she knew him well.

"She'll come around eventually, I expect," Beth said in what she hoped was a soothing tone.

"I'm not optimistic in the least," he said, gloomily. "We've been over and over it, and there's no budging her."

Beth shook her head. Addison smiled at her but without humor. She could think of nothing more to say, so she patted his hand and they turned their attention to the next patient.

❖

"What a pleasant surprise this is," Kerry said as she walked to the table where Abby was seated.

Abby stood up and shook her hand warmly.

"Good day, Chef."

"Good day to you, Miss Eliot." Kerry bowed with mock formality. "What can I tempt you with today?"

"I will happily consume whatever your current special is, though I truthfully have come to see you for a reason unrelated to the Palace's fine food."

After their trip to Mount Tamalpais, Abby wanted to see Norah again. She felt as though she hadn't been convincing enough to change Norah's attitude about the importance of science and wanted to do something else, though she didn't have a clue as to what that might be. Should she invite Norah to go somewhere else? Should she ask her to come to the Society to see what was done there so she could receive a bigger picture than that offered by her own work? It was vital to her that she change Norah's mind, though she couldn't say for certain why this was so. She'd never thought she had to work for anyone's good opinion before she met Norah.

Kerry raised her eyebrows. "In that case, may I suggest that I bring you a dish of cassoulet, and then if you can permit me, say, a half hour, I believe the luncheon crowd may have dwindled enough for me to join you for a bit."

"That would suit me perfectly. But what is cassoulet?"

"It's a stew of meat and vegetables. I'm quite proud of my recipe."

"I trust you're quite proud of all your dishes," Abby said, laughing.

Kerry's pride was one of her most lovable characteristics. In their few talks, it was clear to her that Kerry had found her calling in cookery, especially in cooking at the Palace Hotel, which she never failed to point out was one of the most famous establishments in the world, as well as a premier San Francisco restaurant. It was certainly the center of her life.

As she was finishing her meal, Kerry reappeared with a couple cups of coffee in hand and sat down at Abby's table. Abby was amused to see her flick a couple of stray crumbs off the otherwise spotless white tablecloth.

"I insist on paying for my luncheon," Abby told her. "I won't take advantage of your generosity."

"Very well, I accept. What is it you've come to speak to me about?"

"It's Norah Stratton," Abby said, struck by Kerry's expression of both surprise and profound interest.

"I see." Kerry spoke coolly enough, but she looked closely at Abby. "What of Norah?"

"I thought since she shared your home for a few months, you might know something about her."

"I know *something* about her." Kerry's brown eyes were gleaming. "But, what exactly do you want to know?"

"I had her accompany me on an outing to Mount Tamalpais because I wanted to show her what I do. She's expressed some skepticism over the utility of pure science in general and botany in particular."

"Oh?" Kerry asked, looking confused.

Abby suddenly felt silly, a very unwelcome and unfamiliar feeling. She had no idea what she was asking. She only knew vaguely that her day with Norah had left her wanting more, but she wasn't certain Norah wanted the same thing.

"I'm not sure what I'm trying to say. What moves Norah? What does she like?"

"She likes being a doctor, I know that. Otherwise, well, I'm not sure. Why don't you ask her?"

"I suppose I could. I thought…oh, never mind. I don't know how to make myself clear."

Kerry regarded her for a long moment and said at last, "I think you ought to ask her if you could visit the City and County Hospital and have her show you what she does. Most folks are happiest when doing what they love or talking about it. Rather than worry what she might or might not think of you, focus on her and her work. You'll find out a lot about her that way, I think."

"Of course. I don't know why I didn't think of that. It's so obvious."

Kerry leaned back in her chair, her arms folded as she nodded with a wise smile.

"I'm sure she'd appreciate your interest."

"I swear, Beth. Abby is one of us but doesn't know it yet. She's taken with Norah."

Beth yawned. She wasn't terribly interested. She knew Kerry wanted her to be, but she just couldn't summon the energy. She also knew that if she were more consistently engaged with Kerry, Kerry would be more apt to mind her own business.

"That's nice, darling. Now could we go to sleep?"

Kerry was sitting up in bed with the covers around her waist. She made a sound of frustration and slapped her hands lightly on the quilt, which made a puff of air shoot out like a person exhaling. It was cold in their room, and Beth clutched the covers more tightly around her, wishing for Kerry to lie down and snuggle up to her so that their combined body heat would warm her.

Kerry slid down in bed and put her hand under the covers on Beth's hip, stroking up and down. It was Kerry's signal that she wanted to make love. Beth thought if it would serve to silence her it was worth it, even if she was tired, and then was ashamed of her uncharitable thought.

Kerry nuzzled her neck and slipped her hand from Beth's hip to her breast and squeezed lightly. "Bethy? Are you asleep?"

Beth turned over on her back. "No. How can I be asleep with your talking and your touching?"

Kerry climbed on top of her and moved her body against Beth's. Her voice was muffled in the pillow. "It's a miracle we're home and in bed and awake at the same time."

Kerry was right that this was quite unusual. Beth embraced Kerry and squeezed her back muscles, becoming aroused because of Kerry's nearness. "All right."

Beth inhaled sharply as Kerry's hands roamed over her under her nightgown, her touch at first feather light but then became more demanding. Beth moved restlessly as Kerry touched her all over, finally diving under the covers between her legs where, with her tongue, she made Beth cover her face with her pillow to muffle her cries of pleasure.

When Beth melted into the mattress, gasping, Kerry crawled up to lie next to her, kissing her gently over her face and neck, whispering "I love you" until Beth fell asleep.

Norah was taken aback when she received a note from Abby asking if she could meet her at the City and County Hospital and take her to dinner. That made no sense whatsoever. Norah was convinced that their acquaintance was at an end. Why she was so convinced of this, she didn't know, and she was clearly wrong if Abby was seeking her out. She surely could not be pursuing her romantically. That was impossible. She agreed, however, via a short note back to Abby, wondering that Abby didn't employ the telephone, but the note was endearing.

Shyly, Norah showed her the hospital. Abby was attentive and asked many good questions about the patients, especially who they were and where they came from.

"People with the means go to private hospitals and employ private doctors—like those fellows at the party, Whit and Scott."

"Oh, yes. Them. Of course. But you choose to forego wealthy patients and the fat fees they pay to care for the poor."

"I like to see where I can be of assistance. Esther suggested I come out West to work here."

"New York City must have an abundance of poor, sick people. Why did you uproot yourself and travel all the way across the continent to do what you could do where you lived?"

Norah colored, thinking of May suddenly, but she couldn't see how to explain that to Abby in any comprehensible manner. Abby was staring at her, obviously waiting for an answer. She was so simple without being stupid, with no artifice at all, unlike May, who was entirely artifice. She was seeking friendship, most certainly, and with friendship came the sharing of confidences.

"I was ready for a change. There was nothing to keep me in Manhattan. My mother and father were both gone."

"I see." Abigail didn't appear to actually believe she was hearing the whole story, which she was not, and Norah was grateful she didn't press for more detail.

"Well, if that's the case, then it's San Francisco's gain and New York City's loss." She smiled, and if Norah hadn't known better, she would have gauged her expression flirtatious.

To close this uncomfortable subject, Norah asked, "Where are we to dine?"

"I thought Ramsay's on Market Street. It's respectable. I inquired if they were comfortable with two women dining together, and they said they are."

"Then let us proceed there."

After dinner was over, Abby again walked Norah home, and Norah was touched by her chivalry.

"You seem to believe I need protection," she said, making sure she said it lightly.

"I don't think you do. I'm just being polite."

"I'm not a helpless female, even though I was a bit at sea up on Mount Tamalpais."

Abby peered at her in the darkness. "I apologize if I've given you that impression. I don't consider you helpless in the least. I'm a resident of the City and you're unfamiliar with it, so I think that I can walk you home without you being offended."

"I'm not offended. Oh, bother, let's change the subject. Do you in fact enjoy the City, or is it a trial to you and you'd rather be out in the woods somewhere?"

Abby seemed to consider this question seriously. "I do enjoy it and have made it my home for many years. I love its vibrancy, all the people rushing about. Even at this time of the evening the streets are alive with activity. I enjoy being in the City, but then I like to go out somewhere and to the quiet of the mountains. It's a different feeling, I suppose, not one better or worse."

Norah looked around at the scenery. The principal thoroughfare, Market Street, stretched the length of San Francisco. There were tall buildings, as in New York, though fewer of them. She'd heard it called the Paris of the West, and so it could be. There were museums and music, commerce and culture. And the loveliness of the Pacific Ocean and the San Francisco Bay surrounded it. At that moment, Norah realized she would always live in San Francisco. New York had all the things San Francisco had, even more, but it wasn't beautiful in the same way.

"It's my home now," she said. "I've chosen to live here and make my life here. I don't know why, but it feels safer in a way than New York. People are more easygoing, that's certain."

"Do you think so? I believe folk are friendlier in the West. Since I've never lived in the East, I don't have anything to which I could compare, but I'm glad to hear that you think so."

"Yes, I do." Their eyes met, and Norah tried to discern what Abby was thinking. "You, for instance, are quite friendly."

"Am I?"

"In spite of my tendency to insult you, you remain patient and accommodating."

"You haven't insulted me. Why do you say that?" Abby's confusion was endearing.

"Oh, I don't know. I've been vocal about my misgivings regarding your work."

Norah wanted reassurance that Abby liked her.

"That's not insulting to me. I'm used to people who find the idea of someone spending all her time botanizing rather dotty. It doesn't concern me."

"That's admirably open-minded. When someone expresses anything negative about my being a doctor, I get very upset."

"Well, that's simply ridiculous. As I said, medicine is a noble profession. You perform work vital to humanity."

"Well, that is true, but it's more my being a woman that puts them off. I don't believe people view you in quite the same way." There she was, being contrary and competitive again, and she hadn't wanted to be.

Abby didn't seem to notice. She only said, "I think what I do is worthwhile, but not in the same way as your work. You save people's lives."

Abby gazed at her, her face eager and sincere, and she put her hand over Norah's. Norah looked back at her, her feelings jumbled. She was stuck between wanting to push her liking of Abby aside, or at least minimize it, and wanting to embrace it and return it wholeheartedly. She had no idea where this would lead. She'd lost her heart to May and didn't want to repeat that experience, but she was being drawn ever closer to Abby. What she feared more than losing her heart was Abby not returning her feelings. Abby was companionable, funny, and patient, but nothing indicated that her feelings went beyond friendship.

Norah looked back at Abby with what she hoped was mere gratitude, but she no longer sure what her heart wanted.

Chapter Six

At the March board meeting for the San Francisco Natural History Society, Abby presented her expense reports. When she concluded, Howard Sellars looked around the table and said, "I move that we reduce Miss Eliot's expense allotment by ten percent. I believe Professor Graves has expressed a desire to attend the British Royal Society of Natural History's annual meeting in London, and he will need funds for that."

So that was what he was after. Abby fumed silently.

"One moment," she said. "Am I to understand that I am the only person giving an expense report at this meeting? Am I the only member who is under consideration for a reduction?"

The assembled board looked at one another, and many shifted restlessly in their chairs. Abby waited.

Mr. White, the reptile expert, spoke up. "Mr. Sellars, what's your objective here? I was under the impression that we don't pit our researchers against one another. All are important and all are supported."

Howard tried to look innocent. "Not at all. I am sure we are aiming to increase our international profile, and Professor Graves's presence at the Royal Society meeting will do just that."

"Why would we not merely allocate more money to Graves then? We're able to, are we not? This question came from Harmon, the archeology researcher.

"It's a matter of prestige. Miss Eliot's endeavors, while important, don't give us that."

There was a chorus of objections. *You think you can get away with this easily, Sellars. Not so fast.*

"I move we issue Professor Graves funds for the purpose of his trip to London. We'll use the reserve, and then we can later see if some of the supporters will make it up."

"I second!" one shouted. And after they voted, Sellars hadn't succeeded. As the meeting concluded, Abby saw Sellars glaring at her as though she was at fault for his defeat rather than a democratic vote of the Society's board. She was relieved but didn't doubt he'd be back again at some later time with another proposal to undermine her. She went to her workroom and took up the project she'd been engaged in before the meeting.

She'd taken a trip up to the mountains near Sacramento, the Sierra Nevada, where she'd hoped to find a very rare species of native California cypress. She'd brought it back to the City, along with a few other items, and was well satisfied by her acquisitions. But oddly, she'd missed Norah very much. A few weeks had gone by since Abby's visit with Norah at the hospital.

Roaming the meadows and woods, far away from civilization, observing plants in their natural environment and collecting them had always been her raison d'être and her greatest joy. It wasn't as though that joy was diminished. It was as present as usual, except that along with it was a vision of a dark-haired, blue-eyed woman smiling at her in her sleep.

At random moments, she would see herself turn and say to Norah, "Here, look at this." Or "How are you feeling?" She thought of Norah there with her, camping by a stream and at her side as they walked through incomparable beauty. She wanted Norah to see the world as she did. Why this should be so was a mystery to her.

When she was with Norah, she felt like an awkward country bumpkin with a smooth, sophisticated lady who viewed her with just an ever-so-slight air of amused condescension. Abby didn't feel she meant to be unkind. They were just different. Abby spent her time with people who were the same as her, and when she met those who were different, well, the differences didn't concern her.

Not this time. Norah's difference mattered, but she didn't know why it mattered so much to her. Or why Norah had invaded her mind in the fashion she had. She only knew that she wanted to go on seeing Norah whenever and wherever possible.

❖

Beth was just falling asleep, by herself as it happened. Kerry hadn't yet returned from work. From down the hall, she heard raised voices, then a door slam and angry steps in. She got out of bed and opened her bedroom door in time to see Addison, in his trousers, vest, and shirt, carrying his shoes and a coat, reach the top of the stairwell.

"Addison, whatever is the matter? Where are you off to?"

He turned around, his face troubled, his hair disheveled. "Ask Esther. I'm going out for a walk." He clomped down the stairs, and in a moment, Beth heard the front door close. She turned back into the hall to see Esther standing at the doorway of their bedroom in a dressing gown, which she held closed over her nightgown.

"Esther?"

Esther shook her head and went back inside her room. Beth followed. She sat next to Esther on the bed, who sat with her head in her hands.

Beth patted her back. "What's the trouble?"

"We quarreled."

Beth was glad that Esther couldn't see her face, which broke into a small smile at Esther's offering of what was obvious. "What about?"

"About the child, of course, or rather about marriage. The child is incidental." She closed her eyes.

Beth said, "Addison is still asking you to marry him?"

Esther sighed. "He has progressed to making demands. He says my stubbornness is going to ruin him at the hospital, ruin my good name, destroy the child's future, etc."

All Beth could think of to say was, "Oh, dear."

"He claims that I don't love him enough or in the right manner. I *do* love him."

She began to weep, which surprised Beth, who continued to pat Esther's back and squeeze her shoulder in a wordless attempt to comfort her. "I'm sure he'll return soon. He won't stay angry." Beth hadn't seen Addison get angry very often. He wasn't a choleric man.

"I don't know that he will. He more or less issued me an ultimatum: either we marry or we end our connection."

"Oh, no." Beth didn't know what to say to that, so she only replied, "Well, there is nothing to be done at the moment. I think I must go back to bed and try to sleep. You ought to do the same. We'll see what happens tomorrow."

"Right," Esther said, wiping her eyes and straightening her shoulders. "You must get your rest. Our troubles can't worry you."

Beth returned to her room and attempted to fall asleep, but she was still awake when Kerry returned.

"What's the matter, Bethy?" Kerry asked after hearing her say hello drowsily.

"Everything!" She pounded her pillow.

"Everything?" Kerry asked, putting an arm around her.

She'd climbed into bed, bringing the scents of the kitchen with her, but her closeness soothed Beth. "Scott isn't speaking to me. Esther and Addison are at odds." She told Kerry what had occurred that night.

"Hmm. Too bad. But what about us? All's well with us, isn't it?" Kerry asked, and she sounded as though she doubted it.

"Oh, yes, we're fine. All is well. Don't be frightened, darling. We're an island of calm in a sea of trouble." They embraced, saying to one another what words could never adequately express.

❖

Norah listened to Esther's tale of woe the following week when they were at the hospital. Addison had returned home, but Esther reported they were still at an impasse and not exchanging any more words than were absolutely necessary. As Esther talked, part of Norah's attention remained fixed upon her own concerns.

She and Abby were experiencing their own sort of impasse, in Norah's mind at least. They spent a good deal of time together, and every meeting, every moment was both joyful and agonizing. Her relationship with Abby could lead to heartbreak of another sort than that she had experienced with May. It seemed as though they were friends, but nothing more, yet Norah, without wanting to or even consciously realizing, had started to fall in love with Abby. All the evidence said Abby was oblivious. She was caring and affectionate, companionable and agreeable, but that was all. They seemed destined to go on as they were.

"Let me cease boring you with my troubles," Esther said. "You've not said a word in any case."

"Oh, you're not boring me. I'm just a bit distracted. Please go on." Norah was embarrassed that she'd not been listening closely to her friend.

"No. There's nothing new to say. Neither of us will give in. I'm beginning to bore myself with the retelling of my tale." Esther laughed hollowly. "But how about you? How is your work going? How is your boardinghouse?"

"It's fine. The other women are acceptable. The food is adequate. You *know* how the hospital is. It's hard. I'd like to expand the weekend vaccination clinic to two days, Saturday and Sunday, but I can't do it all myself, and they won't give me any more help."

"It's true. We do what we can, though, and I can't fault myself, nor should you, for not being able to solve all the problems people bring us. Do you not have anything that amuses you or brings you happiness? I'd invite you to the commune for a supper party, but we're not in a festive mood these days. Beth is trying to finish her paper because the medical convention starts next week, and Kerry simply works nearly all the time. You know what Addison and I are up to." She grimaced.

"I'm in love, but it's impossible," Norah said suddenly in a rush of words. The pent-up emotion of the past few weeks forced it out of her.

"Oh. Is it Abby?"

"Yes. It is." Just saying it aloud made Norah more despondent. The reality of her dilemma crashed down on her, and she began to cry.

Esther instantly moved to her side and put an arm around her shoulder. "My dear. It can't be as bad as it seems. Has she rejected you?"

"N-no. It's only that…I don't know how…" Norah took a deep breath to try to bring her emotions under control. "She doesn't know. About how I feel, I mean."

"Well. Hmm, I see." Esther rubbed her shoulder. She appeared to be thinking. "You are going to have to be brave and tell her."

"I have to tell her? How can I do that?" That seemed preposterous.

"Just tell her."

"I can't possibly do that." That idea terrified Norah. Esther drew away so their eyes could meet and put on her stern look.

"You were led by the nose by May, were you not?"

That question stung and made her sound like absolute ninny, which she had been, but she didn't like Esther reminding her of it. "I suppose."

"Well. Abby is nothing like May, is she?" Esther raised an eyebrow.

"Not in the least, but I don't see—"

"You have to take charge. You let May take charge of you and look what happened!"

"Hmph." Esther was likely right, but Norah didn't want to admit it. She rather preferred being a victim so she wouldn't have to be responsible for her feelings.

"Abby doesn't have a clue what's transpiring between the two of you, does she?"

"No. I assume not."

"Then it's up to you."

Norah slumped in her chair and stared at her shoes. Nothing would change unless she made an effort. As Esther said, she ought to tell Abby her own feelings and risk the possible rejection. Nothing would change unless she took a step forward.

"Oh, bother. Why do you have to spend the night there?" Beth was incensed because Kerry had just informed her that she would be staying at the Palace Hotel for a couple of days to be available in case Enrico Caruso wanted some sort of snack in the middle of the night.

The great tenor was in town to perform in the operas *Carmen* and *Queen of Sheba,* and even Kerry, who had no knowledge of or love for the opera, was caught up in the excitement since Caruso was staying at the Palace Hotel.

"Bethy, love, it's a great honor. He's more important, or he's at least as important as some a' them government bigwigs who stay at the hotel. Fermel asked me to take care of him. He keeps late hours, and in case he gets hungry, Fermel wants me to cook him up something to eat. You're busy anyhow," Kerry pointed out.

It was true. The medical convention had begun, and Beth's talk was scheduled for Wednesday, April eighteenth, at nine in the morning. She was very nervous about it and kept obsessively reviewing her notes. She was to speak on food-borne illnesses among children of the South of the Slot area. If she could interest some other doctors in her work, she would perhaps be able to garner more support from the hospital. As a junior doctor she needed the help of more experienced and, she presumed, male doctors to give her work credence and induce the hospital to allocate more money to her research.

Meanwhile, Kerry wouldn't be at home for a few days, starting Monday. They had to make the most of their Sunday, their one day off together for the week. Beth believed it would be better to not be around the commune, if possible. Esther and Addison were still not speaking, and neither appeared ready to give in. Their situation was distressing and poisoned the atmosphere of their once-congenial home. She wished they could resolve it soon.

"Let's go walk along the Ocean Beach."

"Not the baths?" Kerry teased her.

"No. Remember, we're still saving and the beach is free, love."

"Oh course, Bethy. Whatever you desire. Always." She hugged her and Beth felt a bit better.

❖

On Tuesday evening, Norah walked from City and County Hospital back toward her boardinghouse in a fever of anxiety. In the days since her talk with Esther, she'd been mulling over what to say to

Abby. She played imaginary conversations, speculating on what she could say and how Abby would respond.

She'd decided to go to the Society building, knowing Abby would still be in her workroom, bent over the table covered with dried plant specimens, preserving materials, notes, and drawings. She pictured Abby's face when she opened the door.

"I believed you'd be here still, and here you are. The caretaker let me in," she said when Abby opened the door to her knock. Abby's face lit up, which was a hopeful sign. At least her unannounced appearance wasn't unwelcome.

"Why, Norah, what a pleasant surprise."

"May I tear you away from you studies and persuade you to dine with me this evening?"

"I think that's possible." Abby was smiling with what appeared to be genuine pleasure at seeing her, and that gave Norah hope.

Presently, they were seated at a back table in a modest restaurant on Market Street.

After they ordered some roast chicken and tomato salads, Norah fell silent, thinking of what she was about to say. Abby was not a chatterbox, but she could converse quite freely on a number of subjects. Her work, certainly, was something she enjoyed talking about, but she was astute enough to know that it couldn't be a perennial subject.

"There's more activity than usual downtown, I think. My colleague, Harmon, told me that, besides the opera and Caruso, a masked carnival on roller skates is performing at the Mechanics' Pavilion."

"My goodness. Do you like opera?" Norah asked.

"Oh, I suppose, though it's not my favorite style of singing. I prefer the down-home parlor songs with the piano, such as what we enjoyed in February at the commune. That's what you call it, correct?"

"Yes. That's what we call it. You sang very well." Norah said, and she meant it. Abby's rendering of *Greensleeves*, in fact, had first sparked Norah's interest.

"Thank you," Abby said, smiling, as she sipped water.

"That's an interesting household, isn't it?" Norah began to have a glimmer of an idea on how to broach the subject she wished to discuss with Abby.

"I guess. They're all quite friendly and hospitable."

"They are. They were very kind to me when I was staying there. I was a stranger to everyone but Esther, but none of the rest so much as batted an eye. I meant, though, that you don't often find such a disparate group of people living together." This was frustrating, trying to work around to saying something that would convey some meaning besides just aimless gossipy chatter.

"It's one thing having an unmarried couple living together, but Kerry and Beth are something else entirely."

Abby raised her eyebrows and tilted her head. "Oh? Whatever do you mean?"

Norah tried to adopt a breezy, offhand tone. "Kerry's manner of dress, I mean."

"Well, she's a chef." Abby wasn't taking the bait.

"And Kerry and Beth are, well, they're quite a pair."

"They're awfully nice. I especially like for Kerry to make me laugh. She does as good a job at that as she does cooking. She once imitated the head chef, some French fellow, and had me in stitches."

Norah was stymied. Abby obviously didn't grasp the reality of Beth and Kerry's relationship. Or she did but didn't want to come right out and say it. Norah didn't know which it was. This seemed to be a dead-end conversation. She couldn't see a path to come out and tell Abby about herself, Esther's encouragement notwithstanding.

They'd paid their check, and as they stood on the sidewalk, a cable car rumbled past. It was still light out, the weather was mild, and Norah wasn't ready to say good-bye.

"Would you like to take a walk?" Abby asked.

"You've never showed me where you live, you know," Norah said in a playful tone.

"Oh, it's a ways from here and up a hill. I don't think you'd be up to that this evening."

Norah almost said, "Oh, yes. Let's go there." But she thought it might be a little forward to invite herself to Abby's home, though she longed to see it. Abby was right, however. She didn't care to take an uphill hike at that moment.

"No. I'm not," she said, regretfully. "But you could walk me part-way home, though I don't want to make you go out of your way."

"Certainly." And off they went, but Norah could think of nothing to say. Abby pointed out landmarks and buildings, businesses. Finally, they reached the Palace Hotel at First and Market Streets.

"Well. I better get home," Abby said. "And I expect you have to get up early tomorrow?"

"Oh, well, yes. I do. My shift starts at seven a.m."

"Then it's good night, I guess. Happy to see you today, Norah." Abby beamed and shook her hand. "Let's meet again soon." And with that, Abby turned, waved, and strode back up the street toward the Twin Peaks. The pink-and-blue sunset sky outlined their dark masses.

Norah stood staring at her for as long as she could pick her out from the throngs of people crowding the street. Two cable cars passed each other, their bells ringing as the conductors shouted, "First and Market Street, eastbound-westbound," almost in unison.

San Francisco people flowed heedlessly around her as Norah watched Abby until she disappeared, able to pick out her flat, sensible brown hat as she moved up the street. It was much like New York in that she was but one anonymous person among thousands.

When Norah couldn't see Abby any longer, she sighed and turned south on First Street toward her home. The mild weather made the streets of her neighborhood busier than ever, even as night fell. Norah climbed the two flights of stairs up to her room, which was wrapped in gloom until she could light her lamp. She sat on her lumpy single bed, unhappy with her lack of courage, and when she finally fell asleep her dreams were haunted by nameless anxiety.

❖

It was long after three a.m. when Kerry was finally able to crawl into the bed in the lonely if luxuriant hotel room where she'd been spending the last two days. As predicted, Mister Caruso demanded food at one a.m., and she was required to cook for him. He was a vain, pompous man, she observed, and everyone at the hotel from the general manager down to the lowliest bellboy was required to jump when he snapped his fingers. It was well that his performances would be over and he would be gone by the end of Wednesday and she could return home.

She missed Beth horribly but was convinced that Beth didn't miss her nearly as much. She most likely was in a state over her presentation the next day. She pictured her earnest, pretty sweetheart, done up in her best dress and standing in the front of an auditorium with a long pointer and a set of charts and numbers speaking to a roomful of bearded, bemused doctors. Well, she would be wonderful because she could do anything. Kerry pulled the covers over her head, spread out in the huge bed, and instantly fell asleep.

Chapter Seven

A bby loved the old mishmash of a house where she rented a room from an Italian man for less than eight dollars a month. It was near the top of Russian Hill, and she was blessed with a lovely vista of the Bay and the City below. A number of additions had been put up over the years, and on a balmy day, she could take a chair out on one of the roofs to sit and take in the view. It wasn't the same as the view from the Santa Lucia Mountains or from the summit of Mount Shasta, but it was compelling all the same. From there, she could look out at Alcatraz Island and Angel Island and Mount Tamalpais.

After her dinner with Norah, she was wakeful. Something had been unsettled and uneasy about Norah, and Abby had no idea what it was. She respected the privacy of others too much to ask direct questions. She hoped Norah would talk about whatever concerned her and wondered why Norah's moods were so variable. She also wondered why, in spite of that trait, she liked to spend time with her. It was very unlike her to tolerate moodiness.

It was also unusual for her to puzzle about such a thing at length. She generally liked a person or didn't, and that dictated the nature of their interactions. It seemed, although Norah confused her, that she also fascinated her. Norah was serious, then flighty, amiable then prickly, silent or talkative. Something about the occasionally intense focus of her light-blue eyes upon Abby's face made her think that Norah's heart and mind contained a world of unspoken things. And when and how Abby should ever be graced with hearing them, she didn't know and didn't want to ask. She wished she had a way of asking without being too nosy.

Abby came awake with a start. The walls of her little room shook, rattling pictures and items on the tables. It took her sleep-befuddled brain a moment to comprehend that it was an earthquake, and she leapt out of bed and ran to the door as Dr. Friend, the geologist, had advised her and held onto the doorframe to steady herself. The shaking lasted for an unusually long time. This was the worst one she'd ever felt, but it wasn't the first. After what seemed an eternity, it stopped. Dr. Friend also told her the best place to be in an earthquake was up on a hill. She looked around and saw nothing broken, though some books had fallen out of the bookcase. Then another, even stronger temblor occurred, and Abby had to grip the side of the doorframe once more as the house roared in protest and windows shattered and more of her possessions were dislodged from their places.

When it stopped at last, and she'd sufficiently calmed her nerves, Abby dressed and prepared some breakfast and wrapped up a few items for lunch, as the sky was lightening. This was a good day to be early to the Society, as there was always much to do, and today there'd likely be some displacement if not actual damage to their collections that would have to be seen to. She walked down the steps of her house to the street and saw Mrs. Anderson from across the way waving at her.

"Did you feel that, Abigail? That was a stunner. Come see what's happened to my dishes."

Since it was still early, Abby didn't mind a stop before she set off down the hill to work. She dutifully tutted over the damages at Mrs. Anderson's house, and they went back outside where the other neighbors on their steep little cul-de-sac path were gathered, muttering in groups. It had been a much worse shaker than usual. As before, when there'd been an earthquake, she and her neighbors would talk about it with excited voices and questions of "Did you feel that?" and "How long did that last, you reckon?" Abby stayed chatting with them and someone said, "Look!"

Abby looked toward downtown and saw smoke starting to rise in a number of spots. This really could be much more serious than she realized. She ran back upstairs to her room and filled her bathtub, sink, and every single pot and pan she owned with water, in case the supply should be shut off. Then she grabbed her bag of food and started off down the hill toward Market Street. This time she didn't slow down to count the flowers between the cobblestones on Taylor Street.

❖

The bed shook so much that Beth thought she was having a nightmare. She woke up to see the picture on the wall to her right slamming rhythmically and then finally fall to the floor with a thud. After she rolled out of bed she could barely stay on her feet. She made it to the hallway just in time to see Esther and Addison tumble out the door of their room. The three of them stared at one another but said nothing and ran downstairs and out into the street, where it seemed as though all of their neighbors had also appeared, also in their nightclothes. Though it wasn't even light yet, the street was packed with people, and the shaking stopped, then started again in a different direction, like a pogo stick popping up and down. Women and men alike screamed and grabbed at one another to try to stay upright. Between Esther and Addison, Beth couldn't make a sound, but she was held steady. Then the quake stopped, and she heard the church bells from every church in the neighborhood tolling over and over.

She looked at Addison, whose face was white. She'd never seen him show fear, even when they'd been in the Philippines war and the enemy had shelled the fort near their hospital. Even then he'd been calm, urging them to tend to the patients and ignore the noise. His arm was around Esther, who clung to him tightly. The cries of their neighbors dwindled down to scattered weeping. A few of the neighborhood dogs were running about, whimpering.

"Are you all right?" he asked, hoarsely.

"I think so. If I can just catch my breath—"

"Let's go back inside and see if all's well in the house," Esther said.

"Kerry. What about Kerry?" Beth said, filled with panic suddenly.

"Oh, the Palace Hotel is still standing," Addison said with his customary certainty. "That building is indestructible. She's no doubt about to start dispensing drinks to scared guests to calm them down." He laughed a little and Beth calmed.

What he said was likely true. It was yet another of Kerry's boasts that the Palace had been built as a one-of-a-kind structure. They even had their own firefighting equipment. The entire Palace Hotel staff participated in elaborate fire drills, and the in-house emergency fire-fighting equipment had been used to battle small fires in the past. Kerry told them the hotel's general manager often said that if the Palace burned down, all of San Francisco would be destroyed. Recalling Kerry's words made Beth feel better.

As they turned to walk in the house, Beth looked east toward downtown and saw smoke billowing. The skyline of San Francisco had lost its usual profile, though she could see that the huge *San Francisco Call* building on Market Street was still standing. But other buildings she remembered were no longer visible, and she began to be afraid again.

"Addison, Esther!' Beth said and pointed, and their eyes followed her hand.

The three of them stared for a moment.

Addison said in a whisper, "This was a bad one. It looks like some of the buildings downtown fell."

"There'll be folks injured. We best get to the hospital as soon as we can," Esther said. "They'll need us." She brushed her hands across her nightgown, a gesture Beth knew well. Esther was girding herself for battle. They all stared at one another, the reality of the earthquake seeping into their minds and reflected on their shocked faces in an identical manner. But without another word, they began hasty preparations to leave. As she dressed, Beth said a silent prayer of thanks that their home was still intact and another that Kerry would be safe.

❖

It sounded like a thousand freight trains pounding by all at the same time, a terrible scraping and crashing and grinding sound. Norah sat up in her bed, which was jerking back and forth. The walls of her room were vibrating in a fearful way. She couldn't comprehend what was occurring, but she could hear the other tenants screaming. She tore out of the room and down the stairs, fighting with the score of other panicked women, all of them in nightgowns. They pushed and shoved and finally made it out to the street. The shaking stopped, then a few moments later started anew, and as Norah watched, the street itself undulated in waves. It was like a nightmare from which she couldn't waken.

The movement stopped but the noise didn't. All about them, chimneys crumbled and crashed to the ground, and pieces of buildings fell. A large hotel down the street slowly collapsed before Norah's eyes. She turned to look at their boardinghouse. It was still standing, miraculously, but for how long? She turned to the woman standing next to her, whose face mirrored her own terror.

"What in God's name has happened?" Norah asked her, as if knowing the answer would somehow make things easier to cope with.

"Earthquake," the girl said simply. She seemed numb.

Norah still didn't quite understand, but her practical side overcame her disorientation and fear. She'd better get her things out of the rooming house since it might collapse, and she might as well go to work, where there would surely be much to do, and also Addison, Beth, and Esther would be there.

She re-entered, at first only thinking to get some shoes. As she climbed the stairs, they creaked ominously. If she intended to go anywhere, she would need shoes, that was certain. She struggled to tie them as quickly as she could and threw a dress over her nightgown. It would have to do. What else should she take? She owned little and didn't need very much. She sat on the bed, her heart pounding and her mind racing. She took a suitcase and stuffed a couple of dresses into it, another pair of shoes, what little money she had, and her parents' picture. With one last swift look around, she threw on her coat and fled the Miller Ladies' Hotel and Rooming House.

She arrived back on Harrison Street to a scene of utter chaos. People were trotting or running, some dragging trunks or leading crying children by the hand. A solid stream of people was headed west, and Norah understood why. She could see flames, though they were still several blocks away. She heard the clang of fire bells, and the chilly, moist morning air had turned acrid with smoke. She gripped her suitcase and started walking with the rest of them. At least she knew her destination. These poor people were simply fleeing. Then she remembered that Abby lived downtown up on Russian Hill. She stopped, in a quandary as the crowd continued streaming around her.

Where would Abby go? It was possible she'd try to go to the Society. Or did she have to stay in or near her house? There was no way to answer those questions. Norah shook herself and kept walking. She hoped Abby was unharmed but couldn't think how to get a message to her. In any case, she had her duty and she'd better hurry. Perhaps Abby could find her later at the hospital. She quickened her pace, trying not to let the panic of the crowd throw her into a similar state. She needed every bit of courage and calm she could muster.

❖

Kerry woke up when she fell out bed and onto the floor with a smack. The only thing she was aware of was the floor shaking, and when she opened her eyes, she could see the chandelier over her swinging wildly. Some presence of mind caused her to roll under the bed she'd been thrown out of just as the chandelier crashed down inches from her. The carpet muted its impact, and only a few of the light fixtures broke. She lay under the bed, breathing harshly until the shaking stopped. Before she could gather her wits, she heard another roar and rumble, and the room vibrated. When it stopped, she carefully crawled out and around the broken chandelier. In the hallway, she heard shouts and the sounds of people running. She struggled into her clothes, and as she put on her shoes, she saw the time on her alarm clock by the bed. It read 5:22 a.m. Good Lord, she'd been asleep for only three hours. Nevertheless, she was wide-awake now, every nerve on alert. She hurried into the hall where the hotel guests were heading downstairs. The first person she encountered in the lobby was her old friend Teddy Black, one of the bellboys.

"It was an earthquake, Kerry, a bad 'un." She almost mocked him for stating the obvious but only gripped his arm. He pulled her into a quick hug.

"I'm goin' to see if Kendall has any orders." Kendall was Teddy's boss.

"I guess I'll go to the kitchen. Don't know what else to do. See you."

As she traveled through the huge hotel, Kerry thought about Beth and hoped she was safe. She wondered fleetingly if she should simply leave and try to get home to check on her family, but her sense of duty kept her on course.

The kitchen, on the first floor, was a mess. Cooking implements lay scattered everywhere, and pots and pans had fallen off their hooks. She stood in the doorway simply gaping in awe. A couple of porters on the night crew were attempting to clean things up, but their efforts were pitiful in the face of the chaos.

Having no one about to give her orders was a lucky thing, and she thought again about slipping out the back door into the alley. She'd not be missed. As she stood rooted in place, trying to decide, some combination of faith that Beth was safe and loyalty to the Palace overcame her, and she instead hurried to the lobby. Hundreds of guests there were milling about or talking excitedly to each other. She spotted Kendall off to one side, with a group of porters and bellboys gathered around him.

"You there, O'Shea, get over here."

She could do nothing but obey. If she didn't and it got back to Fermel, she'd be in hot water.

Kendall wasn't usually an expressive man, but his shocked expression and jerky gestures said he felt the weight of his responsibility as well as the effects of the earthquake.

"We must get the guests calmed down," he said. "That's the ticket. O'Shea, take three porters with you and get all the booze you can find. And find whatever food you can scare up that can be served cold." Kerry realized that they couldn't start the stoves because there could be gas leaks.

"You boys," he addressed Teddy and the others, "start going around and asking everyone to please remain calm and move into the dining room. Tell them we'll start serving them food and drink as quickly as we can, on the house."

Kerry led the three porters back to the storeroom. "There'll be a lot of them wanting a drink," she said. "Here, get all these bottles and take 'em out to the bar."

She took the last porter into the kitchen with her, and they got to work. She felt steadier now, as she had to concentrate on how to prepare food without cooking anything. She gathered bread and cheeses and various fruits and some cold meats, and they carried it all out to the dining room.

❖

As Abby flew down Russian Hill and into the downtown business district, she prayed that the Society building had withstood the shock of the earthquake. She passed many buildings whose facades had crumbled. If the Society building hadn't survived, the losses would be incalculable: not just her own work but all the precious scientific collections of many years in the making. She raced the fifteen blocks from Taylor Street over Nob Hill and onto Market Street. As she crossed from the north to the south side of the street, she gasped. Scores of people were trudging up the street, dragging whatever of their worldly possessions they could salvage. She saw the huge clouds of black smoke farther south and east and thought suddenly of Norah, who lived in South of the Slot. But she would first see to her responsibilities and then perhaps search for Norah, though how she would do that, she had no idea.

In front of the building that housed the Natural History Society, she stopped and breathed a sigh of relief. It was still erect, seemingly undamaged. But it wasn't yet seven in the morning, with no one about, and she had no key. She walked over to the store next door, which harbored another entrance to the vestibule of the Society building.

The scene inside chilled her. Bricks lay scattered across the floor, and the roof was completely gone. Abby stood rooted in place for a moment, at a loss. Then she turned back into the building next door and climbed the stairs to the sixth floor, where a footbridge connected to the research area of the Society. On that floor, however, the footbridge had collapsed. She raced back down the stairs and to Market Street. Looking from one side to another, she scanned the fleeing crowds for a familiar face, someone from the Society with a key to the main door. She had to get in and see if the collections were safe.

She felt a hand on her arm and heard a familiar voice say, "Abby?"

It was Matthew Stout, one of her cronies from the Hill Tribe.

"Oh, Matthew, I'm so glad to see you!" They embraced, clinging together like survivors.

"Abby, this is a hell of a thing. I'd come down just to sightsee."

"It's good you're here. I desperately need your help. I must find a way to get into the Society."

"Oh, of course. Let's see what we can see." They strode off around to the back alley, Jessie Street, trying doors, but didn't find even a window through which they could climb. On Mission Street, the fires were clearly drawing closer, and they had to work fast before they reached the Society building. They rounded the block and back out to Market, where they saw Howard Sellars at the front door with James, the caretaker, who was unlocking the front door.

"Howard, so good to see you," Abby said, and in this instance, that was true.

"Miss Eliot. I see you're about early."

He was such an idiot, but she had no time to think about that.

"Here's my friend and a friend of the Society, Matthew. We're going to see what we can salvage."

Inside the main lobby of the Society, conditions were worse than Abby had first thought. The grand marble staircase was completely in ruins, chunks of it lying all over the floor. How would they ever make up to the sixth floor?

While Sellars and James looked around aimlessly, their faces registering the shock of the destruction, Matthew went directly to the staircase railing, which was still intact. He jumped on it and shoved it back and forth.

"Abby! The railing is good. We can climb up on it."

"Splendid, Matthew. You're a wonder."

"Now, Miss Eliot, I scarcely think this is something—"

"Howard." She was in no mood for his nonsense. "Unless you're prepared to take charge and actually do something, I suggest you leave Matthew and me to this task and go make yourself useful elsewhere."

"I, uh…very well. Do your reconnaissance, and we will assist in whatever way we can." He conceded in the face of her certainty.

Abby hung her satchel on the horn of the stuffed mastodon who'd miraculously survived the carnage and buttoned her skirt up as though she were about to ride. Matthew grinned rakishly and his spirit buoyed her. His attitude said this was no more a problem than hiking a steep trail up on Mount Tamalpais.

"I'll go first and you follow. I believe we can just haul ourselves up by putting our feet in between the rungs of the railing. He set off, clambering like a monkey, and made it to the second floor, turned, and waved. "All's well."

She followed him, and they were able to reach the sixth floor. It was strenuous work but not too difficult for two people in good physical condition.

They entered Abby's workroom and all appeared to be safe. Then she found the case that held her most precious collections, her type specimens, the irreplaceable museum-designated examples of thousands of species of plants. She'd ordered a special lightweight case to hold them, thinking of a situation during which they would need to be moved, such as a fire. Abby had feared fire from within the building, but not from without.

The type specimens were safe, but the case was ruined and useless for transport. She turned to Matthew, who was at her side, awaiting her direction so he could leap into action.

"I must move these quickly." She looked about the room, spotting her large, sturdy work apron. As she picked it up, she said, "We'll use this and lower them to the ground floor. I have ropes." They went to work, tying the bundles of plants between their protective parchments leaves and heaping them into the apron.

Matthew climbed back down, and together they lowered bundle after bundle of the precious types. Abby looked about her workroom and the small office adjacent. What else could she save? In the office, her possessions were buried under ceiling plaster.

Matthew called up, "Abigail, we must make haste. The fire's getting closer." She was in a quandary. The only personal thing she finally retrieved was her favorite Zeiss magnifier, which she slipped into her pocket. She climbed back down the ruined staircase with the final few types strapped to her back, exactly as she would have done out in the field.

Other Society members had arrived, and they retrieved what they could. Then they gathered out on the street with their salvaged material, and Abby tried to think of what they could do to secure it.

Soldiers were now lined up to prevent people from crossing from the north to the south side of Market, where Abby could see the fire just a few blocks away.

She boldly crossed Market Street and made it to her bank at Ellis Street but found a long line there. She didn't want to wait in line to store the Society's goods in her safe-deposit box; she had to find another way. As she turned, she saw between the buildings that the Fuller Paint Company on Mission Street was on fire, and flaming debris was falling into the open roof the Society. They were running out of time.

She tried to cross back to the south side of the street, but a young soldier stopped her. "Sorry, miss, but no one's allowed."

"Who's your captain?" she demanded.

He pointed to a man a few feet away.

"Captain, sir?" Abby calibrated her voice to the most authoritative tone possible while still remaining polite, and he turned to focus on her.

"I'm Abigail Eliot, curator of botany of the San Francisco Natural History Society, and I must ask you to let me pass so I can save the Society's precious collections." She pointed to the building across the street for good measure. Miraculously, her request worked and he let her pass.

Back at the Society entrance, all were in excited conversation about what to do next. In the meantime, Matthew had arrived with an express wagon and driver and waved from across the street. The soldiers had cordoned off Market Street on both sides as hordes of people struggled past, headed west.

Abby said to the nearest soldiers, "Gentlemen, I've been given leave to cross by your superiors, and these people are with me."

The soldiers looked confused, and one said, "We've been told to keep all back and—"

"Nonetheless, you must stand aside."

He looked unhappy but didn't interfere as she motioned the rest of the Society people across the street with their burdens.

To the wagon driver, Abby said, "Now, sir, what's your fee to carry this, along with myself and one other, to safety?" The wagon driver hesitated, looking sly. The heat from the fires was increasing, and Abby's patience, already frayed, was growing shorter.

"Come along, man. What's your fee?"

He looked at the sky, from which rained ashes and soot, and drawled, "Three dollars." That was an outrageous sum but they had no choice. She looked toward the assembled Society members, especially Assistant Director Sellars. They raised their eyebrows, but not one of them reached into his pocket to offer money. Matthew started to hand her three dollars, but she shook her head and gave the driver four silver dollars. He nodded, and they loaded their material into the wagon. Abby and the caretaker jumped on the wagon with him, and they drove up Russian Hill to her home and, with James's help, carefully unloaded and stored what was left of the Society's precious collections in her apartment.

With that task accomplished, Abby was free to wonder about the fate of Norah and, for that matter, Kerry and Beth and the rest of the inhabitants of the Fillmore Street commune.

Addison, Esther, and Beth managed to get across the City from Fillmore Street all the way down to Potrero Hill and the City and County Hospital in good time in Addison's automobile. They'd honked and edged their way through the refugees streaming up Hayes Street. Everywhere, the evidence of the earthquake littered the streets. Some buildings had collapsed while others next to them appeared untouched. Cable cars stood stopped and abandoned, horse carts overturned. They could see people helping others along who were clearly injured, but they didn't stop.

"We must get to the hospital and treat people where we have the means," Addison said.

What greeted them when they arrived, however, chilled Beth.

Next to City and County Hospital was a second emergency hospital for trauma cases only. However, when the three of them entered the front door, the main lobby of the hospital was overrun with hundreds of people, all in various states of distress. At the front desk, hysterical people begging for help beset Nurse Brett.

"Doctor Grant, thank God you're here. You two as well, Doctor Stratton, Doctor Strauss."

"Who's on duty?" Addison asked.

"That's our trouble. Doctor Peterson from the Emergency is nowhere to be found. The emergency hospital is unusable. We have got one doctor from there and no one—" Nurse Brett was a rock, but in this instance, her stalwart nature was clearly being tested.

"That's all right, Nurse. Who else from City is about?"

She named a couple of the staff doctors, but no one with trauma experience was available. Addison ordered Nurse Brett to find any doctors she could and bring them to the lobby.

Addison said to Esther and Beth, "We can only hope some more doctors will arrive. In the meantime, we three plus the others have to perform triage and first aid."

A few nurses from the night crew appeared, so Addison gave everyone their orders and they set to work.

With a nurse at her side carrying bandages, splints, various ointments, and the essential morphine, Beth took one side of the room and Esther took the other. Addison posted himself at the door to examine the incoming patients.

Beth steeled herself, called on her early training in medical school, and summoned every ounce of her confidence. The sheer number of people crowding their waiting room was overwhelming. She reminded herself that it was essentially quite simple. She was a doctor and must render what aid she could when and where she could.

She quickly lost track of time and, thankfully, any inclination to worry about Kerry. She and her nurse moved about the room quickly assessing which people were in the direst straits and which could wait.

She was startled by a touch on her shoulder. She turned and saw Norah, looking bedraggled but otherwise unharmed, and they embraced.

"It's so good to see you well. That's first, and second, that you've come to help. Later we'll talk, but now, we need your help."

Norah said, "I've come to fetch you. Addison is dispatching us elsewhere. Leave off what you're doing and come with me." Beth followed her.

Addison was deep in discussion with another man at his side, clearly another doctor.

"Beth, Norah, this is Doctor Steele. He's come to see if we can spare a few hands to go downtown, where they're in a pickle. The two hospitals down there have been destroyed, including the one in City Hall. They have injured people piling up in the Mechanics Pavilion."

In Norah's fevered mind, she remembered that last night, when they'd had the roller-skating event there that she and Abby had spoken of. It had been turned into a makeshift hospital?

Addison continued. "Now that we have some more staff here to help, I'm sending you with Doctor Steele. He's also commandeering my auto." Addison grinned ruefully. "At orders from above, all private autos are at the disposal of doctors and other officials who need them."

"What should we take?" Beth asked.

Dr. Steele smiled slightly. "We have plenty of supplies. But we don't have enough doctors. Only yourselves and your good hands and willing hearts."

Beth and Norah embraced Addison and Esther, then followed Dr. Steele out to the waiting auto.

Chapter Eight

Once plied with food and drink, the Palace Hotel's terrified guests became far less troublesome. They were scattered about the lobby and barroom and restaurants in groups, chattering and laughing. The atmosphere had become merry and nearly party-like, so the harried employees dared to slow down a bit and catch a breath.

One of the bellboys ran up to Kerry. "Come see this. It just about beats all."

Kerry, Teddy, and the others followed him out to the sidewalk, where they were greeted by signs of destruction and stunned by the huge numbers of people milling about. The bellboy who'd summoned them said, quietly, "There's lots of fires in South of the Slot. They're runnin' from 'em. Hope the fires don't make it up here."

Then he perked up and said, "Oh, look there." He pointed back at the Palace. There, on the fourth floor at one of the windows, stood Enrico Caruso, who looked down at the crowds on the street like they were seated in the opera house awaiting him to appear.

He threw his head up and started belting out some song in a strange language. Kerry was astounded. His voice was really something, like a trumpet or some other instrument. She looked back at the crowd, and some of the doleful refugees staggering along the street with their worldly goods gazed up at Caruso and even smiled and clapped. Kerry and the bellboys were held in place by the spectacle. Kerry almost forgot how irritating Caruso was because she so admired both his singing and his willingness to entertain the beleaguered citizens of San Francisco for free.

She felt a tug on her arm and saw Teddy put his finger to his lips and motion for her to follow. The rest of the bellboys came as well, and back in the lobby, they gathered once more with Kendall.

"Boys, there's firebrands starting to fall on the roof. Don't talk to anyone. Just get yourselves up there with the hoses and wet it down. Do it real quiet like. We don't want the guests panicked. Off with you, but don't run." Kerry and Teddy strolled over to the staircase like they were going for a nice walk. The Palace's elevators had been turned off, so they'd have to hoof it up eight floors.

As they walked, Teddy said, "You know, I got to hand it to old Kendall. I always thought he was a fussy old stick, but here he is as cool as can be."

"That's true, but I don't see him coming up to man the hoses," Kerry said. She was conscious somewhere in her mind that she was tired, and she still wondered about Beth, but she was also excited: she had another job to do. They made it, puffing all the way onto the roof. There, the famous flagpole stood with the Stars and Stripes flapping in the hot wind. The bellboys, porters, and Kerry unfurled their hoses, and a few of them stopped to gape at the scene to the south of the Palace.

It looked as though everything in sight was on fire. Kerry felt no fear, only a kind of wonder at the enormity of the destruction. Then they set to work hosing the roof of the Palace Hotel to prevent it from catching fire as they dodged the bits of flaming debris raining down on them.

❖

Beth and Norah arrived at the Mechanics' Pavilion, and the police cordon let them through on Doctor Steele's word that they were doctors come to help. Norah wondered what the police were there for, but she supposed it was only natural in such a confused and chaotic scene.

Across the street from Mechanics', the brand-new costly City Hall was ruined, only parts of its big dome still standing. This was as disheartening a sight as any she'd seen so far today. To Norah's shock, it was only nine in the morning. Beth interrupted her revelry to pull her toward the door of the Pavilion. They had work to do.

From the entrance, they could see that every inch of the vast space was covered with bodies. Some lay on stretchers, some on what seemed to be hospital beds, but some on what looked like just mattresses. They followed Doctor Steele around at first, but it was clear that no one was in charge except possibly for one disheveled white-coated doctor who was shouting orders left and right. The three of them walked up to him and told him who they were and asked him what they could do.

"Pitch in." That was all he said.

To Norah, it looked as though there were more caregivers than patients. But there were hundreds upon hundreds of injured people. She spotted a nurse moving among the patients and knew if anyone would help direct her where she was needed most, it was a nurse.

"Nurse Fisher," the young woman said. "Come with me and we can just walk about and see who needs help. I've got supplies here." She indicated the pillowcase tied to her waist, filled with dressings, medications, syringes, and other items.

"Do you have a pencil and paper?" Nurse Fisher asked over her shoulder as she strode forward.

This request befuddled Norah so she asked why.

"We've got no way of knowing who was given what medicine, and we've no system. So we're writing notes and pinning them to the patients saying what treatment was done."

Norah finally located some writing implements and off they went. She could only look for notes on the patients or do her own exam to determine what had been done or not. This was hardly a way to organize any care, but somehow, they managed to treat the patients.

"Who are all these people?" Norah asked, gesturing. It seemed incredible that so many medical people would be mustered in one place at once.

"Some are doctors from the convention that's in town, but lots of them are regular people who are just helping. That man over there told me he's a hotel manager. You saw Doctor Millar?"

"I don't know who that is," Norah said, as they stood up after giving a young girl a shot of stimulant.

"He's the surgeon from Emergency Hospital across the way. I think he was on duty when the earthquake hit, and he made them open up this place and took all he could from the hospital and brought it over."

Norah listened as she wrote a note and pinned it to the girl's blouse where the next person could see it. Then she bent over another woman nearby and said, "Shock. But there's no note. Go get some coffee." Nurse Fisher went off in a flash and returned with a cupful. Coffee was as good as anything to treat shock.

Norah and Nurse Fisher went on to another patient. She was happy that the nurse was talkative. In between their hurried consultations about triage and treatment, the nurse told her, "The doctors went out and got supplies from the drugstores, and then the hotel people came over from three different hotels and brought mattresses and urns of hot coffee and water."

They were absorbed in treating a small boy with a head wound when the Mechanics' Pavilion suddenly gave an enormous shudder. All around, the cry of "Earthquake!" went up. Those who could move had started to race for the exits when Norah heard a loud, hoarse voice roar, "Stay where you." And then the shock was over. Norah continued her rounds with Nurse Fisher, and time ran together. She had no sense of beginning, end, or middle. It was just one more patient and one more treatment, then another and another.

At one point she had to use the toilet and reluctantly left her work to find it. When she came back, she'd lost Nurse Fisher in the crowd. She was also wondering where Beth could possibly be when a policeman came toward her and whispered in her ear, "You're a doc, right?"

She looked at him, uncertain, and nodded. "I'm Doctor Stratton. What—"

"The roof's on fire. Don't tell the patients, but we're going to evacuate through the rear entrance. Dr. Millar gave the order. The coppers will help. Pass the word."

❖

It was a sound Abby knew she'd never forget: the scrape and grind of a thousand trunks being dragged up Hayes Street.

As the fires came closer, the rifle-wielding army men had herded the crowds north of Market Street. The people fleeing the fire were mostly quiet, except for an occasional crying child. They scarcely said anything as they carried their goods as best they could, to what destination, Abby had no idea. Perhaps they didn't either. Their only thought was to get away from the fire. And the things folks thought valuable enough to rescue. She saw a man in evening dress with a silver-headed cane. One woman carried a birdcage, but the inhabitant wasn't a parrot. It was a cat. She even saw men pushing and pulling a piano up the street.

In the relatively short time since she'd gone back up to Russian Hill to secure her specimens and return to Market Street, the fire had moved much farther west and appeared to have engulfed the entire South of the Slot area. The Society building was gone, and that was that.

She wondered again about Norah and steeled herself to think positively. Norah must be at work in the City and County Hospital, and she could go there to look for her. Abby wouldn't let herself entertain the fear that Norah had perished in one of the fires south of Market. That simply couldn't be true.

It wouldn't be a difficult journey because she'd be out of the main flow of the refugees. It couldn't be more than a mile and half as the crow flew. To a member of the Hill Tribe, that was a minimal distance, and it was dead flat. Abby had eaten the lunch she'd so naively packed, thinking of a routine workday, and so was fortified. The journey wouldn't take long, and she could then be assured of Norah's safety.

She reached the City and County Hospital in less than half an hour. The lobby was as chaotic as the streets, but she spotted Esther moving amongst the scores of wounded.

"Hello, my friend. How are you faring?" she asked.

Esther looked up from the patient she was bandaging, and her face lit up.

"Abby Eliot. What a surprise! Are you well? Have you an injury?"

Abby hugged Esther instead of offering her usual handshake; under the circumstances it seemed more appropriate. They were survivors, and it was a gift to find each other unharmed.

"Not at all. I'm well. I've had my adventures today and will tell you about them at some other time. I'm here to see Norah. I was concerned about her."

Esther looked closely at her and didn't answer right away, so Abby grew fearful that something was amiss with Norah. She gripped Esther's arm. "What is it? Did something happen to her?"

Esther said, "Oh no, I apologize. She's quite fine, but she's not here. She was sent downtown to help care for casualties at the Mechanics' Pavilion."

Abby was sorely disappointed and a little frustrated. If only she'd known, she could have walked over to the Mechanics' Pavilion from Sixth and Market in less than five minutes.

"I see. Well, I must find my way there then."

Esther looked at her and nodded. "So you must. Please take good care of yourself. As you see, we're occupied here. I hope we'll see you again soon. Our home on Fillmore is fine. Nothing but light damage to a few items."

"I'm happy to hear that, but I must go. Thank you."

She started back toward the commercial district at a faster pace. It was only a little after noon, but it seemed as though the day had gone on forever since the earthquake had awakened her just after five a.m.

❖

Kendall appeared at the door of the roof and shouted, "Come with me." The amateur firefighters hurried after him, dragging their hoses. He stopped in the stairwell and, with remarkable calm, said, "The south and west sides of the hotel are on fire. Run those hoses down to the second floor and get out on the Jessie Street fires escapes. You two on the west side, you three in the middle, and you two on the east end. Go! For God's sake, boys, we've got to save her. I'll wait for five minutes, and then we'll turn the water back on."

Kerry, Teddy, and another bellboy named Toby ran where they'd been directed, then went to the street level and climbed up the fire escapes. Kerry could see the fires inside the hotel rooms. They strung the hose out and busted the windows, just in time to get in position as the water came gushing out of the fire hose. They got the fire out in one room and moved to the next and put that one out. Kerry and the boys laughed and shouted, "We got that one, by God!"

Kerry had the fire-hose nozzle and said, "Let's go, boys. Over here." She started to drag the hose to the next window, but the look on Teddy's face stopped her.

"Kerry, the fire's coming back."

Kerry ran back to see, and sure enough, a fire was blazing up at the door to the room where they'd just been. They directed the water back in, but behind them and one room over, the fire blazed up and out the window. They felt the heat and turned just in time to stop the flames from reaching them. The water in the hose slowed to a trickle, and they looked at one another, stricken. What had happened?

"Toby, run see what the matter is."

He obeyed her, and she and Teddy retreated from the flames, the useless fire hose hanging from their hands. The heat from the approaching fire forced them to climb back down the fire escape to Jessie Street.

Toby finally returned, breathless, his eyes round with fear. "They're getting the guests out of the hotel, and the fire department took the water. Kendall says thanks and we can go. Er, we must go."

Kerry and Teddy stared at each other, not comprehending for a moment, and then Teddy seized her arm and said, "Kerry, we need to move. Now!" She trotted after him.

Back on Market Street at New Montgomery, even more people were fleeing the fire, which was closing in from both sides. Kerry began to be frightened, but she was still mesmerized by the spectacle. It was beyond belief, for there was their hotel, the huge, world-famous, and revered Palace Hotel on fire. The flag on top of the roof was in tatters, and it too was ablaze. As she stood rooted in place, trying to absorb what she saw, a piece of flaming debris fell onto her. She tried to leap out of the way, but her sleeve had caught fire. She heard Teddy screaming, and then she was on the ground as he roughly rolled her over and over until the flame was extinguished.

She lay motionless and Teddy knelt beside her. They didn't move for a moment as the fleeing crowds streamed around them. *I don't feel pain. Why doesn't it hurt?*

Then Teddy was shaking her and shouting in her ear, "Kerry, girl, we got to go. It's not safe here. We're either gonna burn or be run over, I don't know which. Get up, Kerry."

He hauled her to her feet. She nearly fell back over, but Teddy held on to her and began to drag her down the street.

"Kerry! Keep moving."

In a haze, she said, "Where are we? Where's Beth? I must go find Beth."

"Never mind that. Just move. Come on, walk with me."

They staggered together up the street in a sea of terrified people moving in the same direction, the heat of the fire at their backs.

Norah joined the medical folks and the other helpers as they simply picked up the patients on their mattresses and walked to one of the Pavilion's rear exits. She was frightened, but she saw no flames and knew she must be careful to keep the injured as well as herself calm. The policeman's piece of information was alarming, but her silent counsel to herself seemed to work. A long line of autos was waiting on the street, and the medical people simply loaded their charges into them as best they could, then returned for another patient. She finally spotted Beth with Dr. Steele and Addison's car.

"Where will we go?" she asked the two of them.

Dr. Steele said, "The police have informed me that the army is directing evacuations and have told us to take the injured to Letterman Hospital in the Presidio. We must get out of the downtown area, as the army is going to start laying dynamite to create firebreaks. They turned as one to the east, and Norah saw the fire.

"I'll go with you," she said to Beth and Dr. Steele. They simply nodded in assent, and when they'd gotten two of the injured settled in the back with Norah to look after them, they drove into the masses of people heading west on Hayes Street. Norah's relief at being away from the danger at the Pavilion didn't last long.

"Oh, good Lord, not now," Dr. Steele said, his voice full of exasperation.

Beth asked, "What's the matter, Doctor?"

"You may call me William, as we needn't stand on ceremony. But we're running low on gasoline." Norah leaned over the front seat to look at the gas gauge, which was nearly on empty.

"We must find a drugstore and get some fuel, or we won't make it out to the Presidio. Both of you keep an eye out."

Between observing their two patients, one with a concussion and another with a hastily splinted compound fracture, Norah scanned the left side of Hayes Street as Beth looked to the right. Groups of soldiers were lined up everywhere along the streets, watching the marching crowds.

William spoke in a low voice. "General Freddy Funston's called the troops out, I see. I'm sure those rifles are cocked and loaded." Norah wasn't sure who he referred to, but she assumed he was some sort of high military commander.

"There's one," Beth called, pointing. They eased their way through the walkers and stopped before a storefront reading Walgreen's Drugs and Sundries, and the three of them hopped out of the auto. Two young soldiers immediately pointed their rifles at them, and they instinctively threw their hands into the air.

"Halt!" said one of the soldiers.

"Young man, we're doctors transporting wounded to the Presidio. We need to get some gasoline for our auto," William said.

The two soldiers looked at one another uncertainly. "We've orders to stop looters."

Dr. Steele said, in a stern voice, "You're two good and patriotic soldiers who obey orders. But you can see clearly that we have injured people we're trying to evacuate in the back of this automobile. Kindly allow me through. We're not looters. We're doctors."

He indicated Beth and Norah. Norah didn't know what to do, but she held up her stethoscope as a sign. She thought the bloodstained front of her dress might also help to convince these ignorant and nervous young men. There was no light of comprehension in their eyes, though.

"Doctors, huh," the taller one said.

"I am Doctor William Merstone Steele. At your service. And this is Doctor..." He didn't remember their family names, so Norah stood as tall as she could next to Dr. Steele and said, "Doctor Norah Stratton."

Beth did the same, and the two soldiers seemed to waver, but they were clearly at an impasse.

Beth stepped forward. "Which company are you from?"

Clearly startled, one of the boys answered. "The Tenth Oregon Infantry."

"Commanded by Major Levings of Portland, Oregon?"

The boy nodded.

Beth said, "When you see him, ask him about his bout of dysentery and how Nurse Hammond got him through it back in Manila in ninety-nine."

The soldier boy's eyes widened. "He talks about the Philippines war all the time and told us he had the trots for weeks. How do you—"

"I was an army nurse back then—Nurse Elizabeth Hammond. Give my regards to Major Levings." Somehow her intervention worked, and the soldier hesitated another moment, then lowered his rifle, the other boy doing the same at a nod from his companion.

Dr. Steele said, "Let us proceed," and he marched forward without so much as a glance at either of them. Norah shut her eyes, praying they still wouldn't be shot by the nervous, trigger-happy soldier boys.

Dr. Steele broke the window of the drug store, reached in and opened the door, and they followed him inside. The store was a shambles, and it took some minutes to locate the gasoline dispenser and pour some into a spouted metal can. For good measure, they took whatever medical supplies they could quickly find.

The soldiers were still standing in the same place.

"Thank you, gentleman. Give my best to General Funston." William tipped his hat, but the soldiers didn't smile. They perhaps thought they might be reported for failure to do their duty.

Doctor Steele topped off the gas tank, and they were back on their way.

❖

Abby strode from City and County Hospital back to the Civic Center area, determined to find Norah and verify that she was well.

Then she would see what she needed to do next. The fires were burning to the north and south of Market Street, but she could see that Russian Hill was still safe. Before she'd left her home, she had told her neighbors to take her type specimens farther up the hill to the painter William Keith's house, if they had to, just in case the flames approached. She didn't really care about any of her other possessions.

She had to cross the stream of refugees on Market Street, and once again she was confronted with army men; this time they were letting no one pass. She girded herself and marched up to the one who seemed to be the officer.

"Good day, sir."

He turned his cold gaze on her and she almost faltered but kept her confidence. "I must pass. I'm on my way to the Mechanics' Pavilion."

He glared at her. "No one's getting through, miss. Area's too dangerous. Besides, the Mechanics' is gone."

A wave of terror passed through her, and she was speechless as they stared at each other. "Wha-what do you mean, gone?"

His bushy eyebrows furrowed, and Abby could see his deep frown even behind his mustachios. He wasn't interested in answering her question. That was unfortunate because she was going to get an answer, one way or another.

"Burned, miss. Move on, if you please." For good measure he pulled his rifle across his chest. Abby was finally intimidated, but she still had to know.

"What of the people inside?"

"They was mostly evacuated out to the Presidio, I believe," he said, grudgingly, his face showing the strain of his duties.

She persisted. "Mostly?"

"I don't know, miss. Now if you would please move along." He turned away then, leaving Abby standing in the street at a complete loss as to what to do next.

Where would Norah have gone? To the Presidio with the injured? Possibly. With that she turned and joined the rest of the refugees, and as she started her walk, it occurred to her she'd not thought to bring water and was thirsty. That was imprudent, a novice mistake, and she berated herself silently. She looked about for anyone who might have water, but the grim faces of the people told her nothing. As before, she noted that they marched in silence, the only sounds coming purely from whatever conveyance they were using to transport their belongings.

She saw a couple of women together and pulled up alongside them. "I beg your pardon, but do you know where I might obtain some water?"

Their stoic faces didn't alter as they looked back at her impassively. She thought they might be foreigners who didn't understand English.

"I am looking for water." Abby enunciated carefully.

"There's no water," the shorter blond one said, finally. "Don't you know?"

"Know what?" Abby asked.

"All the water mains broke. The firemen got no water. No one has any water."

"Oh, I see." So here she was, like any other refugee, trudging along Hayes Street with no idea what had become of Norah and not a drop to drink. She put her shoulders back and gauged how far away from Presidio she was. It was more than five miles. Again, this distance normally wouldn't offer any difficulty for her except for the lack of water.

The taller, dark-haired half of the pair handed her a small sliver of foil. "You can try this. It's all we got."

Abby took the small, flat object from her; it was a stick of chewing gum.

"Thank you," she said, touched, but neither woman said any more. No one wanted to waste any energy. As the three of them marched on, Abby unwrapped the gum and put it in her mouth. It was scarcely like a drink of water, but it gave her mouth something to do, so she was grateful.

"Where are you headed?" she asked the shorter woman.

"No place to go but the park. That's were the army keeps telling us to go."

"What for?"

"It's west, and it's safely away from downtown and them fires."

Abby thought carefully. Where would she likely find Norah? How in the world could she know where to look? She tried to quell her rising fear and abruptly decided to return to the hospital and see if Esther had any news of where Norah and Beth could be and if she could likely find water there as well. Abby said good-bye to her benefactors and turned south at Van Ness Ave toward the Potrero district once again.

After a half hour or more, she was once again in the lobby of the City and County Hospital, and after getting some water, she searched for Esther.

"I couldn't find her. The Mechanics' Pavilion burned, but I think everyone got out. The army was somewhat helpful and said they evacuated the injured to the Presidio. Would she be there?"

"I don't believe so. They've got a full staff of army medical people. She might come back here, where we really need more help."

"Well, in absence of any information, I've got nothing else to do, so put me to work."

"That's wonderful. You can help calm people and get them water—what little we have."

❖

"Kerry, girl, you got to move faster. We're falling behind."

Kerry was but dimly aware of Teddy's exhortations. His hand gripping her arm hurt, and she wanted to just sit down or, better, lie down.

"We got to get you to a doctor, but I don't where there's sure to be one. So I'm just following the crowd. I hope they know where they're going. Geezus criminy. Kerry, don't fall."

Kerry felt herself jerked upright. Her head was spinning. Teddy, she thought dimly, tended to gabble when he was nervous or scared. He needed to shut up.

She closed her eyes. She could barely see anyhow, and her burned arm was beginning to hurt horribly. *Oh. There's pain after all. Must be a bad burn.*

Then she passed out for a few seconds, sliding to the ground. She awoke to more of Teddy's ramblings.

"Oh no, Kerry. No!" His voice faded a little, but she could hear him shout, "Hey! Hey you. Hey, stop. No, you got to help me. Please. My friend's burned bad. She can't walk."

The next thing she knew, she was in the back of a wagon, being jolted up and down as it rolled over the cobblestone paving. It reminded her of the earthquake, but it was worse because it didn't stop. Teddy whispered to her, "We got us a ride. Holy crow, Kerry, can you hear me? We're going to the park, he says. He thinks that's where the help is."

She couldn't understand what Teddy was saying, and she just wanted to sleep. She had no awareness of the passage of time, only of the endless bouncing that hurt every time the wagon wheels turned. Finally, mercifully, the movement stopped and Kerry felt herself being lifted. Voices were saying things she couldn't make out. Then she was still, thank God. From the smell of grass, she understood she was lying on the ground. *Oh. I'm in Golden Gate Park.* Then she lost consciousness.

It was like looking upon a large outdoor gathering for a concert or a play. The Panhandle of Golden Gate Park was covered from one end to the other by hundreds of people jostling haphazardly, resting on their salvaged goods. Some wandered aimlessly back and forth. There was no organization, no one in charge, just a mass of stunned survivors waiting for whatever would happen next.

"We've got to see where the hospital is," Norah told Beth. Doctor Steele had driven to the park on the orders of the Presidio commander but had abruptly left, muttering about returning the auto to its owner and ordering Norah and Beth to stay and help. Norah had decided not to argue, since she thought Golden Gate Park was the likeliest place as any for Abby to end up.

She scrutinized Beth, who, on their ride from the Presidio to the Park, had become quiet and distracted. She was likely thinking about Kerry. As they had turned their two patients over to the army medical staff, they were told that the army was preparing to dynamite firebreaks, as the entire downtown area was afire. Beth had gone white, and they had looked at one another without saying anything.

Norah said, "Look at all these people. They all must have walked here. I bet Kerry is around somewhere, maybe Abby too." Beth had only nodded slightly. They were in a sea of humanity, and suddenly everyone stood up and began moving in one direction. Beth and Norah had to go along or be trampled.

Norah could see the reason. Trotting toward them were four horse carts loaded with soldiers and bearing giant wooden barrels. When the first one arrived, one of the soldiers shouted, "Line up, nice and orderly. We've brought water!"

A gasp went up from the people and they surged forward.

All the soldiers raised their rifles, and their spokesman shouted, "Oh no, orderly like, folks. I want women and small children first. You gents wait your turn. No shoving. Everyone will be served."

Beth and Norah joined the water line. As they waited with the rest, Norah asked the nearest soldier where the hospital was.

"Ain't no hospital to speak of. They're bringing all the injured back there." He pointed across Stanyan Street to the park superintendent's stone house.

"Soldier?" Beth asked, "Is there any way to locate people?"

He looked around at the crowd and they followed his gaze. Norah could tell they were thinking the same thing. "How in the world could a person find anyone in this crowd?"

"Back down at Fell and Baker Streets, the *Call-Bulletin* newspaper people are trying to register folks. You might try there."

Norah looked at Beth, who nodded.

"We can check and see if either Kerry or Abby registered. Then we can go to the hospital to help them."

Norah and Beth walked through the crowd. People sat on pitiful piles of their belongings, and children were crying here and there, but otherwise it was quiet.

At the eastern end of the Panhandle, they inquired of the newspaper people how to find someone and were shown who'd signed in. Neither Abby nor Kerry's name was on the list. Disappointed, they left their own names and headed west, struggling through the mass of refugees.

Norah tried to quell her rising panic. The absence of Abby's name on the newspaper's lists didn't prove anything. She said, quietly, to Beth, "They've probably not arrived. It would take a while to walk all the way from New Montgomery out here."

Beth said nothing, her lips pressed together.

A disheveled man appeared out of the crowd and grabbed Norah's arms, shouting in her face, "Where's my Emmy? Where's little Gracie? I lost them somewhere. I got to find them."

Norah shook him off, unnerved. The man was crazy with grief or confusion, looking for his own family.

As they crossed Stanyan Street, the scene became clearer. Beth and Norah gaped as they looked around and then back at each other. On the lawn around the house were a dozen tables, and crowded around each table were small groups of doctors and nurses. They were operating out in the open because they had no choice. They presented themselves to the nearest nurse, who was obviously exhausted, her cap askew and her uniform spattered with blood.

"You can relieve anyone who needs respite. We've nothing here except what we've brought. The doctors are just trying to accomplish the minimum without anything but a little water and some chloroform. As you can see, we've no place to put anyone. She stretched her arm out and indicated the people who were lying on the bare grass, some with family members, some alone. A continuous line of injured staggered toward them.

"I'll perform triage," Beth said. Norah surmised that would give her a chance to look for Kerry. She dearly hoped they could find Kerry and Abby unharmed.

"Very well. I'll be over here." Norah made a round of the operating tables and offered her assistance.

"I don't have any surgical tools, but put me to work."

A haggard doctor merely said, "I could use your hands. That's a help at least. Hold this man still."

The man on the table was half conscious, with a piece of metal sticking out of his abdomen. Norah and a nurse held him as the surgeon extracted the metal, and they tried to slow his bleeding. The screams of the injured filled their ears. They had little chloroform and no morphine. Norah set her jaw and hung on to the struggling man, trying to not worry about where Abby was or what had become of her.

❖

At the City hospital, Abby was worn out from bending and lifting and comforting, and, in some cases, restraining folk who had no obvious injury but were in some sort of deranged mental state. She didn't blame them. This was surely one of the most awful things she'd ever seen. It had taken on the air of normality, though, as she followed Esther or one of the nurses around the hospital lobby trying to make some sort of order out of the disorder. At least it kept her busy and not wondering about Norah. She was certain Norah was safe and merely somewhere lending a hand. That had to be the case.

Esther came over with a tall gentlemen in tow. "This is Dr. Steele," she said. "May I present Abigail Eliot. She's assisting us, but she wants to inquire about one of the doctors."

It was incongruous but oddly normal to shake hands with Doctor Steele amidst the sufferers and medical staff in the City hospital lobby.

"I took Doctor Stratton and Doctor Hammond to Golden Gate Park on the request of the army medical command. The refugees are being directed there, and it was there the army deemed staff was most needed. I assigned myself back here to City so that I could return Doctor Grant's automobile."

Abby looked at Esther. "Go. I know you must set your mind at ease. We'll be fine. I'm sure you can help just as easily in the Park as you can here. But you'll have to walk."

"That doesn't concern me in the least." And it didn't. Obtaining water had revived Abby's flagging energy, and she set off. Before long she was once again swept up in the hordes of refugees on their way west to Golden Gate Park.

It took her two hours to walk from the hospital to the Park, and she was hungry as well as thirsty, having consumed her lunch hours before. She silently gave thanks for her strength and fortitude, forged over years of collecting botanical material in all kinds of environments and weather conditions. She finally arrived at the eastern end of the Park's panhandle area and joined the crowds at the tables there.

"Yes. I can find that for you. Here you are, ma'am." The man at the *Call-Bulletin* table pointed to the name.

There it was on a card—*Norah Stratton*. She was here somewhere. Abby looked around wildly, thinking perhaps to spot her, but it was impossible. There had to be thousands of people on the Panhandle.

"Where's the medical area?" she asked.

"Not sure," the man said. "I think it's over by the superintendent's house."

She thanked him and began to thread her way through the crowd. Abby couldn't really tell where she was and literally used the position of the sun to lead her in the right direction.

She was greatly relieved to make it to Stanyan Street, where she asked a passing nurse where to find the hospital tents.

The nurse looked at her strangely. "We don't have any tents. The docs are over there." She gestured vaguely.

It was late afternoon and the ocean breeze was increasing a little. What would become of the people in the Park that night? But she had little care for strangers. She had to find Norah.

She saw them on the edge of the area, where medical activities were clearly taking place. Norah and Beth were together, kneeling over someone lying on the ground. As she drew closer, she heard their raised voices.

"Beth, no, it's better to let me take care of her. You must not fret. She'll be in good hands. You may sit here for a moment and—"

"No. Norah, I said to leave me to it. I have to save her. It's my duty." Abby didn't know Beth at all well. She remembered a gently smiling, gracious but confident young woman playing gay tunes on the piano that evening a few months before. The figure next to Norah bore but the vaguest resemblance to that woman. Her hair and eyes were wild, and she was almost hysterical. Norah was obviously trying to reason with her.

Then Abby saw over whom Beth and Norah were arguing. It was Kerry. She lay there white and still, her right arm covered with a bandage, and it seemed as though she was severely injured.

"Go look after the other patients," Beth snapped.

"No! I'm not leaving you or Kerry. If you don't calm down, I'm going to get someone who's in charge. You won't care for me having you removed from duty, will you?"

Beth's eyes narrowed. "You would not do such a thing to me."

Abby neared them and spoke. "Norah, Beth. I'm overjoyed to find you two."

They turned and gaped at her. Norah leaped up from the ground and threw her arms around her. As they stood, clinging tightly together, something shifted in Abby's heart. She had never been so happy and so relieved to see a particular person.

"I'm so happy you're alive. My dear Abby. I cannot—" Norah burst into tears.

Abby held her and felt tears at the corners of her own eyes. She took Norah's arm and led her a few feet away. "What's happened to Kerry? Beth seems deeply upset."

Norah's teary eyes took on a wary look for some reason Abby couldn't comprehend.

"Yes. She's gotten a very serious burn. I believe she'll recover, though she's bad off. There's nothing to do but wait and—"

"Beth wants to doctor her? Why is she so distressed?"

"She's just very concerned. I'm trying to convince her to let me help."

"But she's not listening to you?"

"No. She's come undone.'

"Let me try." Abby patted Norah's arm and attempted a small smile. Norah indicated she agreed.

Abby knelt next to Beth, who had Kerry's hand to her mouth and was kissing it over and over, murmuring, "Wake up, my love. Please, could you open your eyes? Speak to me? Let me know you're well."

"Beth. It's me, Abigail."

Beth didn't move or even acknowledge Abby's presence.

"Beth. Please, it looks as though Kerry's passed out. Did they give her morphine?"

"We don't have any morphine," Beth said dully as she continued to stare into Kerry's face.

"I want you to come with me and get some water. Let's leave Norah to watch over her. It looks like you could use a spell of rest." Abby took Beth's arm firmly and got her to stand up.

"I can't"—

"But how about a cup of water, and then you can come right back?" Abby took a firmer hold on Beth's arm, and Beth let herself be pulled away.

"I'm going to go find some water. Do they have a supply here?"

Norah pointed to a wagon and looked relieved that Abby had managed to do what she could not.

"Beth, dear. I'll stay with Kerry. If she wakes up, I'll fetch you right away. Please just go with Abby and take some water and sit down for a moment."

Norah turned back to Kerry, her mind whirling from a combination of relief and dread. Abby was alive and well, which was wonderful. She, however, had just broken down in her arms with a terrible display of girlish nerves. Abby was going to keep asking why Beth was so hysterical over Kerry, and she was going to have to explain what she couldn't explain the night before. That restaurant supper seemed very far away and unreal.

Abby strolled over as though it were merely a normal day at the park and they were all out on a picnic, and perhaps Kerry was just weary from a little too much sun or a few too many glasses of beer. Norah admired her apparent sangfroid.

"I gave the care of Beth over to one of the nurses. Her hysteria's done, and a sort of inertness has overtaken her. I'm not familiar with such mind problems, but in any case, are you able to talk?"

"Yes, of course, but I have to keep an eye on Kerry."

Abby sat down next to her on the grass.

"I'm sure you've had an extraordinary a day, as I have had. As any of us. All of us." Abby's arm encompassed the vast sea of refugees and patients: the rich, the poor, the men, women, and children. Whites, Chinese, Mexicans, businessmen, and laborers were all sitting in the Panhandle of Golden Gate Park after fleeing for their lives and having no idea what else to do.

"I've no doubt that's true," Norah said. "Let us begin with you, however. You reside downtown, where we understand things have nearly been totally destroyed. Kerry was brought in by a man in a bellboy's uniform, who was almost out of his mind babbling about the Palace Hotel burning down."

"Ah, that is horrifying to hear. Well, I can say that my home on Russian Hill is intact, was intact the middle of this morning. I'm going to leave to return to it presently."

Norah wanted to shout at her she would do no such thing, but she held her tongue and let Abby tell her story.

"You risked your life to rescue *plants*?" She was incredulous and angry, unreasonably, immeasurably, angry.

"Well, not precisely. The fire wasn't quite upon us. And they weren't just any plants, they—"

"I cannot believe I am hearing that you, an otherwise sane and intelligent woman, climbed six floors up a railing in a half-collapsed building to find and retrieve dead flowers."

Norah was incensed at what she considered Abby's extremely poor judgment and skewed priorities. She was also overwhelmed with relief that she was safe and deeply annoyed at what she saw as Abby's cavalier attitude.

"Norah. I was never in any real danger. I can't see why you're making such a fuss. I myself was nearly overcome with terror that *you* had possibly perished in the Mechanics' Pavilion fire. I had gone to the hospital to find you, and then I walked back downtown to the Civic Center only to find that everyone was gone and no one knew if all had been safely evacuated. I then *walked* to the City and County Hospital from the Civic Center, thirsty as I have never been thirsty, to look for you! But you weren't there." Abby's voice gradually rose as she talked, and Norah realized she was hearing anguish and fear. About *her*. But she was still angry.

They glared at each other for a full minute without saying another word.

Norah spoke first. "I'm sorry. I didn't mean to raise my voice. It's just that I'm so...I'm—I never—I only thought. Oh my God." And she began crying again. Abby held her and rubbed her shoulder and crooned wordlessly until she was calm again.

"When I was at the hospital, I found out you were here, so I came as quickly as I could."

"I've never been in an earthquake," Norah said, her lips quivering. "I was terrified. My rooming house is gone, my home. I have only what I carried out. I've been trying to take care of people all day." Her words tumbled out, her face buried in Abby's shoulder, the rough broadcloth of her blouse rubbing her cheek. She became aware through her tears and her dismay that she felt safe and cared for in Abby's embrace. Their breasts were pushed together, and Norah was becoming more and more aware of the closeness of their bodies.

"Oh, my dear Norah, I forget that you're an Easterner. I've been in several earthquakes, though none as bad as this. Of course this was terrifying for you. I'm insensitive. Your nerves are hairtrigger after this experience. It's no wonder that you're having a reaction like this. Truly, I'm sorry to have added to your distress by mistake." She hugged Norah tighter. "Now tell me you're feeling more on an even keel. I don't wish to leave you, but I ought to go back home, and I—"

"Oh, can you stay for a short while?" Norah was somewhat ashamed that she was using Abby's guilt and her remorse to keep her there, but now that she had her back, she very much didn't want her to leave.

"For a few moments. Shall we see how Beth and Kerry are getting along? I'm quite surprised at Beth's reaction. I know they're very close friends, but I would have thought that, as a doctor, Beth would be able to keep her emotions under control. It must be all the stress of this unimaginable day." She really had no idea.

"Beth and Kerry aren't friends." Norah said, suddenly.

"They're not?" Abby wore an entirely dumbfounded expression. "But I thought..."

"They're sweethearts. Lovers," Norah said. "That's why Beth was beside herself. That's why I was telling her that I ought to treat Kerry and not her. It's not good for doctors to care for their own family members. As you see, their emotions are engaged and they cannot be clearheaded."

"I see. Well, yes, certainly. That would be the prudent course to take." It was impossible to tell how Abby was receiving this information.

"So I must go see how things are, and then I must get on with whatever must be done for the others, and there are many others, as you see." Norah was pleased that her emotional storm had passed and she was speaking again as a calm and competent doctor. She was scrutinizing Abby for her reaction, though. To her surprise, there wasn't any.

"Are you quite well then? I don't wish to leave you if you're not. I will come back here tomorrow. Where will you sleep?" Abby peered at her, all tender concern.

"I'll find my way to the commune. I expect they will take me in readily."

"That is well then. So good-bye." Abby gave her another brief hug and walked away, leaving Norah staring at her retreating back.

❖

Beth sat on the ground next to Kerry's inert body. She was waiting for her to wake up, and she wanted to be there to reassure her and to reassure herself that she was going to be all right. The doctor who treated her had assured Beth that though it was a serious burn, it wasn't fatal. Beth absorbed this well-meant information and tried to put her thinking into "doctor" mode, but it was impossible. Kerry was in shock and her unresponsiveness was oddly a good thing, she told herself over and over. But Norah was right. She was Kerry's lover, and she couldn't be the doctor at the same time.

She closed her eyes and prayed as she hadn't since her childhood in church with her folks.

"Bethy, is that you?" Kerry spoke in a scratchy, barely audible voice.

"Yes. Yes, my darling. I'm here. You're safe."

"Water." Kerry's voice was coming out in a croak. Beth lifted her head so she could sip from the cup. She sighed and slid back down onto the ground on which she lay. The sleeve of her jacket had been cut away, and a loose bandage placed over the burn. Beth dared to lift it up to look.

The burn was large and extended from the upper part of her arm down to her wrist. In the middle of an angry red outline, it was dead white, a huge blister. She wracked her brain to remember what that meant, but she couldn't. She would have to ask the doctor. She covered it back up with the bandage.

"Bethy, are you well?" she whispered.

"I am, love. I am. You will be as well in time."

"Don't remember much of what happened. I think Teddy saved me though."

Beth was surprised. Teddy, Kerry often said, was a good man, but he was a no-account who'd never be better than he was, a bellboy.

Well, Beth would have to find him and thank him, if what Kerry said was true. She also wanted to get Kerry home to the commune. They didn't need to spend the night here as refugees; they had a home to go to, and it was still standing, as far as she knew.

How to get there was the problem. Addison and Esther were surely still down at City and County. She went off to find a blanket to cover Kerry, but there were none to be had. She had only her shawl, so that would have to do. It was afternoon and getting chilly. It would be colder as the evening approached, and she didn't want either of them to spend the night out in the open. She had to make a plan.

Chapter Nine

A s Abby walked stolidly through the streets of the Western Addition toward the downtown area, she could see the smoke and the flames in the distance. She judged them to be only just past the middle of Market, where the Society was located. As she strode, she thought of Norah, whose emotions once more bounced between cool competence and tears, between anger at her and clear worry. She was as confused as ever. She still didn't know quite what to make of the news of Beth and Kerry, but there was nothing more to be learned at the moment. Abby had confirmed that Norah was safe, and she had other matters to attend to, such as getting back to her home.

She was out of the main flow of refugees so it was possible to walk in the opposite direction, and she was the only one doing so. She reached Van Ness Avenue in good time and once again was confronted with a formidable line of army men and City police. So far, she'd succeeded twice and failed once to cajole the officials into giving in to her, so she reckoned it was worth one more try.

Again looking for the highest-ranking officer, she noticed a knot of soldiers off to one side and saw one in the center who wore a peaked cap with a gold badge. He was very short, but the other soldiers were listening raptly to him so he must have some rank. She knew nothing about army hierarchy, but he was a place to start. As she neared the group of uniformed men, she heard one of them address the short man as "General Funston." Ah, she'd bagged someone important.

"Pardon me, officers," Abby said in as pleasant a voice as she could muster. "Might I be permitted to pass through the line? My home is on Russian Hill and I must return there, where there's no fire's presently and—"

During a short interval the general issued several terse orders to his men, ignoring her, then turned, fixing his sharp blue eyes on her. "Young lady, you'll turn around and march directly back from where you came, to Golden Gate Park, if possible."

"But sir—"

"Madam, be silent. I've no time for nonsense. We're going to be dynamiting the buildings between the fire and here, and no civilians can be anywhere near. You'll be on your way, as we're evacuating these areas at this moment." He broke off to address a question, and it was obvious she was dismissed.

Abby stood for a moment considering her possible courses of actions. She'd left directions with her neighbors on what to do with the type specimens, so she must have faith they would carry them out if need be. She tried to quell her unease. She would return to the park to the assurance of at least some water and some company for the night, if no shelter or food. She was drawn back to Norah as the compass needle points to true north, and as she had no clear alternative, she began the walk back to Golden Gate Park.

❖

"She's stable at the moment, Beth. I just listened to her heart and took her pulse. We've given her water and she's quiet. I suggest we see if any shelter is available for us as night comes on. It's going to be cold, and I've only this wrap with me. You have a shawl, but otherwise, we're not well prepared."

Beth, albeit reluctant to leave Kerry, understood Norah's calm logic and reassurance. Where was Dr. Steele? Would anyone think to come fetch them? Perhaps they could get back to Fillmore Street if they had transportation. She and Norah could walk, but she couldn't move Kerry. Beth made her way through the Panhandle toward the operating tents, hoping to find someone in charge. Knots of doctors and nurses still gathered around the makeshift tables operating by lantern light, so absorbed in their work that no one turned to even acknowledge her.

She spotted a uniformed man watching the crowd, so she decided he might have some knowledge. "Do you have any means to communicate, or do you know where I could find the officer in charge?"

"No, I don't know, miss."

"I'm Doctor Hammond," she said automatically, "and I—"

"Miss, I'm a private. My orders are to keep order amongst the citizenry, and that's that. I'm not a lost-and-found expert."

"Well, yes, then could you tell me if we are to be given any food or shelter this evening?"

"Miss, we can pass out a little water, but that be all. The army is attempting to organize relief, but that won't be here for some time."

Beth gritted her teeth and summoned her steeliest voice. "We've got patients, you know, and—" Something touched her arm, and she stopped in mid-sentence and turned to her right.

It was Scott, and he threw his arms around her. His hair and his clothes reeked of smoke. She stepped back to see him better and was appalled. He had a rumpled jacket over his shoulder and wore a smudged white shirt with a tie dangling around his neck. His face was dirty and streaked with tears.

"It's gone, Beth. All gone." His eyes were glazed, and he didn't appear to be in his right mind. "Whit's gone."

"Is he dead? Dear God, what's happened? Tell me. Oh, but first, you need water. Come with me."

She took him by the arm and led him toward the water wagon. Instead of standing in line, she marched to the front and said, "I'm Doctor Hammond. This patient needs a cup of water immediately."

The man handing out the water blinked at her ferociousness and handed it to her. She sat Scott down on the ground and sat next to him while he drank. The westward breeze was playing up and promised the coming night would be chilly. The long shadows of the trees fell on the knots of people gathered in small groups, sitting on their goods with numb expressions.

Scott downed the cup of water, and Beth returned to get another. He finally lay back on the ground, groaning, his arm over his face, and began to cry. Beth made him sit so she could put her arm around him. His reaction subsided finally and he took a breath.

"We saw the fire coming up Nob Hill. One after another, the houses took flame. All of them, all the mansions. The soldiers told us we must leave. Whit said 'no,' he wanted to salvage some of our things, but it was too late. We were on foot in just our clothes. The soldiers had taken Whit's car, promising to give it back, but he was in a fury and kept trying to fight with them. They said, 'Go on west, get out of here. Are you crazy?' Whit *was* crazy. I couldn't get him to go. We stopped in Alamo Square, but he was so angry. I told him that I wanted to find you, that some folk had informed me that the injured were taken to Golden Gate Park and I hoped you'd be here. He said if I left, I'd never see him again. He intended to get the car and drive down and get on the ferry and leave the City. So here I am. And here you are, safe and sound. I'm so happy about that, but the rest?" He began to sob again.

"Shh, shh." Beth tried to soothe him. "Whit's fine. You'll meet up with him later. Come sit with us." She walked him back to Norah and Kerry.

Kerry was sitting up, looking pale and drawn, cradling her burned arm. Her eyes lit up when she saw Beth and Scott.

"Beth, love, I'm not dead. That's good news. But this hurts like the dickens. Don't we have any painkillers?"

Norah, who sat next to her, patted the shoulder of her good arm. "Shh, Kerry. No, we don't. You must try to hang on."

"Any news?" Norah asked Beth and Scott.

"Not a thing other than here's Scott. You stay here. I'll go round and check on the others and see if there's any one in charge yet. I think the army's supposed to be helping us. I'm going over to see if I can assist, though I'm not a surgeon." She cocked her head in the direction of the operating tables.

Scott put his head on his knees and covered it with his arm. Kerry lay back down on the grass and seemed to fall asleep.

Norah was left alone to wonder about Abby and what her fate might be. Stopping her from heading back downtown seemed as likely as stopping the ocean waves from crashing on the beach. She fought off her worry. Abby was a tough woman who could take care of herself. But Norah was restless and stood up to join Beth in her work of trying to care for patients with only their knowledge, a little sympathy, and a sip of water for tools as scores of people continued to stream into the Park.

❖

They huddled in the darkness. Beth had managed to get exactly one blanket they could share amongst the four of them. The army men had dug a latrine near the park superintendent's house, and they stood in line for that, as well as for a cup of water, but no food or shelter was to be had.

Sitting on the ground, the four of them pressed close together, with Kerry in the middle wrapped in the blanket. Over to the west the sky showed an incongruously normal pink-and-blue sunset, but to the east, it glowed a hellish orange. They smelled wafts of smoke, and bits of ash floated down, but at least Beth knew the fire was far away and they'd have plenty of warning if they had to move. She put her arm around Kerry, who'd begun to shiver violently from the burn. It turned from dusk to full dark, but the ghostly glow of the City's fires lit their faces. Cold and shivering, surrounded by the restless crowd, no one could really sleep. Beth clung to Kerry and waited for the morning, dozing fitfully.

Norah tried lying on the ground, then sitting with her head on her knees, but nothing was any good. She could neither get comfortable nor fall asleep. Her bottom was chilled from the bare grass, she was cold with only her shawl over her shoulders, and she was hungry and thirsty. The night seemed destined to never end.

Scott whispered, "I've a thought. Let us sit under this tree and you may rest against me. Thereby we may keep a little warmer." Norah was too unhappy and too exhausted to decline, and so with the arms of a man she barely knew around her, her head on his shoulder, she fell into a light sleep. In her twilight state, neither asleep nor awake, she saw images of fire and of Abby's face and form. She was afraid and tried to reach out and save her, only to have her disappear and reappear, seeming to be crying out to Norah, but she made no sound.

Norah awoke with a start, not knowing where she was. She was still leaning against Scott, but he was asleep and so his arms had fallen away and she'd grown cold again. She looked around. It was mostly quiet in the strange orange-tinted night, but she still heard faint sounds from the immense crowd of people around them—coughs, low conversations, babies. The wind rustled in the trees.

Where was Abby? What had become of her?

❖

The stream of refugees escaping the inferno downtown was less than it had been earlier in the day, but still dozens straggled and struggled to get to Golden Gate Park. Ambling alongside them, Abby tried to keep her mind on her goal: the Park and Norah. She followed a knot of folks who elected to get to Alamo Square, where someone thought they could get water. It proved true and Abby was fortified to continue.

She never had been so tired. During the many long and difficult hikes she'd taken, she'd always had adequate food and water, cheerful companions, and the promise at the end of rest and a warm campfire, but this was nothing like that. She was exhausted, discouraged, and fearful as well as hungry and thirsty. Her only coherent thought was to return to Norah.

She arrived at the end of the Panhandle on Baker Street at what she estimated was two in the morning. People were camped everywhere, with no organization. She thought the best place to look for Norah would the medical area, where she'd been earlier in the day. Some small campfires lit her way, and she found the makeshift medical tables and tents, still active. Surgeons were operating by lamps held up by nurses. She cursed not having her own lantern. It was extraordinarily difficult to make a methodical search for Norah. She didn't want to disturb the operating teams, and she certainly didn't want to see what they were doing.

She spotted the bulky shadow of the big stone house across Stanyan Street. A huge tree grew on the house's lawn, and it seemed several people were underneath. She took a closer look, and there, under the tree, sat Norah, leaning against some fellow's chest and looking as though she was asleep. Abby's mood plummeted further upon seeing Norah as she was. She almost turned to go but something told her to stay, so she bent to shake Norah's shoulder gently.

Norah jumped and her eyes flew open. Her flailing arms woke up the gentlemen with her, who moaned and shook his head.

"I'm sorry. Norah, it's Abby." She backed away to give the two of them room to come to their senses after her very rude interruption of their sleep. Norah looked at her for a long moment, then stood and embraced her, holding her tightly.

"Oh, my dear. Oh, dear God, you're safe." Abby let herself be held and gradually tightened her arms around Norah. She began to feel much better, at least emotionally. Norah's whispered words of relief and her warm arms made Abby relax.

The strange man rubbed his head and looked up at Abby and said, "Oh, hello, miss. Scott Wilton. We met many months ago." She finally recognized him and was astounded he could manage so polite a greeting.

"I do recall, sir. I'm sorry to awaken you in this manner."

He waved a hand. "Don't concern yourself, miss. After all we've seen today, it scarcely matters."

Norah took Abby's arm and led her a little distance away from Scott. "You couldn't reach your home?"

"No. The army stopped me, and this time I couldn't convince them to let me through. I had to turn back, and all I could think was to return to you."

Norah absorbed this news without saying anything and hugged Abby again as though she would never let her go.

"You must be so tired," she said, finally. "I think I can get you a drink of water but nothing else."

Together they walked back to the medical area, and Norah found Kerry and Beth. They also located some water, which Abby drank gratefully.

"We might as well just sit and wait for morning," Norah said. "I could find a tree for us."

"I would dearly love to sit down," Abby responded, with great feeling.

Norah took her hand and they returned to the giant cypress tree, where Scott had fallen asleep again. Norah sat down beside him, shoving him over a few inches. "I'll do for you what he did for me. Rest yourself against me and we may both get a little sleep." Abby did as instructed. Her head fell back on Norah's shoulder, and she descended into sleep.

❖

Beth was dreaming that she was in the park on a picnic with Kerry and they'd fallen asleep. Suddenly, she woke with a start to see Marjorie Reynolds bending over her. She struggled to pull her mind into wakefulness. The sky was light. It was morning, but that was all she could comprehend. She had no idea why Marjorie was there but was very glad to see her.

Marjorie had been her nurse supervisor when she worked for the army years before. Though Marjorie hadn't approved of her leaving nursing to study to be a doctor, Beth's persistence at maintaining their friendship made sure they'd stayed in touch. Marjorie had formally joined the Army Nurse Corps as an army officer when the corps was formed in 1902, and she had become the head nurse at the Presidio General Hospital, which was renamed Letterman Hospital that year.

"Marjorie? What are you doing here?"

Marjorie, who looked unbelievably wide-awake and was dressed in her usual starched white uniform, said, "Hmph. Elizabeth, if you were still under me, I'd give you such a dressing down for being out of uniform, you'd beg for mercy. In this case, I'll have to let it slide as you are no longer my nurse and there's been a bit of an emergency." She was teasing, something she didn't often do.

Beth unwound herself from the half embrace she'd had around Kerry and sat up, brushing her hair back. She felt as though she'd gotten no sleep whatever, but seeing Marjorie buoyed her up.

"Come, Elizabeth, pull yourself together. We're here to evacuate your patients. This is no place for them."

"Oh my God, it's wonderful to see you. Kerry has suffered a severe burn. She must—"

"All in good time. Meanwhile, up and at it. We have the litters and the ambulances. Let us get this detail organized."

"Have you any water?" Beth asked.

"Oh, of course. Come along."

A short while later, Beth leaned over the litter where Kerry lay and took her hand. "You'll be taken care of, love. Go with the army people. I'll come to the hospital when I can."

Kerry was still pale, but she looked more sad than sick. "Marjorie, ugh. I'm not sure I'll survive—"

"Oh, you." Beth patted her cheek, cheered that Kerry could at least joke about her situation. The lines around her mouth spoke of the pain she was in, but Marjorie had given her a shot of morphine, which had helped.

"You'll come right away?" Kerry asked, her eyes pleading.

The stewards lifted her into the ambulance car and Beth waved. "As soon as I can. Be well!"

She turned to survey the scene in the morning light. There were more people than ever, but at least the army had taken the most severe cases to the hospital. That left the less-serious problems, but there were more of them. She was very hungry as well but had no time for that; she had to find out what fresh emergencies had occurred during the night.

❖

Norah woke up to a gray, dingy light but with her arms around Abby, who still slept. In spite of her fatigue, hunger, and thirst, she felt oddly at peace. It was quite amazing to have the independent, confident Abigail asleep in her embrace like a child. She wished to enjoy their situation a little while before she absolutely had to move.

With a touch on her shoulder, Scott smiled wanly into her eyes. "I see you no longer had need of my help."

"I'm very grateful you were there when I needed you."

"Allow me a moment to pull myself together, and then I will go off in search of sustenance for all of us." He brushed himself off and put on his coat. He'd lost his tie somewhere and his clothes were grass-stained, but he still managed to look well dressed. Grinning over his shoulder, he walked off, disappearing into the crowd.

Abigail stirred, and opening her eyes, she looked taken aback to see Norah. She disengaged herself and ran her hands over her face and tangled blond hair, attempting to smooth it. It was useless, but she still looked beautiful, grave and thoughtful. She took a look around and then returned her gaze to Norah.

"I thought I was dreaming, but it seems I'm not. There was a terrible disaster."

"There was, but we're alive and we're here, out of danger, at least for the time being."

Abby and Norah watched as a large piece of partially burned paper swirled and fell to the ground.

"Scott has gone to see if there's anything for us to eat."

"I hope he's successful because I'm famished. I must eat. Then I must go back to Russian Hill, if I can."

Norah's happiness at being with Abby faded a bit. She was still focused on her own affairs. Well, Norah herself ought to see what else she could do to help with the injured. That was her duty.

When they returned from the latrine, Scott appeared with the news that everyone had to wait in line for food, women and children first, so he couldn't help very well.

"Let's see what Beth knows," Norah said. "Maybe they can accommodate the medical staff separately"

"Excellent suggestion," Scott said, in the manner of someone who'd just been offered the chance to dine at a fine restaurant.

"I'd best be off then," Abby said briskly. "I may return if I'm unable to make it to my home."

Norah took her hand. "Please come to the Fillmore Street house if we're not here. I'm sure you can stay there. I'm going to ask them if I can, as I am homeless."

"Perhaps I will. I'll see you soon," Abby said gently, patting her hand, but then she dropped it and left, leaving Norah staring after her.

"Miss Norah?" Scott said, startling her. "Please allow me to escort you to the food line."

She saw the understanding in his eyes and nodded, letting him place her hand on his arm.

❖

"Army's taking charge, and that's just as well. I urge you to go to your homes, if you've homes to go to," Dr. Steele said to the assembled doctors and nurses. "Come back if you can after you've seen to your families."

He led Norah, Beth, and Scott over to the car. It was midmorning, and there was beginning to be a sort of organization as officious army men arrived and began setting up more latrines, tents, food services, and all other manner of necessities.

The drive across town to the Potrero District was surreal. Bedraggled refugees were still making their way to the parks. The army commander had announced to the assembled medical staff in Golden Gate Park that the Presidio would also be set up as a refugee camp.

Most of the western and northern side of the City was not on fire, but the damage from the earthquake was stark. The buildings were tumbledown. Everywhere, people were cooking on makeshift stoves on the street. The army had posted warnings not to use any stoves or light any flames at all indoors.

At the City and County Hospital, Addison and Esther greeted Norah, Beth, and Scott with relief.

"We've been up all night," Addison said. "Not a wink of sleep. I swear that most of the population of South of the Slot has been here, looking for food and water if not for medical help. We had a water source at least. My God, I need to bathe and shave." Addison had his arm around Esther, who looked surprisingly fresh in spite of their ordeal.

Norah and Beth told them about the evacuation of the Mechanics' Pavilion and Golden Gate Park.

Beth said, "Scott's lost his home. The army men blew it up."

"Oh, my word," Esther said. "You must come and stay with us then. Where's Whit?"

Scott shrugged and wouldn't meet their eyes. "I don't know," he said dispassionately. The others glanced at one another and changed the subject.

They arrived back at the commune on Fillmore Street to find it still intact, but they had no water, and, of course, they couldn't cook in the kitchen, by the mayor's decree. Until the integrity of their chimney was assured, making any sort of fire was forbidden.

"I suppose we'll have to make do with our dishabille for the time being. Let's see how we can improvise some way to cook," Addison said. The five of them pushed, pulled, and finally slid the old iron stove down the front steps on some planks. They had very little coal left, so they fanned out to look for wood. Norah was glad she had so much to do because it saved her from thinking about Abby, at least a little.

At the end of the day, their block took on the air of a holiday with all the neighbors cooking out as well. They laughed and told jokes and their earthquake stories and shared food. The army came by with the water wagons, and Norah felt she'd gotten enough to drink for the first time in over a day.

She wondered about Abby. Their brief time asleep under the tree seemed almost to have not happened. But it had, and Norah was left wondering if they would ever be together like that again. The memory of Abby's body wrapped in her embrace stirred her as she laughed and joked with her friends and neighbors. That morning, Abby had reverted to her customary distance and then, just as usual, had left Norah behind.

❖

Before Abby left the Park, she took time to receive some bread in the food line and made sure to drink a sufficient quantity of water so that she could last for a while. She stuck a piece of bread into her pocket and set off again, walking north on Baker Street to Golden Gate Avenue in hopes of bypassing the fire lines and making it home. She was very tired, but she reminded herself that she was an outdoorswoman and a short sleep on the ground was not unfamiliar, so she would carry on no matter what. She was determined to discover the fate of the plant type specimens that she'd taken such risks to save.

As she walked, she again wove in and out of streams of people headed in the opposite direction. Still they flowed out of the downtown area, dragging their possessions and their children. Smoke filled the air, making breathing difficult. In spite of the discomfort, Abby plowed on but again ran into a line of stern soldiers on Van Ness Avenue.

As she stood composing herself to attempt to persuade them, she saw a man dart out of a store, his arms laden with loot. He attempted to cross the street, but one of the soldiers took careful aim and shot him. He dropped to the ground, all of his booty scattering. Two of the soldiers walked over and one nudged the body with a boot. They nodded and called someone, who wrote something on a piece of paper, which they attached to his body. Abby knew for certain he was dead, and she was horrified and deeply frightened.

She stood still, not knowing what do next. The type specimens were irreplaceable. Abby didn't consider herself emotional, but she started to weep. She cried from fatigue, hunger, and frustration, certainly, but more from a great sense of loss. Struggling to pull herself together, she put her arms up to show she carried nothing and marched over to the nearest officer.

"Sir, may I pass? I'm trying to get to Russian Hill."

He regarded her impassively, but at least he didn't raise his rifle.

"No, miss. We're going to dynamite here again. You must turn back and leave the area immediately."

Tamping down her frustration, Abby started to obey him, but then she remembered that she had no place to go, no place to live. Yet Norah had said to come to the commune and they would take her in. Her self-sufficient soul rebelled at the thought of having to impose on others, but she thought of Norah and her tender looks and comforting arms. She suddenly wanted very much to see Norah again. With no other choice other than the refugee camp in the Park, she said to herself that it was sensible to accept Norah's offer of shelter. That settled in her mind, she turned and retraced her steps, and with each block she trod, she looked forward to rest, to food, but most of all, to seeing the welcoming smile on Norah's face.

Chapter Ten

After dinner, Norah sat with Esther on the front porch as they sipped tea, spiked with a little medicinal whiskey. The commune members kept some hard liquor in the house, though they tended to take only a little wine with their supper. The evening of the day after the earthquake seemed a proper time for everyone to drop their usual practices. Nothing was as usual and might not be for a very, very long time.

"Are you well?" Norah asked, thinking of the baby Esther carried who would be about four months along.

"I believe so, though I've never been so tired. The people just kept coming. Half the time they were just disturbed, partially out of their minds but not injured. We had to soothe them as best we could. There was nothing else to be done." Esther laughed without humor.

"My boardinghouse is gone," Norah said. "It seems I'm homeless."

"My dear, you will stay here as long as you need to. Please don't be concerned."

They were silent for a little bit, and then Norah asked, "Have you and Addison talked anymore of marriage?"

Esther looked away and said not a word. Norah couldn't tell if the question upset her.

"We've not time to think of anything except the next task before us."

"Oh, I suppose that's true. I didn't mean to trouble you, I—" A roar sounded from some blocks away to the east. Norah could tell Esther had heard it as well. They stared at one another, speechless.

"What was that?" Norah asked, but before Esther could say anything, Norah heard a familiar voice.

"Norah?"

She looked around and there stood Abby. "Abby!" She leapt up from her chair and threw her arms around her, holding on tight. Abby slumped in her arms, almost falling down. Norah caught her, and Esther was instantly there on her opposite side. Together they maneuvered her into a chair. Esther went to fetch some more tea and whiskey, and Norah sat down in the other chair to look anxiously at Abby. The hollow sound of distant explosions continued.

"Here now, what's this? Miss Eliot, you look undone." It was Addison, followed closely by Beth and Scott.

"I'm fine. I just must sit for a moment.' Abby said, clearly trying to sound sure of herself but not quite succeeding. Norah scrutinized her and rubbed her shoulder. Esther thrust the teacup into her hands and ordered her to drink, which she did.

The group circled her, waiting for her to gather her strength.

"I was walking back to Russian Hill to my home but was stopped again." She took another drink and rallied somewhat, sitting up straighter. "They're dynamiting the houses on north Van Ness Avenue. That's what you're hearing."

Addison, Norah, and Esther all looked at one another, their expressions mirroring Norah's thought. *They are destroying San Francisco in order to save it.*

Abby gradually gained some color in her cheeks from the tea and whiskey. "I, I was concerned for the material I saved from the Society yesterday morning."

Those infernal dead plants again! Norah kept quiet, though she wanted to scream out her frustration and anger.

"You'll need to stay here with us," Addison said in the manner Norah recognized as his paterfamilias mode. Beth and Esther teased him about it every now and then.

"I couldn't impose—"

Abby had started to speak, but they all protested. Addison turned to Scott. "We've got to make a round of the neighbors and see if we can beg a few mattresses, and if not, we'll go down the street and take them from the furniture store on the corner. Esther, please look up what sort of linens we have available. We're going to have to turn our home into a dormitory of sorts." He and Scott went off together.

"Norah, please stay with Abby," Esther said and gave Norah a knowing look before she too went back into the house to fulfill Addison's orders, Beth with her.

"Are you feeling better?" Norah asked, still patting Abby's shoulder.

"Yes, but I could use something to eat. I'm getting light-headed. Is there something in this tea?" She frowned suspiciously.

Norah had laugh because she looked so stern. She was far from the controlled, confident woman who had been at the party. In spite of her irritation, Norah liked seeing her somewhat at a loss. Norah patted Abby's arm and leaned close. "Whiskey. It'll do you good."

"I suppose it shall." Abby took a good-sized gulp. "I'll take the medicine as prescribed, Doctor."

They grinned at one another and their eye contact held. Norah tried to discern what was in Abby's mind, but then Esther reappeared.

"The men have returned with some bedding. I'll have to put Scott on the couch. You two will sleep in the spare room. Just for the night, we're taking in a couple of women from two streets over who had their ceiling fall in, poor dears. They'll sleep in the front parlor."

Esther rubbed her hands together, looking from Norah to Abby and then back. Her tone told Norah that there'd be no arguments. They were all exhausted, in any case, and they needed rest, not more discussion. They sat together on the steps and the porch of the house consuming their meager dinner and listening to the explosions. No one said much more before they retired to bed.

❖

"Looks to be comfortable. Anything other than the grass looks inviting to me," Abby said as they stood in the bedroom surveying the simple four-poster bed.

Norah swallowed. In the twilight it was hard to tell Abby's expression. The army decree forbade candles as well as indoor cooking. A red glow in the sky shone through the window and illuminated the room just enough for them to see outlines. All was in shadow, including their faces. A single jangling chord of longing rang in Norah's mind as she thought about how near the two of them would be in sleep. At that instant, she thought of May and all that had transpired between them. Yet she attempted to push it aside since this was a different situation. She was also still somewhat angry at Abby for her stubborn bravado.

They took off their clothes in silence, peeling down to their undergarments. Norah's next worry was simply the lack of being able to bathe for several days, but she realized they were both in that state, and she was unlikely to be offensive to Abby. May had been a stickler in matters of cleanliness, and Norah had come to appreciate that trait in a profound way. If any two humans were to be so intimate with their bodies, it was a matter of courtesy to pay attention to oneself. Again she reminded herself, this was not the same thing.

They settled into the bed, which was, as Norah remembered, surprisingly firm and comfortable. And indeed the contrast between the bare ground and a good mattress with linens and a quilt was welcome.

"Good night, sleep well," Norah whispered.

Abby touched her cheek in the dark, gently turning her face toward her own.

"Good night to you, dear Norah. I'm so happy we're safe and we're lucky enough to have a bed to sleep in."

That would have been a perfect moment for a tender kiss, Norah thought as she fell asleep, fatigue and emotional trauma taking their toll at last.

❖

It wasn't a punishment, Kerry reminded herself. She was lying on a thin mattress on an army cot in a ward crowded with two dozen other women in the Presidio hospital because she was hurt and Beth couldn't take care of her. Marjorie had been her usual no-nonsense self but in the end was kind to her, and she couldn't complain about that. In the twilight world of the morphine, her mind jumped around from image to image. She relived the fire at the Palace and being dragged down the street by Teddy.

She missed Beth so deeply. In an alien bed, far from Beth and their home, she experienced a dislocation very like the one she had felt when she was fifteen, after her father had been murdered and she'd gone in search of Addison, who took her in. Then the morphine would wear off and the pain would return. It was like an animal whose teeth tore at her flesh. Though she'd been burned, she would shiver with cold, and no number of blankets helped. She thrashed and cried out, causing the night nurse to hurry over to soothe her. But she would administer no more painkiller until the doctor came in the early morning.

They kept trying to induce her to eat, but it was difficult to keep food down, even the mildest of broths. Kerry almost would have preferred the pain to the vomiting. She could only lie on one side, because of her burned arm and the uncomfortable cot.

She wasn't completely sure what day it was, but she could at least tell it was day because of the light shining through the window. Yet as usual, it was gray and foggy.

Suddenly, Marjorie was standing next her bed. "Kerry. How are you feeling?" Marjorie had just a touch of compassion in her voice.

"How do y'think? I'm either in pain or puking from the drug, and I can't sleep. I want to see Beth."

"Well, you'll have to bear up. The surgeon will be here presently and explain. But I'm certain we'll keep you in here for a while because the biggest worry is infection. Oh, here he is now."

Marjorie kept the doctor out of earshot while they whispered together, which further annoyed Kerry. Marjorie was still Marjorie.

"Young...lady," the army doctor said, hesitantly. "We intend to make you well, but it'll be a bit of time until you're sufficiently healed to return home."

He examined her, which made her grateful the only thing wrong was her burned arm. She couldn't imagine letting a strange doctor see her body and was scarcely able to let Marjorie perform the necessary nursing chores. Kerry longed for Beth even more.

When the doctor left, Marjorie returned and automatically straightened her bed covers and poured her a glass of water. "Major Williams says you're to take as much water as possible and broth every four hours. I'll have to clean your burn and that will—"

Kerry grabbed Marjorie's arm as she pushed herself upright. "I want to see Beth. Please send word."

Marjorie froze and gave her a little glare. "I'll see, Kerry, but Beth is surely taken up with work. You realize you're not the only person in San Francisco who's been injured."

"You understand. I need Beth." Kerry held onto her arm, fixing her with an intense stare as she fought her nausea.

"I do. I know." Marjorie gently patted her good arm before reverting to sternness. "I must get on with my other patients."

Kerry let her go and lay back, trying to stay calm and not vomit again.

❖

The next day, the members of the commune gathered again on street in front of the commune to prepare something resembling breakfast. Addison and Scott had gone in search of wood, and Esther was stirring a pot of porridge. They also had bread and a little over-boiled coffee. The army came around with allotments of water for everyone, enough to cook with and to drink.

"We're going back to City hospital," Esther said, dishing up hot cereal. "What do you say, Norah? Are you able?"

"Yes. I'd like to, very much." Norah glanced at Abby, who was expressionless. Norah wanted to ask her what she was planning to do, but she wished Abby to tell her so she didn't have to ask.

"I'm going to try once again to get home. I'll try a different route," Abby said.

Norah wanted to shout at her not to go, that it was too dangerous.

The soldiers had brought them news as well as water. The fire was still advancing, and General Funston was calling for more dynamite. Mayor Schmitz said civilians were to stay at their homes and follow orders. Period.

Norah pulled Abby aside, out of earshot of the others. "You cannot get to Russian Hill! You heard the army man, didn't you?" she asked, sharply.

Abby didn't say anything. She clearly wasn't used to depending upon others or to listening to them either.

Norah's anger boiled over. "You are impossible! Why in the world are you so intent on risking your life? Why can't you just wait until we get word that it's safe?"

Abby blinked at her, and to Norah's great dismay, she began to cry. "I know you don't understand, Norah. I'm not sure I can make you understand, though I'm sorry to distress you. I should go."

She made as if to turn away and Norah grabbed her arm. "Please don't." She watched Abby's face.

"All right. I won't try again. It seems futile anyhow. I'll head over to Golden Gate Park."

"Oh no, you mustn't. You need not do that. You can stay here," Norah said, aware that her voice was squeaky and pleading.

"I must do something today. I can't just rest here. I'll go crazy."

Norah wracked her brain for something to say. "You and Scott should go look for something for us to eat. There are grocers up and down the street, and they may be open since we've not experienced much damage in the Western Addition."

"I suppose." Abby looked uncertain.

Norah wanted to shake her, but she was grateful that at least Abby had given up on the idea of going back downtown.

Abby had no use for self-pity. Early on, the nuns who had taught and cared for her had instilled the need for not succumbing to such a self-centered and useless emotion. Her life had been a series of puzzles to be solved, and most things fell into place. But not this time. She chafed at not being able to do what she wanted to. It was a strange and unwelcome feeling, and she had to fight down her anger. She resented Norah, though she realized Norah wasn't at fault.

After Addison, Esther, Beth, and Norah left, she went back into the house, restless and at a loss. She combed her hair and brushed her clothes, but it was useless. They smelled of smoke and sweat, as did her body. She was disgusted with herself, but what could she do? There was barely enough water to drink, let alone wash. She thought of Norah's emotions. Her anger and fear had come through very clearly. Abby wanted to calm her, and her agreement to stay at the house had more to do with that than with any true concession on her part. She didn't want to hurt Norah, and though she didn't understand from where Norah's response came, she recognized its intensity. She wandered back down to the front parlor. She supposed it would be better if she and Scott went off on their mission sooner rather later.

Scott sat on the front porch steps, clad in the same dirty clothes he'd worn the previous day. He had a two-day growth of beard and held a bottle in one hand, a cigarette in the other.

"Miss Abigail, lovely to see you. Come join me. We've been left behind so the brave medical people can go save the City."

It was a bit alarming to see Scott drinking so early in the morning. Usually Abby didn't fear drunkenness. In fact, under some circumstances, it could be amusing. She wasn't sure this was one of those times, but she had nothing else to do and no one else to talk to.

"Scott, whatever are you doing?"

"Ah, I'm celebrating." He hiccupped. "I've got nothing left but the clothes I wear and this fine bottle of whiskey. Couldn't drink Addison's supply up, but I found a fellow that I paid the last few dollars I had for this and a couple of cigarettes. Pull up a step." He laughed at his own joke.

Abby sat down and companionably took a tiny sip from the proffered bottle.

"You're a good woman, Miss Abigail. I can tell." He pointed at his head, indicating his faith in his own powers of observation. The smoke from the cigarette made him squint. "I'm thinking you'll fit right in here at the old commune." He took another drink.

"What do you mean?" Abby asked, curious.

"You're a like-minded person, shall we say? They're all freethinkers here, if you know what I mean." He raised his eyebrow and smirked. "They even like *me*. They'd a liked Whit too, if he hadna been such a snob."

Abby thought about the scene at the party those months ago. "Where *is* Whit?" she asked, to keep him talking. At the mention of Whit's name, Scott had fallen into thought, and his mood had abruptly changed from frivolity to sadness.

"Don't know. Maybe he managed to catch a ferry to Berkeley. Who knows?"

"Why didn't you go with him?"

He thought very deeply for a moment. "He doesn't care for me, least not as much as he said he did. He only cares about money."

"What do you mean, 'They even like me.' Who's they?"

He put his head back and seemed to consider her question deeply for a moment.

"You know. Esther and Addison. Most folks don't hold with my type," he said. "But they're fine with Kerry and Beth. They don't care a whit. Ha, ha. 'Whit.'" He started laughing uproariously, then coughed. Abby thought he wasn't making a lot of sense, but something about what he said made her want to hear more. Norah had said something about Kerry and Beth that she didn't understand, and now Scott was hinting at the same thing. Norah had said they were sweethearts, lovers, and Abby didn't know how that was possible for two women. In his drunken state, Scott just might be a little more enlightening.

She prodded him. "What about Kerry and Beth?"

"Oh, you know, they're sweet on each other. They're like a married couple. Me and Whit too. Well, almost, but not quite." He looked sad again. "I thought he loved me, I really did, but he left without me, without a backward look. Men are faithless. Except Addison, he's not. He loves Esther. He don't care that they're not married. He treats her better than many men treat their wives. That's true."

He was rambling, but Abby was still intrigued. *Like a married couple.* What could that mean? She patted Scott on the shoulder and stood up. "Thank you for the drink. But oughtn't we go to the store and find some food?"

He raised his whiskey bottle in a salute, then took another swig. "Here's to you, Miss Abby. You don't be mean to Miss Norah, now. I can tell she likes you."

She stopped abruptly. What was he talking about? He was flitting all over the place, conversation-wise, as drunks would.

"How do you know that Miss Norah likes me?"

He nodded, looking wise again. "She does. I saw that right off at her party. She was starin' at you like you was the hen and she was the fox."

His Southern-sounding analogy mystified her.

"What does that mean?" Abby asked him, keeping her voice light. "Does she want to kill and eat me?"

Scott tilted his head back and gazed at her from under his eyelids. "Not in the least. But I'm telling tales out of school. Why don't you talk to her?"

Abby planned to do just that. She pulled Scott up from the step, made him leave his whiskey behind, and dragged him down the street. At the corner of Buchanan and Market Streets, some twenty minutes away from the commune, they joined a breadline. At the side of the bread truck stood two butchers with chicken carcasses piled on a table, and behind them, men slaughtered more chickens. They waited for an hour, and Scott sobered up, rubbing his aching head and Abby offering him encouragement to keep him talking, but he wouldn't say anything else about Norah.

They at last reached the head of the line, and the soldier said, "Head of household—how many?"

Scott drew himself up and said, "Sir, my wife, her aged mother and father, and her three homeless sisters are in dire need of sustenance." He put Abby's hand on his arm and gave her the smile of a doting husband.

She almost burst out laughing but tried to keep her face arranged in a semblance of polite but definite pleading.

The officer standing by barked, "Three loaves and three chickens."

So they walked back home lugging their precious food allotment. Once there, they tidied up the house and dug another latrine hole in the backyard and threw in quicklime to keep the stench down. Then they wiped down the dishes with damp rags and even swept the front porch.

"Let's fire up the stove so we can have these creatures cooked by the time the rest of them get back," Scott said, seemingly recovered from his previous state. "Do you know how to pluck chickens?" He held up one and looked at it dubiously.

Abby laughed. "I do. You go find some wood and get that stove nice and hot."

He obeyed, and Abby prepared the chickens, thanking those stern nuns and their fondness for making children work for her chicken-plucking skills. They found an iron skillet in the kitchen and some oil and soon had the pieces coated with a crude mix of flour and oil and frying away.

Scott jumped as a spat of oil hit him on the hand. "Curse this. I'm not a cook. That's Kerry's department."

"What is it about Kerry and Beth? Norah said something about them to me. I want to know straight out. What am I misunderstanding?"

He looked at her in disbelief. "You don't know there's some women who love other women and some men who love men?"

"No. I've never heard of that."

"Never?"

"Never."

Scott looked at her, eyes narrowed, didn't say anything. Abby was willing to wait him out, but before either could say anymore, Addison, Esther, Beth, and Norah pulled up in the auto.

Abby watched them as they strolled toward the house. They all waved, but it was Norah her eye was drawn to, and as they drew closer, Norah's smile broadened, and before Abby could think about what she was doing, she walked forward to meet her with a warm hug. Abby thought about Scott's words. *Is Norah in love with me?*

"What have we here? By God, I never thought chicken could smell so good," Addison said. They gathered around the stove to admire the feast being cooked.

In a short time, the group was seated at the dinner table, and during the general merriment, Abby found herself looking more and more at Norah, who appeared to sense she was being watched and would turn to meet her gaze, her blue eyes smiling.

❖

"I had a very illuminating discussion with Scott today," Abby said as they were preparing to go to sleep. The forced prohibition against candles or any type of flame made early retirement a necessity.

Surprised, Norah started and, to stall for time, said, "Scott's quite the talker, I understand, but first tell me of your adventures today."

"There isn't much to tell. We went to get the lovely food we had for supper and worked around the house."

"It was wonderful to come home to supper cooked. We had another very busy day."

They were quiet as Norah brushed her hair, waiting for what Abby would say next, both dreading and anticipating it.

"Scott said more about Beth and Kerry. Essentially he said the same thing you did the night of the earthquake."

Norah's heart nearly leapt out of her chest. Where would this conversation go?

Abby sat in the armchair next to the bed and removed her shoes. She slowly unrolled each stocking, causing Norah's focus to be drawn to her legs. They were long and evidently strong and well muscled. *All that walking.* Her breathing quickened. Abby hung both stockings neatly over the back of the chair and stood to her full height and stretched. Was she doing all of this on purpose? Surely not.

They got into bed, and Abby turned to her with her head propped up on her bent arm. "He told me you were staring at me when we first met. He was drinking earlier today, but I think he was in his right mind. Were you? Staring at me, I mean."

Norah was aware she was shaking slightly from nerves. "If I was, I didn't mean to," she said as calmly as she could.

"Well, it doesn't bother me, if you're worried."

"It doesn't?" Norah had no idea what this meant, but she supposed it was good news.

"No. Scott said you like me. I know that you do." Abby spoke as she always did, her tone even and relaxed. Unemotional. She was so damned hard to read, that was certain.

Norah said nothing.

"I can't impose on you all much longer. I think I might try to find some of my other friends and see about getting a temporary place to live until this all blows over."

It was very typical of Abby to take such a cavalier attitude toward what they were all going through. Norah's heart sank. Abby would leave, and she wouldn't see her for a very long time.

"You don't have to go. You can stay here." Norah couldn't divine Abby's expression in the dim light.

"I'll see. Guess I better ask Addison and Esther since it's their house."

"They don't mind. I swear," Norah said a little desperately.

"Still, better I ask. It's polite. Well, good night." Abby turned over on her side, leaving Norah to stare out the window at the still-reddish sky and wonder what to do next. She lacked the courage to be honest with Abby. The distant roars of dynamite echoed through the night.

CHAPTER ELEVEN

At the bread-and-water line in the morning, they were told the fires were out. A huge cheer went up from the neighbors waiting with them. Hugs and handshakes were exchanged. But the joy was short lived.

As they drove to the hospital, Norah and the others looked around and then at one another in silence. The City seemed to have shriveled. The missing buildings and missing pieces of buildings were heartbreaking. Everywhere lay piles of abandoned possessions. Instead of pedestrians walking about with purpose and streets humming with energy, they saw nothing but death, destruction, and, now that the dynamiting had ceased, a dead quiet. It was raining steadily. Knots of soldiers still stood about or walked around, determinedly ignoring the rain. Here and there a bedraggled civilian would appear, moving aimlessly.

His voice a combination of sadness and resolve, Addison said, "We're alive. We've tasks to accomplish, people to care for. It is, though, nothing I ever in my life thought to see."

Beth said, "Even in Manila, in the war, it wasn't like this."

From the front seat, Esther turned and said to Norah, "I'm truly sorry to have brought you all the way out here, far from your home, only to subject you to this."

Norah was touched, but she didn't want Esther to blame herself. "Oh, you mustn't be sorry, Esther. The earthquake is hardly your fault. Though I wish someone had warned me it might happen."

They laughed, cheered a little by Norah's small joke.

"I fear our worries are just beginning," Addison said. He stopped the car and pointed.

Three large rats scurried across Mission Street.

"The next thing is disease. Some of those rats may be carrying plague." Norah, Beth, and Esther followed the path of the rats as they disappeared, and Norah shivered.

The hospital's director called a meeting first thing. At his side stood an army officer.

"Some people will come here for treatment, but most will not," the director said. "Colonel Shaw is here to talk about the refugee camps and what the next phase of our work will be. Colonel?"

Norah listened to the colonel's speech, but part of her mind kept drifting back to Abby. She wasn't sure that she should even expect Abby to be at the house when they returned later that day. She was such a headstrong woman that she'd likely be off like a shot as soon as she could.

The result of the meeting with the colonel was that the next day, Beth, Esther, and Norah would go back to Golden Gate Park to help with the refugee camp. Addison would stay at the hospital.

As they went around the hospital, collecting what they would need, Norah talked distractedly to Esther.

"Scott has no ability to keep his mouth shut. He doesn't think anything of telling her about me. I never gave him leave to say a word."

"Well, Scott means well, but he's never been one to hold his tongue. Maybe it's a good thing. Abby is a lovely woman, but I believe she would profit by having you challenge her self-control a little. What did you say to her?"

"Nothing! I mean, what am I to say? I don't know how I feel, not really. I'm drawn to her, that's true. I believe I'm in love with her, but she'd think I was just becoming over-emotional because of the earthquake and all the disruption. She's infuriating, but I can't help but admire her. Yet she's so opaque too. She doesn't reveal any of her feelings."

"Well, you have an opportunity here. Fate has thrown you together. And Scott? Well, I'm going to try to recruit him to work at the refugee camp. He can't stay at home drinking all day."

Norah, who wasn't much interested in Scott's problems, continued to focus on her own concerns. "She may leave, though, if she can find another place to stay. Won't you urge her to stay with us?"

"I'll tell her she's welcome, of course." Esther fixed Norah with a meaningful look. "You ought to be the one to urge her to stay. That is, if you want her to." Esther smiled then with a slightly evil gleam in her dark eyes.

"I do," Norah whispered. "I do want her to stay."

❖

It was a singular miracle that the San Francisco Main Post Office on Mission Street was still standing and still doing business. Abby wrote a few notes to some of the Society members and other people, asking for shelter, and gave Addison and Esther's address. She felt better after doing this. The days of frustration and inactivity wore on her. In spite of the fear and trauma of the earthquake, she still longed for useful occupation because it wasn't her nature to be idle. She would return to Fillmore Street and help Scott scavenge for food and fuel for their stove. She wondered why he didn't volunteer to go the hospital, or even the Park, where his skills would certainly be welcome. Well, it wasn't her business. But the two of them could offer as much assistance as possible to their hosts.

She would delay any decision about leaving the commune until and if she received a response from those to whom she'd written. She might as well also write Sellars and inform him of where she could be found.

It was an amazing experience walking through the City to the post office. The earthquake's damage was so arbitrary and fitful. A building would stand seemingly unharmed next to one that had been destroyed. Sometimes disoriented people wandered around, though she heard from the soldiers she talked to that many people had gone to the ferries to escape. The army was joined by national guardsmen and, of course, City policemen. Armed, uniformed men were everywhere. Posters on light poles proclaimed that looters would be shot on sight, and Abby knew too well that they meant that.

As she walked back to Fillmore Street from the post office, inevitably her mind turned to Norah. She was as much of an enigma as ever. Norah seemed at times to be afraid of her, though she couldn't think why. With the others she was companionable, talkative. Could it be as Scott said? She didn't know what to make of his phrase: "She likes you." It seemed fraught with deeper meaning than the obvious. When he was sober, she wanted to ask him what he'd meant, but something stopped her. Maybe she didn't want to know for sure. She'd never been so confused.

Even though she'd told Norah she might leave the Fillmore Street commune, she wasn't sure she wanted to. It just seemed like the appropriate thing for her to do. But then she thought about Norah's request that she stay.

Beth took her stethoscope from around her neck, laid it on her desk, and rubbed her eyes. She didn't think she'd ever be not tired again. The sleepless night in Golden Gate Park followed by a restless night at home without Kerry, but thinking about her, followed by another strenuous day with the injured from the earthquake, had taken its toll. She wondered when she could in practical terms get away to see Kerry and then how she could find transportation up to the Presidio. Addison's auto had again been commandeered to transport the injured, so she couldn't ask him to drive her.

People were still crowded everywhere: screaming babies, folks bleeding from wounds, suffering every ill known to medicine. Beth would look in the waiting room and want to turn around and go hide in a closet.

The worst were the men and women who had nothing whatsoever wrong with them physically but who had apparently taken leave of their senses. The stress of the earthquake, she supposed, but there was nothing they could do.

Addison came to stand next to her. He was always her mainstay when they were at work, the one who could buck her up.

He put a hand on her shoulder. "Beth, are you all right?"

She turned to look him in the eye. "I want to see Kerry," she said simply, "but I don't know how."

"I think we're transferring another burn case to Letterman. You can go along, though you'll have to walk home."

She hugged him. "That's all I need. Thank you."

❖

The ward was dim. On its many windows, the shades were drawn and each bed curtained for privacy. The army's Letterman hospital was just a few years old, and the distinctive hospital smell of sickness, carbolic, and human bodies was present but not yet absorbed by the walls and floors.

Beth asked the duty nurse to find Marjorie for her. She made the nurse believe she was on a medical call rather than a personal one. It was both, really.

Marjorie appeared, looking as composed as ever. "Elizabeth. How good to see you." They embraced.

"I want to know. Before I see her. Tell me."

Marjorie fingered her sleeve before responding. "Well, I predict she'll live."

"That is not what I mean, Marjorie. Tell me the truth. I was there when they brought her to the first-aid station."

"It's not a cut-and-dried thing, Elizabeth. You know how these cases go. It could take a long time for her to come back mentally, even if she heals physically more quickly. There will be a scar, a large one." Marjorie looked at her meaningfully

"I don't care about that. I want—"

"You many not care, but she most certainly will. And I understand the Palace Hotel burned to the ground. It's gone."

"Yes, it is."

"Then Kerry is without the livelihood she's followed since she was fifteen, if I recall. That's bound to exercise a monstrous effect on her beyond the consequences of her injury."

"Yes. I know that. Please take me to her." Beth stood up and put her hands on her hips.

Marjorie took her to a bed at the far end of the huge ward. "Kerry. Beth's here."

She gave Beth an encouraging smile and left.

Kerry was lying on her side, her left arm wrapped in a large bandage. They had to try to prevent infection.

"Kerry dearest?" Beth said, and touched her shoulder.

She turned over. Her brown eyes, usually gleaming with humor and mischief, were dull and cloudy. She surely would still be receiving morphine, as her burn was very large and of the second-degree type but severe, as Marjorie told her. Without morphine, the pain would be excruciating.

Kerry said, softly, "Beth."

Beth kissed her forehead. "It's me. How are you?"

"I thought you'd never come."

"It's difficult. I was able to get a ride today. The City and County is a madhouse. Almost literally." She laughed without humor.

"I miss you."

"I miss you too. But at least I don't have to worry about you. Marjorie will take good care of you."

Kerry made a sound of frustration. "She's the same. Butter wouldn't melt in her mouth."

"Now, Kerry, you know she's more caring than she seems."

"You abandoned me," Kerry said, matter-of-factly.

Beth was shocked. "No, love, I didn't. We had to have you brought here. You couldn't stay in the Park."

"You abandoned me. You don't love me anymore."

"That's not true. You know it's not." Beth was desperate to reassure her, but it wasn't working.

"No, it's true. I've been maimed. I'm not good for anything. You gave me over to Marjorie because you don't care about me."

"Kerry. My love, you don't know what you're saying."

"I'm crazy then?"

"No, that's not what I meant." Beth's composure broke. Three days of constant work, fear, and dismay overwhelmed her. She bent her head and cried into the sheet that covered Kerry. She felt a hand on her back and turned to look. It was Marjorie, who, without a word, took her arm and drew her away.

In her small office down the hall, Marjorie sat her down and brought her a glass of water.

Beth sipped the water, inhaled and exhaled, attempting to pull herself together.

"I wanted to tell you, but it's better you see for yourself. She won't even speak to me. You ought to consider yourself blessed she'll actually communicate with you."

"Is she going to get better?"

"I told you. Physically, yes. Most certainly. Emotionally, I don't know." Marjorie's face was bleak.

Beth took a deep breath. Kerry would recover and return to her old self. There was no other possible outcome.

"I've got no time to think of that," Esther said as she and Norah attempted to organize the medical station in Golden Gate Park. It was nearly impossible, as the refugees constantly bombarded them with demands. The army surgeons from the Presidio had arrived earlier in the day, and after reporting to the officer in charge, Esther and Norah went to work.

Norah's question to her was how things stood with Addison and marriage. She was just making conversation to avoid thinking about Abby and whether she'd still be at home when they returned at the end of the day. In short order, she was so busy she had no time to think of anything at all, as she and Esther began the endless task of diagnosing and treating the thousands of refugees that crowded into the hospital tents.

When they took a moment to have a bite to eat, Esther said, "The situation will settle down in a few days, but then our real work will begin. It will take a while for disease to develop, but when it does, we'll need to be ready."

Norah nodded. If nothing else, all this activity would keep her busy and so she couldn't dwell too much on Abby and the possible declaration of her feelings. Since the earthquake, they'd only deepened, and they were together much more than they'd been previously. Her immediate goal, however, was to keep Abby from leaving the commune.

At last they were able to return to Fillmore Street, and once again, Scott and Abby were there and cooking supper. This time they'd procured a few pounds of pork.

Norah walked up next to Abby as she stood over their outdoor stove frying pork chops. She was methodical and attentive but spared a smile for Norah.

"How are you able to cook like this?" she asked, gesturing to encompass the primitive conditions.

"I've been camping many times. Up in the mountains, we have to make do if we want decent food to eat."

"I see, so you're experienced." Norah grinned.

Abby flipped a couple of pork chops over and turned to face her. "Somewhat. I also like to cook."

"Have you made up your mind whether you'll stay with us?"

Abby didn't say anything for a moment. "As you've pointed out, if I want to stay in the City, I've not got much choice of accommodations. I don't expect that Golden Gate Park is all that much improved since the day before yesterday."

"Things are a little better, but there's no reason for you to go when you can be here. I want you to stay." Norah held her gaze steadily.

Abby didn't answer at first. She flipped the chops onto a plate, then threw a few more into the skillet.

"My only other choice is leaving the City, but I wouldn't just appear uninvited at someone's home so I won't leave for the moment. I've written a few people, but it will take some time to get responses."

Norah was deeply relieved. She squeezed Abby's arm and went to speak with Beth, newly returned from the Presidio. She scrutinized Beth, trying to discern her feelings. "What news of Kerry?" she asked.

"She's resting. They'll make sure she doesn't get an infection."

"When will she come home?"

"I don't quite know. She must stay at the army hospital for a while."

Her voice was dispassionate, but Norah sensed a great deal of suppressed emotion. She didn't know Beth well and didn't like to pry. Beth would confide in Esther if she confided in anyone. In the meantime, night was coming.

❖

Alone with Abby, Norah made small talk to distract herself from her jumbled feelings. She covertly watched Abby as they once again prepared to go to sleep. She desperately wished for a bath, or at least a clean nightgown, but she wasn't going to receive either. It didn't appear to make any difference to Abby.

"I'd kill for a bath right now," Norah said.

Abby smiled but said nothing.

"Doesn't it bother you?"

"I've gone days without baths before in the wilderness. No, it doesn't bother me."

"I suppose we're all in the same boat."

"Yes, we are."

Abby settled into bed next to her. Norah could sense the warmth of her body. She only had to reach across the few inches between them.

"Well, good night," Abby said and turned over.

Norah stared at the ceiling in the dark. Now that they were going to be sleeping together for the time being, what ought she to do next, if anything? She had no idea how to seduce anyone and feared rejection. May had taken charge of the nature and speed of their relations, and Norah had only had to go along with her.

A few weeks after their first kiss, May had invited her to dine, but this time she had asked Norah to come to her apartment and said she would bring some supper in instead of going to a restaurant. When she heard this, Norah grew anxious but intrigued. May welcomed her and bade her sit down on the divan and gave her a glass of champagne. It went straight to her head, and she had laughed and giggled as May made fun of their various common acquaintances and refilled her glass.

"I must eat soon or I'll become too tipsy," Norah said, thinking the combination of tipsiness and anticipation much headier than anything she'd ever felt. May's lips were formed in a secret smile, which she would turn on Norah every so often, and whenever she did, Norah shivered. But May was in no hurry. They drank their champagne and chatted.

May presented each course of their cold supper with a flourish. There were oysters and cold beef, then a gazpacho soup. Finally came strawberries and cream, which May fed Norah in between kisses. May's flat was warm, and Norah regretted wearing a corset, which she didn't often do because of the demands of caring for patients. She leaned back, breathless, and confessed to May that it was making her uncomfortable. May's eyes glittered and she grinned even more.

"Well then, my little one, we must make sure you don't faint. Stand up." Norah obeyed, and slowly and carefully, May unbuttoned her blouse and then her skirt. She stood blushing and trembling as May ever so slowly loosed the stays of her corset and took it off, leaving her clad only in vest and underdrawers.

May stepped back and observed her as though she was an artist looking at a just-completed painting. She tilted her head and then gently touched Norah's cheek. "Better now?"

"Much." Norah was so nervous she could scarcely speak, but whatever was to come she wanted more than anything ever before. May's gaze never wavered as she slowly took off her own dress—a frilly green taffeta that she carelessly let drop to the floor.

She said, "Now we're equal" and gestured to indicate that they were in an identical state of undress.

She moved forward and put her arms around Norah. She was so warm and so soft, Norah nearly fainted again. She kissed Norah's neck from her jawbone to her collarbone and back up the other side to her lips. Her kisses were soft and gentle at first but then became demanding, and Norah answered those demands. May took her hand and led her to the bedroom, where a fire was burning in the grate, making the room quite warm. The fire and their kisses made Norah so hot she wanted to take off her underwear. May seemed to read her mind and did that for her, with many pauses for kisses and soft touches.

Somehow they both ended up on the bed, naked, and as May gently parted her legs, Norah felt first her fingers and then her tongue. She closed her eyes and let the blackness swallow her.

May's promise of much more than kisses turned into a night of stunning revelation and deep pleasure. Norah's fear evaporated, replaced by an overwhelming hunger to repeat the experience and ultimately to learn how to make love to May in exactly the same fashion, wringing identical cries and pleas for mercy as May had elicited from her.

The memory made Norah gasp and look guiltily over at Abby, who had fallen asleep. What would it be like for the two of them to come together as she and May had? How would Abby respond to her caresses? As terrifying as it was to contemplate rejection, Norah had to find out.

Though Abby was maddening, she was fascinating and becoming more so every moment. Fate had thrown them together, and Norah would have to be the one to step forward. It was clear Abby had no more idea of romance or love than a five-year-old. Norah would have to somehow find the courage.

❖

One of the most heartrending aspects of their new station as refugee doctors was the endless parade of people trying to locate their families. The Red Cross had come on site to undertake this stupefying task. Norah and Esther would often treat a patient and in the course of treatment hear a tale of woe.

The man who sat before them about a week after the earthquake was a typical example. He had a badly infected leg and had been wandering here and there in the City, apparently looking for his family, before landing in their medical unit.

"We's never been apart, me and Maggie and our boys. I ain't seen 'em since we was walkin' in the crowds. We got separated. Ouch!"

Esther was attempting to drain his suppurating wound, disinfect it, and dress it before he developed blood poisoning, and Norah has helping her.

When they were done, the man grabbed Esther's arm. "You seen 'em? My Maggie's bout your height but blond and thin. The boys are five and seven year old."

"Mr.—"

"Tate, Ernie Tate. I gotta find them."

"Mr. Tate. You must rest. I'll send the Red Cross over to talk to you," Esther said, giving Norah a glance. At least they could get some help for this man. Many of their patients were so disoriented and traumatized, they had to call army men to help subdue them. One man had nearly strangled Norah.

Esther and Norah went on to the next patient. Gunshot wound. The trigger-happy national guardsmen again. They were worse than General Funston's army troops.

Their patients were packed in like sardines in the crowded tents, with no privacy. As they cleaned and dressed the gunshot, they could clearly hear the interaction between the Red Cross woman and the desperate Mr. Tate.

She took down his name and his former address. Then she asked, "Your wife's date of birth?"

"Uh, she's not my wife," Mr. Tate said.

There was a pause. Then the Red Cross volunteer said, "Well, I can't help you."

"But we's like married. We got the two kids. Please. I need to find them."

Norah and Esther glanced at each other. "Say, there," Esther said. "I'm the doctor treating this man."

That usually got people's attention, and it worked this time as well. The Red Cross woman was an ample lady in her forties, with her hair in a bun and officiousness underlying her surface kindness.

"Yes?"

"Well? Isn't it your job to reunite families?" Esther asked sharply.

The Red Cross lady looked at her for a moment, then said, "Yes, it is, but this man isn't legally married. We have scarce resources. We must see to real families first."

Norah watched Esther closely. She flushed, which was a danger sign.

"Well, I suggest that his family is as loved as any and is as 'real' as those who've taken the step of legal matrimony."

The woman sniffed. "The Red Cross policy is that we assist families first."

Mr. Tate watched this back-and-forth with some interest, as if it were the mythical clash of the Titans.

"I believe your policy is rather restrictive, and it would be in the best interest of those we are trying to help, who've gone through this horrible tragedy, if you treated them with equal attention."

"Doctor," and the woman's emphasis to Norah's ears sounded more satirical than respectful, "I suggest you stick to medical matters and leave the social problems to others."

"You supercilious, know-it-all witch!"

Norah grabbed her arm. "No, Esther, we have more patients to see to."

The Red Cross woman stared at them as they moved on. Mr. Tate had stopped smiling.

"I cannot believe what I heard," Esther said through her teeth. "They've a lot of nerve mistreating people at a time like this. Refusing to help someone because he's not married to the mother of his children."

Norah stared back at her, saying nothing.

Finally, Esther said, "Oh. I see. Well, they need to change their policies is what they need to do."

"Esther, my dear. That's wishful thinking, and you know it."

Esther harrumphed and looked away, but she said no more.

When the day was over, Norah and Esther dragged themselves back to Fillmore Street, looking forward to some food and quiet evening, but that was not what they found.

Scott lay passed out on the couch, Beth and Addison were not at home, and Abby wasn't either. They looked at each other, then down at Scott, who snored away, emitting strong alcohol fumes.

"Well," Esther said, hands on her hips. "This is a fine how-do-you-do. Scott is less than useless, and Abby's nowhere to be found.

We'll have to go in search of something to eat. Doesn't the army distribute food somewhere on Fillmore Street?'

"I suppose. With Scott and Abby taking care of those tasks, I never thought to learn the particulars." She was secretly worried Abby might have again left on her mission to get to her house. If the lingering fires and unstable buildings weren't dangerous enough, Norah feared one of the soldiers would shoot Abby. They heard awful tales and saw the results in their hospital tents, and those were the lucky ones who were still alive.

"Where is Beth? Did she go back to the Presidio again?" Esther asked

"I believe so, but I'm not sure. She's not said much since the earthquake. She was terrified that night, with Kerry so badly hurt."

Esther frowned. "This is quite unlike her. Addison may know something, but who knows when we'll see him? I suppose we ought to commence looking for some food. Is there any water about?"

"I don't know." They checked the kitchen and there wasn't.

Norah was tired, hungry, and thirsty, but they could do nothing but set out to search for what they needed.

It took a good two hours' wait in line for water, then for food, and it wasn't much—just more bread and a few scraps of cheese. The soldiers said they were late to the line, and they'd handed out almost everything they'd commandeered at the neighborhood stores. They received a couple of loaves of bread.

One of the soldiers said there was a bakery downtown that had escaped the fire and was turning out the loaves as fast as it was able.

Waiting in line with the neighbors, they heard many tales of woe, and everyone demanded explanations of the tired soldiers who distributed the bread and cheese and water. They felt like prisoners, which, in a manner of speaking, they were, if only of their circumstances.

The sergeant stood on the back of the water wagon and demanded attention. "You people must understand. We've limited supplies. Relief is coming, but it will take some time. Kindly stop abusing my soldiers."

Norah and Esther looked at each other. Esther shook her head and they went home.

When they arrived, Addison had returned and Scott was awake. He sat on the step smoking another cigarette and looked dreadful.

"You're a sight." Esther told him crisply.

"Have you seen Abby?" Norah asked, but all she got was a tired smirk in response. She glared at him.

Beth arrived in due time but said nothing beyond a brief hello to anyone. She took a bit of bread and went into the parlor, and from the front porch, they heard her playing the piano.

"Addison, what ails her?" Esther asked.

"Not sure, but it may have something to do with this recent dust-up we've had."

"There's no need to be sarcastic, my love. I'm just concerned."

"I wasn't being sarcastic, Esther dear. It's the truth. We're covered in soot. We haven't enough to eat or enough water. We're crapping in a hole in the ground in the backyard. We have more patients than ever and less time and supplies. I would think you, of all people, would recognize that no one is in a very good mood." He nearly shouted the last few words.

Norah had never heard Addison raise his voice, and it was shocking. "Addison! Lower your voice."

"Oh, good Christ. You've got a lot of nerve telling him to lower his voice. Leave him alone." This was Scott.

Esther turned on him, furious. "I'll ask you to shut your mouth. You aren't doing a single thing to make anything better around this house. You're a drunk."

"Oh, yes, that's my sin. I'm just not a saintly self-sacrificing doctor like the rest of you. I'm a bum. Right." He jumped off his step and went into the house and returned with another bottle of whiskey. He tore the cork out and glared at Esther as he guzzled the liquor.

Norah's nerves broke and she screamed, "Stop. All of you. God. Just stop." That got everyone's attention. Usually Norah was quiet.

"Let's not turn on each other. We're all exhausted and hungry and worried about everything and everybody." She thought of Abby as she said this. "We must just try to cope and help each other and not fight."

"I think I'll just get drunk," Scott said. "And not say another word."

Addison looked at him for a moment. "Scott. If you're going to do nothing but drink, you'll have to leave. We can't take care of a drunk because we've got too much else to do. Either quit drinking or go." He spoke without anger, but his intent was there and Scott could see it.

Scott lowered the bottle and stared at Addison, then at Esther and Norah. "Very well," he said. "I'll leave."

He stood up, swaying a little. "I'll just say my good-byes to Beth and be off. I'll trouble you no more. I believe there may be a patch of grass with my name on it in a park somewhere." He drunkenly saluted them and disappeared.

CHAPTER TWELVE

Beth stared at the sheet music in front of her, her hands still on the piano keys, trembling slightly. She struggled to not burst into tears. She'd gone once more to the Letterman Hospital to see Kerry. She felt terrible about neglecting her work, but she had to go. She'd prayed that, by some miracle, Kerry had woken up herself that day. But it wasn't to be.

She'd found Marjorie first and asked her, but Marjorie's face told the truth before she said a word.

"No change. She's stopped speaking to me at all or even asking for you," Marjorie said.

Beth went into the ward and saw Kerry lying on her uninjured side. Kerry didn't move until Beth tapped her shoulder.

Kerry turned over on her back. "Bethy," she said, her voice thready and hoarse.

Beth touched her hair. "Hello, love. How are you feeling?"

"Terrible. When can I come home?"

"Not yet, love. You must heal first."

Kerry's brows came down and her eyes narrowed. "You don't love me anymore, and you don't care if I live or die."

Beth clamped her mouth shut, deciding that argument was futile. She stayed a few more minutes, stroking Kerry's hair and looking into her eyes, hoping she could convey what words couldn't. Then she kissed her good-bye and went away.

"Miss Beth?" Scott's voice behind her startled her. As she turned to look at him, the odor of stale alcohol mixed with the smell of his unwashed body wafted over to her.

"You look awful. Whatever is the matter? Is it Kerry?"

He sat down on the piano bench next to her, forcing her to make room for him.

She had no reason to lie. "Yes, it is. She—"

"They've insisted I go."

"Go? Go where? Why?" Whatever had occurred was serious enough that he couldn't focus for even a moment on her distress.

"They don't want me here."

"Who doesn't?"

"Everyone." He sat with his chin sunk down on his chest, looking like a six-year-old who'd been reprimanded.

"Oh, Scott."

"Because of my drinking."

He was aware of the others' dismay at least, even if he didn't agree with it. "Why *are* you drinking so much?"

"It just hurts. My home is gone, Whit is gone. No more patients. They're probably gone too."

"You're not the only one who's lost a home or a loved one, Scott," she said sharply. "How can you give in to self-pity?" She was angry at his selfishness.

"I don't—"

"Kerry refuses to speak to me." She put her hands over her face.

He put an arm around her. "Oh, Beth. I'm sorry."

"She's hurt and I can't help her."

"What can I do?"

Beth looked at him. "For her, nothing. But for me and for you, pull yourself together. Be a doctor! Come help us. I know you can."

He stared at her for a long time. Then he said, "All right. And I promise you Kerry will be fine. We all, my God, are in such dire straits. You're right."

He was the old sincere, passionate Scott, and she believed him. They hugged.

"Now, please put the cork in that stupid whiskey bottle and let's go speak to the others."

He did as he was told, and they went out onto the porch. The group turned as one to look at them.

"Miss Beth has convinced me to forego the dubious comfort of spirits and instead come and work with you at the Park. I hope you'll consent to let me stay."

They gathered around, hugging him and shaking his hand. Beth was only slightly relieved. She would have to wait because Marjorie said Kerry's recovery would take a long time. She might not be herself for weeks.

❖

In bed, alone, Norah couldn't sleep. Abby hadn't returned by nightfall. Where could she be? Back at Russian Hill? Dead in the gutter, shot as a looter? Her feverish fantasies streamed past her eyes. She nearly jumped out of bed to put her clothes on and go out to search for her, which would be inadvisable. She had to have faith. She had no faith in women because May hadn't engendered any. Abby was nothing like May, though, and Norah would have to be patient. Abby was strong and smart, and she was a survivor. She could live in the wilderness, so the burnt-out City shouldn't present that much of challenge to her. With these thoughts, Norah attempted to bolster her own courage. It was another thing altogether how much she cared.

She woke to someone shaking her shoulder. She turned, and in the dark she could see it was Abby. She sat up and threw her arms around her neck, nearly strangling her.

"You're safe. Oh, my word. I was worried."

Abby hugged her back and said, "I'm safe. Yes. I've returned. I had to."

Norah leaned back to scrutinize her in the dark. "Had to?"

"Yes. For a few reasons. I've a tale to tell. But let that be tomorrow. It's late—"

Norah grasped her shoulders. "No! Tell me now."

She was so adamant, Abby nodded. They sat close together on the edge of the bed. "I left this morning and started toward my home, and Norah, it's truly unbelievable, truly awful…"

❖

Abby walked south on Fillmore Street and then east on Bush Street, and if it weren't for the knots of people huddled on the sidewalks around their makeshift stoves cooking breakfast, she wouldn't have known anything was wrong until she reached Van Ness Avenue. The once-broad boulevard, lined on both sides by some of the most magnificent mansions in the City other than those on Nob Hill, was devastated. The fine houses were gone, not because of the earthquake or even from the fire. The army had blown them up to stop the fire and had succeeded. The difference between west of Van Ness Ave and east of Van Ness couldn't have been more stark.

In a cloud of disbelief, Abby walked on, and then she was in the fire zone. She saw blackened shells of houses, more earthquake debris, and, here and there, bodies. The City she knew had disappeared; it was no longer recognizable. The smell of fire was laced with the smell of decay. It was putrid. She nearly turned back, but she had to finally get an answer.

She was forced to skirt Nob Hill because the soldiers said houses were still on fire there. She could see as she walked on Union Street toward Taylor Street that there seemed to be structures at the top of Russian Hill still intact. She walked faster, her hope rising, and when she reached the footpath, she could tell that her former home was gone, but the houses at the summit belonging to Adam Winters and Henry Long were intact. She practically flew up the hill and pounded on the door of Henry's home.

He flung open the door and pulled her into a tight embrace. "Oh, my dear Abby. We didn't know what had happened to you. No word from you for a whole week.'

"I'm well, Henry. I just was unable to get here, as you know."

"Yes. I know."

"The bundles I gave to Emmett? The type specimens? Are they here?" she asked, every cell in her body bursting with anxiety.

"Come with me." He led her to the kitchen, and there they lay on the floor, tied up and covered exactly as she'd left them.

She knelt and touched the bundles gently, then turned to Henry, tears in her eyes.

"I can't thank you and Emmet enough. It's a miracle."

"It is, Abby. I don't know how we managed. That water you left in your flat? The neighbors had to drink it 'cause, you know, we had none. We fought the fire with soda bottles at the end, with Emmett dangling by his feet out the window and me and Adam holding him. The firemen couldn't make it up the goat track."

"Oh, my word. That's terrifying."

"It was touch-and-go, but we survived."

"I'll have these moved as soon as I can find a good place. You have my everlasting gratitude, all of you."

❖

"So you see, Norah. It turned out my plants were saved."

Norah couldn't tell her expression in the dark, but her voice told her enough. Abby was at peace, relieved. She struggled to understand and not to berate her again for risking her life.

In the silence, Abby spoke. "I know you can't quite comprehend this. I'm sorry to have worried you."

"That's the thing really, Abby. I'm trying to accept what you tell me."

"Oh. That's so wonderful. You can't know how much it means to me. You're not a scientist, so you can't see how important this is."

"What of your home, your possessions?"

"Gone," Abby said, simply. "I've nothing left but what I wear and my favorite magnifier that I'd put in my pocket before I left the Society on the day of the earthquake. And the type specimens too. None of my books, my family mementos. Nothing else."

Norah was quiet for a long time. "We're the same then, in that way. We've lost nearly everything. We're homeless." Abby had managed to save *something* that mattered to her. Norah had nothing.

"Yes, that's true." Abby took Norah's hand. Her palm was warm and smooth, and her fingers intertwined with Norah's.

She squeezed Abby's hand. "Will you stay here?"

"If it's all right with Esther and Addison and with you. I will."

"Yes, we all want you to stay. Especially me."

"Then that's settled. We've must try to rebuild our lives. We have to go forward and not be discouraged. You've got your work with the refugees, and I'll figure out something. They'll surely find temporary quarters for the Society somewhere in the City."

"I would hope so."

"Norah, would you go into the City with me sometime? As hideous as it is, I still want to look around a bit. I might call it sightseeing, though that's a crude way to state it."

"Yes. I'll see if I can get away for a bit in a few days, though we've got so much to do. The Red Cross brings in lots of materials, but we have to fight with them to get it and…"

Abby put a finger to her lips. Norah was so astonished, she could scarcely enjoy the touch, but she stopped talking.

"We should sleep now. It's very late. We can talk some more in the morning." In the dark, Abby took off her outer clothing and once more climbed into bed next to Norah, who moved aside to make room for her. On the one hand, it felt like the most natural thing in the world. Abby's presence was both comfortable and comforting. On the other hand, Norah's pulse began to beat, and she longed to move closer to the warmth emanating from Abby. She wanted to feel that warmth all around her.

What would it feel like if they both removed all their clothing and, instead of keeping decorously to their own side of the bed, met in the middle? What would that be like? What if instead of sleeping they explored each other's bodies? Norah remembered what she and May had done and struggled to rid her mind of those images in order to fall asleep.

❖

With the rest of the volunteer medical staff, Beth, Norah, and Scott gathered in the army's mess tent at eight a.m. on Monday morning a week and a half after the earthquake.

The army's chief surgeon and a civilian flanked the army commander.

"Good morning, ladies and gentlemen. Thank you for taking a few moments of what I know is a very busy day for you. This is a vitally important subject about which we must undertake to inform you. Lieutenant Colonel Torney here—" he indicated the army officer—"will brief you on our sanitation situation. Assisting him is Arthur Reed, sanitary engineer."

"Thank you, sir. General Funston has given me the responsibility for the sanitary arrangements for the entire City of San Francisco. Here we have the largest gathering of refugees aside from those who are currently on the grounds of the Letterman Hospital. While we are seeing to the feeding and housing of our unfortunate citizens, no less important is the subject of sanitation. We'll be depending on you, the medical staff, to assist as much as possible in informing and enforcing our regulations. As you move among the people and see them in the treatment tents, they look to you for information and reassurance as well as medical care.

"As you are no doubt aware, improper sanitation has the effect of creating the ideal conditions for disease. You have the greatest interest in preventing outbreaks of infectious diseases."

He paused for effect, scanning his audience.

"The following measures are in effect, and we will provide written lists for your use and for you to distribute to all your patients and all who come to you for aid. First, no water is to be used other than for drinking, cooking, or what is necessary for medical use, such as sterilization. Second, no citizens may cook or hoard food on their own. They must take meals in the mess tents provided for that purpose. Third, and most vital, the refugees may not dig their own latrines. We must ensure that the conditions whereby flies carry contagion from human waste to food are eliminated at all times. You have to reinforce these measures among the refugees if we are to prevent epidemics."

"Mr. Reed here will describe the measures he has taken and those he will recommend as we move forward."

Mr. Reed coughed and then began in the dry, matter-of-fact tone of a technical expert. "We're fortunate that the Park has its own reservoir, but we've no idea how long the supply will last in the face of increasing population. The army will bring in extra water supplies as needed. The situation of most urgency is naturally the provision of toilet facilities. We're providing fifty sanitary troughs that will be dispersed through the camp on the outer edges." He showed them the location on the diagram. "These will be decontaminated with quicklime and their contents carried away each night. They will be clearly marked for women and for men. They will also be inspected by Lieutenant Colonel Torney's men on a regular basis and cleaned and maintained." He looked back toward the colonel.

"Thank you, Mr. Reed. That, in brief, is our plan at the moment. Thank you for your attention. We'll pass out the orders to you. I would like to see Doctors Hammond, Stratton, and O'Connell, please."

Beth and Norah exchanged puzzled looks. Scott grinned and said, "Since I'm not needed at the moment, I shall head back to the first hospital tent and make myself useful."

Lieutenant Colonel Torney motioned for them to sit at a rough table with himself and the camp commander. "Doctors, I've asked for some more of your time as we need to plan for the inevitable. That is, folk will become sickened no matter how diligent we are."

Beth thought of the typhoid epidemics amongst the soldiers in the Philippines.

"We're already dealing with cases of dysentery," she said.

Norah and the other doctor nodded.

"No doubt. Well. You will need to prepare an isolation tent. Please let us know what supplies will be needed."

"We'll give you a list. The water situation is the most dire, Colonel."

"We're aware, and, as was said, we're endeavoring to remedy that."

Beth, Norah, and Dr. O'Connell walked back to the hospital area near the bandstand and conferred.

"We must be public-health officers as well as doctors," Martin O'Connell said, sounding as though he was not enamored of the prospect.

"It's true," Beth responded. "It's a thankless job, but we must do our parts, as the colonel said. Lest we be overrun with very sick people."

"Beth, may I speak with you? In private?" Norah asked.

Doctor O'Connell politely nodded and walked off.

Beth looked curiously at Norah, who seemed nervous about something.

"What is the problem?" Beth didn't mean to be unkind or short, but her mind was running forward at top speed thinking about preparing for epidemics of cholera, small pox, typhoid, and, God help them, bubonic plague. She had a thousand things to consider.

"I want some time away tomorrow afternoon. I know we're busy and short-handed and—"

"Why?" Beth asked, rather incensed.

"Abby asked me accompany her on a walk downtown." Norah seemed abashed.

"Is that all? Does she know you're needed here? It's all very well for her to ramble here, there, and everywhere. She's got nothing better to do, I suppose. But you?"

"I know it's asking a great deal, Beth, but she's lost everything just about everything she owns. As have I. She asked me to go." Norah looked more embarrassed than ever.

Beth's anger receded somewhat. They were all overworked, tired, and distracted. It seemed like a small thing to ask. She suspected that Norah and Abby were in the very beginning of a romance, as Kerry had predicted. Their vigilance toward one another, their secret looks all pointed to that fact. Beth was inclined to be understanding. No one had much joy these days. She briefly thought of Kerry lying in the Letterman Hospital burn ward, angry and in pain.

"All right. One afternoon. That's all. I'll put Scott to work. It will be good for him after his many months with wealthy hypochondriacs to actually treat real patients with real problems."

She was happy to see Norah smile at that.

"Thank you so much. I won't ask for anything else."

❖

"Will you show me where you lived?" Norah asked Abby. They'd fitted themselves out as though going for an expedition like the one they took to Mount Tamalpais. In a way, Norah believed, they were. They were venturing into no man's land. They would have no water, little shade, and no food. Unknown dangers lurked. Under any other circumstances, Norah's innate caution would have stopped her from making such a journey. But because Abby had asked her and she would be with Abby, it was, like the trip to Mount Tamalpais, something she wanted to do, something she felt compelled to do. She was under the spell of Abby's personality. What would come of it she had no idea. That Abby had specifically *asked* her to come along was puzzling but welcome. Perhaps Abby's stubborn self-sufficiency had waned just a touch. Being needed exerted a powerful pull on Norah. She was happy to be needed by her patients, happy to help them, but this was altogether different.

"I could show you where the house used to be," Abby said with an undercurrent of humor in her voice. "It will, however, as I said before, involve climbing a goat path."

"That's perfectly agreeable to me," Norah said, meaning it.

They set off with their provisions of food and water and a parasol as well, for the sun shone brightly.

Norah had crisscrossed the City between the commune and the hospital a few times, but those areas hadn't burned except sporadically. She wasn't prepared for the look of the City east of Van Ness Avenue. Blackened skeletons stood where buildings had once been. The smell of destruction—of dust and fire and gasoline and singed concrete— was overwhelming. It was only too well illuminated in the bright, benign April sunshine. As they walked, they said little. When she was not looking at ruins, Norah looked at Abby, who was calm but grim. Did she wonder the same thing as Norah—if the City would ever return to normal?

Yet, here and there people were quietly combing through the ruins, searching for something, anything worth saving. The ever-present groups of soldiers and guardsmen roamed around, keeping a sharp lookout. Groups of workers were removing the dead. Astoundingly enough, here and there, stores had been spared and were even open for business. The remaining streetlamp posts held flyers and personal notes, people looking for their loved ones.

They walked California Street, and at the intersection of California and Hyde, they stopped in front of an odd but heartbreaking sight. Dozens of cable cars had been lined up from Hyde to Franklin Streets. They'd been burned, and all that was left were the metal wheels still slotted on the tracks and the brake and grip levers. Abby and Norah glanced at each other, and Abby shook her head.

They reached the top of Nob Hill, and Norah remembered Addison pointing out the mansions of the San Francisco's elite on their way home from the train depot in January.

Now they were all wrecked, fallen, or burned save one. It appeared to have been spared because, unlike the others, it was made of masonry instead of wood. They stood before it, gaping. It was like a dream, a mirage of some sort, incongruous amid the devastation.

"Whose house was this?" Norah asked, in wonder.

"I don't know. Let's ask someone." They looked about and saw a man picking through a pile of wood nearby.

"Sir?" Norah asked.

He turned a stolid, blank face on them. He was roughly dressed, a working man, no doubt. He said nothing, didn't smile.

"Whose home is this that somehow was spared?"

"That?" he said, with some disdain. "That's the Mark Hopkins mansion."

Norah turned to Abby. "Who's that? Do you know?"

"Not sure, but I believe he had something to do with the railroads. Most of the people up here did. That or silver mines."

They walked on to Taylor Street, and on the south side of the street, another structure, or what was left of it, caught their eyes. There was even a man in a dark suit and homburg standing before it with a camera. When they got closer, they could see why.

It was the entrance to what surely had been a very grand home. Two sets of four simple Doric columns stood, likely at one time someone's front door. But behind them was nothing but a panoramic view of utter ruin. To the right, Norah recognized the damaged dome of City Hall. They stood for a while staring at it.

"Would you ladies mind moving to the side so that I may capture the sight that has captured you?" the photographer asked politely, and they did so. They watched him fuss with the camera, moving it in miniscule increments to and fro.

Abby asked him, "Do you know who lived here?"

"Does it matter now?" he replied with some asperity.

"No, I suppose not. It's a remarkable view though."

"That it is. I've taken photographs of many horrifying and astonishing sights these last few days. This one, however, encapsulates the tragedy very neatly."

They looked again. It was true. The only remains of a stately mansion framing the lovely blue sky over the destruction of a once-beautiful city. It was insupportably sad. As always, Norah looked to Abby. Her face was a mask of pain, and a tear glistened at the corner of her eye.

They said good-bye to the cameraman and headed north on Taylor Street toward Russian Hill. Neither of them said anything for a while.

"Abby?" Norah ventured. "Are you well?" They had quickened their pace, or rather Abby had, and Norah was determined to keep up with her, no matter the difficulty.

"No. I'm not," Abby said, shortly. "How could I be?"

Norah wasn't sure what she should say next. "Yes," she said carefully. "It's difficult to even put into words."

"I'm not a city person. I'm a person of the forest and the mountains, but still this is my home too. Even if it doesn't seem so, in nature, there is harmony and reason. Did you know that when there is a forest fire, some things begin to grow immediately afterward? The fire burns out old wood and brush. It's not a bad thing but a good thing. But I can't see any good in this." She bowed her head. "Your home is gone, mine is gone. What do we do next?"

Norah touched Abby's arm to induce her to raise her bowed head and meet her eyes.

"I don't know but we're alive. Our loved ones are alive. Whatever we do next, we'll know when we know. At the moment, it's enough I have a roof over my head and I have work to do. And I have you." Norah wasn't sure where that last sentence came from, but it seemed right to say. It was true.

"Yes. I have you, and I'm lucky to have you. But for the rest...I was always certain about what would come next for me. I went from one occupation to the next without pause or question about my fate. I have no such certainty this time. The Society is not operational for the moment, and I don't know when it will be. For the first time in my life I have nothing to occupy me."

"I can see that's distressing to you," Norah said, "and I wish I had something to tell you, but I can say, if you need something to do, you could help us at the Golden Gate Park refugee camp. We have so much to do, and not all of it requires medical expertise."

Abby looked at her with wonder. "Do you think so?"

"Yes. I'm sure of it. Aren't we on our way to Russian Hill?"

"Oh, yes. Sorry. Let us proceed."

With that, Abby's funk seemed to lift, and she marched off at her usual speed, with Norah at her heels.

❖

At the end of the goat track, the little clapboard houses grouped on the summit of Russian Hill looked peaceful and cozy. They stood in stark contrast to the City below.

'Your plants are here?" Norah asked.

"Yes. Though I do have to determine a better place to store them and a means to get them there."

"How will you get in touch with people to do that?"

"As I've discovered, the post office is running almost in a normal fashion. I'll write to some other Society members."

"That's good then," Norah said, her tone bright and encouraging.

Abby took heart from having Norah at her side to talk to. She never gave much thought to being a solitary person because she was often in company. But it was company starkly different from Norah's. Norah knew little and cared nothing for botany or geology or natural history. Yet Abby wanted to talk to her about everything. Norah would open her blue eyes wide and listen with such intensity that Abby thought she could well read her mind. It was unnerving and wonderful.

Abby thought she ought to leave the City. She couldn't see how she could bear to see the damage every day. She didn't know what else to do, yet Norah had given her an idea that seemed, to her surprise, the better choice. She could stay and make herself useful. The answers as to what next would come when they came. In reality, she also found she didn't want to leave Norah.

"We ought to start back. I think the commune dinner will start, and we wouldn't want to miss that." Norah grinned, referring to the scrounged-up, clumsily cooked fare they consumed with the rest of the group and sometimes the neighbors.

'Yes. That's true." They started their journey, and Abby found herself in a much lighter mood. Yes, the scenery, if it could be called that, was unchanged, but in due time, they crossed Van Ness, and on its west side, the Western Addition looked almost normal, aside from the knots of people huddled around stoves on the sidewalks.

There would be some food, some conviviality, and then later, she and Norah would lie in bed and talk. It was starting to feel as though this was normal life. Abby would write a few letters and post them the next day. She'd check and see if her bank was operating and obtain some money, though there wasn't much to buy, she thought ruefully. Just a few postage stamps. But she could look around and see if some of the stores were open, and she could buy something special to eat for the commune.

Her thoughts were running ahead, but she happened to glance to her side just to see if Norah was there. That was a becoming a habit as well. She was, and the expression on her face was unlike any Abby had ever seen. Norah looked at her quietly, but with such feeling, it took her aback. She didn't quite comprehend it, but she was drawn to it. She returned Norah's eye contact with a look she hoped conveyed her feelings: *I appreciate you, I need you. Being with you makes all this easier to bear.*

When they were back on California Street and headed home, they came upon a man sitting in the dirt and weeping inconsolably. They glanced at one another, and Norah said, "Let's see what ails him. He might be hurt."

"Sir?" Abby tapped him on the shoulder.

He looked up, sniffling.

"Are you hurt?" Norah asked. "Where do you live?"

"I used to live in San Francisco," he said, and went back to crying. Abby couldn't think what to say, and she saw Norah couldn't either.

The meaning of his words sank in. Was there any San Francisco left? For this man, perhaps not. For them, the answer would be yes, there was still San Francisco, such as it was, and Abby touched Norah's arm, indicating they should be on their way. Norah nodded bleakly.

Chapter Thirteen

I want to go home," Kerry said.

"Oh, soon, Kerry, dearest, but I cannot take you home until the surgeon says so. Your burn is still healing."

"If I have morphine, I'm fine. I can't get better here. You know that."

"I want you to try to be patient, love."

Kerry narrowed her eyes. Was Beth telling her the truth? She wasn't entirely sure *anyone* was. She trusted no one. She didn't understand why Beth couldn't just take her away from this dreadful hospital. What good was it for Beth to be a doctor, anyhow, if she wouldn't exercise her authority? She was angry at everyone and everything. The only slightly good thing was that right after a morphine shot, the pain in her arm receded to a dull ache.

Beth sat looking at her hopefully and patting her hand. A tiny corner of Kerry's soul wanted to respond to her, to reassure her she would be well, but the pain and despair was a gigantic black cloak around her mind, allowing no light in. Most of the time, she wanted to die. The rest of the time, she wanted to kill someone, starting with Marjorie, the agent of all her torture.

Every few days, Marjorie took off her bandage and cleaned the enormous blister, causing excruciating pain. She peeled off the dead skin and coated it with oil. Kerry moaned and sometimes screamed or fought back physically, but Marjorie was implacable. To Kerry, she appeared to be without an iota of compassion. Behind her wire-rim glasses, her eyes were glacial, and she never said more than necessary.

Occasionally, she patted Kerry on the arm or hand before she left, but that was all.

After Beth left, Marjorie returned.

"I am not going to clean your wound today. I'm going to change the bandage." Kerry gritted her teeth as Marjorie removed the white gauze, which stuck to the burn.

Marjorie replaced it with a clean bandage and, to Kerry's great surprise, sat down next to her bed and took her hand.

"Kerry?"

"Yes?"

"I want you to see if it is in your heart to not blame Beth for your troubles."

"I'm not. I—"

"Yes, you are. It's not unusual. You've had a bad injury and you've been in shock. You are emotionally as well as physically hurt. You must try to accept your present circumstances."

Kerry turned her head to the side so she didn't have to meet Marjorie's eyes. Marjorie still held onto her hand, but she made no move to disengage. The contact was comforting, though she didn't want to admit it.

"You need not be a fountain of sweetness and light but merely to aim your anger to another direction rather than at Beth. She doesn't deserve it."

That last sentence made Kerry ache with guilt. She'd done a terrible thing to Beth a few years before, and she'd spent much time making it up to her. She never again wanted to hurt Beth, but she didn't want to let Marjorie know she agreed with her.

"Is it time for my morphine shot yet?" she asked, noting her voice was devoid of emotion rather than charged with fury.

"I believe it is. I'll check with the surgeon."

❖

"Beth? Beth!" It was Esther calling her from the door of the refugee tent, where she sat with a mother and three children.

The mother, a poor woman from South of the Slot, very like many of the folk that Beth had interviewed for her research paper, gazed at her with an alarmed, suspicious expression. The three youngsters, aged two to five, were lined up on the army cot where Beth had examined them.

"Yes, Doctor?" she said to Esther, finally.

"When you're available, please come find me."

Beth nodded and returned her attention to the problem before her.

This mother was not able or willing to adequately keep her youngsters clean, and they'd come down with dysentery.

Beth held a bucket with solution of carbolic and said, "Watch me." She put her hands in the bucket and then rubbed her fingers and cuticles thoroughly. She smiled at the oldest child and said, "Now you. I'll help you. "

She picked up the five-year-old's hands and dipped them in the pail, then cleaned each finger and cuticle with a cloth. The youngster goggled at her but thankfully didn't cry. That would encourage the younger siblings to cooperate.

"See?" Beth said to the mother. "In this way, they may clean their hands after they use the latrine and not pass the contagion back to themselves or to each other."

She said, "I see, Doctor." But she still looked dubious. It was likely she'd never paid much attention to the cleanliness of her children before, but this time it could be a matter of life and death.

"You have heard from your husband?" she asked, but the woman nodded in the negative.

"Well, please inquire at the Red Cross tent. I'm sure he'll turn up."

Beth wasn't at all sure of that, but she wanted to be positive.

She went off in search of Esther and found her in one of the treatment tents. Esther took her arm and led her out of earshot of the patients and the other medical staff.

"I'm worried about you. You're not yourself. You're significantly inattentive."

"No. I'm—"

"Yes. You are. I can see it. Is it Kerry?"

There was no use in lying to Esther. She could spot dishonesty immediately.

"Yes."

"Well?" Esther said.

Beth couldn't hide her feelings, she began to cry.

Esther embraced her. "There now. It's not good for you to hold your emotions in check. Tell me about it."

Beth described the situation with Kerry.

"If you weren't so important to our work here, I am sure that Dr. Torney would allow you some time off."

Beth was dejected. "I'm not sure it would matter. She's angry and barely talks to me."

"That doesn't mean she won't come around to her usual self eventually. When may she return home?"

"Not yet. Marjorie is afraid of infection, and in any case, the surgeon hasn't released her. And we're packed in at the commune. She might as well stay at Letterman Hospital."

"Don't worry about that. When the time comes, we'll have to improvise. Why don't you talk to Marjorie and see if you can get Kerry released to return home? That could help improve her outlook."

"Who will care for her? I'm needed here many hours a day. I feel guilty even slipping away for a short while to visit her."

"We'll make a plan. Beth, dear, you won't be an effective doctor if you're worried over Kerry. We could possibly get a nurse from the City and County to help. I can ask Addison."

"If you think so...I'll speak with the army surgeon and with Marjorie. Are you and Addison all right?"

Esther smiled slightly. "With all the chaos of the earthquake, we've not had any opportunity to quarrel, if that's what you mean."

"Have you changed your mind?"

Esther's expression was enigmatic. All she said was, "I'm not prepared to discuss it."

❖

Kerry was aroused out of a stupor by Marjorie.

"I'm sorry, Kerry. It's time to clean your burn again." Kerry stared at her without saying a word. She braced herself, anticipating the pain. She tried to keep quiet, but this was the worst part of her treatment. Kerry hated Marjorie, hated the hospital, hated being in bed and helpless, hated that Beth was not here taking care of her. If hatred could help her heal, that was good, because she had plenty of it. She even hated Teddy, who'd come by to see her, but only once. She was so hateful to him, he never returned. She was sorry afterward and more miserable than ever.

Marjorie returned with her basin and bottles and dressing. Kerry couldn't bear to look at her arm, both because of the pain and the way the burn appeared. From her hand all the way up to her bicep was angry red and mottled with large blisters. Every other day, Marjorie would peel off the dead skin of those blisters and pour something into them that made it feel like her arm was on fire again. She scarcely cared what it was. Then Marjorie painted the raw blisters with oil mixed with something called cocaine. And after that she put on a new dressing. The appearance of new blisters made it necessary to repeat this process every few days.

The first time, Marjorie said, "We have to ensure you don't get an infection." Kerry had screamed and tried not to do so again because it shamed her. It was also necessary for Marjorie to bathe her, and that bothered her even more. Even though she would feel a little better afterward, it was terribly embarrassing. No one but Beth saw her naked. Beth. Again, she thought of Beth, longed for her and silently reviled her for abandoning her. She had no way to reconcile her conflicting feelings.

Marjorie finished her ministrations and then took her temperature. "Hmm. You're beginning to come out of your fever. Today it's only one hundred and one. That's very good. I'll see if we may again feed you some beef broth tomorrow." *We.* There was no *we.* Only Marjorie.

Kerry spoke as though she had cotton in her mouth. "Where's Beth?"

"She's not able to come just at the moment," Marjorie said crisply. "She's going to stay away until you are better."

"Why is she staying away?" Kerry would have shouted had she been able, but she was too weak and too sick.

"You're not an ideal patient," Marjorie said. "You abuse the one person who loves you most. When you're ready to be agreeable, we'll have Beth visit."

"I don't have to be agreeable," Kerry growled. "I'm burned. I'm sick."

"All of which is true. But you will get well. In fact, as soon as your fever breaks and you can eat again, we'll send you home with Beth. It would be nice if you could be pleasant to her."

Kerry turned over restlessly and said, "I'll try, but you tell her to come." She mumbled into her lumpy, thin pillow.

❖

"You can take this list and check on all of these families and see who's in need of attention. Then we can return if necessary. If all's well, then we need not spend time with people who only want someone to listen to their troubles. We do want to know that they're following the sanitary regulations, though."

Norah's serious and detailed instruction secretly amused Abby. She was adorably anxious that Abby not be pulled into dicey situations for which she was unprepared. Abby certainly appreciated that but thought Norah might be somewhat over-protective. Abby was an old hand at taking care of herself, and she certainly didn't need to be treated like a dimwit. Norah clearly had a number of medical issues to deal with among the refugees. Abby could take some of her mundane tasks away.

"Let me have those lists. Please don't be concerned. I believe I can spot children with dirty hands and faces and lackadaisical mothers."

Norah actually smiled. "I believe you can, and that's why I thought it a good idea for you to help us. Other folks are volunteering, and they're certainly not professional nurses, let alone doctors."

Abby went off on her rounds of the encampment and left Norah to her work with the people in the hospital tent who were seriously ill.

The first few visits went well. When she spoke gently to the mothers, they seemed awestruck and cooperative. She saw a few kiddies with fevers and rashes and took note. She was beginning to relax a little, and in spite of her brave words to Norah, she had to overcome some initial nervousness about approaching strangers in their homes, such as they were.

There were suspicious fathers in some of the families. She grasped they were ashamed of the straits they found themselves in, having to receive what they considered handouts and eager not to appear as incompetent heads of households in front of Abby. With these men she exercised the utmost tact.

She stopped to speak with a family group under yet another makeshift shelter of blankets and, in this case, window curtains all held up after a fashion by brass bedstead fragments. How had the luckless family managed to drag it all to the Park? When she got close to them she was overwhelmed by the smell of human waste. She counted three children, ages hard to discern, but the mother held what seemed to be a two-year-old boy in her arms. She essayed a non-threatening smile at the father. She could tell he wasn't sober. With all bars forbidden to sell spirits, she couldn't think where he'd gotten enough alcohol to be drunk two weeks after the earthquake, but there he was. She refrained from wrinkling her nose, but the combination of booze fumes and fecal smell was overpowering. The other families nearby were giving these refugees a wide berth even at the expense of crowding themselves closer.

"Good afternoon. I'm assisting the medical staff today. Have you all had anything to eat?" A silent chorus of wary nods was the response.

"Your boy there? Is he ill?" Abby addressed the mother whose distracted air and furrowed brow proclaimed her distress.

"Hey, you said you ain't no doctor." The inebriated father spoke up, and he sounded belligerent.

"True. I'm not, but I'm helping the doctors, and they're most interested in having anyone who's sick come to the hospital tent right away. Also, I've got a set of sanitary instructions here that I must read to you."

At that moment, the toddler screamed. His mother squeezed him tighter, as though to try to quiet him.

"Ma'am. He looks sick. Let me walk you to the hospital tent so that he can be seen—"

"We ain't going nowhere," the man said, his voice close to a shout. The woman cowered and the other children began to cry. Abby was becoming nauseous. She took a deep breath through her mouth and tried to calm herself. It was ridiculous that she couldn't perform the simple task Norah had set her to.

"I see. Well. Let me read these items to you."

When she got to the part that specified making sure to clean the children's hands thoroughly after they went to the latrine, the mother began to shift her gaze and look everywhere but at Abby. The baby in her arms was mumbling and crying and appeared to be very ill.

Abby tried once again to induce the mother to come with her, but the father stood up, and in spite of her above-average height, he towered over her. She thought he might hit her.

When she located Norah and told her, Norah's expression was grim.

"The boy has dysentery or something worse. I'll have to go back and take a soldier with me."

"Do you think that's really advisable?"

"Yes, it is. Do you think we can let this sort of thing go unchecked? That family could start an epidemic."

"But how—"

"Thank you, Abby. I'll take care of this." Norah brushed past her and left, leaving Abby feeling nonplussed and disliking the dismissal she'd just received.

Abby cooled her heels for what seemed like hours before Norah reappeared. Norah glanced at her, then away, and moved to a row of cabinets, where she opened one to begin examining the contents. "That child is very ill, and I told the parents to cooperate or I would have to have the soldier remove him. The presence of the soldier and his rifle convinced them."

"It's cruel to have to treat people that way."

Norah turned, clearly having heard the censure in Abby's voice.

"Abby, if the mother and father don't keep the children clean and report their illnesses promptly, we could have an epidemic in short order. In these conditions, disease can gain a foothold very quickly. We've no time for coddling people, even if they've just endured an earthquake and lost everything they own. No matter. We have to be strict. You must understand."

"Maybe I'm not fit to be a volunteer in these circumstances," Abby said stiffly, angry at Norah and at herself. Mostly she was chagrined at how incompetent she felt.

"Don't say that. You can do it. I believe in you, but it's important to follow rules. And get others to follow them."

Norah wasn't being unkind, but she wasn't about to coddle Abby. Abby respected her. "I'm not used to having to do that."

"You're also not used to not being in charge," Norah said, with a hint of a smile.

Abby returned her own rueful grin. That was certainly on the mark. This was the bailiwick of Norah and other medical people, and she was a helper. She remembered the scared mother, the smell of baby shit, and the other dirty children. And their scared, angry, drunk papa. It was truly not her usual milieu. Norah was far more competent at this. She wasn't heartless; she was a realist who only cared for the good of all those unfortunate people. She couldn't afford to give in to sentimentality, and Abby was naive. Once again, she thought about the woods and a clear mountain lake and the thrill of finding a new species of plant. She had a supremely easy job. Her life's work was nothing compared to what Norah did.

"I think I'll take up my list and continue on my rounds. If I encounter any more difficult people, I'll be sure to fetch one of the army men."

Norah was grinning widely, beaming, in fact. It was odd in the circumstances, but gratifying. Norah didn't think she was hopeless, and that, for Abby, was enormously satisfying.

"Very good. We'll finish up for the day, and I'll see if we can find anything tasty in the mess tent to take home with us. Rations have been mighty thin on Fillmore Street."

Abby nodded and they went to their separate tasks.

❖

Beth and Scott sat on the little three-legged stools the army had brought in to the hospital tent number two for doctors to use as they saw their patients. They hadn't taken a break for what seemed like hours.

The line of patients was never-ending, complaining of small things such as bruises and serious burns or broken limbs. Scott had somehow found a white coat, and with his dashing mustache and cavalier smile, he charmed or cajoled dozens of people into submitting to his examination.

Beth had a young boy with a fracture before her, and she was trying to set it with the help of his father. The lad was screaming, and his poor father was less than useless because he was so frightened himself. She wished for a nurse to help her, but they were few and busy themselves. She asked Scott, and he requested that she wait for a moment.

"Not that I've forgotten everything from school," Scott said, "but I'm a little rusty on some of the endless ills that human kind is heir to. Especially ones who've had to flee for their lives."

"Scott? Have you thought of what you would do if Whit comes back to find you?"

Scott turned the child in his hands around and listened to his lungs. The little boy coughed harshly. "This young fellow has bronchitis. Nurse!"

After a few moments, one of the white-uniformed helpmeets came to the tent opening.

"Bronchitis. Infectious ward. I want a course of expectorant. Half the adult dose—one teaspoon every four hours." Scott wrote on the chart and handed the boy and the chart over to the nurse. He went to the carbolic pan and dipped his hands in, shook them, and rinsed them with water. Then he walked to the opening of the tent and shouted, "Next." He turned back to Beth.

"No. I've tried very hard to not think of Whit at all. Not of what we had or what we lost. Your wise words told me I must focus on the present. Yes, madam. Have a seat, please, and tell me your troubles." In his incongruously courtly fashion, he led his patient to a stool and then sat in front of her.

He was, Beth recalled, a very good doctor, and she was happy he'd agreed to come help at the refugee camp. He listened to the woman's tale of woe without comment, then listened to her heart.

"Madam," he said, solemnly, "your heart is beating exactly as it should. Your experience of the earthquake may have given you palpitations, but you're fine." She looked at him skeptically but shrugged and went away.

Beth tried not to laugh out loud. Only Scott could get away with such a dismissal of an anxious patient.

He leaned back and sighed. His legs were akimbo and he looked exhausted. "I've never worked this hard, even our intern year."

"Most likely. Now could you help with this, please?"

Scott took the boy in his arms, and in spite of his screams, Beth was able to set and splint his leg. They sent the father and son on their way with instructions.

"Scott, do you think Kerry—"

A young soldier came to the tent. "Excuse me, uh, Doctor? I've a brand-new arrival outside. She's in a bad way and I think she ought to be seen."

He looked uncertainly from Beth to Scott, and his gaze came to rest on Scott. As usual, he assumed the man was the doctor and Beth was an out-of-uniform nurse or some such thing. Scott looked back at the army man, who was a corporal. Beth could tell by the chevrons on his sleeves.

"Yes? What's the trouble?" Scott asked

"Well, I think you should come with me."

Scott made a sound of frustration and stood up, but he took another look at the boy and grinned his most charming grin.

The young corporal had perfect posture. Under his wide-brimmed hat, his blue eyes sparkled and his smile was adorably hesitant. His uniform was neat and clean, and even his gaiters were settled at exactly the same height on his legs. His rifle and his side arm in its holster gleamed from polishing.

"Lead the way," Scott said.

As he followed the corporal out of the tent, Beth shook her head. Perhaps Scott's sorrow over Whit would be assuaged.

Chapter Fourteen

"It says here that the water service has been repaired, though we're asked to practice conservation," Addison announced at supper that evening.

The commune members and guests cheered.

"So that means we can finally bathe," Esther said. "I'll get some clean clothes you can wear, Norah. But Abby, I'm not quite sure what we can do for you since you're so much taller than I am."

"What about borrowing some of Addison's clothes?" Norah asked, and five heads swiveled around to regard her with interest.

After a longish beat of silence, Abby said, airily, "I don't see as I have much choice if I'm to enjoy clean clothes."

"That's settled then," Addison remarked. "I'm happy to donate some trousers and a shirt. Very good. Let us proceed with getting our baths, and I think we can wash some of our soiled clothing at the same time and not run afoul of the City's public works department. "

Norah lay in the lukewarm bath water thinking about Abby, who'd taken her bath just prior to her. She tried to picture what Abby would look like without any clothes on. What came into her mind, though, was yet another occasion with May.

"I think you must come and wash my back, even if you won't join me," May said in her throaty, seductive voice. Norah was still shy.

Though they'd been lovers for a few weeks, it was still all so new and so overwhelming.

"Look at me." May was prone to issuing commands, and Norah would gladly obey.

The body Norah was getting to know in the dark was there before her in bright sunlight, as May had chosen to have a bath in the middle of the afternoon. Norah forced herself to look and hoped she wouldn't blush. She so disliked May's ability to make her feel like an awkward adolescent. Drops of water glittered on May's skin as she squeezed water from a sponge over her arm and her eyes drilled into Norah, her face lit by a welcoming smile.

Norah felt like a lovesick young boy in thrall to an older woman, though May was the same age as she. She swallowed, took the sponge from May's hand, and began to wash her back. If it were even possible, May's half-backward look at her was more seductive.

They had taken their time with the bath but naturally had ended up in bed where Norah had immersed herself in May's clean, warm flesh.

Now she went out into the backyard, where Abby, wearing Addison's clothes, was hanging up her clean, wet clothes on the clothesline. The shirt was a bit large and the pants a bit loose, but the overall effect was attractive with Abby's damp, blond hair loose and spread over her shoulders.

"I feel so much better now," Norah said. Abby turned, and even in the dark, Norah saw her broad grin. Addison's uncollared white shirt glowed in the dark, and the top button was open. With the help of a little moonlight, Norah could make out Abby's quizzical smile and the small indentation between her collarbones.

Norah walked toward Abby carrying her own freshly washed clothes.

"Do you want me to help you with those?" Abby asked.

"That would be nice." They began to attach the clothes to the line with clothespins.

"Do you think they'll dry by morning?" Norah asked

"Oh, I think so. I've often dried my clothes on rocks or tree branches overnight when I've been on a trip."

Norah said, shyly, "You look fine in Addison's clothes. You have the height to carry it off."

"Thanks. I sometimes wonder why I shouldn't simply adopt men's dress. It seems to suit Kerry."

"Oh, yes. I think that would become you." Norah meant her remarks to be simply flattering, but in her mind her words sounded flirtatious, and perhaps that was what she meant to be.

"I guess I'm still too conventional at heart," Abby said, but she sounded regretful.

"Well, we can enjoy them for a short while, I suppose?"

Abby looked at her, clothespin in hand for a moment, then clipped it and said, "There. That's done. Do you want to go inside and prepare for bed? You must be tired from your day."

"I'm all right. I rather like it out here in the moonlight, don't you?'

"Yes. I almost always prefer to be outdoors on a pleasant night. You're not cold, are you? Because if you—"

Abby's words were rushed and she seemed nervous, which emboldened Norah.

"I'm not cold," she said quickly.

They faced each other in the moonlight, and Abby looked at her with such tender concern, Norah was compelled to move closer to her. She stopped a few inches away from Abby, who hadn't moved back but continued to look at her intently.

Norah closed the gap and raised herself up just slightly so their mouths were level. She kissed Abby, who didn't move away and, as Norah kept their lips together, began to mimic Norah's movements with her own lips. Their kiss seemed to go on forever, until Norah broke off and waited silently to see what Abby would do or say.

Abby raised a finger to her own lips and touched them lightly, and her slight grin seemed to indicate she was amused by something. "You're full of surprises, Norah."

"And? Is that good or bad?"

"It's just you."

"Shall we go upstairs to bed?" Norah asked, then realized what that sounded like and blushed furiously. "I didn't...I mean...I don't..."

Abby laughed. "Oh, don't worry. I know what you meant."

❖

In the dark, Abby sat propped against the pillow, her mind careening like a runaway cart. She was bewildered but curious, anxious but amazed. The kiss she had shared with Norah was such a surprise on one hand, yet it seemed inevitable. The emotions it induced were nothing like she'd ever experienced. She wanted to deny what she felt, and she wanted Norah to come to her and continue what the kiss had begun. Abby was sure it was only a beginning. What came next she feared and desired in equal measure. Having Norah in her arms had banished all thought of the rest of the world. The earthquake, the backyard, even the night itself had ceased to exist. Abby never considered that the happiness, the completeness she felt when out in nature, in the woods, waiting for night to fall in the mountains would ever be duplicated by simple physical contact with another human. Yet there it was. With Norah, with Norah's touch.

The bedroom door opened and Norah entered. She stood at the foot of the bed and seemed to be waiting for Abby to speak, for some sort of permission.

"Are you well?" Norah asked in the manner one used to inquire of someone who'd been hit sharply on her head.

"I am. I believe. On one hand anyhow." She paused. She could sense the tension emanating from Norah.

"And the other hand?" Norah asked, her voice low and hesitant.

"I don't know," Abby said, honestly.

"May I come lie down?"

"Of course. This is your room too. By all means."

Norah took off her shoes and settled next to her in bed. She didn't make any further moves. She seemed to be still waiting for whatever Abby would say or do next.

"I'm not sorry I kissed you," Norah said, finally.

"I'm not sorry you did either."

"That's good to hear. I would never, ever want to hurt you or make you unhappy."

"You didn't do either. You don't—It's just, I—" Abby couldn't make sense of her thoughts well enough to put them into words. She was stuttering much as Norah had a few moments before.

"You don't know what to do or what to say?" Norah asked.

"Yes. That's quite true."

"Would it make a difference if I told you I'm in love with you?" It was not exactly a statement or a question but something in between.

"You are?" Abby was both unsurprised and deeply surprised. Scott's words came back to her mind.

"I am. I am deeply and hopelessly and profoundly in love with you."

Abby could think of nothing to say. No one had ever said such a thing to her. It seemed like she'd been handed an enormous responsibility for which she was completely unprepared.

There was just enough dim light in the room to see the outline of Norah's head but not enough to see her face, and Abby assumed Norah couldn't make out hers either. They had only their voices, but there was something else too: a current between them, an invisible connection tying them together. Was this love? Abby didn't know, but she was prepared in the spirit of scientific inquiry to try to find out.

"I see." That was an inadequate response, Abby was sure, but she was incapable of saying more.

"I won't try to push you," Norah said. "I wanted to tell you, though, that our kiss was wonderful, and I'd like to repeat it."

"Oh. Certainly." Abby immediately leaned over and kissed Norah again. Their lips stayed together much longer this time, and their limbs entwined seemingly on their own as their breaths quickened. The same mix of feelings as before returned more strongly. Abby pulled away first and stared into the dark, as though the answers to her questions lay within Norah. Perhaps they did, but she was still afraid to find out though she had no idea why she was nervous. It wasn't an unpleasant feeling; it was more like anticipation rather than anxiety.

"I-I can't go on," Abby said.

"That's all right." Norah's voice was understanding. "We probably ought to go to sleep."

"Yes. We should. Well. Good night." Abby turned away and plumped her pillow.

"Good night, Abby." Norah's reply was soft and tender.

It was only then that Abby remembered she'd meant to ask Norah about what ailed her and caused her to be so moody. She seemed to have received the answer.

❖

Norah couldn't sleep, but that was predictable, she supposed. She was proud she'd voiced her feelings and happy she'd worked up the courage to kiss Abby and at least Abby hadn't run away or ordered her to leave. That was encouraging. But she had no idea what to do next. Waiting for Abby to respond in kind seemed like a dead end. It was clear Abby had no idea what was transpiring between them.

As Abby slept peacefully next to her in bed, serenity and desire were in mortal combat in Norah's soul. Even the faint scent of soap emanating from their warm bodies was arousing. Norah wanted to toss restlessly and she wanted Abby to wake up, but if she did, Norah wasn't at all convinced that she could or should do anything further. From the open window came a faint sound of an owl, and the wind blew in, carrying the inevitable stench of fire. Norah wondered when the smell of destruction would go away and at night she would once again catch the faint tinge of salt air that let her know the ocean was near.

It was obvious she'd have to seduce Abby. If they were ever to be lovers it would be up to Norah to engineer that type of involvement, and she didn't think she had the gumption to do it. She'd let herself be led down the garden path by May, and while that had been a pleasant journey for a little while, it had quickly turned rough. Norah didn't know how to seduce anyone, and she wouldn't receive any assistance from Abby. Abby showed no sign of knowing anything about love in either of its manifestations: the emotional or the physical. She'd received Norah's kisses and declaration of love with the pleasant and composed air of someone being told what to expect for dinner.

She would just have to wait and watch to see what happened. When Abby indicated she was in love with Norah, then Norah would have to take charge. With that thought, she calmed herself enough to fall asleep.

❖

Beth watched Esther rub her hair vigorously with a towel and decided to risk Esther's wrath by asking the obvious question.

"Have you talked to Addison about marriage yet? Have you changed your mind? I mean, after you saw what happened to that man with the Red Cross, I would think—"

"No. I haven't made up my mind."

Esther didn't appear to be overly irritated, or if she was, she seemed more peeved at herself than at Beth.

Esther collected her clothes and threw them in the washtub and poured water over them as Beth waited patiently. "What the Red Cross did to that poor man was an outrage. That woman made their lack of legal ties somehow a sign that she considered that family unworthy of help. She let him go away still in anxiety and uncertainty."

"It's cruel, I agree. But what else can they do?" Beth asked, reasonably. "What if it were you looking for Add—"

"I thought of that. And I know if it were happening to me I would be beside myself." Esther violently swished the clothes in the washtub. "I don't know what I would do."

"I think you need to think of your child," Beth said with some asperity.

"I think of my child all the time, every day, Beth. How could it not be uppermost in my mind?" She pointed to her pregnant belly.

"That's not what I meant and you know that."

Esther stopped beating up her clothes and bent her head. She turned around and looked at Beth. "I want to believe that marriage wouldn't change him. But I don't know. I've seen it change men into anarchists. Ones I never would have believed would treat their women so cavalierly and condescendingly."

"That doesn't mean Addison would! You know he's a different sort of man. Besides, he's not an anarchist. He's not a political poser. He's a good man," Beth said vehemently, thinking of Addison's sadness.

"I know he's good. I love him because of it, because of who he is."

"Then why not give him what he wants and what would be good for all of you, not just the baby."

"I'll think about it," Esther said after a moment.

Beth was satisfied. That at least was progress. Addison was right: Esther was one stubborn woman. It gave her the strength to be the kind of doctor she was, but sometimes intransigence was inimical to love. That reminded her of Kerry. She was due to go back for another visit to the hospital. Probably another painful visit. Maybe if she could bring Kerry home, that would help. She would have to press Marjorie on that point. Kerry needed to be in her own home and surrounded by familiar things and people, especially Beth, and then she'd feel better and become more herself.

❖

"When I told Major Thomas you're a physician, he said we may discharge her to your care," Marjorie said.

"Oh, thank God. When may we come and fetch her?"

"Tomorrow. But Elizabeth, even if you take her home, please don't expect too much at first. I've been watching over her—"

"And I'm deeply grateful to you for that."

"I'm so fond of you two. Both of you. I wanted to do what I could, but to be realistic, Elizabeth, you have got to accept her current mental state. It may not improve for a long time, though her burn is healing."

Marjorie was never one for sentimentality or the sugarcoating of any bad news. Beth appreciated that trait, but she had to have faith that Kerry would be different if she was at home.

She and Addison drove to Letterman Hospital the next morning. Kerry stood on the large pavilion in front with Marjorie, her arm wrapped up in bandages and a dark scowl on her face. That wasn't what Beth expected would be her greeting.

They flanked Kerry on their walk to the auto.

As was his way, Addison tried to lighten the mood. "Kerry. It's wonderful to see you looking so much better."

She turned to him and her face lightened only a little. She was so pallid and thin and quiet, it was nearly a bad joke on his part.

"Yes, well. Leaving this infernal hospital is going to help. I suppose you both know nothing of what it's like to be a patient. You're on the other end of the business. I've suffered enough indignity for a lifetime at the hands of your ilk. The nurses are the worst! Bossy, my word. I knew Marjorie was a bossy shrew, but I didn't know there were many others like her." She sniffed.

Beth looked at Addison, who raised his eyebrows but only said, "We're a full house. We're entertaining Norah, Abby Eliot, and Scott, all of whom are homeless after the earthquake. We've only recently got our water service back. I'm not sure the Spring Valley Water Company won't raise their fees to pay for all the damage they incurred. Esther's been longing to see you despite our endless trials at the City and County and..." He rambled on, and Beth glanced back at Kerry every so often as they made their way home. Kerry wouldn't meet her gaze, though, and stared morosely out the window, saying nothing.

Beth said, "Scott's sleeping in the living room, and Norah and Abby are in the spare room. We're just able to scrape together enough food. The army sets up a depot point down the street, where we must wait in line. The grocers who were open can't seem to keep enough supplies in stock. Now the relief material's coming in and we're able to get more varied food stuffs."

Beth rambled on about domestic trivia as she helped Kerry up the stairs and to take off her clothes. She was appalled at how thin she was. She'd always been wiry and slim, but now she was nearly emaciated. Beth didn't know whether it was her burn that had killed her appetite or her dislike of the hospital cuisine, but whatever the reason, she'd obviously scarcely eaten anything for the few weeks she'd spent in the hospital. She, Esther, and Scott would have to put their heads together and try to conjure something to eat that would be appealing.

"May I take a look at your arm?" Beth asked.

"If you want," Kerry said dully

"My love, let's just get you settled, and then I shall take a look."

Kerry's eyes followed her as she moved around the bedroom, an action Beth had before truly enjoyed as it presaged lovemaking. But Beth didn't think that was the case at present.

Kerry's burned arm was no longer red and blistered. It was scabbed over, but it was cracked in a few places, and underneath, angry red skin glowed. Beth estimated that fifty percent of her arm had received a severe second-degree burn.

She used linseed ointment and a saline/cocaine solution soaked in gauze to clean the burn, though she judged it best to leave it uncovered to hasten the healing.

"How does it feel?" she asked Kerry.

"Hurts."

"How much? A little? Middling? Bad?"

"It's bad, Bethy. It's so bad. I don't remember a time when I didn't hurt." Kerry's bright brown eyes usually glowed with love, but since she'd been burned, her only expression had been one of pain and hurt. At that moment, she widened her eyes in a pleading expression. Marjorie's warning about morphine played at low volume in the back of Beth's mind.

"I'll give you a shot," Beth said.

As she depressed the plunger on the syringe, Kerry's expression changed to dreamy and her eyes clouded. "Good" was all she said, and she lay back on her pillow without another word.

CHAPTER FIFTEEN

A bby preferred not having much time to think. Presently, she had far too much spare time, and that time opened up space for so much speculation about the future. For now, she was at loose ends and had three seemingly unsolvable problems. She was unemployed and had no idea when she might be again at work for the San Francisco Natural History Society. She'd written Sellars and a couple of others on the board of governors but had received no responses. She had no place to live. Despite assurances from Esther and Addison, she was uneasy about being a non-paying guest in their home. At the moment, her only choices were leaving the City to stay in someone else's home for an undefined period of time or refugeeing in one of the camps. Neither seemed to be a good idea. At the commune at least she was close to Norah, which was her third problem. She had no idea where their interactions were leading. Their two kisses, while wonderful, were unsettling. She had no idea what she felt for Norah. She was quite fond of her, but did it go further than that? And if it did, what then? She'd never been tied in such a way to any other person. She was beginning to feel a responsibility to Norah, a wish to make her happy, to not hurt her, to be with her.

They'd spent much time at the refugee camp, and Abby was relieved when she became more practiced at dealing with the refugees and their problems. Norah's encouraging smiles and their close proximity made her happy. But under Norah's smile and behind her professional detachment when they were at work lurked the unknown. Sometimes she caught Norah looking at her, questions in her gaze, watchfulness and what Abby recognized as longing, and it intrigued her.

She'd once again made the trek from Fillmore Street to the post office on Mission Street to see if she'd received any mail, and as before, the walk gave her too much time to think. But she had a choice between being in her head or focusing on the destroyed City. Workmen were beginning to clear the rubble, but that process would take an extremely long time. Abby ached with grief at the state of San Francisco and thought of leaving, to go where or do what she wasn't sure. But then there was Norah.

To Abby's great surprise, the postal clerk handed her two letters, and one bore the return address of Howard Sellars. At last, some news of the Society! Perhaps they'd set up operations temporarily somewhere else and she could join their efforts.

She forced herself to read slowly. After the preliminary and empty expressions of hope for her good health, she focused on the true point of the letter.

So after careful review and much consideration, to my deep regret, I must inform you that the Society no longer has need of your services. Our staff is reduced to the bare bones. I wish you luck in whatever you choose to pursue. You may call at the Mechanics Bank on Market Street, present your bona fides, and draw a money order equivalent to three months of salary—to wit, the sum of $150. Thereafter we may consider your relationship with the Society as severed.

And it was signed by Sellars, only Sellars. She reread the letter, her fury mounting. That despicable toad had taken it upon himself to fire her unilaterally. It was unbelievable. She scrunched the letter in her fist, then hastily straightened it out. She would need to save it. In spite of desperately wanting to take some immediate action, she forced herself to calm down and tore open the other letter.

This was a much different and far more welcome missive, from her acquaintance and host in the Shasta/Trinity area, Arthur Massey. He wrote expressing horror at the events in San Francisco and inviting her out to his ranch for a visit if she needed to get away or was interested in another collecting trip up Mount Shasta.

Abby slipped both letters into her bag and left the post office to walk back to the commune. She couldn't quite bring herself to call it home. It was *not* her home, no matter what Norah said. The invitation from Mr. Massey couldn't have come at a more opportune time. She could get away from San Francisco's troubles and her own. She'd have to jerry-rig collection materials or go buy some. And that reminded her: she would be getting a cheque for her Colorado rents sometime soon. She wouldn't, under any circumstances, cash the Society's or, rather, Sellars's money order. She'd do without. She had some money saved, and she had income and very few expenses at the moment. She'd tried to give Addison some money and he'd flatly refused.

She would write other Society members and solicit their opinions regarding Sellars's decision and proceed accordingly. In the meantime she would take a short collecting trip.

❖

In the darkened room, Kerry lay motionless in bed. She was only slightly aware of the passage of time or the day of the week or even the time of day. The ceiling, the night table, the window with its curtain drawn were in her view, if not in her total consciousness.

The comfort of her own bed and of Beth sleeping next to her at night let only a tiny glimmer of light into the blackness of her soul. Beth was more like a stranger than her lover. They conversed, Beth kissed her cheek and patted her hair, but that meant nothing to her because Beth always left again the next morning

Her life as it had been was over. The Palace Hotel was gone, the restaurant was gone, and she had no reason to go on living. She didn't think Beth would ever view her as anything other than a perpetual patient. That was how Beth behaved toward her, and that was just as well. Kerry was damaged beyond repair both physically and emotionally. Beth likely would never look at her in the same way. The small cuts and burns she'd acquired as a cook were nothing compared to her current state. Her left arm was a solid mass of scab and scar tissue from her hand to her shoulder.

Would she ever be able to use it again, either to embrace her lover or to cook food? She was a right-handed person, but her work demanded both arms and hands. She lifted her arm and flexed her fingers. The movement felt stiff and strange as that action traveled up the tendons of her arm and pushed against the scabs. She was still in pain though it hurt less. She desired the morphine more for its ability to render her unable to think than for its painkilling properties. She was a useless lump of flesh languishing in bed.

When would Beth return? Kerry didn't miss her, but Beth could administer the oblivion of the drug she craved. Kerry turned over in the bed on her good side and stared at the opposite wall, trying not to think.

❖

"You're leaving?" Norah asked, alarmed.

"Yes, when I can. I must wait to get some money and to write Mister and Missus Massey. I have to figure some way of carrying any specimens I may collect since I've lost all my collection equipment."

It was Abby and Norah's turn to find and prepare supper for everyone. With everyone so busy, it wasn't fair that any one person shoulder responsibility for feeding the household. They'd walked to the army food depot and gotten some live chickens and were currently sitting on the back porch plucking them. Norah had watched in awe as Abby had expertly twisted their necks. They had to finish the process so they could roast them. A few potatoes and some carrots would complete the meal. Norah didn't mind sharing the task with Abby. That is, she hadn't minded until Abby had started talking about her upcoming trip.

"How, er, long will you be gone?"

Abby turned over her chicken and ripped the feathers out of its belly. "Don't know. A few days or a week. Whatever is wrong, Norah? You sound unhappy." Abby's tone was brisk and no-nonsense.

"I just didn't expect you to leave."

"Well, I'm weary of the City. I become unsettled and restless if I've not been out in the wilderness for a while. Besides, I have a lot to think about."

There was a pause as Norah waited to see if Abby would continue talking, but she didn't. "And what are you thinking about? If I could be so bold as to inquire?"

"I had a letter from one of the board of governors advising me I no longer had a position with the Society."

"Oh, my word. That's awful."

"It won't stand, but I can't do anything about it at the moment. That's another reason I'm taking a trip."

"But can you fight it?"

"I believe so, but not at present. Oh, here, give me that chicken and I'll finish her."

Abby took the chicken Norah had been working on out of her hands. Norah supposed she'd become impatient since Norah had stopped plucking.

"Are you not troubled by this unforeseen event?" Norah asked, curious as to Abby's apparent nonchalance.

"I suppose, but there's not much I can do."

Norah didn't say anything more, and Abby must have sensed her withdrawal and said, abruptly, "What's the matter?"

Norah's face grew hot. She was embarrassed at how bad she felt that Abby wouldn't invite her to go along on her trip or even discuss this troublesome letter. Norah thought that their closeness would induce Abby to share more with her, but evidently not.

"Nothing," Norah said, aware that it was perfectly obvious that wasn't true.

"Nothing, my foot. You became very quiet all of a sudden, and you haven't moved a muscle. Tell me."

"I'll just miss you. That's all."

"I thought you couldn't leave the City. I wasn't even going to ask. Am I wrong?"

"No, you're right. But it would have been nice if you had asked me. I would like to be with you on one of your trips. Though I wouldn't be much help, I'm afraid."

"Oh, but you would!" Abby wiped the chicken feathers off her own hands and clasped both of Norah's. "I'd love to have you with me!"

"You would?"

"Oh, Norah, I'm just an old hermit in a way. I've never had a friend like you before, and I don't know how to handle myself or what to really say to you. Forgive me?"

"Oh, yes. I do. I wish I could go. Very much. But you're right. I can't leave the City just now." Norah was relieved just a little. Abby wasn't as entirely cavalier as she thought, but still she talked as though they were *just* friends.

"I won't be gone long, and I'll miss you."

"I'll miss you too."

They locked eyes, but just at that moment they heard voices in the house, and with a small hand squeeze, Abby arose and went to greet their companions.

❖

Beth sat in a chair next to their bed, where Kerry lay with her back toward her as she had done in the hospital. "But why won't you come down to dinner? Everyone is glad you're home and wants to see you."

"I'm not ready for company yet. And I'm not hungry," Kerry said with an air of finality that infuriated Beth, though she didn't want to show it.

"I see. Well, I'll bring something up for you later."

Kerry grunted.

Beth didn't know what else to say so she left the bedroom, troubled and disappointed. Kerry had been home for a couple of days, but she was no better than she had been in the hospital. Well, she was physically better, so it wasn't that. It was her mind. Beth was helpless before her tremendous sadness. She had no idea how to comfort Kerry, and nothing seemed to work, except the shot of painkiller she gave her twice a day.

In reality, that seemed to be all Kerry cared about. Beth knew that dependence upon this remedy was a dead end. Back when she was an army nurse, officers would simply drag their recalcitrant troops out of the hospital as soon as the duty surgeon said they were ready. They would have to deal with the consequences as the unfortunate soldiers rid themselves of their opiate cravings.

It was ugly and distressing, and Beth hoped it wouldn't come to that for Kerry. She wasn't sure she could endure to see Kerry suffer like that. She thought of asking Esther or Addison for help, but they were so taken up with their own difficulties and dealing with the refugee problems, she didn't want to add to their burdens. Beth had to take care of Kerry herself. That was her purpose, and no one else should have to bear that responsibility.

The day Abby left for the north, Norah said good-bye to her early before she left for the refugee camp. She struggled to put a brave face on, but it wasn't easy. Abby was cheerful and good humored but appeared to be entirely unaffected by their impending parting, which was most disappointing. Norah would have to endure the separation, but Abby was clearly not going to have any trouble with it. She was as independent as ever, Norah saw, in spite of the kisses they'd exchanged and their secret whispered conversations in bed at night. Abby was not going to be sweetly clingy or sad, no matter how much Norah might want her to be.

At the front door, Abby bent and gave her a nice kiss on the cheek, but it failed to placate Norah. She forced a smile and a wave, but her heart was sore. It wasn't the actual separation, though, that was painful, but more the emotional distance that Abby put between them. In addition to her sorrow at their separation, Norah berated herself for her cowardice. She couldn't make any effort to push their physical relationship forward. Had May made it impossible for her to ever truly love anyone again? It seemed so, and that added another layer to Norah's misery. If only Abby would be more forthcoming and she could be more courageous.

Norah turned away from the door and tried to quash her sad thoughts. She, Esther, and Beth were expected at the refugee hospital very soon. They gathered in the kitchen to wrap some food for their day and drink coffee.

Esther fixed both Norah and Beth with a skeptical stare. "I've never seen such long faces. I wonder if some of our patients are more joyful than the two of you. Whatever is the trouble?" She looked from one to the other, eyebrow cocked. "I wouldn't even trade my aching back for whatever ails either of you." She arched her back, her hands on her hips for emphasis. She was nearly six months pregnant.

Norah was a bit ashamed of herself. She was so caught up with Abby she paid no attention to her old friend and had not even asked her how she felt for quite a while. But while she pondered this, Beth spoke up.

"We must make haste. It's getting late." Norah was surprised at how terse the usually serene Beth sounded. Then she realized it must be Kerry. Beth hadn't truly been herself since the earthquake. But if Beth didn't wish to discuss it, Norah didn't think it was her business to try to force a confession from her. They retrieved the two-horse carriage they rented and rode to the Park in silence, the reins in Beth's hands.

Their first order of business was to see the army commander for the overnight reports.

"Good morning, ladies. I hope you've had sufficient rest. The duty surgeon"—he referred to the army doctor who'd spent the night at the hospital—"says he has six possible cases of typhoid and wants them examined immediately."

Norah felt the familiar dread at the pit of her stomach, along with a sense of excitement. It was always this way. With infectious cases came the thrill of diagnosis, then treatment, but always the threat to doctors and nurses themselves. She recalled that Esther had suffered a bout of bubonic plague several years previously, after being coughed on by a patient. It was important to be vigilant about cleanliness. As they hurried toward the tent with the infectious cases, she was thankful that, at least, the urgency of her work could help supplant thoughts of Abby.

Norah began rounds while Beth and Esther conferred with the surgeon. She heard raised voices and, curious, stopped and returned to the entrance to the tent, where the three doctors stood just outside. They were still within earshot of the patients, but most were so ill, they wouldn't care what the doctors were discussing. Two of the first four people that Norah examined presented with possible typhoid symptoms, but she wasn't ready to make a definitive diagnosis until Esther made her examination. Esther, Beth, and the surgeon came back in the tent and went to the man that Norah thought might be one of the typhoid cases. She joined the three doctors, who were deep in discussion.

Esther picked up his chart and read, "Fever, headache, delirium, temperature 104 at three a.m. Vomiting. It seems clear to me that this is potentially typhoid." She let the chart drop.

Beth asked, "Has the army laid in sufficient supplies of quinine?"

"Perhaps," the army man said. "But we'll want to be sure before—"

"We can't wait," Beth said. "We need to begin treatment immediately if we even suspect typhoid. We can greatly reduce the mortality rate if we do. I've, we've—" she gestured to Esther, "had great success at the City and County Hospital."

The army doctor cleared his throat. To Norah, he seemed very uncomfortable, either because he was dealing with women or civilians or both, she wasn't sure. Knowing how confident both Esther and Beth were, she didn't envy him his position.

"I'm not sure. We will need to see where precisely it is needed and by whom."

Beth said, "You're not at war right at the moment, and we have a camp full of homeless people. Also, it's likely we will see many more cases, given the sanitary conditions. Even with our best efforts, people are digging their own latrines near their camps instead of using the public latrines, so there's the closeness of latrines to their cooking and to open containers of milk, well…We cannot police everyone. You are going to have to give us every single tab of quinine and Wyeth's bronchitis pills you've got.'

"Eh, Doctor? Suppose we just confirm—"

Beth was very close to the army doctor, and she leaned forward, causing him to step back. "Are you mad? We cannot wait for pathologists' tests. We have to act *now*." She almost shouted the last word.

Esther put a restraining hand on her arm. "Doctor? Please lower your voice."

Beth turned to Esther, her fury unabated. "What is the matter with you? Tell this idiot what he has to do."

The army surgeon's brow furrowed. Norah was shocked. She'd never heard Beth speak like that to anyone.

"Doctor?" Esther said, her tone crisp and formal. "Let us discuss this calmly."

"I don't have to discuss this any further," Beth said. "I've made my opinion known." She stalked off, leaving Norah and Esther mystified.

"Doctor," Esther said to Norah. "Let us attempt to get as an accurate assessment of the number of potential victims as we can, and then we'll requisition drugs." She looked at the army surgeon, who nodded, looking relieved.

"My replacement will be on duty shortly, and he can have the commander order the proper medicines brought down from Letterman where they will have a better idea of supplies on hand and where, besides this camp, they might be needed."

"I appreciate your help, Major. Doctor, let us proceed," Esther said to Norah.

"And Doctor Hammond?" Norah asked Esther.

"She may return to duty when she feels able," Esther said, and Norah noted that there wasn't a shred of tenderness in her voice. Clearly she thought Beth's behavior was inappropriate. They had no time to dwell on that, though, as they had a dozen patients to examine.

❖

A few hours later, Norah went in search of Beth and found her near the bandstand. She was sitting on a bench, her head down and her hands folded. The day wasn't half over, and Norah was already exhausted. She wanted Beth to return to help them.

"May I sit down?" she asked, pointing at the space next to Beth.

Beth shrugged. Norah took that to mean she was indifferent, so she seated herself, arranging her dress and sighing. It was good to be off her feet. The bandstand was away from the main refugee camp, and one could almost believe that Golden Gate Park wasn't chock full of homeless citizens. Birds were chirping and flowers bloomed everywhere. The only thing missing was a band tuning up for a performance of John Philip Sousa marches. The bandstand had suffered some damage, and crumbled pieces of it were lying around, but if one could overlook that, the scene was normal.

"We have a tentative count of typhoid cases. We've segregated them, and two of the most experienced nurses are tending to them.

We'll need to help out though." Norah meant that the doctors would have to perform some nursing tasks, especially bathing the patients and handling bedpans. The typhoid patients must have absolute rest. They couldn't be allowed up to go to the latrine, even if they felt as though they could handle it. Norah hoped the Red Cross volunteers might lend a hand as well.

Beth said nothing. She stared dully at her shoes.

"Beth. What's the matter?"

"Nothing."

"That is clearly untrue," Norah said. "Look. We've not known each other that long, but maybe that's just as well."

Beth looked at her curiously.

"I meant maybe you could confide in me more easily. Is it Kerry?" Norah asked. She knew instantly what the answer to her question was because Beth shifted and looked away.

"Yes," Beth said, but stopped speaking. She was not disposed to make this conversation easy. She was likely ashamed of her earlier outburst, which had been so unlike her.

"Well, whatever the matter is, it's serious because it's affecting your work."

Beth finally met her gaze, her eyes teary. "I behaved abominably. Esther very much dislikes those sorts of conflicts. She's probably angry with me."

"She's concerned about you. We both are."

"It's evident I must pull myself together."

"But you must talk about what ails you."

Beth stood up then and paced a few feet, then turned. "I have to handle it myself. Everyone is too busy and overworked. Kerry isn't receptive to me anyhow, so I doubt she'd listen to you or Esther." She spoke this last sentence with such despair and bitterness, Norah was dismayed.

"But she's on the mend, is she not?"

"She is. But she won't get up, and she barely speaks to me."

"She's still suffering the mental effects from her injury?"

"Yes."

Norah said, "One of the doctors at Bellevue studied people who had severe injuries, and he thought their minds were affected far more than we realize. When someone who's recovering physically seems unhappy and distraught, it's because of the injury."

"What do we do?"

"That I can't say for sure, but certainly getting her to get back into some sort of normal life would help."

"Ha," Beth said. "Little likelihood of that anytime soon."

"I'm sorry I can't be of more help."

"Never mind. Thank you for listening."

When Beth left, Norah remained seated on the bench. She was sorry for Beth and Kerry's troubles, but at least listening to Beth had offered a temporary distraction from missing Abby and brooding about what would become of them.

Chapter Sixteen

Much later, Esther and Norah prepared dinner and talked about the day. They could hear Beth playing piano in the parlor. They'd shooed her into the house and wouldn't let her help with the food.

"When do you think we can start cooking indoors again?" Norah asked. "At this rate, we're all going to have dysentery before too long."

Esther laughed grimly and swatted a fly away from the plate of potatoes. "I don't know, but I hope it's soon. How long will Abby be away?"

Norah was startled by the change in subject and then despondent at the mention of Abby's name. She tried to speak serenely though. "Oh, a week at the most."

"And how are you faring?" Esther asked, shrewdly.

"I'm quite well." Norah lied to save face.

"I see," Esther said, sounding skeptical. "I believe you're as well as Beth, who's not well at all." She looked heavenward and sighed.

"Oh, I know." Norah was happy to have the focus taken off her problems.

"The two of you are like mules. You insist that you can handle your troubles." Esther was one to talk about mulishness.

"What about you?" Norah was somewhat incensed at Esther's lack of confidence in her.

"What of me? I've no troubles."

"That's not true. You're six months pregnant and don't want to get married. I don't see that as a trivial issue, do you?"

"Not at all. But with our current situation, we can hardly focus on our petty female dilemmas."

"I agree. My worry may be a petty female dilemma, as you say, but I'm not sure if Beth's is."

"Well, that may be true, but it's up to Beth to come to us for help when she needs it. We must wait and see."

"I gave her a suggestion I think she'll take, but yes, as you say, we must wait and see," Norah said.

Esther looked back at Norah skeptically, but since Norah didn't want to breach Beth's confidence, she merely smiled.

Norah returned to stirring the soup, unconvinced that she could keep her attention on the matters at hand. Her thoughts were often far away with Abby, wherever she was. As much as Norah tried not to, she couldn't help thinking that Abby had left on her trip because she was trying to get away from their situation and away from her.

❖

The flower was out of reach. It was a particularly stunning specimen of Wilkins' Bellflower, perched up on a ledge across a small stream, just beyond Abby's grasp. Abby looked around as though someone might magically appear to render assistance, but there was no one. The majestic silence of Mount Shasta was hers alone, and she mostly preferred that. Yet today it would be better to have some gentleman with long legs and longer arms who could retrieve the prize she sought.

The Wilkins' Bellflower seemed to mock her from its fragrant, grass-encrusted home. She needed that specimen. It was a very rare flower, superior to the one she'd retrieved the previous year from near Tuolomne Meadow. She needn't examine it minutely to know that. She could tell from afar that it was larger, more robust, its purple more vibrant, its leaves plumper. Abby thought for a moment, then set off, poking her walking stick into the ground emphatically. She walked along the stream until she found a spot she could ford, then backtracked and approached her Bellflower from above. She lay flat upon the ground and was able to pluck the prize.

She shook it out and carefully put it in her satchel between two pieces of parchment. Sitting on a small rock, she noted the date, time, and location, as well as the Latin name and common name of her acquisition: Wilkins' Bellflower, *Campanula wilkinsiana*.

Back at her camp, she built a fire and made a simple meal of coffee, bread, and cured beef jerky. By the light of her campfire, she wrote the day's notes into her journal.

Most productive day. I found fine examples of Wilkins' Bellflower and Mountain Lady Slipper. The Harris tract is a superb spot for collecting Cantellids. The weather is cool but comfortable. About 55 degrees, with light southerly wind. Ground dry and wood abundant. Will return tomorrow to the Massey ranch.

She banked the fire and made herself comfortable in her bedroll with her satchel as a pillow. She would go back to the City and its sorrows after an overnight stay with the Masseys. But it wasn't all sorrow; there was Norah. Norah's lovely, sad face appeared in her inner vision. On her ride up into the mountains from the ranch, she'd thought of Norah almost without being aware of doing so. Fragments of conversation drifted into her mind. She even replayed their kisses. The touch of their lips was sweet and alluring. Kissing Norah reminded Abby of how it felt to drink from a cold stream after a long, hot, strenuous hike.

It occurred to her that she wanted Norah here with her. She missed her, missed her voice, her presence. They'd been sharing a bed for a few weeks, so Abby had come to expect her there and, even more surprising, to want her there. She'd never felt that way about anyone before. No one but Norah had ever had such a profound effect on her.

Abby turned on her side, but no Norah was sleeping next to her, and that saddened her and called up other more unfamiliar emotions. She didn't know how to describe them or even what to call them. Unlike her flowers, they evaded classification so she could not put them in nicely labeled boxes.

Abby was certain of only one thing: the answers to her questions lay with Norah. Norah said she loved her. For some reason she thought of the letter from Sellars then, quickly followed by her memory of the conversation with Norah. She wasn't sure why this was important, but she was certain that telling Norah about it had both been helpful to her and important to Norah—a vital piece of information about Abby's mood and life that she felt compelled to share. She had gained no great insight or profound advice, but somehow, the act of sharing it was important. It seemed related to her missing Norah. Was this love? She had no one to ask, no one but Norah, that is.

❖

Kerry forced herself to sit up, then to stand up, and finally to put on some pants and a shirt. She thrust her feet into her shoes and wandered downstairs to the kitchen to look for something to drink. Her burned arm throbbed dully. She shook it lightly, but the ache was unchanging.

The house was empty, which was an odd circumstance considering how many people actually lived there, but it was the middle of the day and they were all away at their various occupations. She was totally alone. She used to have an occupation as well, a fairly consuming one too. But that was gone. Even if her arm still worked properly, she presently had no work she needed to do. The hotel was gone, burned to the ground, the restaurant along with it. There was literally nothing for her to do. She couldn't even cook anything because there was no food in the house, and the household members had to find it and then bring it home each day. She knew this only because Beth told her. She was not part of the conversation, nor did she wish to be.

It was paradoxical: she was deeply lonely, but she had no desire for company unless it was Beth, and even then she could barely face Beth, knowing that she was unable to truly be a partner to her because she had no job or occupation. She couldn't make any money. She was useless, worse than useless. Beth never referred to her situation but would only pat her shoulder or stroke her cheek and look at her in that loving way she had.

Kerry had recently blurted out, "It's gone, Beth. All gone. We're never going be able to save money if I don't work."

And Beth had responded, "Shhh. Right now you must get well and not concern yourself with that."

Kerry rummaged through the kitchen cabinets. She was, in fact, physically better, but she was uneasy and restless. On one hand, she was relieved she would have no more morphine, but on the other she craved the oblivion it brought.

She opened one of the lower cabinets and found a half-full bottle of whisky. She stared at it for a full minute, then took it out and held it in her hand, reading the label. She yanked out the cork and smelled it.

She sat at the kitchen table and set the bottle in front of her. A tiny, distant warning sounded in her brain, but a louder, bigger, more-insistent voice squelched it. The voice said, "You're in pain, you're in dire straits, and a small sip or two won't hurt you. It'll make you feel better." That soothing, agreeable voice helped Kerry focus. She found a glass and poured a couple of inches of whiskey into it, drank it straight down, and in a moment, warmth and peace welled up inside her. She wiped her mouth, put the bottle away, swiped the glass with a rag, and put it back in its place. Then she went outside, sat on the front-porch swing, and watched the street activity on Fillmore for the rest of the afternoon, thinking of nothing at all.

When Norah arrived home in the early evening, Abby was sitting on the front porch of the commune. She attempted to keep herself cool and collected, but she wanted to run up the steps and throw her arms around Abby. When Abby saw her, she stood up with a huge grin and hugged Norah tightly for a long time. Norah's body stirred. They stayed in their embrace for what seemed like forever, but it wasn't nearly long enough. Norah grew self-conscious and stepped back so she could look at Abby.

She appeared well, relaxed and happy, with a bit more color in her face.

"So you're back," she said, realizing she sounded idiotic, but she was trying to cover her excitement.

"Yes, I am, and happy to be. Though I sense nothing much is changed in the City?"

"Well. I suppose in some ways we are still the same. Some of the refugees are leaving the Park, though, and that's a welcome development."

"And you, Norah? How are you?" Abby asked, searching her face.

Abby's scrutiny made her stutter. "I, eh. I'm well. Thanks." Then they were engulfed by the other members of the commune, who wanted to greet Abby and hear about her trip. At dinner, Norah was happy to stay quiet as Abby laughed and talked.

In their bedroom, Abby unpacked the few items she had taken with her. "I lost all my camping gear to the quake, but the Masseys lent me some."

At the word "camping," Norah shuddered. It was yet another reminder of how different they were. Norah sat on the bed watching Abby at her tasks. She was neat, efficient, unhurried. Norah was on edge waiting for Abby to say what? She wasn't sure. That she missed her? That she was glad to be back? Both?

They seemed always in a kind of suspended animation with one another. Nothing was defined, nothing was decided. They moved neither forward or backward but existed as a planet and moon revolving about one another, though which was the planet and which the moon, Norah wasn't sure, yet she was afraid that she was the moon condemned to revolve around the planet.

Norah blamed their stasis on the earthquake. It had made everyone uneasy, as though something horrible might happen at any moment. Members of the commune moved from one day to the next or one thing to the next without any introspection or question or plan. She supposed that made sense when a couple of unexpected but cataclysmic minutes on a Wednesday morning threw routine life into utter chaos.

Perhaps all Norah wanted was some sort of certainty, something to depend on in an uncertain and unstable world. She simply wanted to know if Abby loved her. Sometimes she thought so, but other times she thought not, such as when Abby had nonchalantly left for the north on her trip.

"I guess it was good to get away from what's left of the City?"

Abby didn't answer right away because she was checking her stack of pressed plants. Norah was almost irritated but didn't want to show it.

"It was. I found the lack of soot in the air and the presence of green plants and trees and clean outdoor smells refreshing and soothing." She fell silent. And Norah waited for what she sensed was more but Abby didn't find easy to say. She was on tenterhooks but wanted to be patient.

"I missed you. I missed everyone. God knows, you can't live cheek by jowl with people and not become fond of them. But it was you I missed most of all." She raised her eyes from where she'd been looking distractedly at the quilt.

She sat down next to Norah and took her hand. Norah stopped breathing and concentrated on Abby's warm, smooth palm as she cradled her hand.

Abby seemed to hesitate. "Norah. I don't know what I'm feeling. It's strange, unprecedented for me, anyhow." She laughed quietly. "You could say humans are far more complicated than flowers."

Norah almost snorted at *that* obvious observation, but she kept quiet.

"Most of the time when I'm out collecting, my mind is a blessed blank. I think only of the necessary details of my daily life. Collect my specimens, preserve them. Make a fire, cook something to eat, and go to sleep. Arise the next morning and do the same all over. But not this time."

Norah searched Abby's face for what she didn't know. She held her breath.

"When I was not actively occupied with my work or some necessary camping task, I thought only of you."

"I think about you all the time, except, as you say, when I have to focus on something else. It's been this way for me for a long time," Norah said almost in a whisper.

Abby looked at her quizzically.

"I...I, uh, wanted to tell you the night we dined together, the night before the earthquake, but I was a coward. I wanted to tell you then that I was in love with you."

"I see."

In Norah's mind, that was an entirely unsatisfactory response, and she grew irritated. "I feel it. Tell me you didn't feel it too!'

"Oh, Norah. I don't know what I feel. I don't know what we are to each other. It's out of the realm of my experience or understanding."

"I think you love me. I think you do feel it." Norah was afraid she was being presumptuous, but she didn't care.

Abby stared at her for a long time. "Kiss me again then. Kiss me—"

Norah didn't waste a second but kissed her hard and with much more feeling than she had before. It wasn't a tentative, soft, dry kiss; it was a passionate, demanding kiss. Abby returned it, and they fell on the bed, their bodies moving together. Norah opened her mouth a little, and their teeth clacked. Norah gently bit and nibbled Abby's lip. She dared to press her thigh between Abby's legs just a little. Miraculously, Abby not only didn't withdraw, but she responded. Her body warmed, and her breaths became ragged.

Norah turned them over so that she was on top of Abby. She left off kissing her mouth and kissed her throat and under her ear, the line of her jaw. Abby made a little sound that Norah couldn't interpret, but she decided to keep going. She lowered the strap of Abby's vest and kissed the top of her breast and her shoulder. She reached under the vest and caressed her breast.

Abby abruptly stopped kissing and rolled away from her. "Wait," she said.

She sat up, her shoulders heaving.

Norah followed suit and sat beside her once again. She put an arm around her. Fighting her frustration, she asked gently, "What's wrong?"

"I think I have to go more slowly. I'm sorry. I know this must distress you."

Norah stroked her hair and her cheek. "Abby, we'll go as slowly as you want. I don't wish to frighten you." She clamored for touch and for release but she tried to ignore her need.

Abby turned and said, fervently, "Oh, I'm not frightened. Not exactly. It's just the rush of emotion, the complicated feelings both in my body and my mind." She smiled then to show all was well.

Norah was greatly relieved and remembered how she felt the first time with May. It had been so new and so frightening. She could be patient. She owed it to Abby, and her forbearance would pay off in the long run, she was sure. Whatever her other faults, May had at least been an extraordinarily good seductress, and Norah took those lessons to heart. Their joy would come in time, and she would have to be the one to engineer it, but she had to be careful. And patient.

She pushed a strand of hair away from Abby's face. "Very well. More slowly."

They sat on the side of the bed together, and Norah took deep breaths to calm herself. She stole a glance at Abby, who was looking off into the distance.

"I want to talk with you about something," Abby said. She was still reeling from the feel of Norah's kisses, but her breathing had settled, though she was still unnaturally alert, as though something had been about to happen but she'd interrupted it. She wanted to distract herself, and it seemed as good a time as any to ask for Norah's help with her dilemma about Sellars's letter.

The house had recently undergone a temporary repair of their chimney so that lighting was again permitted. Abby found one of the house's gas lamps and lit it so they could read. Their faces were ghostly and shadowed in the gaslight, but it was a gift after having had nothing but moonlight to see by for so many weeks.

She unfolded the letter and read it aloud to Norah. When she was done, Norah made no comment, seeming to wait for what Abby would say.

"I don't know what to do," she said, and that sentence sounded strange to her. She doubted if she'd ever actually uttered those words before. "I need your help."

"Do they truly want you to leave the Society?"

"There's no 'they' really. I don't think Sellars consulted any of the other directors. He doesn't like me and doesn't care for botany, so he sees this as a good time to be rid of me."

"If it's only Sellars, then, I don't think you ought to worry but instead find your other colleagues and speak with them."

Abby scrunched the letter in her fist, tossed it to the side, and threw her arms around Norah. "Yes, that's it. Thank you so much!"

"It's nothing, truly—"

"It's everything and I'm truly grateful. I don't know if I should sign this paper. I'm not in the least interested in giving up my employment at the Society."

"Don't sign it," Norah said, flatly. "He can't make you, can he?"

"No. He can't. I expect once the Society members can manage to find a new home and we can take up our routine operations, they'll have a board meeting and I can see what the full board has to say."

"It's your salary that's due you, isn't it? But it's meant as a severance?"

"Yes. Most definitely."

"Can you avoid cashing it and just wait to talk to the others?" Norah raised her eyebrows meaningfully.

"Yes. Again, thank you. I mean it."

Norah's grin, winning and tender, gave Abby a warm sensation.

"But I didn't do a thing, Abby dear. You knew the answer to your question."

"I may have, but it seemed prudent to talk to someone about it. It's also a great relief, as I did think about it while I was at Mount Shasta."

"You said you were thinking of me." Norah's voice was teasing.

"I was thinking of both. Thoughts of you were far more pleasant."

"That's good to know. Are you ready for sleep?" Norah asked, though it seemed another question altogether was lurking under that query.

"Yes. Let's go to sleep."

They settled under the covers. Sometime in the middle of the night, Abby woke up to find she had moved close to Norah, whose soft breathing in her sleep rustled her hair. This calmed her, and she fell back asleep feeling warm and peaceful.

"Kerry, dearest, you must at least try to get out and about a bit. Take a short walk, breathe some fresh air. Move about. You were cooped up in the hospital for several weeks and—"

"I don't care to do any of that, Beth, so please stop asking me. My arm hurts abominably."

"I know, love. I've some aspirin and—"

"Oh, bother. Never mind. You don't have the least idea how I feel. Stop treating me so poorly."

"Treating you poorly?" Beth knew that wasn't true, but she didn't wish to start an argument. Kerry had been grievously wounded, and Beth couldn't know the full extent of how that still affected her. Her anger and petulance were understandable. Beth sat down next to her on their bed and patted Kerry's arm, but Kerry made an exasperated sound and turned over onto her good arm, her back to Beth.

"All right," she said. "I'll come back a little later."

Chapter Seventeen

B eth watched Scott watch his friend Corporal Ames bring in some more refugee patients for them to see. The initial trauma of the earthquake was long over, and these days, they faced only the routine human ills folks had always suffered other than the threat of disease brought on from overcrowding. The corporal, whose first name was John, seemed to be recruiting patients just so he could come see Scott.

It was an amusing, flirtatious dance they'd undertaken, and Beth was inclined to be tolerant because she was so happy that Scott was so much more himself than he'd been in a very long time. His separation from Whit had done him a lot of good. Beth didn't even care that Corporal Ames kept them busy by bringing patients if he made Scott happy.

"I'll take this young lady," Scott said jovially, referring to a woman who was anything but young but was charmed by his calling her such. He went to the partition of the tent and into the next section, beaming over his shoulder at both Beth and Corporal Ames. Beth could hear him murmur to his patient.

"Tell me, madam. What ails you today that I may address?"

Beth turned back to the corporal, whose hand rested on the shoulder of yet another grubby little boy from one of the poor refugee families. Under the dirt on his face, he looked scared, but Beth called up her own brand of charm, and soon he was chattering and distracted as she looked at a nasty infection on his hand.

The corporal stuck his head back into the tent. "Excuse me, Doctor Hammond. Someone's looking for Doctor Wilton. Is he available?"

Beth stood up and put her hand on her young patient's back and steered him toward the exit. "Tell your mom and dad to give you one of these pills every day, and then come back here each morning so I can look at your hand." He'd been stoic as she lanced his wound and only looked away from the spurt of pus. She watched the boy walk off and then turned to Corporal Ames and gave a start. Whit was standing at his side.

"Hello, Beth," he said in a friendly manner.

"Whit. It's good to see you looking so well." She shook hands with him rather than hug him, which would have been her normal reaction. She was angry with him on Scott's behalf and wasn't pleased to see him appear when Scott seemed to have finally recovered from his desertion and moved on with his life. She was afraid that Whit's return would reinstate his influence on Scott and no good would come of that.

"Thank you, Corporal Ames. I'll take Doctor Ellsworth to Doctor Wilton." Beth didn't want the corporal to attend this meeting. The young soldier hesitated but must have read her expression because he gave a quick salute and left.

"Scott. Someone here to see you!" she called.

"I'll be done presently," he said.

"Let me take you to our rest area," Beth said to Whit.

"How are you all surviving? The ride uptown from the ferry building was, well, it's horrific."

"It's been difficult but we're fine. As you see, there are thousands of homeless citizens here in Golden Gate Park and elsewhere. Compared to them, we're in the lap of luxury."

Whit rolled his eyes. "I refugeed in Oakland with one of my acquaintances. After they ordered us out of my house, my only thought was to get out of the City. I couldn't persuade Scott to come with me. We had a rather bitter disagreement."

"Scott sees San Francisco as his home." Beth didn't mention that she thought it was much better that Scott thought that way rather than thinking wherever Whit was made his home. That's how she thought of Kerry, and nothing on earth would have ever induced her to leave Kerry.

"Well. Look who the cat dragged in," came Scott's voice, which had a distinct edge to it. He stood at the tent flap, hands on hips, looking at Whit.

"Maybe I'll see you a little later. I'm glad to see you're well." Beth patted Whit's arm and left them.

She returned to work but could scarcely concentrate because she was so concerned, both about Whit's return and about Kerry, who was withdrawn as ever. It had been two weeks since she'd come home from the hospital, but her mental state was unimproved. That reminded her that she wanted to ask Scott if he knew any doctors who specialized in diseases of the mind.

Kerry was always the same, still surly and silent. She'd started to come downstairs for dinner but wasn't convivial. She ate without saying a word to anyone and then returned to their room. Her behavior was excruciating. This was nearly as bad as the time she'd taken up moonshining to make extra money and then lost her job at the Palace Hotel. Beth didn't like reliving those feelings of hopelessness and confusion.

But Marjorie had told her it could take some time for Kerry to really heal. This was one of those times when the experience of a good nurse outpaced her abilities as a doctor. Beth couldn't make Kerry's healing go any faster by prescribing some nostrum or other course of treatment. She had to recover at her own pace, and Beth could do nothing to speed that up. All she could do was worry.

They gathered as usual for the evening meal, but Scott wasn't present. Beth didn't know where he was. He had obviously gone off somewhere with Whit but hadn't even said good-bye to her. When Whit was around, their friendship was markedly different. Beth hoped this was temporary. She watched her companions around the table. Thankfully they were no longer cooking and eating outside. Life was beginning to feel a bit more normal, or as normal as possible with Kerry staring at her plate without saying anything.

Esther was talking about anything and everything other than her pregnancy, and Addison was trying to pretend nothing was wrong between himself and Esther. Beth focused on Norah and Abby, who sat side by side and exchanged warm glances and discreet touches as they passed around the serving dishes. Beth didn't have time to think about what might or might not be going on with those two. She had enough to think about.

She heard a loud crash from the foyer. They all stood up as one, looking at each other as though someone knew the reason for the disturbance. Down the hall they went, and there was Scott, leaning against the front door, his clothes disheveled. He had another whiskey bottle in hand. *Oh no.*

"Here's to the commune!" he shouted. "The best bunch of misfits in California." He raised his bottle in a toast. It was clear he'd thrown the front door open so hard it had slammed against the leaded windows next to it.

Beth stepped forward to take his arm. "Scott, dear. Why not come with me?"

"Hah. Miss Beth, you're a fine young lady. Lovely to see you. If only I could have married you and made my sainted mother happy."

Beth blushed. Scott's Southern accent had returned in his drunken state, and he clearly had no control over what he said. Kerry was staring at him, her brow furrowed.

"Come with me, Scott." Beth led him to the front parlor, where he slept on the divan. She hadn't entered it in a while to allow him privacy and was appalled at how disordered it was. Clothes lay scattered everywhere. She had to push a few off the couch so she could get him to lie down. She propped him semi-upright so he wouldn't choke and then went to get a cold cloth to wipe his face. He was dead drunk, but at least he wasn't with Whit locked up somewhere in a hotel room having a reunion.

When she returned he was already snoring.

Back at the dinner table, she faced five pairs of eyes full of questions. "Whit came back today and sought him out at the hospital in the park. I don't know how he knew to come there, but there he was."

"I hope to never see that man again," Addison said. "I'm glad he survived, but that's all."

Beth glanced at Kerry, who didn't meet her gaze.

They finished their interrupted supper and tidied up. Kerry went directly to the bedroom, and Beth followed her.

"You're still looking after that ridiculous nancy boy," Kerry said.

"Kerry! Whatever is the matter with you?" Kerry didn't answer but kept undressing without meeting Beth's gaze.

Beth answered her own question. The same thing that was always the matter with her these days. Beth thought Kerry had gotten past her jealousy over Scott years ago, but obviously that wasn't the case. Her current state of mind had clearly brought it to the fore again.

"I am, as you see, here with you," Beth said with some asperity. "So I don't know what you're talking about."

"Never mind then." Kerry turned away, got in bed, and pulled the bedcovers over her head, leaving Beth fuming.

"Well, you asked that we go slowly, and I have a feeling we may never go anywhere!" Norah said, trying to keep her emotions in check.

"It's crowded here, and I find myself wondering how we can ever have any privacy."

"We have a room to ourselves," Norah pointed out. "Where we can go and close the door and be alone. Isn't that sufficient?" It seemed fairly obvious that, to Abby, it wasn't. Norah was frustrated in a number of ways.

"I'm not sure. I'm already feeling shy, and all this hubbub isn't helping me be comfortable."

"Whatever can we do?" Norah said. "We're homeless."

"We could go away somewhere."

"That might be a simple matter for you, but not for me. I'm needed here. I'm expected to go back to the City and County Hospital next week, now that there are fewer refugees."

Abby didn't understand what it was like to have obligations because she had none at the moment. She likely wanted to get away from the City again as well.

"Let's not quarrel. I'm sorry, Norah. I do understand, but what are we to do?"

"I don't know. I've no idea." They exchanged a rather neutral kiss before retiring to their separate sides of the bed.

❖

The next morning, Beth shook Scott's shoulder, attempting to rouse him, but he snored on, oblivious. She decided to give up and hope they didn't have too many patients that day for her to handle. She was supposed to help Esther in the infectious tent. She sighed. He'd certainly picked an inopportune time to get drunk. Then there was her heartache over Kerry and the question of their future. They'd be once again tapping savings to pay for their day-to-day needs. Their own home seemed still further off. More important, though, was what would become of Kerry if she couldn't work. What would she do? Beth couldn't see any solution. She went to the foyer to retrieve her gloves and coat, where she heard raised voices at the top of their staircase.

"I swear to you, Esther Strauss, I won't wait any longer. You are out of excuses! The earthquake cannot provide you with a convenient reason to avoid my questions any longer. And you'll have an actual child in about two months. Do you hear me?"

Esther sped down the stairs, rolling her eyes, and joined Beth in the foyer. They were late to depart for the refugee camp.

"I'm not sure he realizes this is a very poor time to have this discussion," she said, grimly.

"You'll have to have it sometime, Esther." Beth thought Esther had had a change of heart after that incident with the refugee and the Red Cross, but maybe not.

"And so you have an opinion as well," Esther said, crossly.

"My opinion is not mysterious to you. I thought you were thinking about it. I think Addison is right."

"Oh, bother. Now where in heavens is Norah?"

"Here." Norah strode down the hallway. "Did you think I'd left without you when I am unable to do that?"

"Oh, not at all." Esther said, clearly not meaning it.

"So what do you think, Norah? Ought Esther agree to marry Addison?"

"That's not for me to say."

Oh, wonderful. Norah didn't want to be involved.

"Someone with sense," Esther said.

Beth was out of sorts for the entire carriage ride over to Golden Gate Park, which was no way to start a long and difficult day of work. Kerry hadn't said a word to her that morning. Scott wasn't even conscious. Esther and Addison were angry with each other again. Whatever relief they'd felt for having survived the earthquake unscathed had long ago evaporated.

Abby bowed out of going back to help at the Park hospital and instead elected to go to the post office so she could see if she'd received any mail and then downtown to the bank to cash the money order for the Colorado rents. It would at least be good to have some cash again. Should she look for another place to live? Matters with Norah were uncomfortable, to say the least. They'd nearly had an argument the night before over the privacy issue. Abby was happy to have the miles of walking to help her think or, at least, try to think clearly about her situation. She really needed to find some occupation and hoped that some of the other researchers had started a temporary facility somewhere

It wasn't that she didn't want to be in Norah's company. She very much did, as long as they were in harmony. Any disharmony made her want to get as far away from Norah as possible. She suspected this was a rather immature view and cursed her lack of experience with intimate human relationships. If only she had someone to talk to, but again she'd so carefully kept her emotional distance there *was* no one.

She could ask her colleague Matthew to risk his life to help her preserve her type specimens, but she could certainly not bring up her difficulties regarding a love relationship with another woman. The only person she could talk to was Norah herself. Then she brought herself up short mentally. That wasn't exactly true. She could probably discuss this situation with Kerry, but she was acting in an entirely uncharacteristic fashion: tense, silent, and not indicating that she even noticed Abby existed, much less saying anything to her. Abby hadn't wanted to cause any trouble, so she hadn't approached her since her return home from Letterman Hospital.

As she walked, Abby saw that gangs of workmen were busily clearing the seemingly endless rubble of concrete, metal, and wood. She supposed that was heartening. Someday the City would return to normal and they would rebuild. What of all its citizens, including her, though? There was more than one kind of recovery, such as the invisible kind. The commune wasn't a cheerful place to be these days with its undercurrents of anger and sadness, as well as its visible indications of discord, such as Scott's return to drinking. Norah's wounded expression that morning had made her heart hurt. But she'd told the truth. It was tough to contemplate anything intimate in a house full of unhappy people.

Abby was overjoyed to find she'd received a few letters. Most were from her acquaintances outside the City, who were worried for her safety, but one, thank goodness, was from the geology expert, Doctor Friend.

Dear Abigail,

I hope this note finds you well. I've heard of your heroic effort in rescuing your type specimens but nothing much since. Reed Harmon and I have found a temporary space in Fort Mason, where you can store your specimens. I was overjoyed to hear you'd saved them. We propose to set up shop there until such time as the board convenes and we can make plans for more permanent quarters. We could use your help if you would be so kind as to meet us at Pier 16 at Fort Mason Tuesday next at nine a.m. If you cannot, we fully understand.

Finally! She could return to some semblance of work in the City. She didn't want to leave with Norah here. This much she knew: they shared a destiny. What that would be and how it would come about, Abby didn't know, but they'd been thrown together by chance, and it was up to them to make of it what they would. She retrieved her small store of cash, and as she tramped back to Fillmore Street, she was a bit happier and decided that it wouldn't be a bad idea to talk to Kerry, if for no other reason than to offer good wishes for her recovery. If, by chance, they could discuss other matters, then she'd ask her advice.

The house was dead quiet when Abby entered the front door. It was impossible to tell if anyone was at home. She went upstairs, listening for what she wasn't sure. There was no sound anywhere. She took a breath and knocked on the door of Kerry and Beth's bedroom, and hearing a low, muttered response, she opened the door.

"Kerry. I hope this isn't a bad time."

Kerry struggled to sit up in bed, her eyes half closed. She looked like she'd been asleep. She wore a sleeveless undershirt, and the extent of her burn was obvious. Abby wondered if it hurt very much.

"No, it's not a bad time. No time is really bad or good. Please sit down."

Abby drew a chair over close to the bed, and though Kerry smiled very slightly, she didn't look well. She was very thin and scrawny, and her skin had a dull tone. Of course she'd not been out of doors at all for weeks so it was understandable. But why didn't she make an effort to get up and about?

"I wanted to say hello and inquire after your health."

Kerry waved a languid arm, as though Abby's offer made not the slightest difference to her. There was a striking and alarming contrast between the Kerry she'd met months before at the luncheon and the one before her now. Abby knew nothing of how someone recovered from a severe burn, but she imagined it was horribly difficult.

"Is it a trial for you to talk? I can leave," Abby said.

Kerry shook her head and asked, "What has this been like for you?"

Her interest surprised Abby, so she gave a brief outline of her earthquake adventures.

"I'll be darned. That took a lot of guts going up in that building when the fire was coming."

"I don't know about that. You braved a huge fire to try to save the Palace Hotel."

Kerry's face clouded and Abby was sorry she'd mentioned it.

"Where's your Society now?" Kerry asked.

"A few people are working up at Fort Mason, but nowhere really. I'm going to join them soon. My plants will be stored there. We can try to organize and inventory things."

"You've got a job to go to. That's good. I don't. I've no reason to be optimistic, nothing to look forward to. My livelihood is gone."

She looked so bereft Abby wanted to hug her, but she didn't know if that would be welcome. "We've all lost a great deal."

"I'm sorry. That's true. Here I am moaning about myself, and you've no place to live."

Abby was glad to see that Kerry wasn't totally absorbed in self-pity.

Kerry fiddled with the bed cover and looked down.

"The Palace restaurant may be gone, but new places will be opening up."

Kerry looked disbelieving. "I suppose."

"Kerry. Do you remember our last talk before the earthquake when I asked you about Norah?"

"Yes. I do."

"Well. It seems she's in love with me."

Kerry's eyes widened, and she sat up straighter in bed. "Is that true? What of you? What are your feelings?"

"I think I'm in love with her too, but that's the trouble. I don't know anything about love."

Kerry actually laughed, and if Abby hadn't been heartened by her sudden change of attitude she would have been annoyed that Kerry was laughing at *her.*

"Abby, no one knows about love. You're not alone. It's not like you learn about it in school as you learn reading and writing."

"You're in love with Beth?"

Kerry's good mood flitted away just as quickly as it had arrived. "Yes, I am."

Abby persisted. "So? How do you know that?"

"It's a feeling. It's something so strong and so deep and so compelling that you cannot *not* feel it. You can't resist it."

"Oh." It still wasn't very clear to Abby, but perhaps she was approaching this subject the wrong way. She couldn't look for facts or logic to convince her. She couldn't look it up in a reference book. Kerry was the closest thing she had to a source of information, but she wasn't especially helpful.

"Well? What was your experience with Beth? How did you know she was the one?"

And at that question, Kerry launched into a remarkable story of the way they'd met and what had transpired.

"She was put in your path for a reason?"

"I believe with all my heart that is true and that we're meant to be together always."

"I find that convincing. For you anyhow. I'm still not sure about myself and Norah."

"It's not easy to explain, but what do you feel when you see Norah? Does she make you feel joy just by reason of her very existence?"

Abby nodded.

"When you're with her, is that all you want, or are you thinking of something else or someone else?"

"Sometimes I think of something else, but never someone else. There's no one else, no one like Norah. She's nothing like anyone I've ever met."

"Beth and I were very young when we met. Adolescents, really."

"What are you getting at?" Abby asked, curious.

"Just that you're not that young."

Abby snorted.

"And you may have a life that you're used to, one that is familiar and comfortable. Norah is unfamiliar, and just maybe she makes you a little uncomfortable?"

"Oh, my. She certainly does. She makes me question everything I know about myself."

"There you have it," Kerry said with an air of certainty.

"My life as I knew it. Your life too, really. All of our lives have been changed into something that is nothing like we've lived before," Abby said.

"That's absolutely true. I see that."

And Abby saw that Kerry had grown pensive. "So perhaps this massive cataclysm has given us an opportunity?"

"An opportunity for what? To be penniless and without employment or homeless?" Kerry asked, her tone bitter and sad.

"Well, maybe that's true, but that's not what I meant. I think I can choose to embrace all that is new and different in my life. I can resist or I can gracefully and happily capitulate—to Norah or to the whole experience. I believe you've given me the insight I need!" Abby was elated, really elated for the first time in weeks, months really.

Kerry appeared flummoxed. "I have?"

Abby took her hand. "I hope you'll feel better, and I don't just mean having your arm heal. I mean I want *you* to be happy. I think you will be, but you just don't see it yet. But now I must go. I don't think I can wait until Norah returns home today. I have to go find her."

Kerry grinned then and said, "Yes. You ought to."

Abby squeezed her hand and grinned back. Then she flew down the stairs and out the front door.

Chapter Eighteen

After Abby left, Kerry lay still thinking about their discussion. It was all very well for Abby to be optimistic. She was more than likely in love; she just didn't fully grasp it yet. Unlike Kerry, she had a reason for living, more than one reason, since she also would have her work. Kerry wondered if there was any more whiskey in the house. She wanted a drink.

But what would that gain her? A little while of feeling better or, more precisely, *not* feeling. That was her goal, wasn't it? She started thinking about Beth's first year of medical school and how she'd nearly derailed their lives and their love because she was so blinkered by her own thinking. Abby's visit reminded her of that somehow. Abby was questioning herself and her choices and her feelings, but she was engaged in her life. Kerry was letting despair take over and direct her actions, just as she had six years previously. And why? Because she was hurt in both body and soul? She wouldn't even let Beth comfort her.

Yet, this wasn't the end of the world. Yes, they would be poor. Yes, she might not find work for a very long time, and it might not be work as a cook. What of it? Beth was secure in her work, and more importantly, as she had found out long ago, she didn't have to always be the one who had to be strong and make everything right. She couldn't, in fact, make anything right. There'd been an earthquake and much had happened, but none of it was her fault. That's what was troubling her so much. She shook her head at her own stupidity. She needed to talk to Beth.

❖

"Well. I'd say you're a sight for sore eyes, but that wouldn't be true," Beth told Scott briskly when he finally showed up mid-morning, bedraggled and contrite.

"Please accept my apologies, Miss Beth, for whatever I said last night. I'm certain I didn't mean it."

"Never mind that. Are we to expect you to take up your life with Whit once more?" She sounded very angry and she didn't like it, but there was really no good reason to try to cover up anything, especially her true feelings, about anything. She planned to put this philosophy into practice with Kerry as well when she returned home. She was essentially fed up with both Scott and with Kerry. And with Esther too, for that matter. She might as well lump Norah in with the rest of them. She didn't know where Norah's mind was, but it certainly wasn't with the refugees who needed assistance. Beth and Addison were clearly the only mature, sensible humans left in the commune. She ought to tell him so later. It might cheer him up, poor man.

"Ah, no. That's not the case," Scott said. He sat down on one of their three-legged stools and ran his hand through his hair. It was already disheveled, and he messed it up even more. The earthquake had cured his rampant dandyism. He wasn't even kempt anymore, Beth thought sourly.

"So?" she said, crossing her arms.

"Whit wanted me to come back to Oakland with him. He has all these plans for opening a new practice. He didn't even seem to remember what happened to us during the quake until I reminded him. Then he got angry and began to demean my character and issue orders to me like I'm a child. Like he used to do."

"Oh, Scott."

"I said no to him. He hated that and we had a huge argument and he went off in a huff and I decided to get drunk."

"You're not leaving then? To be with him?"

"I've no interest in being with him ever again, either professionally or personally."

"Thank goodness!" She hugged him tight even though he still reeked of alcohol.

"Now don't expect me to turn completely bonkers and take up a post at your wretched charity hospital, but—"

"Scott!" Beth dropped her arms, stepped back, and fixed him with a glare. "Stop demeaning my work, the hard work a lot of other doctors do."

His face fell. "I'm sorry. Yes, I'll stop saying that sort of thing. I suppose there's still a little of Whit left around." His smile was rueful. "But I don't think I'd do well at City and County. It's not that I don't value our experience here at the Park, but I don't think I'm really cut out for your type of doctoring."

"I understand, but you needn't make disparaging comments about it."

"You're right." He paused. "I'm going to try to set up my own practice. Not the kind Whit and I had, because I really want to help people. People can pay what they can, and some could be non-paying."

She took his hand. "I'm glad to hear that. It makes me happy."

"I want you to be happy, Beth. *I* want to be happy. Whit didn't make me happy. I realize that now. John makes me happy."

"That's wonderful." They sat in silence for a moment.

"Are you happy, Beth? I'm not sure you are. I mean, God knows all of us could be excused for being somewhat out of sorts with this disaster, but there's more than that. You're not yourself."

He could always read her temperament and moods. To Scott, even her silences gave her away.

"Is it Kerry?"

"Yes." She couldn't disguise her misery and began to cry.

"Oh, no. Oh dear." He hugged her again. "Tell me."

"She isn't getting any better. Well, she is, but she's so withdrawn and so angry, and she won't talk to me. I think she somehow blames me for her trouble. She doesn't think she'll ever work again, and our plans, well, you *know.*"

"She needs occupation," Scott said.

"But she won't even try. She just lies around the house all day. I think sometimes she drinks."

"We know *that* isn't a good sign. Have you confronted her?"

"No, I haven't." Beth sniffed and wiped her eyes. "I don't know what to say."

"You need to give her an ultimatum. Tell her to buck up and stop wallowing in her misery. Look how much better it became for me when I decided you were right to make me come work at the refugee camp."

His eyebrows danced, and Beth had to smile just a little. "My word. She'd be angry if I did that."

"Let her be angry. It may help. Stop coddling her."

"Oh." Beth dreaded the conversation to come, but it seemed as though she had to do something.

❖

Norah walked out on the promenade. All around were tents full of refugees. She was homeless as surely as any of them. She had a roof over head, but it was someone else's roof. She couldn't stay forever, but she didn't seem to have many alternatives. If it were only herself to think of, she wouldn't mind, but their close quarters were stifling progress in her relationship with Abby, which was maddening. If only she could set the scene correctly and get Abby to be serene and not nervous, she was sure she could seduce her. But how would she be able to do that under the circumstances? It was going to take some planning on her part, and as with everything in life, she'd have to choose the right time. She thought hard. She might need to seize an opportunity when one presented itself. She became a bit more optimistic.

She wondered how Abby was faring at Fort Mason. Would this occupation become so all-consuming that she would never be at Fillmore Street? She couldn't tell, but she hoped not. She returned to work, trying to focus on the matters at hand, but her mind roiled.

❖

"Having you back here helping us out is a godsend, Abigail. I cannot tell you how relieved I am that you came through the earthquake unscathed."

"I was lucky enough to be offered a place to live by a friend of a friend." Abby was helping Dr. Friend sort through the salvaged material from the Society. They wanted to have everything preserved and stored properly until they found a new, permanent home for the Society. Sellars had come by the cavernous warehouse at Fort Mason where they'd brought everything and, though he'd glared at Abby, said nothing and addressed his entire conversation to Friend and the others. Abby didn't care. Let him fume. She wasn't about to go anywhere.

As they worked, she and Dr. Friend told their earthquake stories. He was absolutely astonished that she and Matthew Stout had braved the fire and the ruined building to save the types.

"It's going to be a significant chapter in the history of the Society, I can tell you."

"If Sellars has his way, a story will be the only thing left of me." Abby told Dr. Friend about the letter.

"By God, since the earthquake, he's gotten even more full of himself, pompous idiot."

Abby had to laugh. She had no idea how much the other researchers shared her opinion of Sellars. She thought they were all too busy with their research to worry about politics.

"Don't be concerned, my dear. We'll convene the board soon and you will attend and it will be resolved in your favor. Sellars cannot act unilaterally to remove you."

"I'm so reassured to hear you confirm that point. I thought it so, but I wasn't sure."

❖

"You're coming outside with me. I've been all day at the Park, and I need to clear my head."

"But—"

"No 'buts,' Kerry O'Shea. You will come with me. Put your shoes on."

Kerry started to open her mouth to say she didn't feel like it and she was too tired and she was not in the mood and so forth, but something about Beth's tone told her she best go along if she knew what was good for her. Her conversation with Abby was still fresh in her mind, and Abby's words had touched a nerve. She wondered what was transpiring with Beth as well. And she'd not thought to ask after Beth for a very long time because she was so taken up with her own misery. She was selfish and self-absorbed, and that wasn't the right way to be, especially concerning Beth. She was reminded of her promise to herself to talk to Beth. She might as well start now, though she wasn't even remotely in the mood to have a serious talk or go anywhere.

"All right," she said. "I'll be ready in just a moment."

Beth stood unsmiling with arms crossed while Kerry laced on her shoes and put on some pants and a shirt. They sat down on the front porch steps, and Kerry decided it would be prudent to wait until Beth had her say before trying to talk.

"I'm sick and tired of your horrific attitude. I'm tired of your complaints, and I'm tired of your demands, and though I'm sorry for your injury, I see that it is healing well, and I don't see why you have to spend all your days in bed. And you won't talk to me unless it's to snarl."

Beth delivered this speech in a tone that Kerry couldn't ever remember hearing. Years before, when Kerry had lost her job, Beth had been devastated, and she had burst into tears and then ordered her out of the house. This was worse because there were no tears, no emotion of any kind, and Beth had spoken in a cold, level voice.

They sat looking at one another for several moments.

Kerry swallowed. "Er. Yes. I'm sorry. What you say is true. I've been in a bad way ever since the fire."

"Kerry dearest? 'A bad way' hardly begins to describe what you're like."

"I'm sorry," Kerry said again. Under Beth's scrutiny she was wilting and reluctant to say anything more for fear Beth would be angrier. Her good intentions were disappearing.

"Is that all you have to say?" Beth asked. "I've held my tongue because I was concerned about you, but I'm out of patience. What will help you return to some sort of normal life? Tell me what you're thinking. Remember what happened before when you withheld vital information from me?"

Ouch. Kerry remembered very well. "I feel awful that I can't work. I don't have a place to go to work anymore. I've failed you."

"You have not failed me!" Beth nearly shouted. "It's not your fault there was a terrible earthquake, there was a fire, the Palace Hotel burnt to the ground, and you got hurt."

"I know." Beth was right, but why did she feel like she had failed? "Beth. I don't rightly know, and that's the truth. I'm afraid you won't love me anymore because I'm damaged. I'm not the same."

Beth's anger was fleeting, thank goodness. She patted her shoulder. "Don't you see, love? We're together, we're alive. That's all that matters. You mustn't feel bad about things you can't control, and I could never stop loving you."

"I've got a horrible scar, and I don't know if you'll ever, if you'll ever, uh—"

"Love you? Don't be ridiculous. Of course I love you, and I will always want you."

"Sometimes you were so short with me, it was almost as though you were Marjorie and not you. I thought you didn't care about me except as just another patient."

"Oh, Kerry. That's not true. I guess I was defending myself from my own feelings. There's a reason doctors ought to leave the care of their loved ones to others. It's too hard on us. We get upset like regular people. The night of the earthquake when Teddy brought you into the Park, I broke down. I was almost hysterical, I was so scared."

"Oh, Beth, that must have been awful. I was so out of my mind, I didn't notice."

"Don't berate yourself. That's not your fault either."

They hugged, which felt so good to Kerry. She hung on tight and kissed Beth's hair and cheeks.

They put their hands together and it felt like the storm had passed. But not quite, apparently.

"Kerry? You must bestir yourself and get out and start looking for different employment."

Kerry hung her head. "How can I do something else? I wasn't ever anywhere but the Palace. I don't know where else I could go."

"You must try, love. It's not the money that concerns me. It's you. You have to have something to do."

"I know. I guess I'll go downtown and start looking around. Maybe some places will be looking for some help as they try to get going again."

"I know they must be. You have to just go see."

"I promise, Bethy. I promise you I'll find something." Some of her old resolve was coming back. They'd cleared the air and got their feelings out, and all would be well.

"There's one more thing I want from you," Beth said.

Uh-oh.

"You are not to berate Scott or demean my relationship to him. If you're jealous, say so."

"I'm not," Kerry said, protesting, but she remembered what she'd said. She had surely been in a befuddled state if she was getting angry with Beth over Scott. They'd long ago settled that matter. She'd been petulant because of her own problems and took it out on Scott.

"And?" Beth persisted.

"I'm sorry for that too. I like Scott. Mostly."

Beth smiled. "Well, you'll be pleased to know there's no more Whit. I believe this tragedy has had a beneficial effect on Scott. He's more like he was before when we were medical students."

"Oh, that's good." If Beth was happy, then Kerry was happy. Nothing was more important than Beth's happiness. She was glad to return to a state of mind where that was her foremost consideration.

"Abby came to talk to me," Kerry said. "She's in love with Norah, but she doesn't quite know what to do. It's a foreign feeling for her." Kerry chuckled. "She's got no idea what she's in for."

Beth mock-glared at her and shoved her gently. "Oh, you. That's terrible. Norah's been quite scattered and mostly silent. I guess she's having a difficult time with Abby."

"I would think so." Kerry grinned. "Someone must be the initiator, and it has to be Norah. I bet that's not something she's prepared for."

"Kerry. Shh!" Beth wanted to look censorious, but she couldn't hold back her smile. She nuzzled Kerry's cheek. "Thank goodness, *you* knew what to do, or where would we be?"

"I know. It's frightening to contemplate," Kerry said.

"Well, we can only wish them well. They must find their own way." They hugged and kissed again, then sat looking out at the passersby on the street.

❖

"Norah, please, sit down. I want to talk with you." Something about the way Abby said it raised alarms in Norah's mind. She was hesitant but serious. Norah could imagine a number of unpleasant revelations.

"I'm not at all in love with you like I thought."
"There's no way I can be your lover right now. Or ever."
"I'm leaving on a three-month trip to Colorado or Mexico or Canada or New Mexico."
"I've met a man."

Stop. Get ahold of yourself.
They were in their bedroom, and Norah sat on the bed and Abby on the chair.

"I've something very important to tell you." Abby grasped her hands, and Norah waited.

"I've received a letter from an old friend of mine up near Truckee. He's invited me to come stay in his cabin by Fallen Leaf Lake, and I accepted."

Oh no. Norah's mood plummeted. It must have shown clearly on her face because Abby looked alarmed.

"Norah, I don't want you to be sad. This is a welcome development."

"Is it?" Norah asked. "You're leaving. How is that good?"

"Oh, no. I mean for you to come with me."

Abby's expression was so hopeful, Norah was touched. "Abby. I can't go with you. My work is here in the City."

"Norah, just let me try to explain. I thought maybe, just maybe, you could get leave to go away for a week or so. I know you can't be away for too long, but…"

She looked so bereft, the expression on her face was almost enough to make up Norah's mind. Then there was fact that it was a cabin in the woods. But this might be their only chance to be alone. "Tell me about this place."

"Well. Joseph has run it as a resort for many years. Fallen Leaf Lake is not far from Lake Tahoe, but it's much smaller. It's very beautiful, very quiet. Very private." She looked meaningfully at Norah.

"Huh" was all Norah could think of to say. She was torn between duty to her work, anxiety about leaving the City, and her desire for Abby. This might be the only way they could be together. "How do we eat?"

Abby laughed. "There's a stove. We can cook. It's really a building, dear Norah. It's not camping out, I assure you. The only thing is that we have to get there from Truckee on horseback."

"Oh, dear God."

Abby said, quickly, "It's a few hours' trip but not difficult. It's a fairly good road, most of the way. I can show you how to ride a horse, and we'll find a gentle one for you. You know, I think we should spend the first night in Truckee anyhow. It's going to be a long train ride, and we want to start fresh, and—"

"We must still…er, get to know each other better," Norah said. She was imagining what that "getting to know each other" process might be like. She wasn't unsympathetic to Abby's view that the commune was entirely too crowded for real privacy, but somehow she hadn't envisioned their first time together in a rustic cabin in the mountains. Still, Abby's excitement was catching and Norah wanted her to be happy, and most assuredly she wanted Abby to be relaxed and not worried.

She took a deep breath. "I must ask Esther for leave. I can't just come and go as I please. And I'll agree to this if you can assure me that I'll be able to, uh, learn to ride a horse."

"I can and you will. I'll write Joseph right away."

❖

"Would you help me with this, please?" Esther said to Norah. She was roasting a rather large side of beef and needed to get it out of the oven. Norah helped her wrestle the roasting pan up to the kitchen table.

Esther fanned herself and took a huge gulp from the glass of wine she'd poured.

"My word. Sometimes cooking's harder than dealing with patients."

"Well, if you're cooking on this scale, it is. Why isn't Kerry helping you?"

"Don't know where she is. I say that's a good thing. She's finally gotten up and out of the house, and Beth said she's looking for work."

"That's a relief. I imagine Beth's doing better?"

"She is." Esther sat down at the kitchen table, and Norah followed suit. She wanted to ask her the question that had hung over them for months: what about the baby? Or, more precisely, what about Addison and you and getting married?

Almost as though Esther had read her mind, she said, "Well, it looks like I truly have to make a decision. Addison has informed me that if I don't agree to marry him, we are parting company, with him promising to contribute monetarily to the child's upkeep. But nothing else will continue between us. It would be a business arrangement." She took another big mouthful of wine and twirled the glass in her hand, staring at it.

"What do *you* think?" Norah asked cautiously.

"It seems I have to agree to his terms." She upended the wineglass and drained it and set it on the table.

"And, is this distressing to you?"

Esther poured another glass and took a long time to answer. "I'm not one to let someone control me," she said. "And this certainly feels as though he's trying to do just that."

"He never has tried to lord it over you though, has he?"

"No, he hasn't. And I love him, I absolutely do. I don't want to lose him even if I hate being given an ultimatum. He promises me nothing will change. I suppose, for my own sanity, I must believe him. There's the child to think of as well. She ought to have a father."

She caught Norah's eye then, and Norah understood how momentous this statement was. She concluded that now was not the time to say I told you so.

"You and Addison will marry?"

"Yes. It seems that's the only way," Esther said. "You'll be the first to congratulate the blushing bride."

Norah laughed then and went to hug her. In spite of all her doubts, Esther actually looked pleased.

"I have to talk to you about something, Esther."

"Let's sit down again then."

Norah took a glass of wine and gathered her thoughts. "Abby wants me to come away with her into the mountains. For a week, next month."

Esther looked at her shrewdly. "I see. And this is absolutely necessary?"

Norah swallowed and replied. "Yes. It is."

"Are you quite sure you won't decide that life in the mountains is the one for you so you can be close to your beloved?" Esther didn't speak cruelly, but her tone was somewhere between skeptical and amused.

Norah laughed. "Oh, dear God, no. I'm not sure how I'm going to cope in such an environment for just a short time. But she's asked me and I want to go, for her sake, for *our* sake."

Esther nodded. "Well, then I suppose I must accommodate you. I don't think it'll be difficult. The camp is settling down a bit, and we still have Scott helping. I'll ask Addison if he can spare someone from City for a little while. We'll say you need to take a short leave."

Norah grinned at Esther and exhaled with relief. She imagined Abby's joyful reaction to the news. Behind the relief and joy, however, lurked doubt and uncertainty. It could all go wrong in so many ways. Norah could lose her nerve, and therefore their opportunity would be wasted, or Abby could have an adverse reaction to the physical side of love. Norah banished her misgivings and told herself everything would work out.

Chapter Nineteen

"Well. I'm fit to be tied. I never thought to see you again," Davey Moore said to Kerry. "I heard that it was horrific at the Palace that Wednesday, with a lot of folks nearly killed." Kerry had run into her old friend from the Palace downtown sitting outside one of the few restaurants that could reopen amongst the ruins. It didn't look as though there was much business.

"It was a bad day, Davey, and I never hope to have one like it ever again in my life, you best believe."

She rolled up her sleeve and showed him her scarred arm and he whistled. "You got it bad then. Can you still cook?"

"Sure can. Good luck I'm a righty and it was my left arm. Say, do you know where I can ask for a job?"

His face fell. "No, I surely don't. It's no joke. There's a hundred cooks for every spot."

"Well, I'm still up on Fillmore, and I want to work."

"If I hear of somethin', I'll come find you."

Kerry returned to her dreary rounds of the few restaurants that were open. But in every place she stopped to ask, the answer was always the same: "I've got all the staff I need. I could use some customers."

Kerry didn't know which was more depressing, the consistent answers to all her inquiries or the utter ruin of downtown San Francisco. She hadn't seen it since she'd been stuck up at the hospital and afterward hiding out at home.

Fillmore Street seemed fairly normal, even busier than it had been prior to the earthquake. She'd heard that a number of downtown businesses had taken up temporary quarters on Fillmore. She thought she might as well head back there and try her luck, because it couldn't be worse there than it was in the Financial District, or what was left of it. Kerry tried hard to keep her spirits up, but it was difficult. She had to do her best, for herself but also to show Beth she was getting better.

❖

They were at a stable a few blocks away from the commune that hired out horses.

Abby stood beside what looked to Norah like a very large and very intimidating horse. Abby held the reins in her hand and patted the horse's neck. "I came to the realization that you needed some horseback riding lessons before we go to the mountains. First, you want to make friends with your horse."

"I merely want him not to throw me off. I don't need a friend."

Nervousness made Norah speak shortly, but Abby just smiled and said, "Yes, you will do better, though, if you aren't a stranger to him. His name is Old Sam and he's a steady fellow, the stable hand said, so come on, then, and give him a carrot and a little pat on the nose and let him smell you." Abby was in her brisk, no-nonsense mode, and Norah wanted to show her she was up to the task. Her being able to ride a horse was the key to their future happiness. If Abby required a quiet, remote mountain cabin to feel comfortable, then Norah would have to go along as best she could.

She tentatively offered the carrot, and the horse took it in his huge mouth. "Good Old Sam," Norah said, and stroked his nose. He whinnied and shook his head, scaring her.

"Don't worry. That's good," Abby said. "He's pleased with his treat. Now come over to this side and we'll have you mount."

"How am I ever going to ride in a skirt? Sidesaddle?" Norah asked crossly.

"I've thought of that. You must buy a skirt, and I'll alter it so you can ride astride."

"You can sew?" That seemed entirely out of character for Abby and yet not. She could do so many different things, Norah found. She was certainly a wonder.

"Yes. I had to learn to take care of those tasks. The nuns taught me to look after myself even if they failed in their attempts to make me a good Catholic." Abby chuckled.

Ah, yes, Abby's independence. That was one of the things about her that Norah both loved and feared. How in the world would someone so self-sufficient ever need her? Norah recalled May's endless neediness and decided that she preferred the challenge of inducing Abby to depend on her. That the process of calling up need in Abby might result in creating the same need in her was a chance she was going to have to take.

In the meantime, she had to shed her misgivings about the great out-of-doors and let Abby prepare her. Abby had done an admirable job for their foray to Mount Tamalpais. There was no reason to suspect she was not up to the task of making Norah ready for something far more ambitious, but still Norah fretted.

When she was not worrying about the practicalities of getting to and living in a mountain cabin for a week, she was teetering between wild anticipation and apprehension about how to go about initiating their physical relationship. The few kisses and hugs they'd exchanged had been wonderful, but as May had said, "There is much more." While Abby was clearly a worldly woman in so many ways, in this one area she was an innocent, which was both enticing and frightening. Norah hoped she wouldn't be clumsy and Abby wouldn't be repulsed. Norah hoped that she would like it and come to want it. Norah recalled that journey she took herself, with May as her guide. She wanted to have Abby take the same journey but without the betrayal and heartbreak at the end of it.

"Are you ready?" Abby's voice brought her back to the moment.

"I suppose."

"All right. Take the reins in your left hand, grasp the pommel with your right and step into my hand with your left foot, and then swing your leg over the saddle."

Norah took a deep breath and followed Abby's instructions, and suddenly she was sitting atop a horse. He gave a snort and made a quick, jerky move sideways. It surprised Norah, but she hung on. She tucked and tussled with her skirt so it wouldn't be in the way and could see where Abby's skirt alteration would be helpful.

"Now, you kick your heels into his sides to make him go and pull back on the reins to make him stop and to move from one direction to another. Remember, he's used to all this, so he will obey if you're firm about it."

"Firm," Norah said, doubtfully. She made a few of the movements that Abby described, and to her surprise they worked. She cantered in a little circle in the street outside the stable and then grinned down in triumph at Abby, who mirrored her, her eyes shining with satisfaction.

"Take a little ride down the street. Get the feel for it. Use your legs to help steady yourself. We'll take it slow when we're on the way out to Fallen Leaf."

Off Norah went at an easy pace. The motion of the horse was almost tranquil, but it felt odd being on the back of something that moved. She swerved around and rode back to where Abby waited.

"All right. I'll get my mount and we'll take a little ride." She went into the stable and came back out on a glossy black mare. In contrast to Norah's horse, this creature pranced and wheeled. Old Sam had lived up to his name, which made Norah happy. She watched Abby ride her horse, struck at how beautiful the two of them looked together. Abby's competence as a rider was evident.

They rode for an hour out to Golden Gate Park almost to Ocean Beach and then back again. Norah's legs and behind were sore when they finished, and she thought about the much longer ride they'd take out to Fallen Leaf. Well, it wasn't to be helped. She'd just have to endure it.

❖

"While you were lounging around at the hospital tent waiting for sick people, I was out and about and asking for work at every place I could find," Kerry told Beth.

"I was scarcely lounging," Beth said with some heat.

"I know, my love. I was only teasing you." Kerry grabbed Beth's hands and started dancing her around their parlor.

Kerry looped an arm around Beth's waist and held her left hand high and dipped her. "I wanted to show you how much better I feel."

"I see that. Oh, goodness," Beth said as she leaned backward. Kerry brought her upright once more and twirled them around.

"Yes. I'm tip-top, ready for anything." She raised her eyebrows.

"Anything?" Beth asked. "That's a very all-encompassing word."

"Yes, it is," Kerry whispered, then pulled Beth into a close embrace and stopped dancing. She kissed Beth's hair and cheek and ear. Her breath tickled, and Beth felt the familiar longing in her body.

Kerry leaned back so their gazes could meet and waited a moment, then kissed Beth deeply. "I want you, right this minute," Kerry said.

Beth almost swooned because those words had such a profound effect on her.

"Then you must have me," she whispered back. "I'm yours always. I've been waiting for you to show me that truth once again."

"I'm ready to, more than ready. It seems like it's been so long."

In bed, Kerry was more tender and ardent than she'd been for a long while. They kissed more, her touch by turns soft and gentle and firm and possessive. Beth knew she was loved, but she required the hard evidence of it every so often, and Kerry gave it completely and unequivocally. Their recent troubles made their lovemaking sweeter, and Beth wondered why this was so often true. Over the years, when they were in conflict and at odds, after they managed to reconcile and return to harmony, they almost always sealed their rapprochement with passionate lovemaking.

"I'm glad you're feeling better," Beth said, meaning it.

"I am as well." Kerry lay on her back with her good arm around Beth's shoulders and sighed deeply.

"You are and always will be beautiful to me." Beth traced the reddish-brown scar on Kerry's arm.

"You're more beautiful every time I see you, every time we do this. You're everything to me."

Beth held Kerry's gaze and stroked her hair.

❖

Abby enjoyed few things more than making ready for a trip into the wilds. She spent enjoyable hours gathering her collecting equipment, reading maps, scrutinizing train schedules. This time, instead of repairing and cleaning her clothes, she purchased new ones Preparations were essential to success and comfort, and she didn't cut corners. Ever.

This trip to Fallen Leaf Lake was in most ways no different. She had boards to cut and twine to ball and food items to purchase. For this trip, they would have the comparative luxury of a shelter so she didn't have to pack a tent. But Abby had no way to prepare for one significant aspect of this journey.

She was going to find out from Norah, with Norah, the nature of love. That phrase made her smile. Her whole life had been dedicated to nature, especially to its botanical side, but all of it, really, except one element. Humans were most assuredly part of nature as well. Their urge to reproduce was evidence of that. They had that in common with all creation. Humans were a bit more complicated than plants, however, and Abby had spent her life successfully avoiding those all-too-human complications that others had to endure or were able to enjoy. She supposed it was both.

She'd realized at an early age that she was in no way fit to be a wife and mother. But she'd never given any serious thought to the idea of an emotional or physical connection to anyone. Until she met Norah.

They were going off together to a geographical place very familiar to Abby. But their emotional destination was another matter. What would happen when they were finally alone, truly alone, took the upper hand in Abby's mind. She supposed she and Norah were somewhat in the same boat, both of them venturing into unfamiliar territory. Norah was such a city girl, she was surely nervous about spending several days in a rough cabin in the mountains. Abby wondered if she was nervous about other things as well.

Nonetheless she was happy. She was going to share one of her favorite places with someone she loved. She hoped Norah would love it too, but that was far from a foregone conclusion. As for where Norah would take her, she hoped she would enjoy that journey. It would be wonderful if they could both arrive at agreeable destinations. But she couldn't say for sure. She guessed that was the real source of her anxiety. She was used to being very sure of both the trip and the destination. When it came to Norah and her, everything was in question.

The earthquake had upended her life, that was certain, and nothing would ever be the same again.

❖

Norah didn't generally mind train travel. It was picturesque, civilized, and relatively comfortable. And she and Abby could avoid any awkwardness between them by occupying different berths. She thought of climbing down and sliding into the narrow bed next to Abby but thought better of it. They would be at the inn in Truckee in due time. She occupied herself trying to decide if she should attempt to make any small movements beyond a simple good-night kiss there or simply wait until they'd arrived at the Fallen Leaf Lake camp, where they'd be alone. At least at the hotel they wouldn't be in a house surrounded by people they knew.

Norah was in a fever of speculation and anticipation, but she couldn't quite make out what Abby was thinking. She was as friendly and affectionate as ever but gave no sign that she desired Norah with the same fervor that Norah wanted her. Women were often difficult to read, May had told her early on, laughing merrily. Ah, how true that was, and it was especially galling that May had turned out to be like the women she spoke of. Nothing was as it seemed.

Norah looked out the window in the dining car and sighed.

"What's the matter?" Abby asked.

"Oh, not a thing. All's well," Norah said, and grinned for emphasis. Abby's crystal-blue eyes rested on her, but to Norah, her glance contained no heat, nothing beyond friendly concern.

"We'll be in Truckee by midday. We have some shopping to do, and we have to hire our horses. The Green Mountain Inn has a nice dinner service, I recall."

"The name Green Mountain reminds me of Vermont," Norah said.

"Ah, yes. I visited there briefly a few years ago."

After checking in, they went down the main street of Truckee to the public stables to inquire after renting horses. Norah looked at the wooden sidewalks and the dirt street and realized she was indeed in the Wild West. She'd considered San Francisco very Western, but it was far more civilized than Truckee.

As they strolled down the street, Abby said, "Lake Tahoe is becoming quite the popular destination for city folk looking for the mountain experience without having to camp."

"Oh? And do you like it?"

"Too civilized and crowded for me. I prefer my solitude."

"So I gather from everything you told me. You don't need a lot of trippers trampling over your plants, am I correct?"

Abby laughed, but she said, "True, but it's not just that. I would rather be alone out in the woods."

"And this time, you're not alone. You're with me."

"Well. I've come to understand that the presence of a special person with me in a place I love, such as Mount Tamalpais, is altogether different than being surrounded by crowds of holiday makers."

"You didn't love me when we went to Mount Tamalpais," Norah pointed out.

"Yes, but I do now, and I understand that it's special." Norah squeezed her arm.

They took their time picking out horses, and Abby insisted that their saddles and tack be in top-notch condition. It was amusing to watch her haggle with the stable manager, a grizzled type who scratched his head at Abby's demands and looked around in vain for some male companion whom he would be far more comfortable dealing with. But there was none, and Norah secretly enjoyed his discomfiture. They walked on to the dry-goods store, the green grocer, and the butcher, and Norah watched with renewed awe as Abby rapidly chose various food items for their trip.

"We can cook at the cabin, though the stove is small and primitive. I believe we may enjoy some pancakes for breakfast. I'll try to make a meat pie so we'll need some flour. How do you feel about raw vegetables?" She raised an eyebrow.

"I-I don't know. I heard they're bad to eat—"

"Nonsense. We eat them all the time when camping. Raw carrots are especially good. We'll buy some smoked fish, too." Abby grinned at Norah's doubtful expression.

On the way back to the inn, Norah stopped and put a hand on her chest. "I'm a bit short of breath. I must sit down for a moment."

"Oh, it's the thinner air. We're at six thousand feet above sea level. You'll get used to it soon enough."

At the inn, they enjoyed a surprisingly tasty meal of venison and grits. They were quiet, as though both of them had too much to say and didn't know where to begin, which was the opposite of having nothing to say.

Up in their room, Norah was once again gripped by anxiety as to what she ought to do. Or not do. It seemed silly to be standoffish since they'd come all this way to get as close as possible.

They went through their separate nightly rituals of washing and changing into nightgowns, and Norah struggled to keep calm and not stare, but it was hard. They climbed into the four-poster bed with its rough blanket but lovely handmade quilt. It was cool, almost cold in the room. During the day, the temperature was warm, but the night brought on much cooler temperatures. Norah silently hoped the fireplace in their cabin was adequate. She hated to be cold more than anything. With any luck she and Abby would be manufacturing a good deal of heat themselves, and with a roaring fire, everyone would keep warm.

Norah turned her head on her pillow and looked at Abby, who smiled tenderly at her.

"Well, here we are," she said. The pronouncement sounded inane to her ears, and she was sorry as soon as she made it.

But Abby echoed her. "Yes. Here we are. Well, we have to get up early tomorrow and get on the trail. Good night." And they both moved heads at the same time and met in the middle for a kiss.

Norah prolonged the kiss, molding Abby's lips to her own. She put her hand at the base of Abby's neck to keep her in place and kept on kissing her and gently rolled her over on her back, not letting their contact break. Abby's breathing became a little ragged, and she eagerly returned Norah's kisses. In their winter-weight nightclothes and under the heavy bedcovers, they were becoming very warm.

Norah ran her hand down Abby's side over the material of her nightgown until she located its hem. She continued her ardent kissing and lifted the hem of the nightgown until she felt the smooth skin of Abby's thigh. She kept her hand in place for a bit then slowly moved it upward until she connected with Abby's stomach and stopped there. They were both panting. *Good.* Abby needed only to feel the right touch. Norah needed only to be patient, but she must not be afraid to go forward. She very much wanted to move her hand high enough connect with Abby's breast. Once she was there, she believed that Abby would be so aroused they could continue. But she mustn't hurry. Hurrying was wrong. Hurrying could alarm Abby, who had asked for slowness. Norah inched her hand higher. God, Abby's skin was wonderful to touch, just as Norah knew it would be. Her fingertips grazed the underside of her breast, and Abby gave a tiny gasp.

A knock on the door startled them both so badly, they jerked and flew apart.

"Breakfast at seven, ladies. Down in the front parlor."

"Thank you!" Abby called.

They'd sat up, still panting a little but more from fright than arousal. The moment was over.

"I uh, er, think we ought to go to sleep now," Abby said shakily.

Norah was vibrating from frustrated desire, but she said nothing, only weakly nodded her assent.

Once again, Norah had a difficult time falling asleep. *So close.*

CHAPTER TWENTY

Lake Tahoe is over there to the left," Abby said. They were on their horses, ambling down a dirt road. Abby had loaded and tied down their supplies and bags properly in what seemed an incredibly short period of time. More than ever, Norah was conscious of being out of her element.

The scenery, however, was breathtaking. Snow-capped mountains ringed the area. Everywhere, evergreen trees towered over slopes dotted with gigantic gray boulders. The air smelled wonderful, especially after so many weeks of breathing soot from the fire in the City. Norah said so to Abby.

"Yes, I know. That is one of the many reasons I wanted to make a trip out here, to clear my head, to clear my lungs, and, of course, to collect a little."

"What about me?" Norah asked in a teasing tone, though she was suddenly conscious that she hadn't appeared on the list of Abby's reasons for wanting to go to the mountains.

Abby, who rode in front of her, slowed and turned around, looking at her with alarm. "Oh, but of course. I didn't mean to leave you out of my thoughts or my words. You're there, always. Please believe me."

She looked so serious, Norah wanted to kiss her immediately. "I do believe you," she said, with a gentle smile to reassure her.

They resumed their ride. The slow motion of a horse at walking pace was relaxing, and the rocking back and forth made her sleepy. Norah felt lighthearted and joyful because she knew that at the end of the road were shelter and food, and they would be together and, finally, truly alone. She closed her eyes for a moment to think of the rustic room with a cozy fireplace and snug bed where they would sleep and...not sleep. She shivered.

In the meantime, the jaw-dropping views held her attention when she wasn't looking at Abby. Abby was different than she was in the City, more lighthearted, brighter. This environment obviously agreed with her. They chatted, and Abby might point out and name a mountain peak or sometimes a flower or tree, and her enthusiasm was catching. Norah thought about Mount Tamalpais and grinned. She'd had no idea what she was letting herself in for. It had been four months since the earthquake. And it had been only two months before that when they'd gone up Mount Tamalpais.

Halfway through their journey, about noon, they stopped for a cold lunch, and when Norah alit from her horse, she was all too conscious of the soreness in her legs and behind from the unaccustomed horseback riding. She knew she was walking a bit funny, and Abby noticed.

"Is everything all right?" she asked.

"Yes. Just a little sore," Norah said, not wanting to seem weak or out of sorts.

Abby looked at her, eyes slightly narrowed, but said no more.

"How much longer, do you think?" Norah asked.

"I'm afraid we have a good six hours to go. We won't arrive before six thirty. In time for sunset, though, which is not to be missed."

"Oh, that would be wonderful." Norah struggled to sound enthusiastic. All she wanted to do was get off that damn horse and lie down. She wasn't exactly short of breath, but it was still hard to get a lungful of air. They finished their lunch and resumed their ride.

❖

"Here we are," Abby said as they rounded a bend on the path by the lake. The shadows were growing longer as the sun began to set. She sighed deeply, taking in the silvery reflection of the darkening sky on Fallen Leaf Lake. It was almost dead silent. Only a few birds chirped here and there. It was her favorite time of the day, well past the bright midday but not yet twilight. The colors of the sky were muted blue, gold, and pink

She looked over at Norah, who sat on her horse gamely, her back straight but with a hint of strain around her eyes. Abby wondered if it was just the long ride or something else. She'd been very quiet the past couple of hours, and Abby was concerned but also wanted Norah to be forthcoming if something was amiss.

Finally, they were in front of Joseph's cabin. They dropped off their horses and Abby reached back to take Norah's hand. "Come, let me show you before we unpack."

Norah nodded, but her smile barely moved her lips.

Abby tugged her hand, and when Norah didn't move forward, she turned around.

"I-I can hardly walk," Norah said, a note of panic in her tone.

Abby took her in her arms right away. "You're just unused to horseback riding. This was a very long trek for a neophyte. I'm so sorry, but let me help you in so you can lie down. She put her arm around Norah and supported her as she limped up the few steps to the door of the cabin.

Once inside, Abby had her sit in a rocking chair, which she did gingerly, wincing.

"Please just sit quietly for a bit. I must see to the horses and bring in our belongings and supplies, and then I'll see to you, I promise. She kissed the top of Norah's head.

Norah was apparently past speech. Poor girl. Twelve hours in a saddle was too much for her. Abby cursed herself for being insensitive. But there was no other way, aside from camping out overnight, to divide the journey in two, and she scarcely imagined how Norah would have been able to do that.

She hurriedly unloaded the horses and carried everything into the cabin. She gave them their feed and water and tied them to the posts in the yard. At least they weren't sweaty, since it wasn't a hard ride, just a long one. She patted them both gently and said good night and returned to the cabin. It was getting very close to dark, and she had to prepare something for herself and Norah to eat. It seemed like a good idea to just dine on some smoked salmon and bread and be done with it.

Norah had pulled herself out of the rocking chair and managed to get her skirt off. She lay facedown on the bed that was situated in the alcove by the fireplace.

"Let me just build us a fire and warm the place up for us. Then, I promise, I will take care of you."

Norah said something unintelligible, her head buried in the pillow. Abby would have to get her up to make the bed as well. This worry about another person was something new. She'd always been with people who could take care of themselves. Norah appeared self-sufficient, but in this instance, at least, she wasn't pretending. Abby was brimming with worry, not that Norah was seriously hurt, because she wasn't, but because she was unhappy and likely blamed Abby. And Abby felt responsible. This was another unfamiliar feeling, and she welcomed it on the one hand but was deeply afraid of it on the other. It was a burden to feel like she had something to do with another's well-being, that what she did or didn't do could have such enormous consequences. She found she was anxious that Norah not stop loving her. She got the fire going and then tapped Norah on the shoulder.

"My dear, I must have you sit again while I make the bed, and then I have something that will make you feel a bit better."

Norah turned over on her side. "I can't sit. It hurts too much."

"Well, how about if I help you stand?"

Norah shrugged, so Abby helped her to stand up and move to the fireplace, where she braced herself on the stone mantel.

Abby found the bedclothes and made the bed as quickly as possible. Then she put some wood into the little cottage heater stove and lit a fire.

"Let's get your clothes off, and I want to put some arnica on you to ease the pain. I have some aspirin powder as well. Then we'll eat our supper. It'll be a cold one tonight, I'm afraid." She smiled ruefully.

"Who's the doctor here?" Norah asked, and Abby was pleased that her tone carried some of her old fire.

"Well, you are, of course. But even doctors need someone to care for them now and then."

Abby helped Norah lie on the bed and found her tin of arnica. She took off Norah's drawers, pulling them carefully out from under her and over her ankles.

Norah's rear end was bruised and red in many places, and Abby winced. She had certainly been naive about this idea of riding to Fallen Leaf. She took the cream and began to rub it over Norah's body as gently as she could.

From her facedown position, her voice muffled by the pillow, Norah said,

"This is entirely opposite how I envisioned this night would proceed."

Abby sensed a blush creeping over her cheeks, but she laughed.

Norah turned her head to the side so she could be clearly heard. "I wanted you to touch me, but not in this manner. I'm so embarrassed."

"Don't worry about it. It's my fault really. Dragging you this long way up here on a horse when you're not seasoned."

"I've free will and I agreed, so it's my own fault."

Abby finished applying the arnica and was moved to touch the inside of Norah's thighs, where she wasn't quite as bruised.

Norah moved restlessly. "If I wasn't in so much pain, what you're doing would make me turn over and take you in my arms at once."

Abby stopped, unsure what to do or to say. She only knew that she wanted desperately to touch Norah but was afraid of hurting her further. For a few moments, neither of them moved or said anything.

"You know, Abigail. I think you should stop what you're doing and bring me that aspirin powder you promised and then feed me, since I'm starving."

Abby stood up and hastily covered Norah with the sheet and the blanket. "Yes, right away, my lady. At your service."

Abby fashioned some padding with an extra blanket plus a bed pillow on one of the wooden chairs and had Norah sit at the table so they could eat.

"I'm all right. Don't look so grim," Norah said. Just an hour or so off her horse had done her a lot of good, and Abby knew that the damage wouldn't be permanent. She knew the physical pain would pass, but she was more worried about Norah's emotions. She thought Norah would blame her for causing them to take a long horseback ride and for the damage not only to her body but the frustration of their plans for the night, but Abby didn't know how to appropriately bring this point up, so she said nothing.

They ate their supper mostly in silence, only punctuated by the most trivial and innocuous comments. Abby helped Norah get ready for bed and put on her own nightclothes. She was both disappointed and relieved that Norah's pain would preclude any thing other than sleep, but she was happy Norah didn't seem angry. In fact Norah was so tired that she was breathing deeply as soon as Abby got her settled in bed. Abby slipped in next to her and, in the cozy warmth, fell asleep almost at once.

❖

Much to her surprise, Norah was insomniac once again, waking in the middle of the night. Perhaps it was the lingering pain in her rear or the excitement of an unfamiliar place. Mainly it was the bitter frustration. Earlier, Abby's touches while caring for her had nearly undone her reason, but the slightest movement was so painful she had abandoned her momentary intention to turn a little bit of first aid into a prelude to a seduction.

She still couldn't make out what was transpiring in Abby's mind. She was such a perfect cipher. When May had wanted her, it was obvious and irresistible, and all Norah had to do was happily succumb. Then, as the evidence of May's perfidy grew, she had been distraught that she was unable to resist May's touch when accompanied by a seemingly sincere apology. In May's hands, she was a puppet, and her weakness ate at her self-esteem.

Abby slumbered away next to her, unaware and, it seemed, unconcerned what could or would happen. This was as she'd always been and seemingly as she always would be unless Norah changed the nature of their interaction. And what then? That was the unanswered question and what they'd come all this way from civilization to answer. Norah had to be the director, and she couldn't let a sore gluteus muscle deter her. *In the morning.* Exhaustion won and she fell back to sleep.

❖

The first thing Abby saw when she awoke was a small window directly above the bed. It framed a tall Monterey cypress tree outlined by the slate sky, whose blue-gray color indicated it was just before dawn. She was aware of how close to her Norah slept. The warmth of their bodies mingled under the covers contrasted to the chill of the little alcove. She ought to get up and stir the fire to life and get the cabin warm. Norah would surely appreciate that. She put a shawl around her shoulders and shoved her feet into shoes without lacing them. Then she went outside to get some more wood and paused on the little front porch of the cabin to look out over Fallen Leaf Lake.

The lake's surface was glassy, with just a little mist rising. Here and there a small bird chirped, but nothing else disturbed the quiet. Abby thought of the woman still asleep inside and wondered if she could make her happy. She wanted to do that so much, but she wasn't entirely sure she was up to the task. Nonetheless, she wanted to try. She hoped for some direction from Norah on how exactly to act, but so far, not much was forthcoming. Above all was still the puzzling and alarming reality of sex.

Abby let herself think the word because that was what it was. But what did she want and what did she feel? She had the same questions for Norah but again didn't know how to ask them. She shook her head and focused on practical actions. She pumped some water into a pan, thinking of cooking some oatmeal and making a pot of coffee.

Back in the cabin, she stoked the fire to life, enjoying the long-familiar smell of wood smoke, though for a moment it evoked her memory of walking through the ruins of San Francisco. The odors were similar but called up entirely different emotions and memories. One evoked joy and comfort at a campfire with friends in the mountains, whereas the other suggested only destruction and terror and despair.

"Abby? Where are you?" She heard Norah's voice behind her. Her heart began to pound for some odd reason

"I'm making a fire. I'll be there in a moment." She poked at the ashes to turn over the glowing embers, carefully arranged a few small logs and twigs around them, and watched with satisfaction as they caught and flamed. After building another fire in the cook stove and her mind swirling with anticipation, she turned and walked back to the bed.

She stopped and watched as Norah threw the covers aside, grinned, and fixed her with an intent gaze. "Get in," she said, in a firm voice. Abby took off her shawl and her shoes as Norah watched her. The air between them shimmered. Something was afoot, and Abby forgot all about fires and cooking. In slow motion, she slid into bed next to Norah and into her waiting arms. They pulled the covers up to their necks and moved together. After the cold mountain air, the heat of two bodies in bed was a welcome contrast.

Norah kissed her on the mouth, moving her lips over Abby's, licking and even biting gently.

"How are your, eh, saddle sores?" Abby said, her mouth against Norah's as she spoke.

"Fine." And apparently that was all the answer Abby was going to get.

Norah kissed her forehead, her cheeks, her ears, then her neck and around her collarbone, impatiently pushing her nightgown aside. She rolled them over so that her weight pinned Abby to the mattress.

This time there would be no thoughtless inn employee to interrupt. Abby's heart began to pound, her breath grew ragged and rapid, and her body heated. Norah suddenly moved away and Abby was bereft, as though she'd been left in a snowstorm without shelter. "What's...?"

But Norah stared into her eyes, knelt on the bed, and struggled out of her nightgown. "You too," she said, her voice low.

"I..." Abby swallowed.

"Right this minute! It's freezing in this cabin, and I need to be back under the covers. I'll help you."

So Abby got up on her knees and Norah yanked off her nightgown and they dove back under the covers and into each other's arms. There was something compelling about the feel of Norah's naked body. When they had embraced before, Abby had noticed hints of its yielding softness, its warmth and pliancy. But nothing had prepared her for this. Her own body vibrated, and she couldn't seem to hold on tightly enough or get any closer. Her blood beat in her head and between her legs. *Lust.* The word popped into her head. *Lust is what I feel.*

Abby closed her eyes and gave herself over to the experience, to Norah, to her lips and to her hands. Like a magician of love, Norah conjured unique sensations.

The phrase "the word made flesh" jumped into Abby's mind. She'd heard it as an expression of the holiness of Jesus, but now it had an altogether different meaning. Norah's caresses made the word love real. Behind her lowered eyelids, inchoate swirling images, flashes of color populated her black vision. Her head spun as though she'd drunk too much.

Abby had once fallen off a steep trail into a swiftly flowing river and had been afraid, but she had remembered to relax and was carried to the shore by the current instead of being drowned. It was like that when Norah made love to her. She had to not fight but to embrace the feelings, accept the fate, let the currents take her. She wasn't apprehensive any more. Norah said nothing at all but, nonetheless, said everything with her touch.

The nuns had read passages concerning rapture and the ecstasy of the spiritual love of God. These came to Abby's mind, even though she smiled, thinking this was surely far from what they had in mind though the words for it were the same. Abby understood that love as a powerful emotion was more easily conveyed via another person's body than by words, which were inadequate. And there was pleasure, profound, intense physical pleasure that left her weak with gratitude and fatigue.

Norah brushed her hair back from face and smiled and spoke for the first time.

"Are you well? In one piece?" Her expression was tender and triumphant.

"I'm very well, and I think I'm still of intact body, but I'm not sure."

"Ah, good then."

Abby whispered, "I understand. I know why you wanted us to do that."

"I've wanted to make love to you for months. Months. But I wasn't sure it was what you wanted."

"I didn't know that's what I wanted. I want it now. I want you."

Norah rested her hand on Abby's breast. "It's quite the most unique feeling in the world, isn't it?"

Abby pulled her down into a kiss. "I've never felt anything remotely like that. I can't believe I've gone through life thinking that love was something I could, in practical terms, do without. I don't think that anymore."

Norah started to smile again but grew serious. "I wasn't sure, you know, if you'd run away from me screaming."

"I know I'm not the most forthcoming of women when it comes to the matters of the heart."

"You are not, but I was prepared to be patient, and my patience has been rewarded."

"Norah, I do love you, with all my heart, I swear."

Norah put an arm around her and pulled her head onto her breast. "Shhh," she murmured. "Rest for a moment, because we'll begin again." She kissed Abby's neck and brushed fingers over her breast. "We're far from finished."

It took a moment for Abby to comprehend this statement, and she tingled. She grabbed Norah's head to capture her lips. "Oh. Yes. I believe I understand you perfectly, and I hope you'll be patient a little longer with me."

"Abby, love, when it comes to you, there is no limit to my patience."

Chapter Twenty-one

Many hours later, Norah woke up. *Dear God, it really happened. I'm so hungry I could eat one of our horses.* When she stirred, she felt Abby's hand on her back.

"Something wrong?"

"Nothing at all, except I'm starving and was going to get up and find something to eat. Come with me?"

"Certainly."

They sat at the tiny wooden kitchen table wrapped in blankets and nibbled some of the leftovers from their supper. They spoke little but looked at each other steadily with small smiles. Norah was suffused with gratitude and relief. It was a miracle of sorts, though she wondered at her previous doubts. Abby took to lovemaking like she'd done it all her life. That really should be no surprise, since Abby was immersed in the world of nature and was a sensitive, self-confident woman. Norah had merely showed her the way, and she had readily followed.

"I'm happier than I've ever been," Abby said. "I didn't know what I was missing, and that's the truth."

"It thrills me to hear you say that."

Abby took Norah's hand. "I've been transformed. I'm not the same person. I mean I am, but I'm somehow different."

"I am as well," Norah said.

"Tell me. I want to know. I want to hear how it feels for you because I can scarcely put into words how I feel."

"Let me start with a sad story." Norah gave Abby a short explanation of her experience with May.

"Oh, dear. That must have been awful for you."

"It was. I had no idea if I could ever find anyone to love. I was very frightened of my feelings for you and wasn't sure how to go forward." She ducked her head shyly, then raised her eyes to meet Abby's. All she saw was love and kindness. "I was scared."

"Oh, Norah. I was difficult for you to fathom, wasn't I?" Abby laughed a little.

Norah laughed along with her. "Well. Yes, you were, but it was worth the wait to unravel your mystery."

Abby raised an eyebrow. "I see. Well, I may have a few mysteries left for you to solve, but if you've had enough to eat, I have an idea." She stroked Norah's hair.

Norah took her hand and kissed her palm. "I have an idea as well. Shall we go back to bed? I've visited most parts of your body, but I'd like to revisit a few just to be sure."

Abby's giggle was delightful, but she grew serious. "I would like that, but first I'd like to get cleaned up. We had a long, dusty ride yesterday, and while I'm not averse to good honest sweat, especially if it's yours, I think we'd both feel better if we had a bath."

Norah was confused. "Where would we do that? I don't see that there's a—"

"Norah, dear. We have an entire lake outside our front door."

"The lake?" Norah was aghast. *Ice-cold, rocky bottom, creatures in the water, no, under no circumstances.*

"I've done it many times, but usually I have to keep my underclothes on because of the people about. No one's here but us. The water is a little warmer at this time of year, and now the sun's up so you'll—" She must have noticed Norah's horrified expression. "Oh, Norah dear, your face is priceless. It'll be fine, I assure you."

"I don't want fish nibbling my toes or snakes crawling over me or what else I don't know!"

"Norah. I'll be with you. Have no fear. Please, do try to trust me, as I have trusted you."

Her face was so loving and hopeful, Norah squelched her misgivings and took a breath. "All right. Because it's you asking I would very much like to be clean and for you to be clean. There's a luscious little trick I'd like to show you that will be more pleasant if we've bathed. I trusted you enough to get on a horse for you, so…"

"Ah, excellent. Let's find some towels and blankets and some soap."

❖

As Norah stepped into the lake, her shriek would have brought anyone within a mile running, but fortunately, no one was nearby.

"Here, take my hand," Abby said, exhilarated by the water and the scenery as always, but the extra dimension of being with Norah and being naked and their nakedness together practically sent her soaring like a bird. Every cell of her body was alive and aware. She made sure her expression was encouraging, and Norah slowly stepped forward.

"It's easier to just jump in," Abby said.

"No!" Norah was having none of that.

They slowly made their way in up to their breasts, Norah wincing at every step. Abby embraced her, and she relaxed a tiny bit. Their nipples, erect from the cool water, brushed together and surprised Abby. She found herself wondering if they could do in the water what they did in bed but dismissed that notion.

"We need to move or we'll get too cold."

"Yes," Norah said between her teeth.

"If you hang onto me, we can swim out deeper."

Norah stared at her for what seemed like a very long time but finally nodded.

Again, Abby felt as though she'd been given a tremendous gift along with a huge responsibility. Norah trusted her to not let her drown.

Wrapped up together, they glided out in the water until the lake bottom dropped off, and Abby used both her legs and one arm to keep them afloat.

"How are you?"

Norah didn't seem frightened or annoyed, but she had a look of disbelief. "I'm fine. I've never done anything like this."

"Neither have I," Abby said, and they kissed.

❖

Later, they stood on shore drying off a bit before returning to the cabin to get dressed.

Norah was surprised at how refreshed she was, and she had a feeling of accomplishment at having mastered her fear and gone into the lake over her head with Abby to hold her up. That was the key. She watched as Abby propped her foot on a rock to dry her leg. Norah immediately wanted to stroke her firm, well-muscled legs, yet the skin on the inside of her thighs was so soft. Norah shook her head to bring herself back from her memory of making love to Abby.

Abby spotted the motion. "Something wrong?"

"No, not at all. What shall we do now?" Norah grinned at the imagery in her mind.

"Well, how would you like go out for a little hike and I'll show you around some more and we can, um, look for plants."

"Oh. *That* again," Norah said, but she smiled to show she was teasing.

In the woods that ran along one side of the lake, Norah trailed behind Abby, who'd brought along her collecting gear and was serious and purposeful. Up on Mount Tamalpais, she'd been more casual. She strode swiftly on the trail until something caught her eye and would stop and take out a magnifying glass and perhaps mutter to herself and yank the plant from the ground and press it between two pieces of board and proceed to write up notes. Norah was content to watch her at her work. Abby's enthusiasm had previously been inexplicable but was now endearing, and she supposed that was how love changed things. Love. That was what they said and what they felt. At least, Norah assumed Abby felt it too. What would be next after this mountain idyll, she had no idea, but for once, it didn't matter to her that she didn't know. She was happy in the present, happy to be with Abby in her element. They'd made the essential connection between their bodies and their souls. Norah recalled that she'd brought a book with her with a poem she wanted to share with Abby because it expressed so well what was in her heart.

That evening, in the light of the fireplace, they sat on the divan close together.

Norah said, "I want to read you something." Abby played with her hair and stroked her cheek. Even those simple gestures of affection turned Norah's mind to the love that they would soon make, she hoped, and she shivered.

She opened the book, *Sonnets from the Portuguese.*

"What is it?" Abby asked.

"Elizabeth Barrett Browning. Poems. She wrote them all for Robert Browning, you know. She was in love with him."

"Ah, love poems," Abby said. "Seems right for us."

Norah found the page she was looking for and read aloud:

When our two souls stand up erect and strong,
Face to face, silent, drawing nigh and nigher,
Until the lengthening wings break into fire
At either curvèd point,—what bitter wrong
Can the earth do us, that we should not long
Be here contented?

She finished reading the poem, then closed the book and put her hand over it before daring to turn and look at Abby. She found Abby staring at her intently but thoughtfully.

"'What bitter wrong can the earth do us'? Truly. I thought that before, a few months ago, right after it happened. But it isn't like that, is it, love?"

"I don't know." Norah didn't exactly take Abby's meaning and wanted her to keep talking. "Tell me."

"The earth didn't wrong us. It put us together for us to find one another in a way we couldn't before."

"Yes. It did." Norah's heart soared. "So that we can be 'pure spirits,' like the poem says."

They leaned forward at the same time and kissed over and over.

❖

Norah didn't want to spoil the mood of their trip, and so when they went back to the City, she asked Abby no questions, nor did

Abby say anything about what the future would hold. They took up their separate occupations. A few days after their return, when it was time to retire for the night, as soon as they closed the door, Norah pinned Abby against the wall and kissed her desperately.

"I want you," she said, hoarsely. "I don't care if there are people about."

"Yes," Abby said in a dreamy voice, kissing her back. "I can't resist you. I could no more stop my feelings than we can stop the sun from rising and setting."

They struggled out of their clothes as fast as they could move and dove under the covers, smothering their giggles in the pillows. When Abby moved between Norah's thighs and began to lick her, Norah put a pillow over her face to stifle her screams, which made them laugh even more.

Afterward, they lay in the dark close together. Norah turned to nuzzle Abby's neck and murmured, "Tell me what you think of this now. What you think of us."

"I would never have guessed I would be so enamored of someone. It's only now, having your love, that I understand how empty my life was, how disconnected from the most important human feeling there is: love. I was bereft without being aware of it. I could no more do without you now than flowers could survive without sunlight or water."

She turned and took Norah's face in her hands and kissed her for a long time.

Norah said, "If you keep kissing me like that, I shall not let you go to sleep. I'll have to have you again."

"To have someone. I never knew what that meant. It means to keep someone close both in body and in soul. There is no difference between the two of us or between us."

Norah stroked Abby's hair and settled her head on her shoulder. "No, love. There is no space between our souls or our bodies, and there never will be again. You're mine and I'm yours. Forever."

❖

At the hospital, Esther waddled about the wards, sometimes touchy, other times radiant. She was due very soon. Norah asked her what plans she and Addison had. She understood that Esther had agreed to marry Addison, but Norah took the position that she'd believe it when she saw the minister and heard their vows. Until then, Esther and Addison's marriage was purely theoretical.

"Well, we will marry, but after the birth of the baby. I don't want to be in a wedding gown looking like a hippopotamus. Addison is content that I've agreed and importunes me no more. In fact, he's full of nothing but talk of the baby, whom he assumes will be a boy. I dearly hope it'll be a girl." She laughed, but Norah saw she was no longer fretful now that she'd made her decision.

"I'll be needing to find a place to live. You won't have room with the baby in the house."

"Nor would I imagine you would care to be awakened five times a night by a crying infant. I'm not looking forward to it myself but..." She spread her arms wide. "What's to be done? Nothing."

"Will you be seeking a domicile with Abigail?"

That question came out of the blue, and Norah didn't know quite what to say. "I'm not sure."

Esther cocked her head and smirked knowingly. "I can tell that you've become lovers."

"You can?" Norah was aghast. Abby had begged her not to say anything to the commune members.

"Of course. You don't think I can tell when a woman is in love and being loved?"

"I didn't think it showed. Abby would like us to be discreet."

Esther snorted. "Hmph. I don't think Abby realizes that she looks at you as though you're a fresh pastry she's aching to devour."

Norah blushed but wasn't disturbed. Esther was far too astute not to notice the change in their manner with one another. But the problem still remained: what would the future hold?

Abby came to the hospital to see her, and Norah took her out to the courtyard so they could have some privacy. Radiant, Abby looked as though she was bursting with some item of news.

"I wanted to share with you as soon as I could." They sat on one of the benches, and, obviously excited, Abby grasped both of Norah's hands, shaking them slightly.

"What is it, love, that has you so lit up?" Norah asked, amused.

"Well. As you know, we don't have a permanent place for the Society, but some of the donors got in touch with the board of governors and proposed that work still needs to be conducted while we look for a new home. They've decided to finance a collecting trip for me to South America. I can scarcely believe it."

"South America," Norah said, struggling to keep her voice from shaking.

"Yes, Norah dear. It's an amazing gift, and they're supporting me for three months."

"Three months?"

"Yes. I've been to South America once, but that was scarcely enough time to do much of anything. I'm going to the Andes. I can get a local guide and...Norah what's wrong?"

Abby had finally noticed that Norah hadn't said a thing except to numbly repeat fragments of Abby's sentences. She'd gone dead quiet, and to her dismay her eyes were filling with tears.

"What about me? What about us?"

Abby looked at her as though she had no idea what Norah meant. "I don't understand what you're asking."

"We've not settled anything. You're just going off on this trip, without me, for three months Just like that?"

"Well. Yes. It's my work and—"

"The devil can have your work." Norah stood up. She was conscious she was being unreasonable. But the sudden news and the prospect of Abby blithely going off without her for that length of time without so much as a fare thee well or "what do you think?" infuriated her. She turned away and said, "I think you ought to go now."

"Very well." Abby's voice was cool. "I'll see you later today."

Norah just managed to wait until she was sure Abby was gone and burst into tears.

❖

Abby was flummoxed. She'd thought Norah would be pleased for her, but instead her reaction was exactly the opposite. It was stunning. She had no idea what to do or what to say. It seemed like their vacation at Fallen Leaf Lake had turned Norah into a different person. Abby felt different herself, certainly. It was at once a sense of freedom and a kind of a prison to be so intimately tied to another human being. She loved Norah and loved being with her, but she'd no idea that their love gave Norah a say in her comings and goings. No one in her life had ever had that sort of influence over her.

In the back of her mind, she was aware that the prospect of an overseas expedition offered her a way to get away for a bit from a situation she still found a little terrifying. Love came with all sorts of expectations she'd never considered, such as your lover might not want you to leave. Ever.

That was untenable because it would mean that Abby couldn't pursue her passion. She'd never entertained the slightest inkling that loving Norah and loving work would come into conflict. But it was obvious she had to do or say something to try to repair the damage, and she had no clue what that would be. Since they'd left San Francisco for the Sierra as friends and came back as lovers, Abby was reluctant to disclose this fact even to their housemates at the commune. It was the most private information she could imagine. She didn't for some reason even want to tell Kerry, even though she knew Kerry would understand. Kerry and Beth apparently had no qualms about anyone knowing of the nature of their relationship. She envied them that, but it wasn't for her.

She was going to have to try to sort this out with Norah herself. She felt like she was on a hike in unfamiliar country with no map or compass to show her the way, an unwelcome and unusual feeling.

They had supper as usual, and Norah would neither look at nor talk to her, and it was surprising how painful this was. For the past few weeks, Norah had had nothing but eyes for her all the time when they were in public, and when they were alone in their bedroom, well, they could scarcely sleep for the desperate need to touch each other. The prospect of being deprived of Norah's attention was unwelcome. Even worse was the knowledge that Norah was angry with her. No other person's anger had ever made the least difference to Abby.

Norah said not a word to anyone and after supper had gone directly upstairs. Abby was on kitchen cleanup so she stayed to complete this task, and she ached to be able to talk to Norah, though she didn't know what she would say. She was more concerned that she hear from Norah exactly what was wrong so she could fix it.

CHAPTER TWENTY-TWO

Norah lay on her back on the bed, then jumped up and began to pace about the room. She looked out the window down at Fillmore Street. The street business went on, oblivious to her pain and confusion. It would be wonderful if Abby would discern the reason for her dismay and apologize, cancel her trip, and begin the important search for a place to live with Norah. That would be ideal, but Norah couldn't see how that would occur. For one thing, she had to admit, she'd voiced no request to Abby that this was what she desired. Still, Abby should have known she'd be upset at the news of the South American expedition.

Norah kept telling herself this wasn't May all over again. Abby and May bore no resemblance to one another whatsoever. She turned away from the window and stared at the closed door, willing Abby to walk through it. She would come, Norah had no doubt, but the wait was excruciating. Norah lay back down on the bed and stretched out her arm, imagining Abby lying next to her waiting for her touch, wanting her. She began to cry again. She'd wanted to present herself as calm and in control of her emotions, but that was evidently not to be.

At long last, the bedroom door opened and she heard Abby say tentatively, "Norah?" She turned over, and Abby approached the bed slowly, looking as though she was expecting another earthquake to begin.

"Hello," Norah said, tearfully.

Abby sat down on the edge of the bed but didn't touch her. "Norah, could you tell me your trouble? I'm sorry if I'm the source of it."

Norah took her time rearranging pillows and settling herself against them. It gave her a chance to gather her thoughts.

She spoke carefully, as though a misplaced word would forever destroy any chance of them reconciling. Maybe it was true. "You came and informed me you were leaving for three months."

Abby's brow wrinkled in consternation. "I thought you'd be happy. I thought you'd be excited for me."

"You know nothing about women, do you?"

"I guess not, even though I *am* one."

For the first time, Norah detected a note of pique in Abby's tone, and it oddly reassured her. She'd become convinced that Abby inhabited a world of pure logic, a place divorced from intense emotions and wants and needs. Norah might have introduced her to the sexual dimension of life, and Abby might have professed love for her and believed that it was true, but it was fairly clear she had no real grasp of all its ramifications.

" I would have rather you came and asked me about taking such a trip, talked to me about it first, instead of just announcing you were going."

"Oh." The light of comprehension shone in Abby's eyes. "I'm truly—"

Norah held up her hand to stop Abby. "We've only just begun, I know. It's all new for you, and for me too, but we must talk with one another, and talk honestly. I want very much for us to discuss our future, and we can't do that when you just tell me what you're going to do."

"Oh," Abby said again. She hung her head, which made Norah feel she was being too harsh.

"Look at me, Abby." Abby raised her eyes, and Norah was touched by the pain and regret she saw there.

"You're not a monster, and I didn't mean to imply that you are. But I want to know if you understand that there is now a 'we,' not just a 'you' and an 'I.' Or that is what I want there to be."

"Oh, that is what I want as well, Norah, my dear. It just doesn't come naturally to me to think that way. I've been on my own for far too long. I'm a dimwit."

"Abby, darling, don't be so hard on yourself. I've got my own faults. I shouldn't have been so angry with you without explaining why. I feel like you're abandoning me."

"Oh, no. Norah, dear, not at all. I very much want to come back to you."

"I don't want you to go."

"Yes, but it's my work. I must go."

"No. You're choosing to go."

Abby shut her mouth in frustration. "Well, then what do you suggest?"

"Could you delay for a time? May we make some of our own plans first? We can't stay here. You know that. We must find a place to live. I want that to be a place for us to live together." Norah put heavy emphasis on the word "together."

"Together?" Abby spoke the word as though it was in a foreign language. Perhaps for her, it *was*.

"Yes. Together. And I have an idea."

"Wait. We are to live together, just ourselves?" Abby asked.

"Well, yes, of course. What else?" Norah was becoming angry all over again.

"I've never lived with anyone or only just as a visitor for short stretches. I've always been on my own."

"Precisely the problem," Norah said.

"Yes. I suppose so. I've got to start thinking of you and me. 'We,' as you said."

"That is my hope," Norah said with as much tenderness as she could summon.

"Well. Then, my only answer to that is yes, we shall live together, but first I must go to South America."

"Abby Eliot, are you not listening to me?"

"I. Er. Yes. I'm listening."

"Really?" Norah fixed her with a hard stare until her shoulders fell. "Then listen to me. I don't want to stop you from going, but could we settle our lives a little before you leave me?"

"All right. Tell me." Abby folded her hands and prepared herself to listen.

"Are you going to make a commitment to me? Forever?"

"Forever?" The mask of cooperation fell away.

If Norah hadn't been so serious, she would have laughed. "Yes. I'm in love with you. I want to be with you for the rest of my life. I must hear from you how you feel."

"I feel the same but…"

"But what?" Norah was exasperated and a bit fearful as well. Her self-sufficient botanist was finding it difficult to let go of her independence.

"How will I know if this is going to last? I mean, life is uncertain. Anything can happen."

"Yes. And what is your point, precisely?"

"My point is this, Norah dear." She took Norah's hands and made sure they had eye contact. "I've never in my life had to be responsible for anyone but myself. And here we are talking about being as one for eternity. I'm having some difficulty seeing this for myself. Forgive me, love. I only want to make you happy, but I'm terribly afraid I can't."

"Well. I have no idea if I can make you happy either, but we can try. And I'm sure you know that, as a doctor, I'm very familiar with life's uncertainty." She was a little acerbic in that last sentence, but Abby deserved to know she wasn't the only realist in the room.

Again Abby looked abashed and said, "Oh. Yes. Of course. All right, then it's settled. We're to be together, in one home. I suppose I could delay the trip for a while until we're more settled."

Norah grinned with obvious relief, and Abby relaxed. She seemed to realize that it wasn't that difficult after all to make another person happy but that, first, you had to find out what she wanted and what she thought.

"The City's government is building temporary housing, cottages, around the City for the refugees," Norah said. "We need to apply. We're not sleeping in the park, but we are essentially homeless. We can stay in one of the earthquake cottages until we can find a more permanent house."

She waited for Abby's answer. It seemed an eternity, but finally Abby said, "That's it then. We'll move into an earthquake cottage— what a funny name—and…" She looked expectantly at Norah.

"And then you can make your journey to South America and come home to me." She spread her arms out and Abby came into them. They clung together. The storm had been weathered. They both jumped when someone knocked on the door.

Beth's voice came from hallway. "Abby, Norah? So sorry to disturb you, but you must come downstairs to talk with all of us for a moment. Addison and Esther are making an announcement, and so are Kerry and I."

"We'll be there soon." Norah said, then turned to Abby and asked, "Shall we tell everyone about us?"

Abby hesitated, but then she grinned. "Why not? That's something else I'm going to have to get used to, so I may as well start with these folks who've so kindly sheltered me for these past few months."

"Yes. We have to start somewhere."

In the parlor, everyone was arranged on various chairs and divans except for Addison, who stood beside Esther's chair as she sat with her hands folded over her giant belly. Abby and Norah found a spot next to Scott.

"It's good to see all of you looking so well," Addison said. "There have been a few times since the quake that I wasn't certain we all would survive, and I don't mean survive the quake but survive each other.'"

"Addison, darling, no speech. Get to the point," Esther said, and everyone laughed.

Addison looked momentarily put out, but he recovered. "Ahem. Yes. Let me tell you the reason for having us all gather here. I want to invite you all to our wedding, which will be soon. Esther has agreed, finally, to marry me."

The group clapped and cheered.

"Now. Esther has asked that we wait until after the birth of the baby, and I've assented because it's truly a miracle that she agreed—"

"Addison." Esther had a warning tone in her voice.

"Ah, yes, to be sure. At any rate you're all invited as honored guests."

Kerry spoke up. "I've got some news. Davey Moore has asked me to come and cook in the new restaurant he's starting. We'll be here on Fillmore Street first, but when the downtown is rebuilt, we'll move." She held Beth's hand as Beth beamed at her.

Beth said, "As we've worked in the refugee camp, I've begun collecting data for a new research project the City and County has agreed to support. They want me to present at the rescheduled medical conference in two months. It is very soon, but we have, ahem, a wealth of information."

Norah cleared her throat. "Abby and I will be moving soon. I'm going to apply for one of the earthquake cottages in the Presidio."

"You know you'll have to get to City and County Hospital somehow. Perhaps by horseback?" Abby said, and everyone laughed.

"We'll see about that," Norah said and glared at her, but then broke into a grin.

"Since we're all making announcements, I have one," Scott said. "In view of the large change that is coming to the commune, I've concluded I must find my own place. I've found another doctor's practice to join, and he's offering me lodging as well. We'll be in the Outside Lands, if you can believe it. This fellow thinks that's where the future growth of the City is."

"What about Corporal Ames?" Beth asked archly.

"He won't be far away," Scott said, and he winked.

"That's all settled then. The wedding will be in few weeks, after the baby's born. We'll have it here at home in the backyard. We've come through a very trying time, for everyone. Our beloved City was nearly destroyed, there was much suffering everywhere, including," he cleared his throat, "here at the commune." He paused as though thinking about the difficulties they'd endured.

"But that's all behind us now, and we've nothing but prosperity and happiness to look forward to."

Norah took Abby's hand in hers and squeezed it as they looked lovingly at each other.

The End

About the Author

Kathleen Knowles grew up in Pittsburgh, Pennsylvania, but has lived in San Francisco for more than thirty years. She finds the City's combination of history, natural beauty, and multicultural diversity inspiring and endlessly fascinating. Her first novel, *Awake Unto Me*, won the Golden Crown Literary Society award for best historical romance novel of 2012.

She lives with her spouse and their three pets atop one of San Francisco's many hills. When not writing, she works as a health and safety specialist at the University of California, San Francisco.

Kathleen can be contacted at kathy-sophia@hotmail.com.

Books Available from Bold Strokes Books

18 Months by Samantha Boyette. Alissa Reeves has only had two girlfriends and they've both gone missing. Now it's up to her to find out why. (978-1-62639-804-7)

Arrested Hearts by Holly Stratimore. A reckless cop with a secret death wish and a health nut who is afraid to die might be a perfect combination for love. (978-1-62639-809-2)

Capturing Jessica by Jane Hardee. Hyperrealist sculptor Michael tries desperately to conceal the love she holds for best friend, Jess, unaware Jess's feelings for her are changing. (978-1-62639-836-8)

Counting to Zero by AJ Quinn. NSA agent Emma Thorpe and computer hacker Paxton James must learn to trust each other as they work to stop a threat clock that's rapidly counting down to zero. (978-1-62639-783-5)

Courageous Love by KC Richardson. Two women fight a devastating disease, and their own demons, while trying to fall in love. (978-1-62639-797-2)

Pathogen by Jessica L. Webb. Can Dr. Kate Morrison navigate a deadly virus and the threat of bioterrorism, as well as her new relationship with Sergeant Andy Wyles and her own troubled past? (978-1-62639-833-7)

Rainbow Gap by Lee Lynch. Jaudon Vickers and Berry Garland, polar opposites, dream and love in this tale of lesbian lives set in Central Florida against the tapestry of societal change and the Vietnam War. (978-1-62639-799-6)

Steel and Promise by Alexa Black. Lady Nivrai's cruel desires and modified body make most of the galaxy fear her, but courtesan Cailyn Derys soon discovers the real monsters are the ones without the claws. (978-1-62639-805-4)

Swelter by D. Jackson Leigh. Teal Giovanni's mistake shines an unwanted spotlight on a small Texas ranch where August Reese is secluded until she can testify against a powerful drug kingpin. (978-1-62639-795-8)

Without Justice by Carsen Taite. Cade Kelly and Emily Sinclair must battle each other in the pursuit of justice, but can they fight their undeniable attraction outside the walls of the courtroom? (978-1-62639-560-2)

21 Questions by Mason Dixon. To find love, start by asking the right questions. (978-1-62639-724-8)

A Palette for Love by Charlotte Greene. When newly minted Ph.D. Chloé Devereaux returns to New Orleans, she doesn't expect her new job, and her powerful employer—Amelia Winters—to be so appealing. (978-1-62639-758-3)

By the Dark of Her Eyes by Cameron MacElvee. When Brenna Taylor inherits a decrepit property haunted by tormented ghosts, Alejandra Santana must not only restore Brenna's house and property but also save her soul. (978-1-62639-834-4)

Cash Braddock by Ashley Bartlett. Cash Braddock just wants to hang with her cat, fall in love, and deal drugs. What's the problem with that? (978-1-62639-706-4)

Gravity by Juliann Rich. How can Ellie Engebretsen, Olympic ski jumping hopeful with her eye on the gold, soar through the air when all she feels like doing is falling hard for Kate Moreau, her greatest competitor and the girl of her dreams? (978-1-62639-483-4)

Lone Ranger by VK Powell. Reporter Emma Ferguson stirs up a thirty-year-old mystery that threatens Park Ranger Carter West's family and jeopardizes any hope for a relationship between the two women. (978-1-62639-767-5)

Love on Call by Radclyffe. Ex-Army medic Glenn Archer and recent LA transplant Mariana Mateo fight their mutual desire in the face of past losses as they work together in the Rivers Community Hospital ER. (978-1-62639-843-6)

Never Enough by Robyn Nyx. Can two women put aside their pasts to find love before it's too late? (978-1-62639-629-6)

Two Souls by Kathleen Knowles. Can love blossom in the wake of tragedy? (978-1-62639-641-8)

Camp Rewind by Meghan O'Brien. A summer camp for grown-ups becomes the site of an unlikely romance between a shy, introverted divorcee and one of the Internet's most infamous cultural critics—who attends undercover. (978-1-62639-793-4)

Cross Purposes by Gina L. Dartt. In pursuit of a lost Acadian treasure, three women must not only work out the clues, but also the complicated tangle of emotion and attraction developing between them. (978-1-62639-713-2)

Imperfect Truth by C.A. Popovich. Can an imperfect truth stand in the way of love? (978-1-62639-787-3)

Life in Death by M. Ullrich. Sometimes the devastating end is your only chance for a new beginning. (978-1-62639-773-6)

Love on Liberty by MJ Williamz. Hearts collide when politics clash. (978-1-62639-639-5)

Serious Potential by Maggie Cummings. Pro golfer Tracy Allen plans to forget her ex during a visit to Bay West, a lesbian condo community in NYC, but when she meets Dr. Jennifer Betsy, she gets more than she bargained for. (978-1-62639-633-3)

Taste by Kris Bryant. Accomplished chef Taryn has walked away from her promising career in the city's top restaurant to devote her life to her five-year-old daughter and is content until Ki Blake comes along. (978-1-62639-718-7)

The Second Wave by Jean Copeland. Can star-crossed lovers have a second chance after decades apart, or does the love of a lifetime only happen once? (978-1-62639-830-6)

Valley of Fire by Missouri Vaun. Taken captive in a desert outpost after their small aircraft is hijacked, Ava and her captivating passenger discover things about each other and themselves that will change them both forever. (978-1-62639-496-4)

Basic Training of the Heart by Jaycie Morrison. In 1944, socialite Elizabeth Carlton joins the Women's Army Corps to escape family expectations and love's disappointments. Can Sergeant Gale Rains get her through Basic Training with their hearts intact? (978-1-62639-818-4)

Before by KE Payne. When Tally falls in love with her band's new recruit, she has a tough decision to make. What does she want more—Alex or the band? (978-1-62639-677-7)

Believing in Blue by Maggie Morton. Growing up gay in a small town has been hard, but it can't compare to the next challenge Wren—with her new, sky-blue wings—faces: saving two entire worlds. (978-1-62639-691-3)

Coils by Barbara Ann Wright. A modern young woman follows her aunt into the Greek Underworld and makes a pact with Medusa to win her freedom by killing a hero of legend. (978-1-62639-598-5)

Courting the Countess by Jenny Frame. When relationship-phobic Lady Henrietta Knight starts to care about housekeeper Annie Brannigan and her daughter, can she overcome her fears and promise Annie the forever that she demands? (978-1-62639-785-9)

For Money or Love by Heather Blackmore. Jessica Spaulding must choose between ignoring the truth to keep everything she has, and doing the right thing only to lose it all—including the woman she loves. (978-1-62639-756-9)

Hooked by Jaime Maddox. With the help of sexy Detective Mac Calabrese, Dr. Jessica Benson is working hard to overcome her past, but it may not be enough to stop a murderer. (978-1-62639-689-0)

Lands End by Jackie D. Public relations superstar Amy Kline is dealing with a media nightmare, and the last thing she expects is for restaurateur Lena Michaels to change everything, but she will. (978-1-62639-739-2)

Lysistrata Cove by Dena Hankins. Jack and Eve navigate the maelstrom of their darkest desires and find love by transgressing gender, dominance, submission, and the law on the crystal blue Caribbean Sea. (978-1-62639-821-4)

Twisted Screams by Sheri Lewis Wohl. Reluctant psychic Lorna Dutton doesn't want to forgive, but if she doesn't do just that an innocent woman will die. (978-1-62639-647-0)